THE PHOENIX LEGACY

Three unforgettable novels of passion,
romance and adventure, THE PHOENIX
LEGACY is the story of the House of DeKoven
Woolf, born to rule and sworn to destroy a
dazzling empire of the far future. It is a story
of the grandeur of love and the cruelty of
war, of proud men and passionate women as
far away in time as the heroes and heroines
of the Bible, and as close as the dreams and
desires of our own hearts. It is a story of our
children's children's children, building an
empire that spans the stars . . .

**Also by M. K. Wren
and available from NEL:**

THE PHOENIX LEGACY
Book I: Sword of the Lamb
Book II: Shadow of the Swan

House of the Wolf
Book Three of the Phoenix Legacy

M. K. Wren

NEW ENGLISH LIBRARY
Hodder and Stoughton

Copyright © 1981 by Martha Kay Renfroe

First published in the United States of America in 1981 by Berkley Books

First New English Library Paperback edition 1986

British Library C.I.P.

Wren, M.K.
    House of the wolf.——(The Phoenix legacy/
    M.K. Wren; bk. 3)
    Rn: Martha Kay Renfroe   I. Title   II. Series
    813'.54[F]   PS3573.R43

    ISBN 0 450 39378 X

Printed and bound in Great Britain for
Hodder and Stoughton Paperbacks, a
division of Hodder and Stoughton Ltd.,
Mill Road, Dunton Green, Sevenoaks,
Kent (Editorial Office: 47 Bedford
Square, London, WC1B 3DP) by
Cox & Wyman Ltd., Reading.

SYNOPSIS

PART 1: APPRENTICESHIP
OCTOV 3244 TO JULY 3253 A.D.

The Lord Alexand DeKoven Woolf is destined by birth to occupy a unique position of power in the Concord of the Loyal Houses, the monolithic and essentially feudalistic government that is the matrix for all human civilization in the thirty-third century. The Concord, despite its outward appearances of stability and prosperity, is suffering severe internal stresses, primarily manifested by chronic "uprisings" among the Bonds, its serf/slave class. The Concord is, in fact, threatened with the specter of a third dark age.

The Elite, the Concord's ruling class, however, remains myopically oblivious to that threat. Alexand does not, and he accepts as an obligation, not a privilege, the power to which he is heir. He is the first born of Lord Phillip, member of the Concord's Directorate and First Lord of the House of DeKoven Woolf. Alexand is also the grandson of Lord Mathis Daro Galinin, Chairman of the Directorate and the most powerful man in the Concord, and at the age of seventeen Alexand becomes indirect heir to the Chairmanship when Galinin's only direct heirs are assassinated. Those assassinations precipitate a political crisis, and Alexand is not alone in suspecting Lord

Orin Badir Selasis, whose ambition for the Chairmanship and antagonism toward Phillip Woolf make him a bitter enemy of the Houses of Woolf and Galinin.

In the highest echelons of power there is little room for love, but Alexand finds it in Lady Adrien Camine Eliseer. He loves her from the moment they meet, as she does him, but political necessity comes between them; both are committed to marriages—but not to each other. Four years pass before an unexpected chain of events alters the political situation, and Alexand and Adrien are at length betrothed.

Yet before the wedding takes place, Alexand makes a decision whereby he forfeits not only his heritage of power, but all hope for marrying Adrien.

Alexand is near the end of his traditional tour of duty with Confleet, during which he has been involved in quelling fourteen major Bond uprisings, each a searing nightmare in his memory. The catalyst of his decision is his brother, Richard, victim of a crippling neurological disease that will inevitably kill him before his twenty-fifth year. Rich becomes a recluse while still in his teens and devotes himself to the study of sociology, his principal subject the Bonds and Bond religion. Using the Fesh pseudonym of Richard Lamb, he earns a University degree in sociotheology before he is twenty. The Bonds with whom he works in his research regard him as a holy man and call him Richard the Lamb.

As a sociologist, Rich recognizes the critical instability of the Concord. By chance he discovers what he considers the only hope for its survival: the Society of the Phoenix, founded in the Centauri System by survivors of the Peladeen Republic, which was crushed by the Concord. Little is known about the Phoenix in the Concord, and the few who are even aware of its existence generally dismiss it as a pirate clan with revolutionary overtones, but Rich learns its true purpose: evolution, not revolution; to *save* the Concord by forcing on it a long-term process of social evolution toward a representational government providing "a maximum of individual choice, opportunity, and judical equality within the limits of a stable system." Rich becomes a member, well aware that this makes him a traitor in the eyes of the Concord, and the penalty for treason is death.

Phillip Woolf has loved his two sons passionately, as he

loved little else in life, but he proves incapable of acceptance or tolerance when at length he learns that Rich is a Phoenix member. It is Rich himself who reveals his "treason" to his father. His disease is only days or weeks from its lethal culmination, and he has two missions to accomplish before he dies. First, to act as an envoy of the Phoenix to Woolf and Mathis Galinin, to give them a true accounting of the Phoenix and its aims. Second, as Richard the Lamb, to become a saint in the Bond pantheon by offering himself as a martyr in a public execution. His purpose in this is to prolong the life of the Concord by sacrificing what little life is left to him. As a saint, he will have profound influence on the Bonds after his death, a pacific influence he hopes will mitigate the emotional chain reactions that precipitate the bloody uprisings plaguing the Concord and contributing to its instability.

But Woolf angrily renounces his son; he cannot believe Rich's purpose in becoming a martyr is anything other than to instigate a disastrous revolt. When Alexand comes to Rich's defense, Woolf turns against him, too, calling him as much a traitor as his brother. It is then that Alexand makes his decision to follow Rich into the Phoenix. He realizes that he is only heir to power, not yet in possession of it, and by rejecting him, his father renders him politically impotent and incapable of altering to any degree the ruinous course upon which the Concord is embarked. He chooses to sacrifice his marriage to Adrien and his very existence as the Lord Alexand to the cause for which Rich offers his last precious scrap of life and for the hope that the ultimate catastrophe of another dark age can be averted.

Rich has his apotheosis, and Richard the Lamb becomes a saint. On the following day the Lord Alexand "dies" in the crash of a Confleet Scout on Pollux.

PART 2: METAMORPHOSIS
JULY–AUGUS 3253 A.D.

The Lord Alexand dies and Alex Ransom is born. At Phoenix headquarters on the island of Fina on Pollux in the Centauri System, he meets its governing Council, including three friends of Rich's: Dr. Erica Radek, Chief of Human Sciences; Ben Venturi, Commander of Security and Intelligence; and Dr. Andreas Riis, founder of the Phoenix, chairman of the Council, and creator of the Society's ultimate secret weapon, the matter transmitter.

Alex also meets an enemy: Councilor Predis Ussher.

Phase I of the Phoenix's General Plan hinges on establishing a member in the Concord's ruling hierarchy through whom the social reforms vital to the Concord's survival can be initiated. Before Alex's arrival only one member is likely to be recognized as a Lord by the Concord: Predis Ussher, who claims to be the son of Elor, last Lord of the House of Peladeen. But Alex offers a better alternative if the Lord Alexand—an heir to the Chairmanship—can be resurrected, and Ussher does not welcome him. There is no immediate confrontation, however; Phase I will be achieved only by forcing the Directorate to the bargaining table with a show of military force. The Phoenix isn't yet prepared for that encounter, and beyond that, its primary offering—and threat—is not yet operational: the *long-range* matter transmitter (LR-MT). At present the MT functions only within Einsteinian limits and is not feasible for interstellar distances.

Alex's real identity remains the secret of the Council pending a breakthrough on the LR-MT, and he is assigned to Fleet Operations, the Phoenix's military branch. But his identity is guessed by one member who is not on the Council: Jael the Outsider, who joins the Phoenix shortly after Alex. Before Jael leaves Fina for duty with Security and Intelligence on Castor, he warns Alex to beware of Ussher because he is not only a threat to the future of the Phoenix, but, quite literally, a killer.

PART 3: GAUNTLET
DECEM 3257 TO JANUAR 3258 A.D.

Four years after the Lord Alexand DeKoven Woolf "dies" to join the Society of the Phoenix, Alex Ransom is First Commander of Fleet Operations and a member of the Phoenix Council. He has also continued Rich's work among the Bonds, calling himself the Brother of the Lamb and preaching the same message of peace and submission.

The uneasy truce between Alex and Predis Ussher is shattered when Andreas Riis at last makes a breakthrough on the LR-MT. Ussher makes his move, an anonymous tip to the SSB, the Concord's secret police, and Alex and Andreas are arrested. The security lid on Andreas is so tight all Ben Venturi's attempts to find out where he is being held fail, and Alex endures nearly a month of "interrogation" before Ben succeeds in arranging his escape.

When Alex returns to Fina, he finds Ussher in control, firing the members with grandiose ambitions whose underlying purpose is the fulfillment of Ussher's personal ambition to become Lord of the Centauri System. But without Andreas and LR-MT, the "loyals" can't openly oppose Ussher for fear of precipitating a schism that would destroy the Phoenix. After a close brush with poison, Alex realizes Fina isn't safe for him and makes plans to leave Fina and set up an independent base of operations elsewhere from which a rescue attempt can be made once Ben locates Andreas.

But before his departure, Alex learns something that drastically alters his future course of action: Adrien Eliseer is to be betrothed to Karlis Selasis, the spoiled and willfully cruel son of Lord Orin Badir Selasis. Alex realizes that he had deluded himself these last four years in thinking he had accepted losing Adrien. He knows now that he can't accept her marriage to Karlis and meets secretly with her at her private retreat on Castor. She welcomes his resurrection as a miracle; her love for him did not die, even though she thought him dead. When they part, Lile Perralt, Eliseer House physician and a Phoenix agent, becomes their sole line of communication.

PART 4: EXILE
JANUAR–AUGUS 3258 A.D.

Alex goes to the city of Helen on Castor and is nearly caught in an SSB trap. He is saved by Jael, who takes him to his father, Amik the Thief, head of the Brotherhood, a loose organization ubiquitous among Outsiders, the unofficial class constituting the criminal and fugitive elements in the Concord. For a price Amik provides the equipment for Alex to set up his headquarters in a cavern called the Cave of Springs (the COS HQ), which is eventually equipped with a complete communications and monitoring center and MT terminal, and staffed with thirty-four loyals from Fina.

Plans for the Eliseer-Selasis wedding proceed, and Alex is helpless to stop it. But Adrien makes her own plans to escape immediately after the wedding ceremony to the convent of Saint Petra's of Ellay where she will be hidden behind the convent walls and the veil of a nun. She anticipates Orin Selasis's wrath and knows she must hide herself well, especially since she is pregnant with Alexand's twin sons. She entrusts this information as well as her plan of escape to Lile Perralt, but he dies before he can relay them to Alex.

Adrien thus seems to disappear into vacuum, and both Alex and Orin Selasis initiate searches for her. Selasis charges his Chief of Security, Bruno Hawkwood, with the task of finding—and killing—her.

While Alex and the loyals search for Adrien and for Andreas Riis, Ussher strengthens his hold on the Phoenix, and two months later, in June, he announces a military offensive against the Concord to take place the following Januar, a brief, but intensive surprise attack limited to the Centauri System. With it Ussher expects to drive the Concord out of Centauri—not to bring it to the bargaining table as delineated in the General Plan.

The search for Adrien finally focuses on Saint Petra's, and Valentin Severin, one of the COS HQ loyals, enters the convent as a novice to find Adrien. The search for Andreas also bears fruit, leading to the Detention Center in Pendino, a Confleet base on Castor. On the same day that Alex and Ben embark for Pendino to rescue Andreas, Bruno Hawkwood is at Saint Petra's where he kills a novice he believes to be Adrien. Alex and Ben succeed in rescuing Andreas, but Alex is hit with a laser beam that nearly destroys his right arm. He is transed to the COS HQ, but his relief at finding that Andreas is unharmed and mentally clear turns to despair when he learns of the murder of the novice at Saint Petra's. He cannot doubt that Adrien is dead, and under the combined assault of the wound and his grief, Alex collapses.

CAST OF CHARACTERS

Alexand DeKoven Woolf
(Alex Ransom)

First born and heir to the First Lordship of the House of DeKoven Woolf, indirect heir to the Chairmanship of the Directorate

Richard DeKoven Woolf
(Richard Lamb)

Alexand's younger brother

Phillip DeKoven Woolf

Alexand's father, First Lord of the House of DeKoven Woolf and member of the Directorate

Elise Galinin Woolf

Alexand's mother, the daughter of Mathis Galinin

Theron Rovere

Lector; Alexand's and Rich's tutor

Fenn Lacroy

SportsMaster in the House of De-Koven Woolf and Phoenix agent

Mathis Daro Galinin

First Lord of the House of Daro Galinin and Chairman of the Directorate

Orin Badir Selasis

First Lord of the House of Badir Selasis, member of the Directorate, and bitter antagonist to Woolf and Galinin

Karlis Selasis

First born of Lord Orin Selasis

Adrien Camine Eliseer

Daughter of Lord Loren Camine Eliseer of Castor, and Alexand's Promised

Lectris and Mariet

Adrien's Bond servants

Amik the Thief	Also known as the Lord of Thieves, head of the Brotherhood, a predominantly criminal organization prevalent in the Outside
Master Bruno Hawkwood	Orin Selasis's chief henchman, also known as the Master of Shadows
Dr. Lile Perralt	Eliseer family physician and a Phoenix agent
Sister Thea	A nun of the Order of Faith, Supra of the Convent of Saint Petra's of Ellay on Castor
Malaki	Elder Shepherd in the Eliseer Estate Bond compound

SOCIETY OF THE PHOENIX:

Dr. Andreas Riis	Founder of the Phoenix, chairman of its Council, and creator of the matter transmitter
Dr. Erica Radek	Council member, head of the Human Sciences Department
Ben Venturi	Council member and commander of Security and Intelligence
Predis Ussher	Council member, head of Communications, who claims to be the son of Elor, last Lord of the House of Peladeen
Emeric Garris	Council member, commander of Fleet Operations
John M'Kim	Council member, head of Supply and Maintenance

Marien Dyce	Council member, head of Computer Systems
Jan Barret	Leftant Commander in Fleet Operations
Valentin Severin	Assistant to Erica Radek
Jael	New member of the Phoenix, its first Outsider

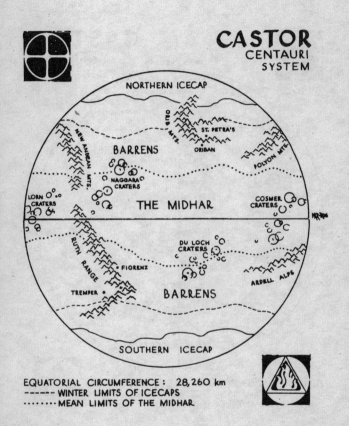

CASTOR
CENTAURI
SYSTEM

NORTHERN ICECAP

OLD MTS.

ST. PETRA'S

ORIBAN

BARRENS

NEW ANDEAN MTS.

POLYON MTS.

NAGGARA CRATERS

LORN CRATERS

THE MIDHAR

COSMER CRATERS

DU LOCH CRATERS

RUTH RANGE

FIORENZ

ARDELL ALPS

TREMPER

BARRENS

SOUTHERN ICECAP

EQUATORIAL CIRCUMFERENCE : 28,260 km
------ WINTER LIMITS OF ICECAPS
········ MEAN LIMITS OF THE MIDHAR

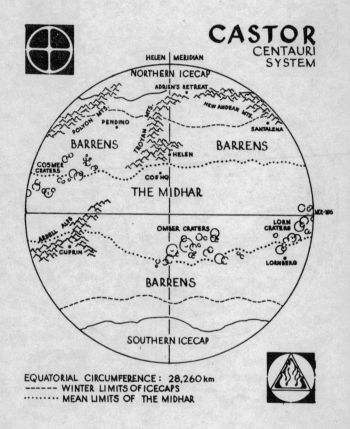

CASTOR
CENTAURI
SYSTEM

HELEN | MERIDIAN

NORTHERN ICECAP

ADRIEN'S RETREAT

NEW ANDEAN MTS.

POLYON MTS.
PENDINO

TROYAN MTS.

SANTALENA

BARRENS

HELEN

BARRENS

COSMER
CRATERS

COS HQ

THE MIDHAR

MER-106

ARDELL ALPS

LORN
CRATERS

OMBER CRATERS

CUPRIN

LORNBERG

BARRENS

SOUTHERN ICECAP

EQUATORIAL CIRCUMFERENCE : 28,260 km
------ WINTER LIMITS OF ICECAPS
.... MEAN LIMITS OF THE MIDHAR

POLLUX
CENTAURI SYSTEM

LEDA MERIDIAN

POLLUXIAN OCEAN

LAMONT

AMAZONIA MTS.
RIOLLEGROO
WEST PANGAEA
HIMALYA MTS.
ALPS
HAMIDROPOLIS
DRAKONIS
LEDA
TEL-HAMID
KRISTAE
PANGAEAN STRAITS
SIMONSVILLE
HALLI-COURT
CORIS MTS.
PANEASTY DESERT

PETROVNA
CAUCASIAS MTS.
SUMMER VALLEY

SELAMIN SEA

EAST PANGAEA

FINA
COMARGIAN STRAITS
ORIFEL
COMARG
OMEGA
SAHREAST MTS.
SAHRA RIFT
SAHRA MTS.
SAHRWEST MTS.
COMARGIAN PENINSULA

POLLUXIAN OCEAN

EQUATORIAL CIRCUMFERENCE : 42,240 km

Contents

HOUSE OF THE WOLF

PART 5: NADIR

●IOIOIOIOIOIOIOIOIOIOIOIOIOIOIOIOIOIOIOIOIOIOIOIOIOIO●

PHOENIX MEMFILES: DEPT HUMAN SCIENCES: BASIC SCHOOL
(HS/BS)
SUBFILE: LECTURE, BASIC SCHOOL 28 MARCH 3252
GUEST LECTURER: RICHARD LAMB
SUBJECT: POST-DISASTERS HISTORY:
THE MANKEEN REVOLT (3104–3120)
DOC LOC #819/219-1253/1812-1648-2833252

When the Mankeen League Lords met in Mosk in 3104 to sign the Charter, they also elected a Council of nine members, and to contemplate the character and fate of those nine men is, to a great degree, to contemplate the character and fate of the League itself.

Lionar Mankeen was, of course, elected Minister of the Council (he refused to be called "chairman"), and his character and fate are well established. Second only to Mankeen, the foremost of the five landed Lords on the Council, was Alric Eads Berstine, whose Home Estate was in Omsk; he held land grants on an area east of the Ural Mountains, sharing that border with Mankeen, as well as similar grain franchises, and a friendship of long standing. The relationship was so close that Mankeen signed Contracts of Marriage between his daughter, Irena—his favorite child, it's said—and Berstine's first born when Irena was only four years old and her Promised, Aldred, only eight.

Irena was nineteen when the marriage took place in 3115, and I wonder if Mankeen didn't even then regret the impulse that led him to sign the contracts so early. At that point, five years before his final defeat, the League wasn't faring well, and neither was his friendship with Berstine. The worlds weren't faring well, for that matter; the extraterrestrial colonies had been evacuated or abandoned, and the revolt had become a vicious civil war fought out on Terra's war-scarred surface. Irena and Aldred were childhood friends, but apparently little affection carried over into their marriage. Aldred was not as convinced of Mankeen's ultimate victory as his father, and Alric was losing his confidence. Mankeen later—too late—recognized his old friend as a consummate opportunist who was not inclined to stay overlong with a foundering ship. The crisis came in 3118 when, for reasons never entirely clarified, Aldred sank a knife into Mankeen's chest, missing his heart by centimeters.

Mankeen's guards reacted with a barrage of laser fire that killed Aldred instantly. Mankeen survived the knife thrust, but his friendship with Alric Berstine didn't survive the death of his son, however deserved it was. Berstine renounced Mankeen and surrendered to the Concord, and he was one of the few League Lords whose House survived.

Another councilor, also Lord of a landed House, was more loyal to Mankeen, and his House paid the price. Myron Holst Desmon held land grants on most of the Missour River drainage in central Noramerika, and although he was among the last Lords to join the League, he was one of the most loyal to Mankeen. He was also one of the three Lords who accompanied Mankeen on his final voyage toward the sun. Afterward, his first born, Danis, managed to trade his and his family's lives for a merger with Olin Fallor, whose lands adjoined his on the north, and who treated the Desmons despicably. Danis survived the merger by only three years, and his death, officially listed as suicide, probably occurred when he tried to kill Olin Fallor.

Another landed Lord and councilor who remained loyal to Mankeen and joined him on that final flight was Owen Alis Arnim, who held sheep and cattle franchises and a large land grant in north central Conta Austrail. His wife and three children accompanied him on Mankeen's death flight, and few of his remaining relatives— or even his Fesh and Bonds—survived the Mankeen Purge. His holdings were awarded to the House of Hamid, which under the aegis of the Selasids was very much a rising power at that time, and within ten years of the end of the Revolt occupied the House of Tadema's seat on the Directorate.

Another agrarian House on the League Council was that of Bernar Po Kien, whose Home Estate was in Ningsi in central Sinasia. Kien was, like Mankeen, the descendant of a "native" Lord appointed by Ballarat, and traced his dynasty back ten generations before the Wars of Confederation. The dynasty ended with Kien, who would undoubtedly have joined Mankeen on that last flight, but he was killed six years earlier at the Battle of Paykeen. His holdings were absorbed by Titus Vanevar, a Cognate House of Omer.

The third Lord who accompanied Mankeen on his last flight was Winston Grenwell Pratoria, one of the two mining Houses on the Council. His Home Estate was in Sudafrika, in Pratoria, from whence the House name was taken; his predecessor was one of the Fesh commanders awarded Lordship by Ballarat. Pratoria apparently inherited a talent for tactics and took an active part in Mankeen's military campaigns, after 3112 serving as Cormoroi's second-in-command. Perhaps for that reason, his House suffered particularly during the Purge. His holdings and basic metals franchises were given to the House of Cameroodo, which was also very much a rising power, and a few years later Lerenz Cameroodo was sitting on the Directorate in the Adalay chair.

The other mining House on the Council was that of Lore Videl Valera, whose Home Estate was in Cracas, Sudamerika. He was one of the first Lords to join the League, and one of its most outspoken partisans in the beginning, but his enthusiasm waned quickly, although he didn't work up the courage to break way until Berstine left Mankeen in 3118. Valera joined Berstine in his renunciation of Mankeen and surrendered to the Concord, but he didn't fare as well as Berstine, perhaps because he wasn't as adroit an opportunist. The House of Valera and its holdings were a few years later absorbed by Ivanoi.

There were only two industrial Houses on the Council, and both were Mankeen partisans for palpably selfish reasons. Karol Zleski Delai, whose Home Estate was originally in Victoria but was moved to Varsaw during the Revolt, held computer franchises that put him in direct competition with Omer, a Directorate House that was systematically forcing Delai into bankruptcy. Obviously, Lord Karol had his reasons for fighting for the emancipation of his House, but whatever his motives, he fought hard for the League and was killed on the battleline in the last Battle of Toramil. His first born, like Danis Desmon, managed to make a bargain for survival, with Omer in this case, and in the resulting House merger, Delai's descendants fared far better than Desmon's.

The other industrial House, and the last of the nine original Council Houses, was that of Lord Aram Sejanis, whose Home Estate was in Stanbul. The name of Sejanis has since become synonymous with treachery, and for good reason. The House was a Cognate of Selasis with franchises for the manufacture of certain cast-metal parts used in Selasid ships, and until Aram became First Lord, the relationship between the two Houses was peaceful, with the previous Sejanid Lords carefully avoiding antagonizing the Goliath of Selasis. Lord Aram, however, was an avaricious and ambitious man who thought to play the role of David. He was among Mankeen's most zealous partisans in the beginning, but later became the first League Lord to renounce Mankeen. That was in 3112, and it's never been clear why he chose to do so at that time; the League was then in a good position strategically and still a potential winner in its contest with the Concord. Sejanis, however, was to a great degree responsible for the change of the tide of the League's fortunes in that year. He wasn't satisfied simply to desert the League and surrender to the Concord, but took with him information and strat plans that led to Cormoroi's shattering defeat at the Battle of Pollux.

For a while it seemed that Sejanis had made a good bargain. Lord Bernar Selasis took him under his wing and treated him magnanimously, which perhaps should have served as a warning to Sejanis. Apparently it didn't, and he enjoyed the fruits of his treachery for five years before he met his death in a fall from a balcony in his Stanbul Estate. Few people accepted his death as an accident, especially when Selasis moved so quickly afterward to consolidate the House's holdings with his own. But there was no great outcry for justice on Aram's behalf. Despite the fact that he gave the Concord its first major victory, Aram Sejanis was as much despised by the Lords of the Concord as he was by the Lords of the League.

Before the end of the Revolt, Mankeen had become accustomed to renouncement and desertion. By 3118 a third of the League Houses had been destroyed, their holdings absorbed by Concord Lords, and another third had deserted and surrendered, most of them suffering the same fate. And in that year, while Mankeen was still recovering from the stab wound dealt by Aldred Berstine, his wife joined the exodus. Lady Lizbeth sought sanctuary with her father, Lord Tomas Lesellen, but she didn't go alone. Feador, their first born, and Julian, their third son, accompanied her. There is evidence, although Concord histories play it down, that Mankeen not only didn't oppose this desertion, but insisted upon it. Leo, the second born, and Irena did not go with their mother and brothers to Bonaires, and I can't believe they weren't given a choice. They chose to stay with their father and finally join him in his last voyage, as the remaining third of the League Lords chose to remain loyal to him to the last battle, however hopeless.

CHAPTER XVI: Augus 3258

●I●I●I●I●I●I●I●I●I●I●I●I●I●I●I●I●I●I●I●I●I●I●I●I●I●I●I●I●I●I●

1.

Erica Radek checked the S/V screens to see that they were on total opaque from the outside. A hulking man stood guard near the cubicle; from all appearances, he hadn't moved a muscle since Jael posted him there. A "blade," Jael called him, a paradoxical term; the man wore the usual Outsider's knife, but it was obvious he didn't depend on that to carry out his duties, but on the imposing X^2 holstered on his hip and the metal-studded gloves covering huge hands that curled menacingly even in relaxation.

She turned and went to the chair by the bed. As a psycho-sociologist, she should be making use of the fund of information available to her now on the Outside, its customs, traditions, behavioral codes, and people. "Members" would be more apt. Like Dr. Cedric Eliot. What had brought a man so skilled and dedicated to his work into the Brotherhood? She'd been apprehensive about the staff in Amik's infirmary; this wasn't a case to be trusted to incompetents. But Eliot had been a pleasant surprise—if anything in these last four hours could be called pleasant.

6

She sagged back in the chair, letting her eyes close.

Three hours in surgery, and there was so little they could do. The muscles and tendons had been repaired to some extent, bone cultures implanted, skin grafts made. But Alex needed vascular and neural implants if the arm and hand were ever to function at anything close to a normal level. Dr. Eliot didn't have the facilities or the expertise for that kind of surgery. It was all they could do to save the arm.

And what was so bitterly galling was the knowledge that the specialists and equipment necessary to treat this wound properly were available in Fina.

She opened her eyes and looked up at the biomonitor screen on the opposite wall. The moving lines spelled a general state just short of deep shock. Dr. Eliot had hesitated for that reason at giving Alex a sedative after he came out of the anesthesia, but it became a necessity, the lesser of risks. It was imperative that his arm be kept immobile, but even restraining straps didn't contain his desperate thrashings. Eliot had been at a loss to understand the uncontrollable emotional reaction, recognizing it as a response to something more than physical pain. Erica hadn't tried to explain it, but she understood it.

The cubicle still seemed to echo with those agonized cries. She looked at Alex, half her mind still operating on the level of a physician. He lay in a nulgrav bed, enveloped in an invisible bubble of controlled warmth, a respirator mask covering half his face, mechanically pacing his breathing. Taped on the inside of his left elbow was a tube to supply saline and nutrient solutions; electrodes for brainwave monitoring and emergency cardiac shock were attached to his forehead and chest; a biomonitor cuff was strapped to his left wrist, its readings projected on the wall screen. His right arm was bandaged from the knuckles to the deltoid muscle, tented in bacteriostatic gauze, a rack of inverted plasibottles mounted above it with eight tubes looping down, disappearing under the bandages, meting out protein-enzyme solutions.

Barring infection or rejection of the grafts, the arm would heal. How well it would function, she couldn't guess, but she doubted he'd ever be capable of full digital apposition.

But the arm wasn't her real concern.

She had seen Alex Ransom weep, and knew what that

meant. The locks on the mental chamber where he'd jailed his grief for Rich, for his mother, and even in some senses for his father, had broken with this new grief. Erica had warned him years ago that the locks wouldn't hold forever, but he'd been unwilling—or unable—to open them himself and endure the natural process of recovery.

Now he was under a double assault, both mental and physical, and the rigidly disciplined control crumbled in the face of that devastating combination. His last coherent words were, "Let me go—in the name of mercy, let me go. . . ."

He meant, *Let me die*.

And Andreas Riis was free.

She focused on the thought, trying to recapture the relief and joy she felt when Ben brought him through the MT. The day they had worked for and anxiously awaited for eight long months; Andreas was free, and because she loved him, the relief was still there. But any hope for the future of the Phoenix was dimmed. Whatever his virtues, Andreas wasn't capable of leading the exiles back to Fina. Not to a Fina occupied by Predis Ussher.

She reached out and touched the motionless hand lying against the sheet, finding it cold under her fingers. It was a personal conviction that the survival instinct is too strong to be easily overridden, and when existence becomes that intolerable, the victim is justified in asking the mercy of death. She wasn't sure she was capable of offering that kind of mercy; it had never been asked of her. But it didn't matter; she had no choice. She *couldn't* be merciful. Not to Alex Ransom; to the Lord Alexand.

But he *wanted* to die. The question that haunted her now was whether it was within her power to keep him alive.

She tensed, aware that she wasn't alone, feeling a chill of fear; this was the realm of the Brotherhood. Then her breath came out in a sigh of relief. Jael. She wondered how long he'd been standing behind her.

"Are you well, sister?" He came up beside her and stood looking down at Alex.

"Yes."

"And Alex?"

"We managed to save the arm."

Jael turned to face her, and she wasn't deceived by the lack of emotion in his black, hooded eyes.

"Will he live?"

"He'll survive the wound."

"You slip my questions."

She pulled in a deep breath, suddenly so bone-weary, she wondered if she could stand.

"I can't answer your questions; not the real ones."

He nodded slowly. "That's answer enough."

"What about Andreas?"

"He's resting now. We set up an S/V cubicle for him. The 'cells' didn't hold much favor with him."

"I can understand that. Does he seem—I mean, is he—"

"He's clear and straight down the line. Ben had a long talk with him, skimming the general stat, then Andreas had a head session with Lyden and Bruce, and he's ready to dive in."

"I must talk to him before I go back to Fina."

"Erica, it'll hold. He needs rest, and so do you. Ben said he'd wait on for you at Fina; he left an hour ago."

She nodded mechanically, then after a moment frowned. "Will you be here with Alex?"

"I can be, but I brought Carl Roi from the COS HQ. He's a Grade 6 medtech."

Erica looked out through the haze of the S/V screens and saw a face-screened man standing a little distance from the Outsider guard.

"Yes, I know Carl. Thank you, Jael. I hadn't thought that far ahead."

"You've had enough to think on." He looked down at Alex again. "He left some tapes with me. Called one a death testament. Asking fate, damn it; he kept asking fate."

"Are the tapes private?"

"Not the one with my name on it. I've called an Exile Council meeting tomorrow; we'll hear it out then."

She noted that "*I've* called," but the assumption of command implied in it didn't surprise her.

"When will the meeting be?"

"Talk that out with Ben. Any time the two of you can shake loose." He looked up at the biomonitor screen. "The tape . . . he talked about the Peladeen Alternative."

That didn't surprise her either. "With you as the prospective First Lord of Peladeen?"

"Yes." He stared fixedly at Alex; the sighing of the respirator paced out a short silence. "Erica, we can't be taken down to that alternative."

She pulled herself to her feet, exhaustion dragging at her like a tangible weight.

"Then hope Lady Adrien is alive, Jael. There's nothing more important to the Phoenix right now than finding her."

He hesitated. "And if she *is* dead?"

She heard the words, the answer to that question, in her mind: *If Adrien is dead, Alexand is dead.*

The tears came unexpectedly, and she was too tired to stop them. Jael said nothing; he only offered a supporting embrace and an understanding silence, holding her until it was over, until she had herself under control again.

She was thinking of Val Severin when she finally looked up at him. "Jael, I like to delude myself that if I'd ever had a son, he'd be the kind of man you are."

He laughed. "What can I do with a gim line like that? Come on, I'm taking you back to the Cave and waving you off to Fina. You've had a week in a day."

She nodded absently. "I should talk to Carl."

"I've already lined him in, and he talked to Dr. Eliot. And I've set up a schedule; there'll be a Phoenix medtech with Alex every hour, every day, and they'll be armed. Besides, I laid edict, and so did the old Ser, and I'll keep one of the blades on watch here, too. Alex is as safe as a babe."

She touched that still hand once more and turned away. "All right, Jael."

"Hold it in faith, sister."

She smiled faintly as she stepped out of the cubicle, remembering to activate her face-screen.

"I do. I hold you in faith."

2.

It seemed a frozen tableau, the meeting of the Exile Council. Alex always called it that, and the name held. Jael sat at one end of the table in the rock-walled conference room with the portable speaker before him. He didn't have to listen to the words; he had them all laid to memory. But at the last words his breath caught and he swallowed at the tightness that closed his throat.

". . . and to you, Jael, friend and brother . . . fortune."

Jael reached out and turned off the speaker, then let the silence run a while longer until he had himself under hold again. Erica and Ben were watching him, waiting, but Andreas was still staring at the speaker.

Jael said, "I won't call that an 'advisory command.' At least, I'll leave off the 'advisory.' He laid the lines, and I intend to run the gant like he read it. And I intend to hold down his chair until he comes to claim it."

He waited then. If anyone showed any tooth, it would be Ben, and he'd be the hardest to bring around. Ben looked up, meeting his eyes, then gave him a crooked, humorless smile.

"Jael, there's a hell of a lot in that tape I don't like, but there's nothing I don't agree with. That includes your holding down his chair. Did you think I'd draw blades with you over that? I accept the alternative Alex put on that tape as exactly what he called it: the only viable alternative. That includes you as his second-in-command and heir apparent."

"Thanks, brother. Erica?"

She'd been watching Andreas, who had at length turned his gaze from the inert speaker and focused it vaguely on Jael's face. She roused herself to answer him.

"Jael, you know I'm with Alex. Could I be with him and against you?"

"No, sister, I don't think so." He looked at Andreas, who took a long breath; it came out in a sigh with the weary weight of defeat in it. He turned his palms up.

"All of this . . . Predis—what's happened in Fina . . . I can't deal with it. It just doesn't make *sense*." An introspective frown, then he shook his head. "No, it makes sense; I can understand it objectively. But I can't deal with it. Alex said I must be the . . . spiritual leader of the Phoenix. That's burden enough. I leave it to you, Jael, to assume the burden of secular leadership." He put his hands on the table and leaned forward as if to rise, but for a moment hesitated, his eyes fixed on the speaker. Then, seeming to remember his purpose, he pushed back his chair and came to his feet.

"Excuse me, I have to get to . . . the lab. . . ."

None of them questioned that or tried to stop him. Jael said to Erica, "This meet's over. Maybe you should go with him. If he needs words, they'll have to come from you."

She nodded and went to the door, resting a hand on Jael's shoulder in passing. She didn't say anything, and a silence that seemed to emanate from the rocks themselves filled the vacuum of her departure.

Finally, Ben asked, "Have you heard from Val since yesterday?"

"She called an hour ago; that's after the cloister curfew. She didn't have much, Ben. She's only been inside for two weeks and she hasn't hooked into any of the in-lines. I guess novices are supposed to stay shut unless they're asked, and except for prayers and penances, they don't often get asked. She's planting microceivers to pick up conversations she can't sit in on. One of them cost her fifty prayer penances; she got caught out of proper place. Anyway, she has a name for the novice who got pinned. Sister Betha."

"Which doesn't tell us anything."

"No, but Betha was new to Saint Petra's. Val doesn't know *how* new. She says time is relative there. They talk about something that happened twenty years when as 'lately.' But she's inside, Ben. Just hold on to that."

"Yes, I guess we have to keep reminding ourselves of the things we should be grateful for." Then he looked at his watch. "Jael, I'd better get back to Fina. Anything else you want to line out now?"

"No. It's all been drawn, brother."

3.

Mathis Galinin rose and looked around the circle of Directors. Preoccupied faces, he was thinking, as his no doubt was. The wintery afternoon sunlight heightened the colors in the tapestries on the Chamber wall, but even that warm light couldn't make those heroic scenes seem anything but faded ironies. Nothing is so stale as the glory of vanished empires.

"My lady and my lords..." He glanced at Honoria Ivanoi, wondering why he'd never noticed that she still wore black after all these years, and wondering why he should notice it now. "We'll adjourn for today and resume tomorrow morning at 10:00. Thank you."

A burgeoning of muted dialogues accompanied the exodus. Galinin turned to Phillip Woolf.

"Phillip, meet me in my office, if you will. I have something to discuss with you."

Woolf paused. "Nothing...serious, I hope."

"Nothing disastrous, at least. Excuse me—Lord Cameroodo, a word with you, please."

The tall, dark-visaged Lord of Mars stopped at the Chamber doors.

"Yes, my lord?"

Woolf didn't stay to hear the conversation; he knew what was on Galinin's mind. The same thing that made James Neeth Cameroodo even more intently sober than usual, and had occupied this august body for the better part of a day. Toramil had been rocked by a major Bond uprising only three days ago, and from all reports the compounds, and the city itself, weren't entirely quiescent yet. Cameroodo was in Concordia to ask—rather, to demand—Confleet intervention on a large scale. He called it, with no apparent self-consciousness, a "punitive force."

In the columned entry hall, Woolf's brows came down in an impatient frown when he saw the milling crowds of reporters. They wore DeKoven Woolf badges, but generally he allowed them the freedom they claimed as Independent Fesh.

13

Still, at moments like this it would be a pleasure to order them all out of the Hall.

But a show of temper of that sort would only give Selasis and his cronies satisfaction. And, he thought, as he caught a glimpse of Selasis barging through a cluster of mike- and vidicam-armed reporters, rob him of the satisfaction of seeing Selasis suffering their insistent attentions.

Woolf's jaw tensed at the shouted questions. They had nothing to do with the Directorate meeting; they were concerned with the rumors surrounding the Lady Adrien's death.

"My lord . . ."

He turned to see Captain Martin Sier of his House guard standing at attention, backed by two more Woolf guards. A sign of the times. Conpol had advised the Directors to maintain personal guards even within the Hall.

"Captain Sier." He said nothing beyond that recognition of his presence. The reporters were surging toward him, and he set off down the side corridor, striding past the waving mikes and ogling lenses. Sier and his men were hard put to keep up with him or to fend off the jostling reporters.

"No, I have nothing to say," Woolf insisted, never breaking pace. "When the Directorate has made concrete decisions concerning the situation on Mars, I'll have a statement, and not before."

That brought on a new verbal bombardment, but he looked neither right nor left, the firm set of his mouth eloquent of determination. The babble of questions seemed endless. Would they never recognize his silence as unyielding and turn on someone else? Didn't they—

"My lord!"

The shriek of alarm gave him warning. He never knew its source; perhaps one of the reporters.

He spun around, catching a flash of light reflected in the downward thrust of a blade as a man launched himself out of the crowd. The sharp pain across his left forearm triggered an explosion of anger—not alarm or fear—and his responses were instinctive, automatic, and savage. His hand locked on one flailing arm, his knee came up, smashing into flesh, eliciting a wail of agony; a jerking twist on the arm pulled the man around, then a kick to the back of the knee, a heaving turn, and the man was briefly airborne, spinning to a shuddering impact with the floor.

Pandemonium was loosed. The reporters were half panicked, half delirious with joy at this supremely newsworthy event, vidicams and mikes taking in every detail. Within seconds, ten Directorate Guards plunged into the tumult to aid the House guards. Woolf's features were taut with cold fury; his burning gaze sought the ranking Directorate guard.

"Leftant! Clear the corridor!"

"Yes, my lord!"

"My lord, your arm—"

Woolf spared Captain Sier one scathing glance, and the captain's face went red, reminded that his Lord had dealt with the attack with efficiency and dispatch, and with no help from his guardsmen. Woolf glanced down at his arm. It was a shallow cut, streaking across his left forearm, sending red threads down the back of his hand. He wasn't cognizant of any pain yet; the anger was too consuming.

"Who is he?"

The hapless assassin lay in a foetal position, moaning in pain. The two House guards pulled him to his feet and held him, while Sier searched him.

"There's no ident, my lord."

Woolf's mouth tightened in annoyance. The clamor was fading as the Directorate guardsmen unceremoniously pushed the reporters back with volleys of shouted orders.

"Let me see that." He held out his hand as one of his guards leaned down to pick up the knife. It had a silicon blade to slip past the metal detectors at the Hall entrances. He tossed it back to the guard and turned his attention to the man who had wielded the knife.

And he felt the anger draining from him, leaving only a desolate weariness.

Man? He was little more than a boy. This would-be killer of Lords wasn't more than eighteen.

"What's your name?"

The youth swallowed, finally finding his voice. "I . . . I won't tell you my name."

"Not that it matters; the SSB will answer that easily enough. But for the God's sake, will you tell me why you came bumbling in here trying to jab that knife into me? If you wished to see me dead, surely you could've been more imaginative and more intelligent about it."

The youth lifted his chin defiantly.

"None of you fat, soft-bellied, money-hungry Lords will listen to reason! You live off the fruits of slavery, bloating yourselves on riches bought with the blood of the enchained masses! The only language you know is violence and brutality. I've come to speak to you in your own tongue—with blood and death!"

The guards reacted with shocked dismay, and Sier's arm came up to silence him with the flat of his hand, but Woolf stopped him.

"Sier! That's exactly what he wants." He was beginning to feel the pain. "You mindless young fool! Tell me if you found *me* fat and soft-bellied while you lay wailing on the floor after attacking an unarmed man. And what 'enchained masses' do you speak for? The Bonds? Is that it?"

The boy was only capable of a quick nod.

"I suppose you belong to the ROM." Again, a silent nod. Woolf took a step closer. "Let me try to make something clear to you, although, considering your behavior, I doubt you're intelligent enough to grasp it. Your inept attempt to kill me doesn't disturb me nearly so much as your ignorance. I suggest you study a little history, beginning with Lionar Mankeen, and I suggest you inform yourself on the Galinin-Woolf-Robek resolution."

He blinked in confusion. "The . . . what?"

Woolf coldly repeated himself, adding, "A code of standards for humane treatment of Bonds, my youthful illiterate. *I* helped draft that resolution, and I can't be held responsible for its failure. If you want to strike a blow for the Bonds, it would be better aimed elsewhere, and by the God, learn to speak for yourself! Don't spout nonsense parroted from someone else. If I must have my life jeopardized, damn it, I won't have it done in the name of ignorance and inanity!"

He stopped, realizing he was losing control, and his disgust was as much for that as for the erstwhile assassin. Finally, he waved his hand in a gesture of dismissal.

"Let him go, Captain."

Sier's jaw dropped. "What, my lord?"

"Let him go." He turned on the Directorate guard leftant. "That's an order. Holy God, he's only a boy, and a fool at that. He isn't worth the effort and expense of taking to trial."

The youth nearly collapsed when the guards released him. He stared at Woolf in stunned disbelief.

"I—I don't . . . understand."

"Of course you don't. Now get out of my sight and out of this Hall. Leftant, let him pass."

"But—but, my lord—"

"Leftant, I have serious problems to deal with; I haven't time for trivia. Sier—come along. Lord Galinin is expecting me."

"Thank you for calling, Phillip." Olivet smiled out from the screen, her concern reflected only in the deepening of the lavender cast in her eyes. She was in the nursery; Woolf could see Alexandra and Justin behind her building castles of glowing blocks. Olivet wouldn't let them hear or see her anxiety.

"I just didn't want you to find out about it on the vidicom 'casts, Olivet; the reporters enjoy sensation too much."

"Well, I'm sure it must have seemed rather sensational." Then her smile almost faded. "You're sure your arm isn't—"

"It's only a cut. I'll have Dr. Stel take care of it as soon as I get home, and that should be within an hour."

"All right, Phillip. Now, you mustn't keep Lord Mathis waiting. Give him my regards."

"I will. Goodbye."

The image faded from the screen as he rose and left the desk to join Mathis Galinin in the chairs at the windowall. He had wrapped a handkerchief around his arm, but it kept slipping; he frowned as he tightened it.

Galinin smiled wryly. "The young man should have chosen one of the truly soft-bellied Lords for a target."

"The young man hadn't the sense he was born with."

"Apparently not. Why did you release him?"

Woolf let his head fall back against the cushions of the chair. Why, indeed?

"I don't know. He simply didn't seem worth the bother."

"A man who tried to assassinate a Directorate Lord?"

"Perhaps it was unwise, but he was only a boy spouting nonsense."

Galinin's rumbling laugh surprised him.

"In fact, it was an eminently wise decision, Phillip. It will serve to make the ROM an object of mild contempt or even humor. You're quite right; he wasn't worth the bother. However, I'm sorry about the cut."

Woolf laughed. "At any rate, you'll understand the slight delay in my arrival. What was it you wanted to talk to me about? Toramil?"

"No. I hope the unrest settles, but I'm afraid this week's disturbances are only a prelude. I don't like Cameroodo's attitude; he's being particularly hardheaded. I'm going to talk to him privately this evening, but I doubt I'll change his thinking. That isn't what I wanted to talk to you about. I finally got the truth from Commander Cory about Andreas Riis's escape."

Woolf leaned forward intently. "Then he *did* escape."

"Yes. Five days ago. That fool Cory didn't want to admit he let Riis slip through his fingers; he tried to make it seem he'd died. That might be acceptable for public consumption, but I won't tolerate having the truth withheld when *I* ask for it. Cory has learned that lesson the hard way. He's no longer Commander of the SSB. He's been exiled to a minor post on Perseus."

"So we've lost Riis."

"Yes, and never succeeded in breaking his conditioning. However, I'm told the SSB psychocontrollers found the experience educational."

"I'm sure. Has anyone any idea how he escaped?"

"Oh, yes. There was no dearth of information on that once I got past Cory. Of course, no one knows how the Phoenix found out he was in Pendino, but there were plenty of witnesses to the actual escape. They all agree that Riis and his two rescuers disappeared into vacuum."

Woolf's eyebrows came up. "Oh?"

"No doubt it's true, and I'm afraid we must assume the matter transmitter exists as something more than a mathematical theory."

"Two rescuers? Why was it necessary to send rescuers? Why didn't Riis just disappear long ago?"

"Well, for one thing, I assume they didn't know where he was, and apparently this device isn't the quasi-magical thing it might seem. The two men had to gain access to the Pendino DC from outside. It was only then that the vanishing act occurred."

Woolf rose and went to the windowall to scowl out at the Plaza, barred with long afternoon shadows, the Fountain of Victory a frosty froth of white.

"Damn Cory! To have Riis and then lose him—it's intolerable!"

"I'm surprised we kept him so long. There's one aspect of this I find particularly interesting—the names given by the so-called inspectors, or, rather, one of those names. The ranking member of this duo called himself 'Major Ransom.' Perhaps you'll remember that a man named Alex Ransom was with Riis when he was arrested."

Woolf nodded. "He escaped soon after their arrest, didn't he?"

"It was nearly a month later. Yes, he escaped."

"Wasn't he betrayed again?"

"Twice more, in fact, but the SSB didn't manage to recapture him."

"There's efficiency for you."

Galinin laughed. "Don't be too hard on them. They're up against an extraordinary adversary in the Phoenix, and perhaps in Alex Ransom."

Woolf regarded him curiously. "Have they any further identification of him?"

"No, and all the SSB files on Ransom have disappeared. At first, they considered him simply a menial, since he was flying Riis's 'car when they were arrested, but they began to wonder when he was betrayed to them twice more."

"Time enough for them to wonder. Apparently someone in the Phoenix thought him at least as important— or undesirable— as Dr. Riis. You think the 'Major Ransom' who rescued him is the same man?"

At that, Galinin shrugged. "I can't believe the name was chosen at random, but if this is the mysterious Alex Ransom surfacing again, I'm wondering why he used his real name— or real pseudonym, probably—for this mission."

Woolf considered that a moment, eyes narrowed. "It does open some interesting areas of speculation. The name means nothing to the Concord. If it carries a message, it would seem to be intended for the Phoenix."

"Yes, and it may be another indication of schism within the Society. Someone tried to put Ransom out of the way. Perhaps he's trying to establish the fact that they didn't succeed. But whoever he is, he may not surface again. One of the DC guards hit him with a laser beam, but he vanished before the extent of his injuries could be determined."

Woolf frowned in annoyance. "Who *is* he?"

"He's piqued my curiosity, too. I find myself hoping he did survive so I might eventually have an answer to that. All we can be sure of now is that he's a friend of Andreas Riis's. A good friend. He risked, and may have lost, his life for him."

"We'll have to be careful or we'll have a popular hero on our hands. How much of this will you make public?"

"The fact of the escape, but not the means. We'll simply say that two armed men, disguised as SSB officers, took Riis out at gunpoint, but I want nothing said about the probable use of a matter transmitter. The Fesh are close enough to panic as it is."

"Will you mention the name used by one of the rescuers?"

Woolf was half joking with that question, but Galinin considered his answer quite seriously.

"Perhaps I will, Phillip. Something's happened in the Phoenix; a power struggle. We can assume that on the basis of these betrayals, and since Riis's arrest, their military program has expanded at an alarming rate. I can't believe that name was used gratuitously, and if Ransom is with Riis, I think we'd do well to help him get his message through, if that's his purpose. I'd rather deal with the Phoenix under Riis's leadership. At least he's not an entirely unknown quantity."

"Is there anything else I should know about this?"

Galinin shook his head, absently working at the gold Concord crest ring on his left hand.

"No, but I'm concerned about the direction the Phoenix seems to be taking. Confleet is convinced they're building up for a major military campaign."

Woolf said coldly, "The peaceful Phoenix is showing its talons. Perhaps Rich misjudged it after all." He was aware of Galinin's inquiring scrutiny, but chose to ignore it, and after a moment Galinin turned to look out at the Plaza.

"At any rate, we may have to deal with this taloned Phoenix in the future. I hope it doesn't come to open revolt. We can defeat them, but we're rocking on the edge of chaos now, and it would be a costly war, considering the degree to which they've infiltrated the Concord."

"I hope it doesn't come to that," Woolf responded with a flat inflection, and Galinin seemed to recognize his unspoken plea for a change of subject.

His white brows were drawn in a frown as he said, "I've reached a decision on another matter, Phillip. I've decided to cancel the Concord Day ceremonies in the Plaza this year."

Woolf stared at him, stunned. The Plaza ceremonies had marked the celebration of Concord Day for a century and a half. Then the shock passed, giving way to numb resignation.

"It's unfortunate psychologically."

"I don't like it, but Conpol has been pressing me. They don't think they can maintain order. It's their attitude that forced me into the decision more than anything else. Take a hundred thousand Bonds and Fesh, three thousand Lords and their families, add five thousand nervous Conpol and Directorate guards, and disaster is almost inevitable." He gave in to a long sigh. "It's only one of many small surrenders. Bit by bit we surrender the Concord, and we don't even know what we're surrendering it to. But—" He glanced at Woolf's arm, "—if something like this can happen on an ordinary day in the Hall of the Directorate, I can't risk what might happen on Concord Day with that many people and armed men crowded together."

Woolf turned and gazed out the windowall again. There were only a few people in the Plaza this late in the day; it seemed peculiarly bleak under the cold, clear sky.

"I should be relieved not to have to endure the ordeal again. I assume other celebrations won't be affected?"

"No, and I'll plan special public entertainment, but only in small groups. You'd better have your broadcasting branch work out some vidicom programs for the evening. We'll discuss it in detail later, but you might give it some thought and get your producers thinking."

"I'll see to it." He paused, glancing at his watch. "Mathis, will you join Olivet and me for supper? We're dining alone tonight—for once."

Galinin grimaced irritably. "I'd enjoy that, but I have James Cameroodo to contend with this evening. But I'm anticipating the newscasts tonight. I'm looking forward to the screened account of the Lord Woolf singlehandedly putting down an armed assailant."

Woolf groaned. "I would manage to get attacked in full view of a covey of reporters."

"You might be a candidate for a popular hero, yourself."

"Never. I'm cast as the villain in this life." He started for the door. "Goodbye, Mathis."

"Goodbye, Phillip. Be careful."

When the doors closed, Galinin frowned. He'd never before felt an inclination to add that cautionary admonition. It seemed quite natural now.

4.

Valentin Severin bit back an expression of annoyance as her foot caught in the hem of her habit, nearly sending her—and her armload of clean linens—tumbling onto the steps. The word she'd almost spoken wouldn't be appropriate in the cloister of Saint Petra's of Ellay.

She readjusted her load, freeing one hand to lift her skirt as she continued up the stairs. Don't *hurry* so, she admonished herself, hearing the words in Sister Herma's unctuous tones. In the Holy Mezion's house, one must comport oneself with dignity out of respect for Him. Herma could make a breach of decorum sound like a mortal sin.

Frustration usually focuses on trivial annoyances when the real source is beyond hope of control, and Val found annoyances enough here. Sister Herma was one.

Stone stairways were another, and somehow she wasn't

suitably impressed that these were dished with nearly two hundred years of *dignified* footsteps. And it was difficult enough to accustom herself to stationary stairs without the added burden of negotiating them in a flowing, floor-length habit, and difficult enough to find her way through the shadowy corridors without the veil that enveloped her in a blue fog.

At the top of the stairs she stopped to catch her breath. She was trembling, and that index of the state of her nerves dismayed her. But there was due cause for it; she'd endured eighteen days of convent life, and it seemed like eighteen weeks, but she was still no closer to accomplishing her mission. And after what Jael told her about Alex, about that wound...

The Phoenix had failed him at every turn where Lady Adrien was concerned, and now the burden of failure fell most heavily on Val. She was the only one behind these walls, the only one with any hope of finding the Lady Adrien.

She *is* alive. How many times a day did she tell herself that? She is alive; she must be.

But all Val had to show for her eighteen days' incarceration was a name that meant nothing in itself—Sister Betha—and the fact that Lectris was still at Saint Petra's, which meant as little, and twenty-five microceivers planted in various places in the cloister where they might pick up conversations between the Sisters from which a mere novice would be excluded. So far, they had provided only that name and hours of stultifying boredom listening to the tapes in the after-curfew privacy of her room.

In regard to the sensational tragedy visited on Saint Petra's in Sister Betha's death, the Sisters cautioned curious novices not to be afraid and to pray. Pray for Sister Betha's soul and that of the benighted person who had desecrated the Holy Mezion's house with violence. They wouldn't even identify him, as Conpol had, as a Bond gone inexplicably insane, nor did they mention the fact that Conpol had found no trace of the crazed desecrator at Saint Petra's. The novices were more inclined to talk among themselves about the tragedy, but Val soon learned that they knew no more—in fact, much less—about it than she did.

She heard footsteps, the measured pace adopted by all these veiled women. She shifted her load and started down the corridor, imitating that *dignified* pace and studying the nun as she approached, trying to identify her. Val was learning the visual cues, but it was a slow process; another source of frustration. This one she didn't know, but she nodded respectfully.

"Good morning, Sister."

"Good morning, Sister Alexandra. Lord bless."

Val sighed as the footsteps faded behind her. They all seemed to recognize *her* easily enough. She paused at a cross-corridor, looking down toward an area of brighter light, hearing the sound of children's voices. The morning play period. She could reach the linen storage room faster by continuing along this hall, but she decided on the longer route via the arcade overlooking the play court.

The court was of interest to her as the site of Sister Betha's murder, and because Lectris had returned to his duties there after two days in the infirmary for treatment of his leg wound. Val took every opportunity to look for him, but she'd never seen him talk to any of the nuns. Watching Lectris from within the cloister was a futile endeavor when her opportunities were so limited, but it was something concrete, and in the hushed, ritualized world of the cloister she grasped at any straw simply to preserve her sanity.

Still, she doubted anything would preserve it if it weren't for her nightly contacts with Jael. She hadn't realized how important he had become to her, or how much she would miss him, until this exile into the cloister.

Sunlight glared through the intricate screens guarding the arcade, casting a weave of shadow patterns on the stone. She looked down into the court. Lectris was there, kneeling in a bed of flowers, alone and intent on his task. Four nuns were supervising the children: teachers. None of them were novices, and she was totally convinced, after eighteen days, that Lady Adrien could only be here as a novice. Passing herself off as a full nun would be all but impossible; there were too many matters of custom, ritual, and attitude that no outsider could understand or imitate.

She caught a movement out of the corner of her eye and saw a veiled figure come out of one of the side corridors, cross to the screen, and stand looking down into the court, apparently unaware of Val, some ten meters away.

A novice. Val had eliminated all but fifteen of the thirty-six novices simply because they were too tall, and of those fifteen, she had managed to get VP ident that eliminated five more, but that still left ten likely candidates.

This novice was one of the fifteen who fell within the height range, but she was far too heavy. Val didn't know her name; she seemed even more reclusive than the other Sisters. Val identified her as "the plump one," and that extra weight eliminated her as a possibility. Lady Adrien had never suffered the problem of obesity, and this woman—

Val frowned, inwardly cursing the habit. From the white koyf framing the face, a cape-like drape extended to the waist, and the habit itself fell from the shoulders in loose folds, unfitted, unbelted, all the way to the ground. As unflattering, she thought bitterly, as it was successful in disguising the figure under it. But now, as she studied the novice, she realized her bulk wasn't simply a matter of overweight, and she chastised herself for having blithely classified it as such. For one thing, the diet in the cloister would make overweight nothing short of a miracle.

She remembered a monitored fragment of conversation between two nuns; something about Sister—what was the name? Iris. That was it. Sister Iris was excused from certain duties because "her time is almost at hand." Val had taken that euphemism to mean one of the Sisters was near death, but perhaps another kind of "time" was indicated.

The novice's head turned in her direction, and Val looked away, down into the courtyard, watching the jubilant choreography of the children in a circle game.

The novice was pregnant.

There was a certain irony in that, but she suspected there was also heartbreak for the novice. The irony was that one didn't expect a nun to be pregnant. The loose habit hid her pregnancy not only in a physical sense, but because it was a *nun's* habit. Yet nothing in the rules of this Order precluded membership because of pregnancy, and it probably wasn't so unusual in the Sisters of Faith.

There was a lesson to be learned here: Don't take anything for granted.

Val glanced obliquely down the arcade and found it empty;

the novice had disappeared into the cloister. At any rate, whether by virtue of plumpness or pregnancy, she was still eliminated from the list of possibilities.

Val sighed, feeling the weight of her load. Sister Herma would give her a lesson if she didn't get these linens put away, and that would mean more hours in the chapel saying penances on aching knees.

5.

Tickings and swishings, metronomic electronic pulsations; the rhythms never stopped, never faltered, and seldom changed their cadences.

He floated in an electronic womb, suspended in soft warmth, webbed in multiple umbilicals; tubes to force air into his lungs and pump it out; tubes to carry moisture and sustenance into his body; still more tubes to carry the wastes of living away.

They were keeping his body alive.

There had been a time when he was wracked with despairing resentment at that, when he was still capable of wondering why. Why did they refuse him what he sought?

He passed a threshold of tolerance somewhere in the endless, monotonous transitions from awareness to unawareness, the myriad small deaths and births. Beyond that threshold, the mental circuits ceased to function, etched to fragments, neural rags that could no longer carry the impulses, that diffused energy in errant, aimless patterns.

They couldn't keep his body alive forever.

He could only wait; there was no alternative to that.

And waiting asked nothing of him. Impatience exists only within a temporal framework, and he'd been freed of the reference grid of time; the matrix of memory had collapsed. Memories came only in sensory fragments, sensations divorced from the rational processes that would give them meaning.

He experienced memory fragments of another limbo when existence had also been separated from time and locked with a pattern of fear and pain. He might still be in that limbo. The pattern of fear and pain was still constant.

ar James Neeth Cameroodo so particu-
him in some senses more than Selasis,
wields more real power.

power over Cameroodo, which is one
pies a more prominent position in the
ns. We should, I believe, be grateful for
r Cameroodo; otherwise, we'd have two
ly threatening factors to deal with, and
f a challenge as it is.

ost concerns me is motivation.

erstand. His compounds are dismal sinks
ivation because he considers it unprof-
anything else, and because he is too
to care how his guards and overseers
and efficiency as long as they do it. The
nanization in Selasid compounds are
dvertent.

of dehumanization in Cameroodo com-
ul and systematic.

derstand that, too, even if I haven't
fying it, and there's the source of my

iders himself a religious man and he
ally as any Bond, the divinity of the
r questions it, and he will maintain it
a. He sees the status quo as a morally
sible premise. He might disapprove of
s, but will remain loyal to him and his
the status quo without, I'm convinced,
motives. Selasis defends what is pre-
oodo defends what he regards as di-

ascendancy over his Bonds, and he
ive pronoun equally sanctioned. They
to his possession by divine right, and
nale for him to maintain them in the
cannot see them, in any sense, as
human beings. If he were to recognize
destroy the rationale, and his psychic
and solely dependent, upon it. In order
ale, he *makes* objects of his Bonds
tic dehumanizing processes.

But the fear had become vague and unfocused. He didn't know what he was afraid of until it was upon him. It surfaced only in those transition periods on the brink of unconsciousness and semiawareness, taking the old shapes, the terrifying images, of his nightmares. They floated out of the darkness, aligning themselves in the familiar lattice of horror.

Yet when they were gone, fear was also gone. That asked a temporal framework, too; one that included a future.

Pain was ultimately the only constant.

Pain was pure sensation demanding no ratiocination, no temporal framework; it transcended both thought and time. It was aboriginal. It antedated and survived the mental processes that drew the demarcations of time. It would be the last index of his existence, as it had been the first.

They couldn't keep his body alive forever.

He looked out through the misted, distorted prism of vision that only occasionally functioned, and that was a matter of indifference. There was nothing he had to see, or wanted to see. Except the screen. His eyes gathered images, but they were only phenomena of light. All sensory input met a looped circuit within his mind.

Except the screen.

He understood the screen. He watched himself abstracted, reduced to points of light trailing glowing, undulating lines endlessly across a blackness. Those points and lines were the total of his being. He existed there, not in the embryonic husk whose only purpose was to provide a vessel for pain.

The lines would stop finally; he waited.

PHOENIX MEMFILES: DEPT HUMAN SCIENCES:
SOCIOTHEOLOGY (HS/STh)
SUBFILE: LAMB, RICHARD: PERSONAL NOTES
5 JUNE 3253
DOC LOC #819/19208-1812-1614-563253

I've just finished a report on my latest sojourn to the Cameroodo compounds in Toramil, and take no satisfaction in it. Nor certainly any satisfaction in Toramil.

The Lord James Neeth Cameroodo frightens me.

That, however, I can't put in so many words in a properly written field report. It's a highly subjective reaction that I can't objectively validate.

I can report conditions in the compounds, of course; the squalid subsistence level at which Cameroodo Bonds are forced to exist, the inadequate housing, clothing, and basic sustenance. Infant mortality is twenty percent higher in Cameroodo compounds than in Galinin compounds, for instance; the mean age of death is forty-five as compared to sixty-two. Yet work hours lost due to illness are thirty-four percent higher in Galinin compounds. That doesn't mean more Galinin Bonds suffer illnesses, only that Cameroodo Bonds aren't allowed to take time off from work because of illness. Not until they're incapable of working, and Cameroodo Bonds have a name for the compound infirmaries: the places of dying.

And I c
Bonds mu
hour, that
ships and
more vulr
units as
"Pairings'
Bonds ar
spring—
especially
are taker
reared ir
pounds,

I'm
ligion in
defying
"soft lib
the risk
one ins
oversee
because
even st
by it, a
anism.
gently
forms
herds
to ano
seers
flocks

I
even
these
perio
shift.
agon
made

Y
or a
facti
syste
still

So why do I f
larly? And I fear
although the latter

He also wields
reason Selasis occ
Society's calculatic
Selasis's power ove
divergent and equa
Selasis is enough c

Perhaps what m

Selasis I can und
of cruelty and depr
itable to make ther
lacking in empathy
maintain discipline
processes of dehur
cruel, but oddly ina

But the processes
pounds are purpose

Perhaps I can u
succeeded in quanti
fear.

Cameroodo cons
accepts, as fatalistic
status quo. He neve
with his dying breat
sanctioned and defer
Orin's moral excesse
passionate defense of
recognizing his real
cious to him; Came
vinely sanctioned.

That includes his
considers the possess
are objects entrusted
it is vital to the ratic
status of objects. H
comparable to him as
them as such it would
foundations are built,
to maintain the ratio
through those system

I must somehow—and soon—put Cameroodo in a more objective framework; he must be entered as a prime factor in our equations. If we do succeed at some future date in negating Selasis, then Cameroodo will become an independent factor, one that I'm afraid has thus far been underestimated as a negative—and threatening—quantity.

CHAPTER XVII: Septem 3258

●II●I●I●I●I●I●I●I●I●I●I●I●I●I●I●I●I●I●I●I●I●I●I●I●

1.

Jael left Erica in a medical head session with Carl Roi and Dr. Eliot; they didn't seem to miss his going. Outside the cubicle, he stopped for a word with the blade on guard.

"Corb, I'll be back in an hour. If anything comes down 'com me."

"I got your seq set on my 'com, Jael," he answered, eyeing his Drakonis Bond garb curiously.

Jael's costume attracted more looks as he rode the pedway down the hall, and the same kind of curiosity. What sort of gim was Jael running in Bond weave?

They'd never believe him if he told them. Jael the son of Amik nobbing with Shepherds, laying his life for stakes and coming away with both hands empty.

Alex had said the Bonds must be warned. So Jael was making a run at it. This was his first pass today, and it wasn't as difficult as he expected. The medallion and the words opened the doors, even if the one was a fake. But the words were true weight. He had been to the underground city of Semele on

Dionysus to see the Elder Shepherd Mahmed. The old man treated him like he came in the wake of saints, and perhaps he did.

When Jael reached his apartment, he set the sec-systems and went over all three rooms with a montector. He hadn't set foot here for two weeks, since before Alex Ransom moved into that ticking cubicle in the infirmary.

No change. Erica said it with a shake of her head. Twelve days, and no change, and maybe that was something to be grateful for. Jael had seen enough death; something happened around the eyes when it was close. It was in Alex's eyes now.

Jael went to the comconsole in the salon and called the COS HQ frequency. Telstoi was waiting.

"Tel, I'm staying over at the old Ser's until Erica's ready for an escort. Val should be calling in the next half hour. Give me an interconn here when she does. You have the 'com seq? My apartment."

"Yes, sir, I have it."

"Thanks, Tel."

Jael cleared the frequency settings, then went into the bath, stripping off his Bondman's clothes as he went. He only had time for ten minutes of Gam Chi calisthenics and a shower before a buzz recalled him to the comconsole. The exercises were a well entrenched habit he'd let slip lately, and that was asking fate. He needed to be on top, physically and mentally, more than ever now. He wrapped a towel around his still wet body and reached for a headset.

"Yes, Tel."

"Your call from Val, sir. Go ahead."

"Jael?"

He took a quick breath, wondering, as he always did, at the sudden tightness in his throat. He'd been right all those years ago. A green-eyed Fesh sweet, and a heart-holder; that more than anything.

"Are you well, sister?" Then, with a short laugh, "Sorry. That name probably rubs wrong."

He was relieved to hear her laugh; it sounded easy and without too much of an edge.

"Brother, from you it sounds good, and I'm well, other than being in my usual state of near frenzy. You'd better talk to

Erica about transing another medical package."

"Val, you haven't tossed down all those pills already?"

"Not quite; don't worry. How's Alex?"

He braced himself to answer the question. "No change. But he's no worse."

There was a brief pause; he could almost see her nodding acceptance of all the implications in that.

"Well, I've finally got something to report from here, Jael. At least *that's* a change."

"Thank the God. What is it?"

"All those hours of eavesdropping on the Sisters's gossip paid off finally. I have something more on Sister Betha. Jael, she was a *Bond*."

He stared at the lights on the console, wondering why those words seemed so incomprehensible. If Betha was—

"You better lay it out for me, Val."

"I picked up three of the senior Sisters talking in the pantry—that seems to be a favorite gossiping spot—and Sister Betha's murder came up. They refer to it as her 'passing.' Anyway, one of them put forth the theory that the assassin, the 'insane Bond,' was someone out of Betha's past. She said, 'After all, Betha *was* a Bond. Perhaps *he* was the real reason she came to Saint Petra's to begin with.' Then she went on to say something about how everybody *knows* how uncontrollable Bonds are when it comes to 'bodily desires.'"

Jael managed a laugh, but it was short-lived.

"But how did they know Betha was a Bond? You said every Sister's past life is a closed chapter. No one but the Supra's lined in on it."

There was a hint of impatience in her tone. "Jael, I'm sure no one *told* them she was a Bond. They knew the same way you'd know. How long does it take you to read anyone's class just from the way they act and talk?"

"Point, sister. Five minutes, usually, but I've never tried to read anyone in a nun's suit."

"Well, that might take you *six* minutes. The Sisters probably aren't as quick, so give them a couple of days. But they had somewhere around *four months*. That's something else that came out in this conversation. They were trying to remember exactly when Betha entered the cloister. The consensus was that it was just before Saint Budh's day, and that was 10 Avril."

"And Lady Adrien disappeared 3 Avril." That was only thinking in words, and he didn't expect a response. He went to a chair and sank into it, pushing a hand through his damp hair. "Oh, 'Zion, that's the first ray of light we've had since . . . Val, the Master of Shadows made a slip. Betha had to be *Mariet*. He'd be going on height and weight, and Mariet was Adrien's mannequin." Then he stopped, frowning. "Unless Mariet wasn't the only Bond novice at Saint P's."

"But she *was*. Jael, Saint P's isn't closed to Bonds, but the number who apply is infinitesimal. The odds are against there being two Bond novices here at the same time, and I know none of the rest of the novices are Bonds. Well, there's a couple I can't vouch for personally, but I've asked around—subtly, of course—among the ones I'm on good terms with, and there aren't any Bonds. Not now. That means Mariet isn't here any more, and *that* means—"

"It's a true-weight ray of light, and thank the God. Thanks to you, sister."

She hesitated then, and he heard an uneasy laugh.

"Well, I wanted to give you that first, because I have more to report, and it's not so encouraging. I told you I'd eliminated all but two of the novices for one reason or another—height, weight, VP ident. Well, today I . . . I got voice recordings from the last two."

Jael pulled the towel up around his shoulders, feeling a chill in the air.

"And you eliminated them, too?"

"Yes. I've eliminated *all* the novices. But, Jael, I can't believe Lady Adrien would be here as anything but a novice. Not unless Thea's hiding her in a secret dungeon. It doesn't make sense. Lectris is here, Mariet *was* here—I'm convinced she was Betha—so Lady Adrien *must* be here."

"Val, I know." He could understand her desperation, but the hint of panic in her tone cut to his heart. "Let's look it over on a cool slant."

"Maybe *you* should look it over. I think I'm past a cool slant."

"All right, have you looked at this? Maybe after Bruno pinned Mariet, Adrien left Saint Petra's."

"No, not if she's one of the novices. I run a head count every day at sunrise and sunset vespers. There were thirty-seven novices before Betha's murder, and thirty-six afterward, and no new novices have come in. That would never be kept secret."

"Then the gist must be in the elimination process."

"Jael, I've gone over every piece of information I have, and every novice, time and time again."

He said lightly, "And I thought you were gimming us all this time while you lounged off the days."

That brought a laugh, even if it was brief.

"Of course I was. Saint Petra's is just a resort spa in disguise. All right, Jael, I'll start at the beginning again. I've missed something, but the God help me, I don't know what it is. I'll start on the tall ones. Maybe one of them is wearing padded shoes. Does SI have any detectors for that?"

"I'll check with Ben." He leaned back in the chair, his smile fading into an introspective frown. "Val, there's more here that doesn't make sense. Why is she still in hide? She must know Selasis already buried her."

"Maybe she's hoping for a contact with Alex—with the Phoenix—before she makes a move."

"She isn't making the contact easy."

"Of course not. We can't be sure how much she knows, and even if she's sure Selasis is satisfied *now* that she's dead, what if something turned up to make him realize Bruno made an error? I wouldn't be breathing easy if I were her."

"No, I suppose not. Well, at least you're behind the walls, Val. You'll line in on her sooner or later."

"But how much time do I have? Later may be too late. Too late for . . . for Alex. Jael, I've been thinking about . . ." She hesitated, then went on firmly, "We've talked about it before, and I know you don't agree with me, but I still think I should try to approach Sister Thea and show her the medallion."

· "Val, we have to assume Thea's protecting Adrien with all she's got. You go to her with that medal and tell her to show it to Adrien, what can she do? If she takes it, she's admitting Adrien's there, and your word that you're friendly won't carry any weight. In her place, I'd toss you and the medal out of Saint Petra's on the minute. Remember, she's already seen a murder in the cloister, and you can tally what that did for a peace-loving Sister-hermit with seventy-some years on her."

"Jael, I know, but I—I've got to do *something*—"

"Oh, Val . . . little sister, I know you're holding on with your fingernails, and there's no one there to reach out a hand to you. Please . . . don't let go. You may have to go to Thea before the last card's down, but we won't run that gant unless we're pushed to it."

He listened through a silence, then heard a resigned sigh. "I suppose you're right. Well, I must get to the day's collection of tapes and hope I don't fall asleep right when Sister Herma tells Sister Helen she's decided that obnoxious new novice Alexandra simply will never become a proper nun. A disgrace to Saint P's. Damn, this is ruining my knees, you know."

He laughed at that. "Then behave yourself, sister; they're your best feature. With the exception of that upper-caste nose, and certain other features . . . in between."

"Oh, Jael, please—not while I'm locked in a nunnery."

He took a long breath. "Yes. Well, it's a little monkish around here. So, get to your gossip and stay off your knees if you can. And thanks for the word on Betha. That gives us all a new lease on hope." He hesitated, feeling his throat tightening again. "Val, I'll be here waiting for you. Always."

Her voice was only a whisper. "I know. Fortune, brother."

"Fortune . . ."

2.

It was becoming increasingly difficult to remember the security procedures. Today, Erica forgot to call ahead to Ben before she transed from the COS HQ. She'd been too preoccupied with medical indices, with the data that spelled out a medical paradox. The wound was healing—slowly, to be sure, but it was healing—yet the patient was on a long, inexorable downward slide; psychologically, totally unresponsive, physically, only weakly responsive.

Twelve days. The exiles at the Cave of Springs would have

been totally demoralized except for two factors: Jael and the LR-MT.

Jael had assumed command of the COS HQ from the moment Alex surrendered it, and none of the exiles took exception to it; he made it seem both natural and inevitable. There was no breakdown in discipline, no changes in duties or schedules, and, above all, little free time for anyone. The COS HQ staff was, if anything, busier now than before Alex's collapse, and Andreas had plunged with that intense concentration that always amazed her into the LR-MT. Two more Fina physicists had joined him and James Lyden and Caris Bruce, and together they retreated into another world whose language was numbers and equations. From that world, messages occasionally emerged to give hope to the exiles. Tentative plans for an experimental test were already being made.

But Alex lay in his guarded cubicle, drifting in and out of consciousness, always out of her reach, evidencing no awareness of her or anything around him, except the biomonitor screen. He seemed to understand its function, and she knew why he watched it; she knew it wasn't in hope. Not hope in the usual sense.

Erica only realized she'd slipped up on the security procedures when she transed into the Fina MT room and found Ben waiting for her at the door. She looked over at the two techs manning the console. There were always two on every shift now, and both these men were loyals.

"Hello, Phil . . . Chan. Thanks for the ride."

Chan Orley was hurriedly clearing the orientation board. "Any time, Dr. Radek. How was your trip?"

She knew the real meaning of that question and shrugged uncomfortably.

"Nothing's changed. Hello, Ben."

He only nodded, wearing that typical, faintly anxious frown as he walked with her into the corridor.

"Erica—"

"I know, I didn't call you. I'm sorry."

"Well, Mike Compton signaled me, and I happened to be close by; the Council meeting just adjourned."

The corridor was busy for this late hour. Erica automatically noted postures, gestures, voice levels; the aura of urgency was all-pervading, but it didn't surprise her. Predis Ussher was a master at mass manipulation. He engendered and sustained that urgency and used it to negate doubt.

"What about the Council meeting, Ben? Was anything said about yesterday's convenient power failure?"

He laughed caustically. "Of course not, and I kept my mouth shut through the whole damn meeting. You'd have been proud of me."

"Didn't anyone mention the newscast? Predis may have cut Fina off, but not the outside chapters."

"The rumors are floating around, but no one on the Council was going to put it up to him, and like I said, I was a good boy and didn't say a word. Not even when he announced a change in the timetable for the offensive."

Erica looked up at him. "What kind of change?"

"What do you think? He's moving it up. This isn't for general publication yet. He says it's tentative."

"That means he wants to make the announcement himself at the next rally."

"Probably. That's scheduled for tomorrow. Anyway, that should take everybody's mind off the fact that the SSB finally admitted Andreas *did* escape."

"Predis is adept at creating diversions. Did the newscast mention the names of Andreas's rescuers?"

Ben's frown at that was one of mild puzzlement.

"Yes, as a matter of fact, and we didn't have a chance to add anything to that script; Woolf was sitting right on top of the whole broadcast."

"As long as they mentioned 'Major Ransom.' What's the new date for the offensive?"

"Concord Day: 14 Octov."

She felt the chill of pallor in her cheeks, and knew she wasn't successful at keeping her dismay hidden.

"Ben, that's only a little more than a month."

He nodded bleakly. "Thirty-seven days."

3.

Predis Ussher carefully separated two loops of the gold braid crisscrossing the front of his blue uniform; he didn't shift his gaze from the mirror when the door chime rang.

"John, that must be Jan Barret. Unlock the doorscreens for him."

John M'Kim raised an eyebrow, then went to the door. "I have work to do, Predis. I'll be on my way."

"Very well. As for the uniforms, I'm pleased. Rather impressive, don't you think, Rob?"

Hendrick was examining the other uniforms on the rack in the center of the office. He looked across at Ussher.

"Quite impressive, Predis. Hello, Jan."

M'Kim spared Barret a distracted nod in passing. "Excuse me, Commander, I must get back to my office."

Ussher was facing the mirror again, studying his reflection critically. "Lock the doorscreens, Jan."

Barret complied, his gaze shifting from Hendrick to Ussher to the clothes rack.

"What's all this, Predis?"

"Our uniforms. What every properly attired member of the Phoenix will be wearing during and after the offensive." He pivoted toward Barret. "Rob, show Jan his uniform."

Hendrick shuffled through the uniforms, then pulled one out and hung it at the front of the rack. Barret eyed it dubiously, noting that it was less ornate than Ussher's; there wasn't as much gold braid.

"Where did you get these?"

Ussher walked over to the rack, a private smile of satsifaction hovering around his lips.

"John M'Kim procured them, of course, from a number of sources. The insignia and that sort of thing is applied here in Fina."

"Who's going to be wearing these things?"

"Everyone, Jan. These are samples of the various styles." He pulled out another uniform, devoid of braid. "This is for the rank-and-file members, for instance. Of course, our double idents won't be sporting these for a while."

"Holy God, Predis, we've never needed uniforms, not even in FO."

Hendrick's chin came up pugnaciously. "Listen, Barret, it's not up to you—"

"Calm down, Rob," Ussher said sharply, then favored Barret with a sympathetic smile. "Jan is a man of action. He doesn't understand the importance of appearances, and perhaps that's to his credit. In the end, it's always action that counts."

Barret couldn't think of a response to that. He stared at the uniform designated as his, trying to picture himself in it, but the image only seemed faintly ludicrous.

"Since when have appearances been so important to us?"

"Among ourselves they aren't," Ussher assured him. He went to the chair by the mirror where a cloak was draped; the same light blue as the uniform, with a darker blue lining. "We're above such concerns," he went on, turning to the mirror as he draped the cloak around his shoulders with a whirling flourish. "But the Phoenix is moving out into the worlds now, and appearances are very important there. You're a Second Gen, Jan; it's hard for you to understand. In the outside worlds, no one will take an army in slacsuits seriously, but put that army in uniforms, and it will command attention and respect. It's a matter of basic psychology."

Barret watched Ussher's hands smoothing the material, adjusting the drape.

"So we're an *army* now."

Ussher stiffened and turned slowly.

"No, we're not an army, but we must speak in terms the people—and the Lords—of the Concord will understand. Really, Jan, I thought you'd be pleased."

"I'm sorry, Predis, I . . . it just doesn't seem right."

Hendrick said curtly, "Barret, if the chairman says it's right, then it is. He knows more about these things than you ever will."

Barret turned angrily on Hendrick. The damned yes-sayer. Why did Predis put up with him?

But he didn't always. Before Barret could get a word out, Ussher cut in, "Rob, haven't you anything else to do? John said Dr. Hayward hadn't sent him the last of the specifications on the new pulsed lasers."

Hendrick's handsome features reddened. "I'll talk to him." He started for the door, sending Barret a cold look.

"And, Rob..." Ussher waited until Hendrick had unlocked the doorscreens. "I want a report on that—the lasers."

"You'll have it tomorrow."

When Hendrick had departed, Ussher removed the cloak, tossed it on the chair, and went to his desk.

"Lock the screens, Jan."

Barret swallowed his resentment at that offhanded order; it never seemed worth making an issue of. He set the lock, then crossed to the desk, waiting while Ussher checked a requisition sheet.

"Predis, is this what you wanted to see me about—the uniforms?"

He put the sheet aside. "That was the main reason."

"Then if you don't mind, I'll get back to FO. Commander Garris and I were meeting with the TacComm staff."

"I said that was the *main* reason. I also wanted a report on your department's preparedness status."

"You've had reports every day from every subdepartment and unit in FO—"

"I know, and I've read them all very carefully." His understanding smile made Barret feel embarrassed at his own impatience. "It's just that statistics don't always tell the whole story, Jan. Will you be ready?"

He shrugged. "Yes. We'd be better off with the 1 Januar deadline. For one thing, you can only rush a training program so fast. I have thirteen hundred volunteers from other departments; that's a third of our personnel. If they don't get adequate training, we'll all be in trouble."

"Yes, I know, but there are advantages in the Concord Day date that override the disadvantages. Perhaps the volunteers should be concentrated in the ground crews."

"For the God's sake, Predis, they'd be as much of a liability there as in the flight crews."

There was a short silence, and Barret was inclined to apologize for his curt tone, but Ussher nodded reassuringly.

"Of course. At any rate, I have complete faith in you, Jan. If anyone can bring FO to optimum strength, you can."

Barret didn't try to answer that, except to say, "We have two more raids lined up; if they go well, we'll only be eight percent short of optimum. Armanent will be tight in terms of quantity, but the new lasers will offset that. We should be able to field a fleet of approximately 330 Falcons and 150 Corvets. About a third of them will be hangared at the Rhea base."

Ussher smiled with evident satisfaction.

"Nearly five hundred ships—a fleet to rock Centauri! I can always count on FO. Jan, we'd be lost without you."

Barret let the words slip without thinking. "Especially with Alex gone?"

Ussher seemed to freeze; his smile faded slowly.

"The Phoenix doesn't depend on any single man. Ransom wasn't indispensable."

"And Dr. Riis?"

"I said *no* man is indispensable. His loss was a tragedy, of course, but the Phoenix survived it."

Barret sighed, his brief defiance fading with that expiration of breath. We've survived, he thought, and yet...

"Jan? Is something bothering you? Please, don't hesitate to unburden yourself to me. Something *is* bothering you."

"Only...rumors, Predis."

Ussher's eyes narrowed, but he was still smiling.

"Well, then, perhaps you should tell me about them and let me put your mind at ease. After all, if we can't be honest with each other, where are we?"

Barret was sorry he'd let the conversation take this turn, but he couldn't just cut Predis off without an answer.

"I've heard rumors about the power malfunction last week, that there was a newscast during the—the blackout about Dr. Riis."

"Am I to understand the coincidence has been given some deeper significance?"

"Well, yes. They're saying you...engineered the failure to make sure no one in Fina heard the newscast."

Ussher averted his eyes, as if to hide the hurt chagrin that briefly seemed to slip out of control.

"*They* say. You've *heard*. Really, Jan, I never thought you, of all people, would be taken in by this malicious gossip. You know where it starts."

"Predis, I didn't say I was taken in. It's just that—well, I just wondered."

"Exactly. Jan, that's what they want. They want people to 'just wonder.' If anything out of the way happens around here, it gets blamed on me. Like that unfortunate incident when Commander Venturi was wounded. No one gives me a chance to defend myself; no one has the guts to accuse me to my face. And in that case, I wouldn't be surprised if some of Venturi's so-called friends didn't set up that ambush. But *I'm* the one who gets blamed."

Barret frowned, feeling the heat in his cheeks, and he wasn't really sure whom Ussher meant by "they" and "so-called friends."

"I'm sorry, Predis, I didn't mean—"

"I know, Jan. Actually, I'm glad to know what's being said behind my back, and it certainly isn't your fault."

Barret hesitated, then, "Predis, I talked to one of our agents in Leda who heard the newscast. The SSB said Dr. Riis *had* escaped. He was rescued by two men. One of them called himself Ransom. That's . . . what they said."

Ussher's easy laugh was the last thing Barret expected.

"Well, that wasn't the story they told week *before* last. Jan, you don't trust any news item the SSB puts out, do you? The old divide-and-conquer ploy; sow doubt among the enemy. Besides, if Dr. Riis *did* escape, where *is* he? Where's Ransom? Can you answer me that?"

Barret shook his head. "No."

"Of course not." Ussher glanced at his watch pointedly. "Jan, I have a departmental staff meeting coming up. If you'll excuse me. . . ."

Barret nodded, reminded that Garris and the TacComm staff were still waiting for him.

"I have work of my own. Goodbye, Predis."

If he responded, it wasn't before the doorscreens clicked on between them.

Uniforms. Barret wondered why the idea rankled so much.

Undoubtedly, they were necessary. Still, it didn't seem right.

But there wasn't time to worry about it. Concord Day was only thirty-two days away.

4.

PUBLICOM SYSTEM BROADCAST #20958-C-2 DIR/CON
TRANSCRIPT: SPECIAL NEWS BULLETIN 20 SEPTEM 3258
POINT OF ORIGIN: CONCORDIA

ANNOUNCER: We interrupt our regularly scheduled programming to present this special address by the Lord Mathis Daro Galinin, Chairman of the Directorate of the Concord of Loyal Houses. We take you now to the Hall of the Directorate in Concordia.

(Music: Hymn of the Concord.)

(Pan: Plaza of Concord toward Hall of Directorate. Zoom to windowall of Chairman's office.)

(Cut to interior, office. Closeup: Lord Galinin at desk.)

(Music out. Fade to office pickup.)

ANNOUNCER: The Chairman of the Directorate, the Lord Mathis Daro Galinin.

THE CHAIRMAN: Citizens of the Concord, it is not my custom to come before you personally to discuss events within the Concord. However, I'm sure you're all aware that the situation on Mars is very grave, and I'm informed that unfounded rumors and exaggerated accounts of the disturbances are being circulated that have fostered a climate of fear and doubt throughout the Two Systems.

As an instance, I've been told that a rumor is now circulating that the Lord James Neeth Cameroodo was killed in the initial outbreak. To this I can reply with perfect assurance that Lord James is alive and unharmed. I spoke with him by SynchCom only a few minutes before this broadcast.

Rumor also has it that the atmobubbles in Toramil were damaged, and again, the answer is an unequivocal no. Toramil's habitat systems are intact. There was a brief failure in Almath's systems, but it was immediately remedied with emergency power sources, and *no* casualties resulted.

Even the actual casualty rates have been grossly exaggerated in some accounts. I consider such morbid rumor-mongering thoroughly reprehensible, even treasonous, and I've chosen to speak to you personally today in order to set the record straight, to explain to you what has actually happened, and what is being done.

First, I must be entirely honest with you; the situation is indeed serious. However, you must bear in mind that the seriousness of these uprisings is due in part to the fact that all human habitation on Mars is dependent upon artificial environment systems. The memory of the revolt in the Ivanoi compounds on Ganymede is painfully clear. The staggering death toll there was a result of damage to the habitat systems. It was actually a minor uprising; it was devastating *only* because of its location.

We have a similar state of affairs on Mars. Were these disturbances taking place on Terra or Pollux, the situation wouldn't be nearly so serious. Drastic measures, such as evacuation, certainly wouldn't be called for, and I consider evacuation an extremely drastic measure, not only for the people directly involved, but because it could engender general doubt and fear and even panic.

For this reason, I hesitated at giving that order, but I had to face the fact that a special element of danger exists on Mars. With the possibility of failure in the habitat systems foremost in my mind, I ordered the evacuation of all but key Concord personnel from the ten Martian cities. I also ordered evacuation of all but key personnel allieged to the House of Daro Galinin and advised other Lords with holdings on Mars to do likewise.

I'm pleased to inform you that the evacuation is being carried out by Confleet, with the assistance of the Selasid

InterPlan System fleets, in an orderly fashion, with very little panic or confusion. Terran, Polluxian, and Lunar Conpol units have been brought in to aid the Martian units in maintaining order and preventing potential looting in evacuated areas, and a full Confleet wing has been dispatched to assist in containing the violence still in progress.

I can also report at this time that the uprisings have been entirely contained in three Martian cities: Almath, Chryse, and Rubivale. Some violence still persists in other cities, but the worst of it is centered in Toramil, where Conpol and Confleet forces are concentrating on an offensive sweep to isolate the insurgents.

I would also like to mention that Lord Cameroodo has refused to leave Toramil or evacuate anyone allieged to his House, and in this he demonstrates a positive attitude that all citizens of the Concord would do well to emulate.

Let me assure you, strong measures have been taken to control these disturbances. There is no cause for panic or uncertainty. Above all, I must emphasize that the evacuation is a *temporary* measure, and primarily a *precautionary* one. And let me further assure you that the Directors and all Concord officials are keeping themselves alert and fully informed on every aspect of these disturbances, and that every available resource is being brought to bear to bring them to a swift conclusion.

I ask all citizens of the Concord to remain calm and to refrain from listening to, or spreading, unfounded rumors. We are passing through a troubled era in history, but the Concord has survived greater perils. The times demand courage and faith. The Concord wasn't built by cowards and pessimists; courage and faith are our heritage from its founders, our forefathers. Remember, we are the forefathers of future generations. They must find inspiration in us as we do in our predecessors.

And now, I ask that each of you add your prayers to mine; I ask you to pray with me for an end to the dissension and for the restoration of order and reason.

May the All-God and the Holy Mezion grant us all peace.

(Pan: Full view of office.)

(Music: Final chorus, Hymn of the Concord.)

*(Cut to exterior: Fountain of Victory. Overlap and fade to
studio and announcer.)*

ANNOUNCER: You have just heard an address by the Lord
Mathis Daro Galinin, Chairman of the Directorate. Stay
tuned for an updated report on the Martian uprisings with
a special feature on the arrival of the first evacuees in Concordia, Norleans, Coben, and Tokio.

5.

"Cameroodo is collapsing! Mars will soon be lost, my
friends! Lost! The Concord totters on the brink of chaos, and
our time is coming!"

Predis Ussher gripped the railing of the comcenter deck with
both hands as if to brace himself against the tangible power of
the massed cheers that surged up from the sea of faces, beating
against the stone walls, crashing against his ears like a tumbling
surf. He stood alone on the deck, resplendent in his blue-and-
gold uniform, looking out over the close-packed, blue-clad
crowd, at the open mouths, the waving arms, the boundless
joy and hope.

They were his. They *believed*.

Nearly five thousand men and women crowded the hangar,
like a blue sea around the black islands of the ships that waited
to lift off toward their destiny of conquest and victory.

The people were with him, one with him, extensions of his
mind and body. Not even Erica Radek, standing near the deck,
watching as she always did—not even she could quench his
exaltation today, nor that of this multitude.

They were *his*, body and mind.

He raised his hands, and the sea subsided.

"My fellow members, the Lord Galinin asks the citizens of
the Concord to pray, and well he might. He'll *need* those
prayers; he'll *need* the All-God's help. But for the Concord,
it's already too late. Mars is doomed! The evacuation has begun; the cities that once glittered in the midst of the red deserts
will soon be as empty as the deserts themselves. Only Cameroodo, of all the proud Lords who held sway on Mars,

remains to battle chaos to the end. He will not win that battle, my friends! He *cannot* win!"

The cheers exploded around him. His voice struck out into the rush of sound.

"Galinin seeks aid of the All-God, but I ask you, who does the All-God choose to favor? The Concord? Can you doubt whom the All-God chooses to bless when within twenty-four days of our offensive, Mars has erupted in violent uprisings demanding a concentration of Conpol and Confleet forces unprecedented since the War of the Twin Planets? The Concord is staggering, fighting with every available resource to save Mars. What will be left to join the battle to save Centauri? What except a shattered remnant of its vaunted fleets? And we will strike like a storm, without warning. We will rouse the silent, enchained masses, and they will swell our ranks by thousands, by millions! The people of Centauri will rise up and say to the proud Lords of the Concord—*no more!* We will live in your chains no more! We will set ourselves free, and the Republic will live again! The Peladeen did not die! Freedom did not die! Freedom is the Phoenix, the immortal bird rising from the ashes of death! The Republic of the Peladeen lives; it lives in victory!"

He lifted his arms, calling up the thunder of straining voices, turning slowly to encompass them in the beatitude of his outstretched hands, his head thrown back, flame-hued hair seemingly tossed in the storm wind.

And he shouted, *"Victory!"*

They took up the word hungrily, letting it give shape to their formless clamor, and as each voice found the word, it became a rolling, rhythmic tide, the three syllables pounding out in crashing cadences, drowning everything except that one word, drowning even Predis Ussher's unleashed laughter.

"Victory!...Victory!...Victory!...Victory!..."

6.

The white beads slipped through her fingers, one by one, her lips moved, tolling the silent minutes with prayers.

Val Severin knelt in the first row of pews, and before her

the chapel altar vanished into distanced shadows; tiers of gilt
saints and seraphim winged into the hallowed darkness that
swallowed up the light of the altar candles. There wasn't even
enough light to trace the interlaced arches to their culmination
above her, and in the cavernous spaces meant to hold the echoes
of the orchestral organ, there was no sound except the whispers
of her penances.

Her knees ached unmercifully against the stone floor, and
yet she wondered sometimes if she didn't unconsciously seek
these hours of prayer penances. The solitude in this chapel was
different from that of her small room; less constricting spatially,
at least.

And easier. Face it, she admonished herself bitterly, in that
room the transceiver was waiting, and she never thought she'd
dread her few nocturnal minutes with Jael, but she did now,
because every call meant admitting another day of failure.

I'm slipping, brother, slipping over the edge. Hold on to
me. For the God's sake, give me your hand. . . .

Forty days and nights behind these walls, twenty-six since
Sister Betha's death, since Alex Ransom's surrender to pain
and grief. And twenty-two until Concord Day. She tolled the
days with her prayers, pale, lightless beads, moving one by
one through her fingers, and with every day she felt herself
slipping nearer the edge of some incomprehensible abyss—

"Sister Alexandra?"

The voice took her breath. She hadn't heard anyone approaching. In all this huge silence, not a sound had reached
her mind.

Sister Herma. That precise, clipped inflection was unmis-
takable. She stood in the aisle at the end of the pew. Val looked
up at her, wondering as she always did what kind of face hid
behind that veil.

"Yes, Sister Herma?"

"Did you know it's past curfew?"

I *am* slipping, Val thought distractedly. She hadn't even
heard the chapel chimes ringing the curfew hour.

"No . . . I didn't realize . . ."

"I think you've done penance enough to satisfy the All-God,
my dear. You'd best get to bed now."

Val rose, teeth set against the pain in her knees. At the aisle, she genuflected toward the altar, touching the first two fingers of her right hand to her forehead, then her heart, executing every movement carefully with Sister Herma looking on. Then she turned and nodded respectfully.

"Good night, Sister Herma. Lord bless."

"Good night." A hesitation just long enough for Val to take three steps up the aisle. "Sister Alexandra . . ."

Val turned warily. "Yes, Sister?"

"You know, my dear, I've been wondering if—well, if you've really found your answer at Saint Petra's. Many young women who come here find the convent *isn't* the answer for them, and there are so many ways to serve the All-God and the Holy Mezion outside the convent."

Val stared through the haze of her veil, restraining the impulse to tear away that other veil. Herma wanted to put her out of Saint Petra's. She was suggesting with her usual blunt subtlety that Val leave voluntarily.

Never.

She almost spoke the word aloud. You'll have to throw me out first. Not until I've accomplished my mission here, until *I've* finished with Saint Petra's, until . . .

She said meekly, "Sister Herma, I'm here because I found no other way that satisfied me to serve the All-God and the Holy Mezion. I'm sorry I seem to cause you so much trouble; I don't mean to, and I'm trying to learn the ways of Faith."

"Yes, I'm sure you are, my dear, but it seems to be so difficult for you."

"I never expected it to be easy, but I haven't given up, and I would hope the Holy Mezion hasn't given up on me so soon. He always answers my prayers with hope."

Herma's sigh whispered in the shadows. "Then that's as it should be. Good night, Alexandra. Lord bless."

Val bowed her head and turned. "Good night, Sister Herma."

She felt the eyes behind that veil on her every step of the long passage up the aisle. She walked circumspectly, restraining the overwhelming urge to break into a run, to escape those unseen, all-seeing eyes, her hands clasped under her sleeves, so tightly interlocked, they tingled numbly. The distance seemed lengthened by the night shadows; demons of frustration and fear seemed to flit on the periphery of her vision. At length she reached the ponderous, carved-wood doors that pivoted on rumbling hinges, willfully resisting her trembling muscles. She heard a muffled whimper as she pushed them shut, and didn't at first realize it was in her own throat. The doors closed with a dull thud, and she stood with her back against them, both hands in fists pressed to her forehead, shivering as if the darkness were cold; the veil suffocated her.

I'm slipping, slipping. Jael—oh, Jael, help me. . . .

Her hands locked on her koyf; she jerked it off with the veil and cape, tossing her hair free. Before her, the long, arched hall, dimly lighted at amber intervals with stabile shimmeras, stretched to a dark infinity, and she began running toward it, koyf and veil clenched in one hand, the other holding back the snare of skirts, the beat of her footfalls quieted by the soft-soled shoes.

The shimmeras made dull streaks on her retina, her heart pounded ever faster with her footsteps, the habit beat about her legs, billowed behind her. The stairway. Soft footsteps pounding against stone, jarring through bone and flesh from heel to skull. The stairs turned. For every level, three right-angle turns. Stone steps, dished with dead footsteps; two centuries of dead footsteps.

Three turns. An empty, soundless hallway. Three more, step upon step. Hot pain shot along her leg muscles, hissed out with every breath; the amber lights jigged in the reddening shadows. Three more turns to the third level. Nine steps; turn. Three steps; turn. Nine more to make the holy number three sevens.

Jael, brother . . . help me.

She faltered on the seventeenth step, fell on the eighteenth, hands bruised on the twenty-first, and that was all that stopped her head from smashing against the stone tier.

She lay in a heap of pain, every panting breath burning, her cheek against the stone, cold and wet with tears. It was a long time before she could hear anything for the pounding of her heart and her gasping breaths; a long time before she could be sure no one else had heard the intolerable sounds of running feet, of panting breath, of weeping.

If Sister Herma heard it, if she found her here like this—

Val pulled herself up slowly into a sitting position on the top step and put her back against the stone wall while she delved into a pocket for a handkerchief.

To hell with Sister Herma.

At any rate, it was past curfew. Herma and the other Sisters charged with maintaining the purity of Saint Petra's novices would have completed their curfew rounds. They never made a second check.

Val wiped her tear-wet face and blew her nose as quietly as possible. She was still shaking and her eyes felt swollen shut.

Panic. It was that simple, and this wasn't the first time it had gotten the best of her. She was walking a tightrope with the medication: calmers to keep her from going hysterical; drenaline to keep her going in general, to compensate for the sleep lost every night while reviewing monitored conversations or to stubborn insomnia.

Val rested her head against the wall and looked down the empty, doorless hall. At a distance of five meters, a shimmera cast a gloomy pool of light. Finally, she pulled her skirt up over one knee; a watch was strapped there. She couldn't depend on the chapel chimes; occasionally she needed to know minutes, not just hours.

It was 18:20 TST. She was more than an hour late calling Jael. That wasn't so unusual, but he would worry. Still, she made no move to rise. She couldn't let him hear her voice now; he'd recognize the aftermath of panic, the tears in it.

Besides, she wasn't yet ready to admit another day of failure, nor to broach—again—the alternative of approaching Sister Thea with the medallion. That was a decision reached over her beads in the chapel. The time was coming for that last resort.

She unfastened the stiff collar of the habit, her fingers seeking the medallion. Perhaps she'd wait until tomorrow night to bring that up. A doricaine and a good night's sleep—she could survive one more day.

The medallion was in her hand. She wasn't even conscious of unclasping the chain; she did it so often in moments of privacy.

The lamb. The pale light glowed lovingly on the fine contours of the tiny figure. A smile touched her lips. She hadn't really been a close friend of Richard Lamb's, but he had a gift for making everyone feel close, and he had entered the Phoenix at a crucial time in her life. She'd been a member for two years and was suffering doubts about it. Rich had stilled those doubts even though she had never spoken to him about them. It was simply that she couldn't doubt any cause Richard Lamb espoused. He was so gently, truly just, he seemed to make anything he was part of unassailably right.

She turned the medallion over and felt a cold weight taking form under her ribs. When she looked at the wolf, she always saw three small pill bottles in her hand.

Cyanase.

Yet Alex believed her when she said she didn't know what those pills contained. He didn't for a moment doubt her.

She held his life in her hands then, and she held it now. Would he believe her again, believe she—

Her hand closed on the medallion.

A sound.

Her heart began pounding anew; she didn't move, hardly breathed, listening past the dull thudding in her breast.

Footsteps. But the Sisters *never* made a second check.

A soft, irregular padding; she began to relax a little. Someone coming out of the novices' wing. At least she'd be in a position to bargain; neither of them were supposed to be out of their rooms after curfew.

Still, there was something unnerving about the slow, halting approach of those footsteps; the back of her neck prickled. She waited, unblinking eyes fixed on the empty section of hall lighted by the shimmera. She couldn't have guessed how long she waited, listening to the footsteps falter and stop, proceed hesitantly a while longer, stop again, approach again. She didn't know what she expected to see, and somehow she wasn't surprised that it was an apparition.

A faceless woman in a flowing white gown, long raven hair falling about her shoulders, catching silken lights, her left hand against the wall, sliding along it as her halting steps took her forward out of the shadows into the pallid glow of the shimmera. She stopped again, right hand pressed to her body, a sound escaping her, a sighing cry.

The God help me, I've gone over the edge. . . .

At first, that was Val's only coherent thought. But that sound, that muted cry, jarred her back to rationality. It seemed so solidly real, and the woman was moving into the light now; perhaps that robbed her of her ghostly aura.

Her white raiment proved to be nothing more than the shapeless white nightgown issued to every nun at Saint Petra's, and she was faceless because she was using a face-screen. That was odd, but certainly not supernatural.

The light gave further elucidation. It delineated the swollen curve of her abdomen and explained the faltering step, the cry of pain.

Sister Iris. The pregnant one. She must be in labor.

Val felt a brief return of panic. Nothing in her experience had prepared her for a contingency like childbirth. Still, she stayed calm enough to realize Sister Iris needed help; that was why she was wandering the halls after curfew.

Val rose, forgetting her koyf and veil, but taking the few seconds to fasten the medallion around her neck; she'd have secured that if she were dying.

"Sister Iris, can I help you?"

She seemed to freeze, head turned toward Val, weight pressing on the supporting hand against the wall, and Val chided herself for coming so suddenly out of the shadows to frighten her.

"I'm sorry, I didn't mean to startle you. I was just coming up from the chapel. Please . . ." She put out a hand to her. "Let me help you."

Sister Iris still didn't move; her voice was pitched low, as Val's had been, but it had all the tension of a shout in it.

"Who *are* you?"

Val couldn't answer. She was too close to shock.

Two things hit her at once. First, the light catching, throwing sparks of color from a ring on the hand against the wall. Sparks of blue and red; sapphire and ruby.

And that voice.

She had listened so long for that voice, she wondered if she wouldn't have had the same reaction even without the recognition conditioning. With it, those few words exploded like a bomb in her mind.

But it was impossible. Sister Iris was pregnant.

"Oh, no . . ." The words slipped out, and in a flashing moment Val understood the aching, ironic *possibility* that couldn't be denied because it was so tangibly self-evident. And she understood, but took no comfort in the realization, that Bruno Hawkwood had made the same error.

"Who are you?"

She drew back against the wall, hiding her left hand under her sleeve, that sibilant query rife with desperate defiance. Val reached for the clasp of the medallion, hands shaking, keeping her voice down when she wanted to shout aloud.

"Oh, forgive me, my lady, it was just such a—*Wait!*"

Val reached out for her, caught her shoulders, and held on desperately simply to keep her from bolting.

"My lady!" The frenzied whisper echoed in the amber silence. "For the God's sake, look at this! The medallion! I'm from the—oh, damn!" She couldn't say the word; her conditioning stopped her. *"Alex Ransom* sent me. He told me to tell you it was blessed by a saint, oh, *please*—look at it!"

Her resistance ceased suddenly; she sagged against the wall, dark hair falling forward over her shadow-face as Val pressed the medallion into her small, cold, trembling hand.

Val waited, breath stopped, saw the hand move finally to turn the medallion over.

"Alexand . . ."

She was falling. Val managed to ease her down to the floor where she slumped against her, huddled over the medallion, body wracked with muffled weeping. It was like holding a lost child, she seemed so small and frail, and Val felt all her own anxieties and frustrations pale against the lonely terrors echoed in that constrained sobbing.

Six months. Half a Terran year.

What kind of nether hell had it been for her?

But it was over, her hell and Val's. And Alex's. Val was weeping, too, although she was hardly aware of it. She was only conscious of a fountain of laughter within her that took the form of tears.

Jael, brother, I've found her—I've found Adrien Eliseer. . . .

7.

She had been dozing; "skimming sleep," Jael called it. Erica Radek shifted in the chair, cramped muscles complaining. It was 19:30 TST. She looked across the bed to the biomonitor screen, realizing she'd been closer to real sleep than dozing.

Alex hadn't moved; he seldom did. Only regular periods of "exercise" consisting of electrode-induced contraction of the muscles prevented atrophy. What concerned her at the moment was his respiration rate. She had removed the oxymask, another therapeutic measure designed to force his body to keep working for itself. Part of the time, at least.

He was breathing well enough; shallowly, and a little erratically, but she expected that. She rose and stood looking down at him, automatically checking the web of wires and tubes surrounding him, the thermostat of the heat shell, the feel of his forehead under her hand, an instrument she trusted as much as the biomonitor. Just as automatically, she checked the five capped pressyringes on the control panel at the head of the bed. They were always ready for any emergency brought about by a change in his condition.

But there was no change.

At least there seemed to be none at first.

For a long time she stood watching him, her eyes occasionally flicking up to the screen.

It came at irregular intervals. A nearly invisible movement behind his closed eyes. Nightmares, perhaps. She watched the brainwaves. A dream-state pattern, or so it seemed, and she took hope from that; he hadn't even shown evidence of dreaming for two weeks. Yet the brainwaves displayed a slight peculiarity in contour; there were anomalous elements of waking, high-anxiety states in them.

She took his left hand in hers and heard the ticking of his monitored heartbeat quickening. She watched his chest rising and falling, heard the whispers of breath, felt his hand stir in hers. She considered calling Dr. Eliot, but decided against it, foreseeing nothing she couldn't deal with, knowing he was presently involved with a serious knife wound.

But the brainwave configuration—it worried her because she didn't understand it; she didn't understand what was happening in the dark recesses within his mind to which he had retreated.

She uncovered the pressyringes, not even sure which of them she might need. Not the stimulant, at least. The one nearest her was morphinine. That he would need; as long as he was in a comatose state, he'd been given nothing for pain.

Alex... Alex, are you there?

She didn't speak the words aloud, afraid to do anything, hesitant even to move. His breathing was becoming labored, the exhalations accompanied by faint moans, the only sounds she'd heard from his lips since that first night. His hand moved in hers, pulling away, and she let it go, watched it move against the sheet as if he were trying to reach out to something or someone. She paced her own breathing carefully, warned by a hint of lightheadedness that she was so intent, she was forgetting to breathe.

He was trying to speak.

Erica watched the tentative motions of his lips fixedly, as if she might read the half-formed words. Perhaps it was only an unconscious contraction of muscles; perhaps she only wanted to believe he was trying to speak. Faint sounds formed with the motions of his lips now. Still, she couldn't make sense of them.

"Alex? Can you hear me?" She whispered the words, leaning close to him. The ting of his monitored pulse beat faster, a small sound that seemed inside her head; her ears would burst with it soon if—

Adrien.

Finally, Erica recognized the word he was trying to say, and she felt an aching within her, a painfully palpable sensation. If that was what he was waking to, waking in hope of finding...

She didn't speak again. Perhaps he *had* heard her, heard a feminine voice and translated it into Adrien Eliseer's.

His head moved against the pillow, face contorted; he still tried to speak the name through panting breaths. Erica shifted her attention from him just long enough to reach for the morphinine syringe, and in that brief time he surged up out of the bed, ripping wires and tubes loose, his right arm wrenching against the restraints.

"Adrien! Adri——"

The pain stopped him. Erica held him as his body curled spastically, strained cries hissing through his clenched teeth. She forced him back onto the bed, and it took all her strength to keep him still long enough for the morphinine injection.

It began to take effect within thirty seconds. She felt the cramping tension in his muscles loosen and glanced up at the screen. The erratic pulse and respiration rates gradually slowed. Finally, she could let him go, but she didn't let herself relax. She pulled back the sheet to assess and repair the damage, restoring tubes and electrodes, checking the bandages on his arm, cutting away a section at the elbow soaked with reddish secretions that meant he'd torn some of the unhealed skin grafts. She used an antiseptic spray and made a hasty temporary bandage. By the time she restored a semblance of order and covered him again, he was lying with his eyes closed, his breathing and pulse rate nearly normal.

She couldn't say the same of her own as she stood at his left side, waiting, wondering whether he would slip away from her back into unconsciousness again.

At length, he opened his eyes.

She wanted to cry his name, to shout a prayer of thanks, to weep, to embrace him. But she only stood silently, watching and hoping.

His pupils were contracted with the morphinine, and she knew he was seeing little more than indistinct lights and shapes. He was trying to focus his eyes, frowning a little, and she was beginning to dread the moment when that vague gaze would find her, dreading that he wouldn't recognize her. And yet he did. It took some time, and she dared to speak now, sure he wouldn't mistake her voice for any other.

"Alex, welcome back," she said softly, and her eyes blurred with tears when he finally smiled weakly, and his hand moved, seeking hers.

"Erica..." A slurred whisper of sound caught on a long, trembling sigh. Then she heard the ting of his pulse rate quicken. He was trying to speak, to tell her something, but he couldn't seem to shape the words.

"Slowly, Alex. Just relax. There's plenty of time."

He managed a nod at that, and took a long breath.

"Shh . . . she's . . . al——" For a moment, frustration got the better of him, then he took another breath and tried again. "She's . . . *alive*. I saw . . ." A frown, then; he seemed bewildered. "Nn-no. I didn't *see*. But . . . I *know* shhh . . ."

Erica couldn't respond. She knew exactly whom he meant with that feminine pronoun, and the affirmation that Adrien Eliseer lived stunned her. She didn't know how to answer it. But he didn't seem to expect a response, and when he spoke again, the words seemed to come more easily.

"Pain . . . she was in pain. But she . . . wasn't . . . afraid. I don't understand. But I . . . I *know* she's alive. Erica, she's *alive*. . . ." He turned his head away, covering his eyes with his left hand; he was weeping, and he didn't want Erica to see the tears he couldn't stop.

No more could she stop her own, and she could only hope he was right. She found herself murmuring meaningless assurances, the words falling into a lulling, hypnotic pattern. It was still possible; Adrien might still be alive. She *must* be if these words, these tears, weren't to be his last.

The weeping ceased at length; he was slipping away, but not into unconsciousness, only sleep. The brainwaves recorded a typical deep sleep pattern, all vital signs stable, reflecting only a general weakness due to long illness.

A miracle.

She tried to understand it both medically and psychologically as she went around to the other side of the bed to bandage the arm properly. She had to work carefully; several times he stirred and nearly wakened. Then she made careful notations on the chart, and it took an inordinate amount of time. Her thoughts kept wandering from past to future, from despair to hope. Her hands were shaking when she filled a fresh pressyringe with morphinine and put it with the others, ready for the time when he wakened again.

Reaction set in, and when she sank into the chair, she was crying. She propped her elbows on her knees, head in her hands, and let it run its course.

When Jael came into the cubicle half an hour later, the tears had spent themselves, but there was still evidence of them, and he had no way of differentiating relief from grief when it took that form.

"Erica? For the God's sake, what happened?"

She rose, hushing him with an upraised hand. "Nothing happened—I mean, everything." She was half laughing, half crying, but Jael's anxious bewilderment sobered her. "I'm sorry. He's all right; he's *sleeping* now. He regained consciousness and recognized me, Jael. He *talked* to me."

Jael's shoulders sagged in relief. "Thank the God. I thought perhaps I came too late with the news."

"What news?" she demanded sharply.

"Val finally called. I came straight from the COS HQ."

Erica was hard put to keep her voice down.

"She found Adrien—she *found* her!"

"Who's telling this spin, anyway? Yes, she found her."

Erica looked at Alex with a chill of wonder. He knew. How? It didn't matter; some phenomena could only be accepted, not explained.

She said absently, "Forgive me for ruining your story, Jael."

"Well, you haven't heard it all yet, and you'll never glim the end of *this* one. I'll lay any stakes on that. The Lady Adrien just gave birth to slightly premature, but healthy and hollering twin sons. Now, does that clear a few questions in your head?"

Erica stared at him, and at first it cleared nothing; it only created a blank void.

"Gave . . . birth . . . ?" As she said the words, it began to make sense, and for some time she couldn't speak for all the questions and answers coming together in her mind. Jael was right; it cleared quite a few.

Again she looked at Alex, relieved to find him still deep asleep.

"Jael, he didn't know she was carrying his—*sons*, did you say? Twins?"

"Identical twins. No, of course, he didn't know. He'd have lined Val in on something that obvious, and besides, Alex is a gentleman born. He'd never knowingly let his Lady run that gant. She's a straight blade, Erica."

"So she is." Then, with a frown, "A multiple birth and a first pregnancy—were there any complications?"

"Val says it went off without a catch. Val's with her, by

the way. In the hospital, I mean. The medal turned the card with the Lady, and she laid word with Thea. Val's moved into the same room with her."

"Thank the God. Jael, I must talk to Adrien—I mean at the hospital. Val will have to set up an MT fix for me. I'll have to call her." Then, with a glance at Alex, whose sighing exhalation of breath reminded her to lower her voice, "Can you get a medtech—"

"Carl's outside, sister. As for Val, she can probably take a call now; it's the night shift there."

"Then, come on. I'll have to talk to Carl first." She was almost out of the cubicle before Jael stopped her.

"What about Alex? Don't you think you should line him in? At least that his Lady's been found?"

She turned and looked down at that gaunt face that seemed so much at peace in its repose now.

"I don't have to tell him. He . . . already knows."

PHOENIX MEMFILES: DEPT HUMAN SCIENCES: BASIC SCHOOL
                                        (HS/BS)
SUBFILE: LECTURE, BASIC SCHOOL 4 AVRIL 3252
                        GUEST LECTURER: RICHARD LAMB
                        SUBJECT: POST-DISASTERS HISTORY:
                        THE MANKEEN REVOLT (3104–3120)
DOC LOC #819/219-1253/1812-1648-443252

I think one of the most tragic figures in the Mankeen Revolt was Commander Scott Cormoroi, the tactical genius who gave Mankeen the might to make a Rightness of his ideals. I wonder at what point in the long war Cormoroi first realized it was hopeless. Fairly early, probably; he was a highly intelligent man, and his early training in science undoubtedly made him fully capable of recognizing hard facts. And I wonder at what point Cormoroi realized that the greatest impediment to the Revolt's success was Lionar Mankeen himself.

Mankeen, like Pilgram and Ballarat, had a talent for motivating people, and despite the defections that plagued his cause in its later years, those who renounced him were in the minority. The devotion he inspired among his faithful had almost religious overtones, and it isn't surprising that the Bonds made him a saint. But, unlike Pilgram and Ballarat, Mankeen had no talent for consolidating his gains.

He didn't seem to know what to do with them. Time and again Cormoroi won territories by dint of tactical brilliance and courage, only to have them lost again months later.

63

Mankeen couldn't seem to formulate a consistent policy for the occupation of these territories. Too often he tried to initiate sweeping social reforms in situations where the immediate need was for order, not freedom, and the result was anarchy and unnecessary loss of property and lives. In some occupied territories, his administrators—usually League Lords—in desperation imposed order by harsh means that resulted in counterrevolts. Thus Cormoroi was continually in the position of trying to maintain an advancing front while looking over his shoulder for attack from the rear, and the tragic abandonment of many of the vacuum colonies can be attributed to Mankeen's lack of organization and control. If there had been even one man among the League Lords capable of effectively consolidating Cormoroi's gains, we might live in a very different world today. But there were none, and Mankeen, who should have taken the spiritual role in this campaign—should have been his own Colona or Almbert—constantly undermined himself and the Revolt with ill-conceived reforms and conflicting directives to his administrators.

I couldn't hold it against Cormoroi if he had chosen to wash his hands of Mankeen. Yet he didn't. Scott Cormoroi continued fighting Mankeen's hopeless battles until the last one, the Battle of the Urals, and when that was lost, Cormoroi was among those who joined him in his death flight to the Sun.

Cormoroi was a man of honor. He was also Mankeen's closest friend, and beyond that, he believed fervently in the ideals Mankeen tried, so ineptly, to realize.

Most of the passengers on that final flight left lettapes behind for friends, relatives, or posterity. Mankeen, oddly enough, did not. Cormoroi addressed his parting message to a brother, James, his only surviving relative, or so he thought. In fact, James had died a year before, but the news of his death had never reached Cormoroi; James was allieged to Reeswyck, a Concord House. At any rate, Cormoroi's message was the most eloquent of the lot, and has since been the most quoted.

Cormoroi, at the age of seventy-three, facing his death and looking back on his defeat, tells his brother, "Human beings can't go on forever living as slaves. That's what it was all about. At least, for me. We lost, finally, and the price was high, both for the losers and the winners. I know that. But, James, we had to try. We had to try."

The Concord was more fortunate in its leadership, although it couldn't boast a military commander with anything like Cormoroi's genius, but it had an administrative leader of extraordinary ability in the Chairman, Arman Galinin. He wasn't as inspiring a leader as Mankeen—he left the spiritual aspects of leadership to the Archon, Bishop Nicolas III, who proved very effective at it—but Galinin was a strong personality and one of those men who seem to rise to adversity.

It was Galinin who formulated the Charter of the Concord of the Loyal Houses and used it to forge a new order and cohesion among the Lords in the chaotic aftermath of the League's initial military assaults. The Concord Charter is, of course, essentially the Articles of the PanTerran Confederation reiterated, yet it served to unify the Confederation at a crisis point when it was in very real danger of dissolving, and that was undoubtedly its purpose. The Court of Lords met in Octov of 3105 in Victoria—which became Concordia before they adjourned—to sign the Concord Charter, and from that point the Concord presented a united front to the League, and could thus take full advantage of its superior numbers and industrial capabilities. Galinin continued to be an astute and forceful leader, and was backed by an equally forceful Directorate, on the whole, and, as I've noted before, the power structure came through the Revolt virtually unaltered. There were only three changes on the Directorate during this period, which, considering the number of Houses destroyed, merged, or absorbed, is remarkable. One Directorate seat that changed hands probably would have done so under any circumstances. The House of Tadema was failing long before the Revolt began, and with Selasid backing, it was almost inevitable that Hamid should take that chair. Lagore Lao wasn't exactly displaced; it simply merged with Shang, but certainly its First Lord was displaced. Adalay was the only undisputed victim of the war; that old landed House was forced to give way to the emerging House of Cameroodo with its multiple metals franchises.

One could wish that Arman Galinin had taken advantage of this time of crisis to slip a few liberalizing reforms into his Charter—and he *was* philosophically a liberal—but he undoubtedly realized that even a hint of liberalism would smack of Mankeenism and jeopardize the unity so vital to the Concord's survival. In fact, to civilization's survival. And Galinin can't be held responsible for the reactionary attitudes on the part of the surviving Lords that have brought us to this new period of crisis nearly a century and a half later. That he managed to maintain order and the existing social structure through the catastrophic stresses of the Revolt is a miracle in itself and a tribute to his ability and foresight. There was really nothing he could have done to counteract the inevitable extreme conservative reaction to Mankeen's extreme liberalism.

Above all, Arman Galinin can't be held responsible for the Purge. That holiday for mass murder and unrestrained violence was in no way sanctioned by Galinin, the Directors, or the top echelons of Conpol and Confleet. Men and officers in both the latter were unquestionably responsible for a great deal of the destruction and slaughter, however, while House guards must take the blame for most of the rest of it, and they didn't always act without orders from their Lords, although no Lord ever admitted giving such orders.

The Purge—which began immediately after Mankeen's death and lasted a month—was as much a threat to the survival of the Concord and civilization as the Revolt itself. It is, in fact, an indication of how close we came to another dark age. And there was a lesson in that vicious and bestial exercise of vengeance that the Lords should have heeded, and that is how easily externally imposed (in contrast to internally imposed) behavioral controls fail. The lesson was ignored, perhaps because too many Lords themselves suffered a failure of internal controls, and of course had few external controls imposed on them.

At any rate, Arman Galinin brought the Concord through the Mankeen Revolt and the Purge, but both had taken a bitter toll. Not only were nearly a billion people killed—a quarter of the population—but humankind had retreated to Terra, all the extraterrestrial colonies abandoned, except for Pollux, which was for a time and for all intents and purposes forgotten. Civilization had taken a giant step backward to a stage of development approximating that of a century before, even though MAM-An, nulgrav, and SynchShift were available. But they didn't make the war-shattered Concord of the post-Mankeen period any less a planet-bound culture. The Lords had to rebuild, both literally and figuratively, their Houses on Terra before they could consider rebuilding on the other planets or satellites. It was half a century before that became possible.

That was a crucial half century in Centauri, of course, and although the brave experiment of the Peladeen Republic was abruptly and cruelly culminated with the War of the Twin Planets, the very fact that it existed will have repercussions in the future. And, among other things, the Phoenix is a product of that experiment. It seems ironic in a way that if the hopes and potentials of the Republic and the Phoenix are ever realized, it must be attributed in an indirect, almost inadvertent, manner to Lionar Mankeen.

CHAPTER XVIII: Octov 3258

1.

The bed, covered and curtained in satinet and silk, was an excellent example of Early Kao-rossic, with its cantilevered canopy. The chair Erica had pulled up for herself was carved ebony, and if it were in fact a Starenza, which Alex didn't really doubt, it couldn't be less than three centuries old.

Amik was a gracious host, as always, and Alex appreciated the apartment provided him for these last five days, especially when he compared it to the sterile, ticking cubicle in the infirmary. Yet in a short time he would leave these luxuriously appointed rooms for the rock-walled chambers of the COS HQ, and he couldn't muster a grain of regret at the exchange.

He sat on the side of the bed, while Erica, oblivious to the fact that she was occupying an heirloom, shaped a strip of gauze into an overlapping spiral around his right arm. His left hand strayed to his throat, encountering the fine chain that seemed so familiar to his touch, but it wasn't Rich's medallion that hung there now. The betrothal ring. Ten days ago it had been brought to him with a promise: when they were finally

68

reunited, an exchange would be made. The ring was simply an assurance, proof of Adrien's living, as the medallion had been another kind of proof to her.

He had wept when he first heard her voice in a static-ridden interconn; dust storms in the Barrens. It didn't matter. All he cared about was her voice. Since then, he'd spoken to her at least once each day, and always found it difficult not to weep. For so many years he had considered himself incapable of tears, but they came all too easily now. He had journeyed too near death to return unscathed, and somewhere on that journey he had learned to weep again.

Erica glanced up at him, perhaps responding to some subtle symptom of tension, asking with the silent lift of an eyebrow if her ministrations were too painful. He responded with a shake of his head.

It *was* painful, even with the analgesics. The bandaging always followed fifteen minutes of what Erica called "exercise." Alex wouldn't dignify it with that term. *She* did all the exercising, moving the arm through short, repetitive arcs, turning it a few degrees this way, a few that, flexing the wrist up and down. He might call it therapy, but not exercise; that implied voluntary movement, and he was capable of no more than a jerking contraction of the thumb and a grand total of ten degrees flexion at the elbow.

He looked away from Erica and her work, his left hand seeking the reminder and solace of the ring.

Today was the promised day of reunion. A few hours. Adrien.

And Richard and Eric.

He pronounced the names in his mind as he had in every waking hour for the last eight days. Erica had waited two days before telling him about his sons, waited until he had recovered enough to dispense with the life-support systems. He wondered if she thought the shock of learning he'd become twice at once a father might precipitate a relapse.

It had no effect at all, as far as he could determine, and perhaps that was because he didn't really believe it. It was so incomprehensibly incredible, it didn't reach him.

The first born Adrien had already named. Richard. She told him the child had been named when it was conceived, and even now when he thought of the calculating risk she'd taken—that he *let* her take—the realization dizzied him.

She asked him to name the second born, and he did. There was no question in his mind about the choice of a name. It had come without conscious thought, as if the decision had been made long ago, and perhaps it had been; made when he first came to Fina and found Rich's dearest friend waiting, made when that friend was forced to bring his griefs to him and bear them with him.

Yet Erica Radek's namesake, an infant, a human being to be called Eric—Alex could accept that, and Rich's namesake, as a premise in some system of reality as he accepted the existence of the electron, but it didn't touch him as part of his own reality.

Time, Erica assured him; it will all make sense in time. And he had enough to make sense of out of the twenty-six days he'd absented himself in pursuit of death. On the table by the bed were ten tape spools; only ten out of the hundred capsule reports Erica had provided to bring him up to date on Fina, on Predis Ussher's offensive, and on the crises that had occurred in the Concord.

He frowned, remembering that there had been more to occupy him in the last ten days. His body. He resented its weakness bitterly, yet Dr. Eliot kept using the word "miraculous." Erica had set up a rigid schedule of rest, graduated exercise— *real* exercise for the parts of his body that still functioned at his command—and diet that included massive doses of vitamins and protein, and he had adhered doggedly to that schedule, but he refused to call the results of those ten days miraculous. Not when he was capable of staying out of this elegant museum-piece of a bed for no more than five hours at a time. Today it would be six.

He wondered how many hours his body would allow him by Concord Day. It was only fourteen days away.

Erica had reached the wrist, which had taken the brunt of the laser beam, and he was forced to concentrate on keeping the arm immobile. He would be glad to have it covered and dreaded the time when the bandages would no longer be necessary. He wondered if he would ever accustom himself to those riven scars, patched with sickly white grafts, etched with livid suture lines. He watched Erica's face, noting the tightness around her mouth.

He asked, "Is it so distasteful?"

She looked up at him, startled, until she saw his faint smile; her breath came out in a sigh as she made another spiral.

"Of course not, Alex. I've seen worse than this."

"So have I. That's . . . a little tight."

She eased the tension as she worked a loop around the base of his thumb.

"Better?" Then, at his nod, "I'm amazed at how well you're tolerating this. It makes me doubt every personality matrix I made on you." The last of the scars disappeared under the bandages, and finally she cut the strip and taped the end inside his palm.

"Erica, did you count this in your data?" He touched the ring against his breast. "And Andreas? Andreas alive and free, and the LR-MT within days of proof?"

"Yes, I counted them, and that revives my faith in my science to some degree." Then she rose and picked up his robe from the end of the bed. "You'd better get this on."

He came to his feet, reminding himself to move slowly, and submitted to her help with the robe. Brocaded velveen in a deep blue; another offering of his gracious host's. The arm caught in the sleeve and he winced as it treated him to a new spasm of pain.

"Damn. Retribution, Erica. Did you count that?"

She frowned, studying him. "What do you mean?"

"'The Holy Mezion metes out justice in the mirror of injustice.'" He pressed the waistband closed awkwardly. "I hope Jael doesn't forget to bring my clothes. I'd feel a little ridiculous parading around the COS HQ in this."

"He won't, and I won't let you pass off that retribution business so lightly. Not when I think you really believe it."

"Well, perhaps I've spent too much time with the Shepherds these last few years, and that reminds me, you didn't bring the capsule on yours and Jael's time with them. You won't put *me* off on that. I must know which of the Shepherds you've seen, and which the Brother must see in the next two weeks."

"I'll discuss that with you tomorrow, but no sooner, and you won't embark on any sojourns as the Brother for at least three days. Now, Alex, that isn't just a medcal opinion, it's an order."

"Erica, we only have fourteen days until—"

"I can count, too, but I—oh, damn. Who's that?"

The argument was cut short by the warning chime that meant someone was entering the salon. Jael, perhaps, Alex thought, or hoped, as he checked the vis-screen by the door. But he was wrong.

"Amik," he told Erica. "Your face-screen."

"Oh, Alex, I gave that up with Amik long ago."

"There's a servant with him." He reached up to turn on his own 'screen, then fumbled at the doorcon with his left hand. Amik was crossing the salon like a brocaded mountain, streaming a fumerole of smoke from his jeweled cigar holder.

"Ah! Up and about, my friend. A small miracle, that."

Alex was tired of the word and distracted by the youth trailing after Amik, carrying three slacsuits on hangars. Amik didn't wait for permission as he led the way into the bedroom. "Come, Jaro, put them in the closet there. Thank you. You may go now."

Jaro nodded and hurried out of the room. The three of them waited until the outer door closed behind him, then the face-screens went off, and Alex went to the closet.

"These aren't mine. Jael was supposed to—"

"My dear Alex, a little patience, please," Amik said in a pained tone. "It seems my son said something, very much in passing, about bringing clothes for your departure. Now, I've seen your wardrobe, such as it is, and I've noticed that you invariably wear slacsuits of a standard design in which the shirt is pulled on over the head. I've had some experience with laser wounds—vicariously, I'm pleased to say—and I've also kept myself well informed on your wound in particular."

Alex found himself a chair, annoyed at the need for it, annoyed at the aching of his arm that seemed to intensify with the attention so offhandedly given it, and, above all, annoyed at Amik. He remained pointedly silent as Amik continued his exposition.

"Well, it occurred to me that standard slacsuit design would create unnecessary problems, even discomfort, for you, and it also occurred to me that my tailor was sitting about idly at the moment, collecting his 'cords, and wasting his time entertaining certain young women, and his imaginative powers creating self-dissolving veils."

Erica laughed at that, but Alex was so distracted, he didn't at first realize why.

She put on a mockingly sober expression. "Well, Amik, I hope you remedied that."

"Naturally. I put him to work designing these slacsuits. One can't, I suppose, do much about the pants, but Cobrik managed to improve on the shirt." He went to the closet, and pulled out one of the slacsuits. "So. You see, he's opened the shirt all the way up the front and put in simple pressure fasteners, and to further facilitate life for you when the bandages come off, Alex, I had him line the inside of the right arms with this rather exquisite material. Soft as sea air. I acquired quite a stock of it in a recent . . . uh, business transaction."

Erica went to Amik and took the slacsuit. "The color is nice. That's what I'd call a true Terran green. Terran moss, perhaps."

More like Castorian barrengorse, Alex thought.

"Come, Alex, try it on. I'll help you." Her smile faltered then, as if she realized that wasn't the best thing to say at this particular moment.

"I thought it was designed to relieve me of the need for help."

Amik shrugged elaborately. "Did I say that? I simply assigned Cobrik the task of making it easier for you—"

"To dress myself?" He rose and went to a drawer for underclothing—also provided by Amik—saying over his shoulder, "The break-point test, then, for Cobrik and me."

Neither of them offered any assistance, which compounded embarrassment with discomfort, but pride precluded his asking for what wasn't offered. Childish, no doubt, he chided himself, teeth set as he awkwardly pulled on the pants and fumbled at the waistband fastener. The shirt he managed with relative ease, pulling on the right sleeve first, aligning the front opening with the tab snap provided at the neck, then pressing the front closed. As he slipped on the shoes, he was grateful that he didn't have to contend with formal boots, and wondered if he ever would again. Finally, he turned to the mirror on the closet door to see that he had everything on straight.

Erica said softly, "Very handsome."

Alex felt all the resentment sagging out of him, remembering a night—how many years and eons ago?—Master Webster fussily draping the Lord Alexand, and Rich, looking on, making the same comment in almost exactly the same tone. Rich, watching from his nulgrav chair, enduring even then the chronic pain that would finally become unbearable.

Alex turned and met Amik's eye with a smile.

"Cobrik has passed the test, Amik. I'm grateful to him, and to you."

Amik flashed his golden grin and puffed out a perfect smoke ring.

"Well, perhaps I'll reward him with a new challenge: *edible*, self-dissolving veils."

That broke the tension with laughter, and if Alex was frowning slightly when he turned again to the mirror, it had nothing to do with Amik's kindly presumption.

"I have a challenge for him, Amik. A uniform. Pale blue, trimmed in—in anything but gold braid."

"You can have platinade, if it suits you. Of course, you understand that Cobrik is a man of rare talent, and his services carry a high tax."

Alex reminded himself to smile at that, and, as he turned from the mirror, put the remembered image from the tape capsules out of his mind: the image of Predis Ussher in his gold-decked uniform. But Ussher was right; the Concord wouldn't take an army in slacsuits seriously, or a man who still called himself First Commander of Fleet Operations. Costuming is a tool. Phillip Woolf's words.

"Forgive me, Amik, but I'm not yet recovered enough to indulge you in haggling. Whatever Cobrik's price, it will be paid, and silver braid will do. Let's adjourn to the salon. I'm tired of looking at that bed."

They followed him into the salon, another elegantly appointed room whose luxury only seemed oppressive. Amik found a chair that suited him and sank into it with a sigh. Then he straightened abruptly. "Ah! I nearly forgot half my purpose here." He searched various pockets in his robes, while Erica watched him curiously from a couch nearby, and Alex, still standing, took a quick look at his watch. Jael was late.

"Ah. Here it is." Amik proffered what seemed at first only a piece of cloth.

It was a glove. Alex took it, feeling his guard come up against resentment again. It was lined with the same downy material as the right sleeves of the slacsuits, but it was the outer material that held his attention. Black, with an opalescent sheen; it seemed to be some kind of thin, flexible leather.

"And is this intended to hide the scars?"

Amik only shrugged. "If you wish to hide them. Alex, in the Outside, scars aren't *hidden*. A Brother who hasn't a few scars to exhibit by the time he passes puberty will go out of his way to acquire them. Such things are relative. That leather, by the way, is something quite special, and in rather short supply. That, my friend, is the hide of a creature native to Castor, the belnong. It's a symbiont with the Marching For——"

"The *belnong*, did you say?"

"Yes. You know of it?"

Alex laughed, remembering the first time he'd heard that creature's name. In a rose garden, in another life. *Alex, I'm tough as a belnong....*

"Yes, I know of it."

"So. At any rate, the leather has extraordinary qualities. It's as flexible as your own skin, and has a slight grain; it will protect your hand without impairing movement or gripping ability."

Alex wondered if there would ever be much movement or gripping ability to be impaired in that hand, but the thought inspired no resentment now. He pulled on the glove, a slow and cautious process, but even though it was a little tight over the bandages, it didn't add to the pain once he had it on. He found a curious resolution in it.

"Amik, I'll never be parted from it. Again—thank you."

Amik waved that aside uncomfortably. "Don't weigh me down with more gratitude. I'm too old for such burdens." Then, with a quick shift of subject, "Jael tells me Ferra Severin has at last accomplished her mission. I assume I'm crossing no lines. In fact, I'm sure I'm not, since my close-mouthed son was my source." Still, there was a hint of courteous inquiry in that.

Alex eased into a chair, turning his body slightly so he could rest his right arm on his thigh. "You're crossing no lines, Amik."

"Ah. Then your Lady is well?"

"She's well, and she'll be with me soon in the COS HQ." Then he added lightly, "We're a family now, and even if our home must be a cave, it's fitting that we be together—Adrien and I and our twin sons." He saw Erica's eyes flash questioningly toward him. Conditioned or not, neither she nor Jael had presumed to risk trusting Amik with that information, but Alex considered it an offering of gratitude in the form of an expression of faith. Amik deserved that much.

Amik coughed out a cloud of smoke, and even when he recovered, stared blankly at Alex. Then his black eyes narrowed in speculation, that giving way to a wistful smile with only a hint of irony in it.

"So. Well, I'm...delighted. Almost in tears, in fact. I'm a sentimental man, as I told you before, and to see two fated lovers reunited and at the same time blessed with...*twin* sons, did you say? By the God, it has all the makings of a legendary *chan d'amor*. My friend, to think that you're now a father...*twice* a father—it staggers the imagination."

Alex found it so staggering he didn't want to talk about it further. Perhaps it was becoming more real now; it was beginning to reach him. He welcomed the door chime if only because it would conclude this conversation.

Erica went to check the vis-screen by the door, then switched off the sec-system and unlocked it. She didn't turn on her face-screen.

"Hello, Jael."

Alex rose—too fast. He blinked away the fleeting dizziness as Jael came in and, after a quick survey, turned to Amik.

"Wave-offs made, Father? I'm about to take your star guest away."

Amik smiled wryly at that oblique dismissal as he got himself to his feet. "I've had my say, Jael, and I've business to attend to." As he passed Erica, he made a courtly bow. "And you, gracious physician, I hope some day you'll take supper with me. It would honor me and my humble house."

She smiled at that. "Perhaps I shall, Amik, some day."

"The time is yours to name. Alex, rest yourself. And fortune." Then to Jael, "You, my son, I will see when next I see you. Step light."

"You, too, Father." He locked the door after Amik, then turned to Alex. "I just got off the 'ceiver with Val, brother. All clear at Saint P's. Trans is scheduled for 03:00. Two hours from now."

Alex took a careful breath. "Thanks, Jael. Now, what about our trans to the COS HQ?"

"Gather up your worldlies. Your escort's on line."

Erica started for the bedroom. "*I'll* gather your worldlies, Alex."

He nodded distractedly. "Thanks. Jael, did you . . . talk to the exiles?"

"I called a general assembly yesterday. They're lined in on you and every stray thread of the Ransom Alternative, Your Lady and first and second born are expected and prepared for."

"How did they react?"

"Well, some of them already had the Ransom Alternative tallied close enough. It hit some as a surprise, but you can rest easy on one thing—no one was unhappy about any part of it."

Alex had left it to Jael to disclose the Ransom Alternative to the exiles, and perhaps there was an element of cowardice in that. Or perhaps his uneasiness derived from an awareness that he was leaving something behind; something to which he could never return.

"Does it . . . change anything with them?"

Jael eyed him a moment, then when Erica emerged from the bedroom, relieved her of the burden of Alex's wardrobe.

"Did you think it wouldn't, brother?" Then, with a short laugh, "Change never was an evil in itself. Now, come on. They're all waiting."

2.

Another homecoming.

In Alex's mind, Andreas's homecoming was still a recent memory; he had lost most of the intervening five weeks, and as he stepped out of the MT, even the few days he did remember seemed to fade, and this homecoming became an extension of the last, one in which joy was allowed to run its course without being truncated by grief.

Only for a brief moment as he looked around the comcenter chamber did he feel a cold shadow of reminder. That black, impending dome of stone. But the black angel no longer rattled the locks of its confinement. Perhaps it was dead or, sated, had left him in search of other prey. Perhaps it was only quiescent.

That was a matter of indifference to him now. Nothing would spoil this homecoming.

The black dome echoed with laughter and welcome. Andreas was at the MT waiting for him, shouting to the others, as if it were a revelation, "Here he is!"

And Ben, pumping Alex's left hand, the blunt, tough lines of his face creased into a smile, his words lost in the jubilant confusion as the exiles pressed closer. Alex took their hands, savoring the familiar names, each calling up remembered mutual experiences. Yet something *had* changed. He read that in their eyes, and it became more apparent as the initial emotional charge spent itself. A hint of uncertain deference subtly different from that they had always shown for Commander Alex Ransom.

Change never was an evil in itself. So said Jael the Outsider with the succinct wisdom of an Elder Shepherd, and the real purpose of the Phoenix was to effect change on an entire civilization. They accepted this change, accepted him in his true identity. His problem, as the immediate excitement waned, was to keep Alex Ransom alive. In *their* minds, not his.

It was accomplished more easily than he expected. Commander Blayn initiated it. Another Falcon had been captured; perhaps he'd like to see it. When Blayn addressed him, with only the slightest hesitancy, as "sir," Alex responded casually, as if he'd never been, or even thought of being, addressed as "my lord." In the background, Jael deftly reinforced the establishment of a functioning norm with quiet suggestions that reminded the exiles of their duties and sent them willingly back to them.

It became a tour of inspection, and when Alex met the exiles in this context, it was as their commanding officer. Erica, Jael, and Ben accompanied him on the tour, Jael assuming the role of subaltern and guide. No part of the COS HQ was excluded, and Alex could be entirely honest in his expressions of approval; Jael kept his troops in close trim. The tour included the physics lab where Andreas explained the planned LR-MT experiment. It would take place on 6 Octov. Less than a week.

"It's rather crude, really, Alex. We've fitted *Phoenix Two* with some fairly sophisticated observational equipment, however. We'll send her into the Solar System just outside the Asteroid Belt, I think. Caris, wasn't that what we decided on finally?"

Dr. Bruce nodded. "Yes. The chances of Confleet observation are a little higher there than in the outer sectors, but we wanted to try it as close as possible to a strong solar gravitational field."

Andreas said, "I'd like to try it near Sirius A. That would be a better test; a stronger gravitational field. Besides..." His eyes seemed to slip out of focus for a moment. "It can—'t must—take us to the stars again, you know. Beyond Sirius, beyond Altair, beyond..." Then he roused himself, frowning slightly. "However, we have to face our existing power limitations. Anyway, we're transing a flare. The MT here has already been modified for LR trans, and getting the spare parts for that put us in the larceny business again." He sighed ruefully.

Alex glanced at Jael. "What has Amik added to his collection now?"

"The Unicorn Chronicle Arras. Twenty-eighth century, the old Ser tells me. School of Fatim-Karma."

"Lazar Hamid's most precious possession." Alex smiled coldly. Legend had it that Hamid's great-grandfather had broken the House of Kazmirin to put his hands on that tapestry.

Perhaps there was justice in this larceny. "Then you'll simply trans a flare from here into observational range of the *Two*?"

Andreas laughed. "Simply? Well, yes. Our biggest problem was a power source. We need far more power than our generators can produce. Fortunately, we need a very short burst of it, and again we're reduced to larceny of a sort."

"What sort? It might get a little awkward at the bargaining table if the Directors find out we've been systematically looting the Concord's finest art works."

"Not that sort, I'm happy to say. The solar power beams, Alex. Actually, we'll only purloin a microsecond of Lord Drakonis's treasurehouse of power. We've equipped *Three* with a reflector and built a receptor here on the surface. *Three* will simply intercept one of the power beams with its reflector at an angle to deflect the beam to our receptor dish. The trans will be triggered automatically."

It was Alex's turn to question the term "simply." The mathematics behind that brief encounter between beam, ship, reflector, and receptor had undoubtedly taken up a great deal of comp time, and the tolerances would be measured in milliseconds and micrometers, but to Andreas it was only a mechanical problem.

The tour continued and ended finally in a small chamber opening off the back wall of the sleeping section. Alex remembered it as a natural chamber they had enlarged for storage purposes. A woman of middle age with short, white-streaked hair was waiting there. He knew her. Mistra Jenna Cromwel, medtech, Grade 7. What he didn't know, until Jael informed him, was that she had specialized in pediatrics before joining the Phoenix. The conversion of the storage room into an apartment and nursery had been entrusted to her.

Alex was feeling the strain. He hadn't spent this much time on his feet without rest before, and the emotional drain was taking its toll, too. He looked around the converted storage room numbly. Across the middle of the floor a metallic bar was inset for S/V screens that would divide the room into two sections when activated. The right-hand section was furnished with a double bed, a comconsole, and a straight chair placed in front of a low chest over which hung a mirror. There were cosmetic containers on the chest, and he smiled a little at that, sure that the drawers contained feminine apparel. On pegs in one wall, Erica had hung his slacsuits beside three smaller suits; on the floor under them were two pairs of slip-on shoes. He had no doubt they would all be exactly Adrien's size. A tiny crystal bottle on the chest caught his eye, and he went over to examine it. Perfume; one of the House of Sidarta's finest: Primaraude.

He looked around at Mistra Cromwel and smiled his appreciation, then finally forced himself to look at the other half of the room.

Heat lamps and thermcarpet, a sink with water outlets, three storage chests, the stone walls sprayed with plasment in a soft yellow; it seemed incredibly luxurious for the COS HQ. In the center of the space were two small, railed beds. Infant cribs.

"Lady Adrien will find everything she needs here for the twins, sir, and I'll be available at any time if she needs help, or even just baby tending."

Mistra Cromwel was smiling with genuine anticipation, and Erica engaged her in a brief, bantering exchange on frustrated maternal urges. Alex's throat felt so dry, he wasn't sure he could speak, yet he knew he must say something, and knew he should be relieved at the solicitude displayed for Adrien, a nonmember, a First Lord's daughter, far more an outsider here than Jael would ever be.

But his arm was aching miserably and he felt the warning sensation of looseness at his knees, as if the joints wouldn't hold unless he concentrated on them.

Those two waiting cribs. It wasn't fear he felt in looking at them, yet the reactions were very similar, and Mistra Cromwel was smiling at him with a secretive sympathy he found oddly annoying.

She said, "It may seem a bit primitive to Lady Adrien, sir, but I think we've supplied all the necessities."

"And more." He managed a quiet laugh then. "I was thinking it was rather extravagant. As for Adrien, don't forget she's coming here from six months in a convent. Jenna... thank you."

Jael suggested an Exile Council meeting, and Alex knew

it was at Erica's prompting; he caught the nearly wordless exchange between them before Jael deftly delivered him from this room.

Alex accepted the suggestion gratefully, and when they finally reached the conference room, he welcomed the closing of the doorscreens and, above all, a sturdy chair under him. Erica sat on his right, watching him closely, but apparently satisfied; she made no comments. It devolved into an informal conclave among friends rather than a formal Council meeting. Not that their meetings had ever been marked by formality; only a defining structure of priorities that was absent now.

Still, there was no idle reminiscing, and most of the conversation was carried by Jael, Ben, and himself, and centered on Concord Day—two words that embraced a spectrum of meaning too wide for adequate expression.

It was also a process of reacquaintance on a deep emotional level, and in that Alex was particularly conscious of Andreas. Erica had assured him that the eight months in Pendino hadn't changed him except to inflict a certain amount of mental scarring, which was to be expected, and which he had dealt with very well.

After half an hour, Alex was satisfied, yet in all that time his mind was strangely divided; nothing that transpired here was lost on him, and he knew he would reexamine everything said here later and find no gaps in comprehension. But all the while another part of his mind was intensely focused on time; he felt the flick of digits from one second to the next even without looking at his watch, and when he did check it, he was seldom more than a minute in error in his mental estimate.

Adrien waited at the end of the passage of seconds.

The problem of protecting the Drakonis power plants on the Inner Planets seemed especially disturbing to Andreas. It meant exile forces engaging Phoenix forces; brother against brother. But finally he surrendered to the necessity of it. At least fifteen more Falcons would be needed, according to Jael's computations. They would have to come from Amik.

Alex agreed as he looked once more at his watch, keeping his breathing spaced, hoarding his strength, questioning and listening, probing problems and solutions, weighing probabilities and alternatives, while that other part of his mind counted out the seconds.

Whoever was speaking had his full attention. He looked at them, listening, but saw always behind their faces another face in a thousand remembered moments: the child-woman who had materalized in a casual vortex of cruelty to restore Rich's fallen crutch and silence Karlis Selasis's callous laughter with nothing more than her contempt; the seeress of the rose garden who looked at the world, and at him, with clear, unmasked eyes and offered her love as a hope, not an obligation; the fair cygnet become a swan, moonlit in pearls, taking her stand as an irreducible pillar of reason and integrity in an encounter of insanity; his Promised, veiled in gold, cheeks streaked with prescient tears; and finally, his bride, his armed princess with the blue light of the moon-Pollux like silk on her skin, offering again her love as a hope in the chalice of her body.

Alex was listening attentively as Ben outlined an alternative solution to the difficult and complex problem of abducting seventeen people, the First Lords of Centauri and their immediate families, in an extremely short span of time. No other means had been devised to protect them from potential "accidental" bombing—on Ussher's orders—of their Estates. Perhaps there would only be sixteen to worry about; Lazar D'Ord Hamid was scheduled to be in Concordia for a Directorate meeting. He would probably go alone, and because of the cancellation of the Plaza ceremonies, it was unlikely either Eliseer or Drakonis would be anywhere except in their Estates.

Mike Compton was on the MT, and Alex had instructed him to give them five minutes' warning before the trans. Alex carefully considered alternatives for a multiple kidnapping, but his gaze shifted from Ben to the intercom on the table exactly two seconds before the screen lighted and Compton's face appeared on it.

"Commander?"

He touched the transmit switch. "Yes?"

"Five minutes, sir. Everything on sequence."

"Thanks, Mike." The screen darkened as he caught Jael's eye and recognized the restrained anticipation there. "Well, Jael, our cloistered women are about to arrive." Then he rose and addressed the four of them. "Please, come with me. I want you to meet . . . my wife."

Those words caught in an unexpected constriction in his throat. He went to the door, remembered to reach for the doorcon with his left hand. In the comcenter, the exiles were gathering again. The monitoring crew was still conscientiously on duty, and the others seemed a little ill at ease, as if they weren't sure they should be here. Alex reassured them with casual comments, a nod or smile in passing. He'd have called them into assembly if they hadn't already assembled themselves.

He stopped two meters short of the MT chamber, staring into its emptiness, his mind no longer divided; it came into tight focus so that nothing outside that cube of emptiness registered, not the people around him, not even Compton's radio exchange with Val and the words that would have warned him that the long count of seconds had at length reached zero.

A puff of air set in motion, the space was no longer empty. She was looking directly at him as if she knew exactly where he'd be standing. She looked away only for a moment when Erica guided her out of the MT. They weren't strangers; Erica had spent a number of hours at Saint Petra's these last ten days, and the bond of friendship already established between them was clear. Alex didn't find that surprising.

Erica took the white-blanketed bundle Adrien held. He heard Erica say something about taking them to the nursery, out of the confusion, but the words were only sounds in his ears, and if on some level he realized that solicitously handled bundle was something other than an inanimate object, that it was one of his *sons*, his awareness was still too tightly focused on Adrien for the realization to sink in. She was wearing the blue habit of the Sisters of Faith, but the veil and koyf had been discarded, and her hair fell free around her shoulders, sheened with satin reflections.

Then Val emerged from the MT. Jael was waiting for her, but after a few words surrendered her to Erica, and both disappeared somewhere in the murmur of voices behind Alex; Val clothed in blue like Adrien's tw—

Val had been carrying a white-wrapped bundle, too.

Alex didn't look around to see where she had gone; he didn't look away from Adrien's face, from all the remembered faces that flickered out of memory across a long skein of years, merging into the image he saw in this here and now.

Seeress-child, fair cygnet, my pearl-starred swan, gold-veiled Promised teaching me the lessons of tears and joy, Selaneen princess steel-boned and armed for blood, my bride in planet-light. . . .

He went to her and held out his left hand. When her hand rested in his palm, bird-light, warm with life, he said softly, "Welcome to exile, Adrien."

She smiled at that, looking around her, up to the black dome of stone, then finally back to him.

"I've *been* in exile, Alexand. Say welcome *home*."

3.

3 Octov.

Alex crossed the park in the central plaza, moving at a slow, shuffling pace, the hood of his Bondman's cloak drawn up. Under the helions, the trees cast mottled shadows on the pavement. It was night in Helen, but still two hours before the compound curfew.

The trees looked too green in the lights; mutated Terran trees that had forgotten seasons here where life was shielded from winter. In Concordia the trees would still be showing the bones of their branches, misted in the vibrant hues of spring. The city would be decking itself for Concord Day.

But there would be no ceremonies in the Plaza this year.

It was hard to imagine that. Of all the symptoms of failure in the Concord—and he was acutely aware of all of them, from the bankruptcy declaration made by the House of Alfons Stedmark yesterday, to the temporary closure of the University in Leda resulting from the student riots there the day before, to the abortive Conpol conscription mutiny in Saopallo the week before, the 107 Bond uprisings erupting in the Two Systems during the last month, and today, the food riots in the refugee camps in Stanbul and Norleans, two of the hastily organized centers for housing the millions of refugees from Mars, where a semblance of order was only now beginning to emerge from the rubble of planet-wide disaster—yet he found the cancellation of the Plaza ceremonies most disturbing. As an event, it was trivial, but as a symbol, it was staggering. A capitulation to fear.

And only a few weeks ago, Phillip Woolf had been attacked and wounded in the Hall of the Directorate. That index he still couldn't regard objectively.

He glanced up, then fixed his eyes on the pavement. An Eliseer House guard was approaching. Alex concentrated on his role, depending on peripheral vision and his ears to warn him if the guard made any unexpected moves, but he passed without even a break in step. Alex looked around at him, then quickened his pace as he moved out of the park.

He felt more anxiety tonight than he ever had in this compound, Eliseer's Estate Compound A. It wasn't the guard. It was something intangible, something pendant in the air like a vaguely familiar odor. There were only a handful of Bonds in the plaza tonight, yet two hours before curfew, it should be crowded, and the few Bonds he saw were quiet, almost furtive, scurrying hurriedly down the paths.

The fear had reached even into the Eliseer compounds.

The chapel loomed ahead, golden light gleaming in its narrow windows, and it seemed a warm and inviting haven. There were few havens left.

Once inside, he paused to let his eyes adjust to the dim light and his senses adjust to the other-world aura of the place, savoring the pungent odors of candles and incense. A few worshipers knelt in the pews or at the altars along the side walls, but Malaki wasn't among them. Alex reached up with his left hand and unfastened the medallion. A new clip had been affixed to the medal itself so he could remove it and replace it on the chain with one hand. He turned the medallion so the lamb was uppermost and walked down the aisle toward the vigilant image of the Mezion above the altar, paused to bow to it, then went to the door of Malaki's visitation room. The response to his knock came without hesitation.

"Come in."

Malaki was standing at the table in the center of the small, candle-smoked room that was so much a miniature of the chapel in its austerity and primitive decorations. The shelves lining one wall were filled with jars of roots, herbs, and varicolored powders, and the Shepherd was grinding dried leaves with a mortar and pestle; the rhythmic grating stopped as the door closed behind Alex, and Malaki's age-scored features lighted with recognition. He put his pestle aside and came around the table, while Alex held out his left hand and the medallion.

"Malaki, I come in the Name of the Lamb."

The Shepherd knelt, took his hand and pressed it to his forehead, and when he straightened, a tremulous smile was on his lips.

"My lord, it's been so long." Then, when Alex pushed back his hood, "You've been ill."

Alex went to a chair by the table and eased into it. "Yes, I've been ill, my friend, but I'm recovering."

Too slowly, he added to himself, with a flare of annoyance at the weakness in his legs. This was his first appearance as the Brother; only a beginning. A schedule had been drawn. In the next ten days, he would make forty such visitations. He'd been relieved to learn that neither Jael nor Erica had yet seen Malaki, instead concentrating on the more unstable Hamid and Drakonis compounds. This seemed a fitting beginning; it was a Rightness.

"Please, be seated," Alex said. "Have you been well?"

Malaki went to his chair behind the table. "The Holy Mezion smiles still on these old bones. But you . . ." He frowned as his sharp eyes moved from Alex's face to the black glove. "You've been injured."

"Yes, Malaki."

"What kind of injury?"

His tone was so oddly businesslike, Alex almost smiled. "It's a laser wound, but—"

"A moment, my lord."

Alex watched curiously as Malaki went to this herbal shelves and, after a brief search, returned to his chair and proffered a small jar.

"My lord, this is an ointment for burns, but it's also helpful with laser wounds. The mixture was given me by Father Josha, who came before me in this chapel. He had it from Father Ra, and he . . . well, nobody knows who first made it. I think you'll find it will ease the pain a little."

Alex took the jar and studied it. The clear plasex showed a milky paste with a pale green cast. He put it in an inside pocket of his cloak, and said, "Thank you, Malaki. Something to ease pain is a blessing always."

"A simple remedy made by a simple man." He smiled faintly. "But try it before you put it aside."

"I will. I'm not as skeptical as some; I don't underestimate your 'simple' remedies, and I'm grateful for this one." He paused, taking a long breath, letting his sober attitude serve as a warning. "My friend, I've come to you with sorrowful news tonight. I've told you before that a time of war may be coming."

Malaki sighed and thrust his hands into his sleeves. "That time is near, then?"

"Yes. Eleven days. It will begin on Concord Day."

"The Holy Mezion help us all." He closed his eyes in a silent prayer, and when he looked up at Alex again, asked, "Who will make this war?"

"A . . . false prophet. I know him, and he's an evil man. Nothing he says can be taken as truth."

Malaki hesitated, his eyes shadowed in their deep sockets. "Who will this false prophet make war against?"

"Not you or your people; not the Bonds. He'll say he battles *for* you, as Lionar Mankeen did, but in fact he only makes war to fulfill his own ambitions. He makes war against the Concord." Then, seeing that made no sense to Malaki, he added, "He makes war against the Lords; all the Lords."

"Against . . . the Lords? But that's a mortal sin."

"So it is, but this man is infested with a Dark Spirit. I've come to warn you that when this false prophet begins this war, he'll try to make all the Bonds in Centauri join in the revolt and take up weapons with him against the Lords." He leaned forward to emphasize his words. "Malaki, that must not happen. You know it would mean bloodshed and suffering for everyone. Lord Eliseer has been kind and just to you and your flock. You cannot let them rise against him or the Concord."

The old man blinked, still bewildered. "But why should we rise against Lord Eliseer? How can this man, this Dark Spirit, make us do so?"

"By lies, by illusion, by false miracles. In the confusion

and alarm of war, people won't stop to think; they'll act out of fear, and this man has devised a means of rousing the Bonds that will seem supernatural. On Corcord Day all through the compounds voices will come from out of nowhere, from the very air. At least, that's how it will seem. He wants you to think these voices come from the Beyond, but they come from him, and there's a simple and mechanical explanation for them. The voices will come from microspeakers." He reached into his shirt pocket and took out a standard speaker. "Listen to this, Malaki."

The Shepherd frowned intently at the small disk while it blurted its message:

"This is the voice of the Brother. It's a recording made on a device similar to those used daily by the Fesh and Elite to carry messages."

Alex shifted the rewind ring, then handed the speaker to Malaki.

"Touch that depression in the center. There—" He waited while the speaker repeated its message. "You see, it's only a mechanical device."

Malaki nodded as he returned the speaker.

"I've seen such things; the Fesh sirras use them. So this is how the false prophet hopes to make my flock rise up against Lord Eliseer?"

"Yes, except the speakers he'll use are so small twenty would fit in this one. Hundreds of them have already been hidden in the compounds, and they'll be activated *not* by touch, but by a radio beam from a great distance. You can understand how it will seem to your flock; the voices will apparently come from nowhere urging them by all they hold sacred to kill and destroy, to set themselves *free*."

Any promise in that word didn't reach Malaki, not when it was equated with death and destruction.

"I see," he said dully.

"You must warn your flock, Malaki, and I leave it to you to tell the other Shepherds in the Eliseer compounds here in Helen. My time is short, and I won't be able to talk to all of them myself."

"I'll tell them, my lord."

"When you do, and when you warn your flock, you must

be very careful. If you talk too openly of war or microspeakers, the guards might hear of it. They'll call in the SSB, and you might be questioned. You can only tell them your source of information is the Brother, but that won't make the questioning easier. For one thing, my friend, the SSB considers me imaginary."

Malaki managed a faint smile at that, but his dismay at possible involvement with the SSB made it brief.

"It is said that truth has many faces, each as true as the other. I'll find a way to warn my flock . . . carefully."

"You must reach all of them. Concord Day will be a holiday; they'll be free for the day, and you won't be able to reach them then. They must be warned ahead of time."

"They will be. What should I tell them to do?"

"They must ignore the voices as if they didn't exist. The guards will probably order all Bonds to their quarters when the war begins, and they must obey. They must do exactly as they're told, or the price will be paid in blood."

"They'll obey."

Alex let his eyes close briefly. "I hope so."

Malaki leaned toward him, watching him anxiously. "My lord, are you . . . ?"

"I tire easily, Malaki, but my strength returns. Don't be concerned about me."

"I won't. You're Chosen of the Mezion, and He watches over you. Still, I'm sorry you've had to suffer."

"Perhaps it's a Testing." He paused then, sorting the mixed scents of candles, incense, and herbs. At some time, many times, Rich had sat in this same place, smelling the same warm scents, generation upon generation, past and future, coming together in memory and hope in this small, flame-lit room.

And in another room a few hundred kilometers away, buried under the star-lit desert, Adrien lived. She *lived*, and with her their pledge to generations past and future; their sons.

They were real to him now. He had held them, awkwardly with one arm, felt the pulse of life in them, heard their cries and the sounds meant for laughter, seen the light of cognizance, however potential, in their cloudy blue eyes, recognized already the signature of individuality in their faces and behavior even though they were such uncanny mirror images of each other.

There were three people in all the worlds whom he wanted to know about those infants, whatever happened on Concord Day. Phillip Woolf was one, Mathis Galinin the second, and the last was the Elder Shepherd Malaki, who had been a faithful friend to Rich, the first born's namesake, and to Adrien, their mother.

But at length Alex rose. He couldn't tell Malaki now; he couldn't even tell him Adrien was alive, although he knew how much the old man had grieved for her. The danger of attracting SSB attention in the process of warning his flock was too real to be ignored. The Brother rewarded his faithful with the risk of agonizing interrogation and probably death. What would the omniscient Mezion think of that kind of justice?

He knew what the Brother thought of it, but Alex Ransom had no choice. Malaki would know about Adrien, about the twins, but not now.

Not until after Concord Day.

"Malaki, I must go. If we don't meet again, I ask this boon of you: Remember my words as you remember my brother's."

Malaki rose, and there was a solemn grace in his posture, an inherent dignity; his somber gaze was fixed on Alex.

"I can't forget you or your brother. Your words will be remembered as his words are, and if we don't meet again in this world, we'll meet in the Beyond, the Mezion willing."

"The Mezion willing. Thank you for your help and your faith, my friend."

"It's your due, my lord."

"No, it isn't. It's a gift, and I'm profoundly grateful." He turned and crossed to the door. "Peace be, Malaki."

The door slid open, and as he passed into the amber gloom of the chapel, he heard Malaki's parting, "Peace, my lord."

4.

Alex was breathing hard when he transed aboard *Phoenix One*. Vic Blayn was near the MT, waiting; he snapped an order over his shoulder.

"Sargent Hansen, accelerate for SynchShift. Random course. Commander, are you all right?"

Alex nodded as he stepped out onto the condeck, automatically scanning the screens before he looked back at Mike Compton on the MT console.

"Mike, you have fast reflexes. Thanks."

Compton gave him a crooked smile. "I've had a little practice on this thing, sir."

Blayn was still frowning at his commander, thinking how incongruous he looked in the maroon Drakonis Bond cloak.

"Sir, what happened?"

"Luck, Vic; the worst kind. Lord Drakonis made an unscheduled inspection tour of the compound."

"Damn. The place was full of guards, I suppose."

"Yes. Before you reach SS entry, I want Mike to trans me to the Cave. The LR-MT experiment is scheduled in a few minutes. I want to be there."

Blayn checked the SynchShift countdown clock. "There's plenty of time before we reach entry. I ordered SS because we picked up a scan on a Confleet patrol. Did any of the Drakonis guards see you?"

"Quite a few, as a matter of fact. It gave me a chance to test my legs sprinting. I was stopped for an ident check outside the chapel." He studied the radial scanners, absently reminding himself that he must take another analgesic. "I won't be at the COS HQ long, then I'll trans back to Danae; I have two more compounds to visit there today. Mike, check with Bergon. He'll have to set up an MT fix for me again."

"Yes, sir. The apartment will probably be safe. He said he'd be clear for two hours."

"Good. Are you oriented for the Cave?"

"Any time you're ready."

"I'm ready. Vic, give me an all clear when you're out of SS." He stepped into the MT cubicle, frowning across at the radar screens. "That patrol is pulling up on you."

"I know. We're . . . ninety seconds from SS."

"Then I'd better be on my way. All right, Mike."

"Yes, sir. Transing—"

Compton's voice was cut off, replaced by a roomful of voices. As Alex left the Cave of Springs MT, Jael was the first to greet him, extending his left hand in welcome.

"Well, brother, we wondered if you'd make it."

Alex searched the intent crowd gathered around the monitoring consoles.

"I was wondering myself for a few minutes. Where's Andreas? Oh—there he is. What about Ben and Erica?"

"They're both neck deep in Fina, and there's nothing they can do for this gim."

Alex nodded, but his attention had shifted to the tunnel leading to the sleeping quarters; Val Severin and Adrien were emerging. Adrien was wearing a slacsuit, and her hair was tied at her neck out of her way; a towel was tucked into her waistband, and as she came in, she was wiping her hands on it. The midday meal was just finished.

Alex knew how she occupied her time while he transed across space from one Bond chapel to the next, or even when he returned to the COS HQ to immerse himself in continuous working conferences with the exile staff. He could manage eight working hours a day now if he remembered to stop for at least one full hour of rest. Adrien's time was to a large extent taken up with the twins, but if any of the exiles expected her to spend her free time sitting idly waiting to be served, as they might think befitted her title, they soon discovered their error. She insisted on paying her way here with work, and further insisted on what was generally termed scullery duty. She was qualified for nothing else, she informed Mistra Cromwel, and she could free those who *were* qualified to concentrate on the real work of the COS HQ. And so the Lady Adrien Eliseer Woolf spent her days in a cave, cooking, scouring, laundering, and seemed quite content with it all.

Alex was smiling when she turned and found him in the crowd, his focus of awareness narrowing, as it did every time he saw her, as if it were a fresh discovery each time. She crossed the comcenter to him, studying him with a clinical eye that reminded him of Erica, and he asked the question that had been uppermost in his thoughts since he arrived.

"How are the twins?"

Adrien smiled obliquely. "Napping with full stomachs, and I don't think they've grown more than ten centimeters since you saw them this morning."

Dr. Lind's quiet voice sounded from the ampspeakers, creating a hush in the chamber.

"Zero minus two minutes. All sequences on schedule."

Alex took Adrien's arm. "Come, I want to talk to Andreas."

The greetings offered as they moved through the crowd were absent and unintentionally distant. The tension was almost tangible, voices muted more by mutual consent than by necessity. The only one present who didn't seem to feel the tension was Andreas Riis. Lyden and Bruce were seated on either side of him, both displaying more anxiety than Andreas, who seemed totally relaxed, his spare body slumped in a chair at the consoles, his eyes focused vaguely on one of the screens before him as he spoke into his headset mike.

Alex heard the name Leftant Cary. That meant Andreas was in contact with *Phoenix Two*; a very long-distance conversation. *Two* was in the Solar System outside the Asteroid Belt waiting for a miracle that Andreas would call a fact.

Alex asked, "Any problems, Dr. Bruce?"

"No, not yet, anyway." He was listening to his own headset. "*Three* is on intercept course with the power beam, and no hint of patrols in the area."

"Thank the God. Dr. Lyden, don't tell me you're nervous?"

Lyden grinned sheepishly. "Of course not. I've only had three calmers today."

His SynchCom conversation concluded, Andreas swiveled his chair around.

"Alex! You transed in just in time. A few more minutes and we'd have had to decline trans; the MT would be somewhat occupied. How are you feeling?"

"Very well, Andreas. I needn't ask about you. You look fit as a twenty-year-old."

"Well, I am feeling rather fit at the moment." He frowned, hearing someone call his name, and looked past Lyden to Telstoi, who was on the SynchCom console. "What's that, Tel?"

"Sir, you're still transmitting."

"I am?" He reached up and switched off his headset mike. "Forgot about that thing." Then his smile returned as he looked up at Alex. "How's the Brother's tour going?"

Dr. Lind's amplified voice intoned, "Zero minus one minute. All sequences on schedule."

The murmur of voices around them stopped, then resumed

at a lower tone, the tension collectively increasing.

"Andreas, I can't muster any interest in the tour now."

Andreas turned back to the console almost indifferently, and Alex smiled to himself. No doubt Andreas would be willing to let the experiment take place without witnessing it. He knew what would happen. If there were any problems, they could only be mechanical.

"Well, there won't be much to see here," Andreas said, "except on this screen. It's coupled with the *Two*'s vis-screens. The flare we're transing should emerge within range of their vidicams, so we'll see it here. It's pressure activated; it'll go off when it hits vacuum. This screen is only for effect, really. The important data will come from the recording instruments; they're a bit more accurate than the human eye." He surveyed the intent techs at their screens and consoles and smiled faintly. "Actually, we're all only for effect. When *Three* intercepts the beam and it hits our receptor, it'll trigger the MT automatically. It's in the hands of the machines now."

From the ampspeakers came the words, "Zero minus thirty seconds."

Alex felt the quickening of his pulse and knew it was in part simply a response to the countdown, to any countdown. But it was also a response to understanding, knowing how many years had gone into creating a flash of light in space, knowing what that flash could mean for years to come.

This day, 6 Octov 3258, would be a date to be memorized by generations of school children, like the first Terran satellite, the first manned landing on Luna, the first MAM-An generators, the Drakonian Theory, and the first SynchShift ships. And perhaps some of those children would be the descendants of today's Bonds, who knew nothing of history except the history of saints taught them by their Shepherds. And perhaps some of those children would live on the planets of stars brought within human reach by the LR-MT.

Andreas leaned back, lips pursed thoughtfully. "Dr. Lyden has come up with an idea we may be able to put into effect with our available energy sources, Alex."

Alex was listening, but, like everyone else in the cavern room, his eyes were fixed on the screen. Andreas was still the exception.

"It would be a kind of amplifying device, actually," he went on, oblivious to the taut silence around him.

Lind's voice again: "Zero minus eight seconds."

"We could expand our load-energy ratio by a power of ten if it works out, and we can probably set it up in a few months if we can get the equipment for the modifications."

Alex couldn't restrain his laugh, but if Andreas wondered about it there wasn't time to explain.

"Five . . ."

Finally, Andreas turned to look up at the screen.

"Four . . . three . . ."

"Well, we'll have a look at the fireworks now."

"Two . . . one . . ."

The black chamber was silent except for the machines.

". . . zero."

A soundless blossom against the star-speckled black, it expanded in shimmering silver, dissolving to dust and invisibility with the unreal suddenness of vacuum explosions.

It seemed anticlimactic.

There should have been a thunderous rumble. There should have been a chorus of trumpets trembling the air with C major chords. There should have been a roaring ovation, cheers wrung from thousands of exalting throats.

But there was only that brief, silent, silver flowering.

Everyone in the chamber seemed to share the sense of anticlimax as starred blackness restored itself on the screen, but a few seconds later the silence broke with realization. There was no thunderous roar or trumpet chorus, but there were cheers, and if their numbers were less than thousands, there was exaltation enough.

Alex put his arm around Adrien, heard and felt her grateful laughter, it was one with his, while Andreas looked around with a faintly perplexed smile at the shouting, gesticulating, back-slapping, hand-pumping, laughing exiles.

"They seem surprised, Alex."

"Not surprised, Andreas; overwhelmed."

Alex stared at the screen, in his mind re-creating that brief explosion. There would be no fireworks over the Plaza this Concord Day, but perhaps this small flower of light—a feeble echo of those grand displays—would bring the fireworks back to the Plaza next year.

He closed his eyes, his hand tightening on Adrien's, listening to the exuberant celebration around him, feeling suddenly detached from it.

Concord Day was eight days away.

5.

When Alex entered Amik's sanctum, the Lord of Thieves was on his feet, an unusual enough occurrence, talking to a lean, sinewy man with a predatory stance and dark features accented by a curled beard; he was dressed in brocaded red velveen, his boots scrolled in elaborate designs like the jeweled knife sheath at his waist.

Alex stopped inside the door. "I'm sorry, Amik, I understood you were alone."

"I will be shortly, my friend. It's good to see you."

Amik wasn't actually seeing him; at least, not his face. Alex was face-screened as he always was in Amik's realm, and that seemed to heighten the other man's curiosity. He surveyed Alex with an extraordinarily cold and penetrating eye, but in this case appearances would be deceiving; Alex was clothed as a Bond.

"Benino." Amik addressed himself to the swarthy man in a soft, potently callous tone Alex had never heard. "I've made my say, and you've made yours. You had a clear run, but you stood back."

Benino stiffened. "Brother, I never crossed your lines. By the God, I didn't!"

"I've made my say. Now, go with!"

The man hesitated, then turned and strode out the door, passing within a meter of Alex, his glance like a chill wind at the back of the neck. When he was gone, Amik lowered himself into his chair with a sigh of annoyance and took a 'com from a pocket in his robes.

"A moment, Alex." And into the 'com, "Tergo, see to Benino. I'll have no more of his lies." Then, having verbally signed a man's death warrant, he put away the 'com and smiled benignly at Alex. "My friend, you look a bit gray around the edges."

Alex speculated only briefly on Benino's crime or fate as he tossed his cloak on one of the couches and found himself a chair, easing his right arm into a relatively comfortable position.

"I'm only a bit tired around the edges. And you?"

"Healthy and well content, I'm glad to say. May I offer you something? A little Marsay, perhaps?"

"Nothing, thank you. I've come to do some haggling, so I'd better keep my head clear."

"Ah! So you'd haggle with me again? Wonderful. It's always a challenge to haggle with a gentleman born." He studied Alex's attire with a lifted eyebrow and added, "Although I must say you hardly look the part."

Alex laughed. "Protective coloration, Amik."

"So. You've been among the Bonds again." He sighed prodigiously. "Perhaps some day you'll tell me what you find so fascinating about those unfortunate souls."

Unfortunate. Alex recognized his weariness in the weight the word seemed to carry. His tabard was the green and yellow of D'Ord Hamid, and he'd be glad to have it off; the Hamid compounds offered no pleasant memories.

"Perhaps one day I can assuage your curiosity, Amik."

"And perhaps I'll tally it myself one day. But you said you came to haggle. I prefer to get business out of the way first, then we can relax, and I might even talk you into sharing a bit of Marsay with me. So. What is it you have to offer, and what do you expect—in your usual extravagant manner—in return?"

Alex laughed, noting the gleam of anticipation in Amik's black eyes. "You know what I have to offer. Jael's already demonstrated it for you. What did you think of the plasimask?"

"Mm. Well, it was of passing interest. I suppose it might have its uses."

"It does. For purposes of disguise, it's unparalleled. It blends with any complexion, can be built up to a depth of a centimeter without becoming obvious or stiffening or cracking, can be worn up to twelve hours comfortably and longer with less comfort, and is unaffected by perspiration or moisture, but easily removed with a mild solvent."

"Very impressive," Amik commented, looking not in the least impressed, "but the Brothers have done very well in the line of disguise without this invention of yours, however remarkable it might be."

Alex nodded and said offhandedly, "Well, one can always change to a better method if the price is reasonable."

"Price? Already you're broaching the matter of price?" He reached into a cloisonne box on the table beside him, extracted one of his slender cigars, and inserted it in the jeweled holder. "And I'm not yet convinced I'm interested in what you have to sell."

"No, I didn't mean *my* price. I meant the price *you* would ask of your customers when you sell the product."

Amik took time to puff his cigar alight. "Ah. Then we're talking in terms of a franchise?"

"We're talking in terms of the outright sale of a product. The formula, Amik. Jael assures me that you have the facilities—'here and there'—to manufacture the plasimask. I know you have the facilities to distribute it, and I doubt an infringement on the House of Sidarta's franchises will inhibit you *or* your customers. And the markets for the plasimask certainly aren't limited to the Brothers for purposes of disguise. Consider its potential as a cosmetic. You know very well the Ladies of the Elite and more affluent Fesh would pay almost any price you care to ask for it."

"Possibly." With that cautious admission, Amik moved to the next stage of the ritual. "So. Assuming I find this product of interest, what are you asking in return?"

"Only two things, Amik, and they're both short term. More in the nature of loans and services. First, I'm expecting certain . . . guests next week, and, as you're aware, the Cave of Springs offers very little in the way of guest facilities."

"Then you're asking me to provide lodgings for them?"

"Yes. I'm also asking that the lodgings be strictly forbidden to the Brothers. The privacy and safety of my guests must be maintained at all costs. I'll provide the people to tend their needs and guard them, but I must be sure they'll be safe from the Brothers."

Amik studied him a moment, puffing slowly on his cigar.

"These must be very special guests. How many are you expecting?"

"Three families; six members in one, seven in another, four in the last."

"Mm. And how long will they be staying?"

"I don't know exactly, but no more than a few days at the most."

"I can certainly lodge that many here and make them quite comfortable, but I must know who these guests are before I agree to assume any responsibility for their safety."

Alex sighed. "Yes, of course you must, but I'm laying edict where these people are concerned, and even on the information I give you. I must ask your word that you'll protect them as you have me and . . . my physician."

"My friend, you have it. I won't betray your confidence, or your guests."

"Thank you, Amik. The guests will be the Lords and immediate families of the three resident Houses of Centauri—Eliseer, Hamid, and Drakonis."

Amik didn't seem surprised at that; he only pursed his lips and nodded absently.

"Well, that's an interesting assortment, and if I've tallied correctly, there will be seventeen altogether?"

"That would be the maximum, but Lord Lazar probably won't be among them; he's scheduled to be in Concordia. Lady Galia may be absent, too; she's made tentative plans for a trip to Paykeen. If she goes, she'll take Patricia and Annia with her."

"So I may have *only* thirteen Lords and Ladies and their offspring to worry about. Interesting, indeed. Knowing your gentlemanly sensibilities, I assume you're not abducting them for lowly purposes such as ransom or extortion. Now you've given me something else to wonder over. But you said you were asking *two* things in return for the formula."

Alex replied with studied casualness, "I want to use twenty of your Falcons for a twenty-four-hour period. That's all."

Amik's eyes widened in astonishment. "Twenty Falcons, and the man says that's *all!*"

"There's also the problem of crews. I'll provide the navcomp and command personnel, but I need some weapons techs and gunners."

"Ah! Not only twenty Falcons, but crews, too! My friend, I always thought you a little mad, but now I wonder if you aren't *totally* mad."

Alex laughed appreciatively. "Before you get too concerned about my sanity, remember I only want the Falcons and crews for a twenty-four-hour period, and in return, you'll collect a handsome profit on the plasimask for years to come."

Amik subsided, languid eyes cool and calculating now.

"Possibly, but weapons techs and gunners imply a military engagement of some sort. What can I expect in the way of losses during this twenty-four-hour period—or, more to the point, are you going to cover them?"

"No. That's part of the bargain."

"Sometimes, my friend, you're not only mad, but quite unreasonable."

"Unreasonable? You *may* lose a ship or two, or have a few damaged, or lose a few gunners—and you have my word we'll protect them as if they were our own—but the monetary losses are negligible compared to the long-range profits you'll reap on the plasimask. No, Amik, if anyone is being unreasonable, it's you."

The Lord of Thieves loosed a rumbling laugh at that.

"Perhaps neither of us could truthfully be called reasonable men. All right, you've stated your demands, now I'll tell you what I'm prepared to offer. I'll provide lodging for your guests, with due secrecy and protection, for *three* days. No longer. But for the second item—I can't risk twenty ships, or even partial crews, in a venture whose purpose I don't know. I'm not Confleet, my mad young friend. I haven't unlimited supplies of Falcons or trained crews to toss about."

Alex only nodded as he crossed one leg over the other. "How many *are* you prepared to offer?"

Amik paused, studying him intently. Then, "Well, I might be able to spare . . . say, ten Falcons."

Alex frowned impatiently. "That isn't enough. I do have another option open to me for solving this particular problem. I can let Confleet take care of it for me, but for reasons of my own, I prefer not to do so."

"Confleet? Ah, that was a piece of bravado, and hardly worthy of you."

"It wasn't bravado. Amik, have I ever been less than honest with you in our haggling?"

He shrugged. "Apparently not. Very well, I accept the existence of that rather fantastic alternative, but will Confleet provide accomodations for your guests?"

Alex had to laugh at that. "No. Perhaps we should bargain on that point separately, and if so, I'll retract the offer of the plasimask and present something else as my part of the exchange. I won't give up the formula for a few day's lodging for a handful of people."

Amik's sigh was redolent of weariness. "My friend, I've other things to occupy me, you know. I haven't time to go through all this again. Would you be satisfied with . . . twelve ships?"

"Twelve? No." He paused, frowning. He'd come hoping for fifteen, but he didn't intend to be *that* honest with Amik. "I might accept eighteen."

"That's still too many. Fourteen. Holy God, that should be enough to wage a small war."

"I won't risk any of my men or ships in an operation made hopeless by inadequate forces."

"So. Fifteen, then."

Alex still stood firm. "This isn't a matter of simple profit. It's far too important for compromise."

Amik puffed at his cigar, eyes narrowed to slits.

"Seventeen. My last offer, and when I say it's my last offer, I mean exactly that."

Alex appeared to consider the number, then finally capitulated with a sigh of resignation.

"All right. I only hope—but never mind. Seventeen it will be. By the way, the ships should be painted and marked to pass as Confleet vessels."

"Oh? Anything else—*by the way?*"

"No." Alex smiled amiably. "Nothing else. You'll have the formula within a few hours."

"Good, and when will you need the Falcons?"

"A week from today. Concord Day."

"I'll make arrangements to have them available. So. The

bargain is struck. Now will you have some Marsay with me?"

Alex acquiesced willingly, and while Amik busied himself with the bragnac, he rose and moved restlessly around the room, pausing at the niche that held the Ivanoi Egg. He pressed the blue diamond at the top and watched the golden segments open, the swan emerge and arch its neck, the musical mechanism providing a sparkling accompaniment. He wondered what Elise Woolf would have thought of having this favorite possession of hers gracing the sanctum of Amik the Thief. No doubt she'd have found ironies in it to delight her.

"Your Marsay, Alex."

He turned and took the glass Amik offered. "Thank you, and a toast to a bargain struck."

Amik raised his glass before taking the first sip. "To a well made bargain." He studied Alex a moment, then glanced at the Egg. "A lovely piece of work. Tell me, do you regret its loss?"

Alex sent him an oblique glance. "Loss? I don't know what you mean."

Amik laughed as he sank again into his chair. "No, of course not. So. Concord Day is your great day of reckoning. And what hangs in the balance then?"

Alex pressed the diamond again and watched the Egg repeat its smooth flowering and closing.

"My life, perhaps. Possibly the fate of civilization."

Amik raised an eyebrow. "I've studied some history, and few civilizations have fallen as the result of one day's events."

"True. Still, it's probable that what happens on Concord Day will have a noticeable effect on the future of our civilization one way or another."

"And I don't suppose you'll tell me any more about it?"

"Not now, at least."

Amik nodded and sipped at the liqueur. "Well, my friend, I know something about the Phoenix and about you, and from that I can deduce at least the general direction of your plans. The Lord Alexand doesn't intend to stay buried forever. I'm curious about one thing: should that resurrection be accomplished, what can this old thief expect of the Lord Alexand?"

Alex turned to face him, feeling again that equivocal sense of regret.

"Amik the Thief has lived his life outside the law of the

Concord. The Lord Alexand will be bound by oath to uphold that law."

The answer didn't seem to displease or surprise Amik.

"So. That's as it should be."

"Is it? Of course the Lord Alexand might hope Amik the Thief would consider retiring from his present occupation, but he couldn't ask it of him."

"The future is uncharted country, my friend. All things— or at least *nearly* all things—are possible. I'll make a toast now." He lifted his glass, looking up at Alex through its golden prism. "To you, Alex, a straight blade and a gentleman born. Fortune, brother."

Alex raised his glass, and when he could trust his voice said softly, "And I offer a toast to you, perhaps not a gentleman born, but a gentleman to his soul."

6.

In the dim light, Adrien smiled and sang softly a song she'd learned long ago in her mother's arms; one of those songs passed down from one generation to the next thoughtlessly, with no cognizance of its antiquity.

"Sleep, little one, now comes the starry night. . . ."

She held Eric at her breast, laughing as his eyes opened to sleepy slits, but the song didn't distract him from his primary purpose of sustenance. Strange sensations, she was thinking, watching the movements of his tiny mouth, pleasurable in so many senses. But nothing was strange to the mind still embryonic behind those deep blue eyes.

"Lullay, lullay, my little tiny child. . . . For your waking, the sunlight bright . . ."

How strange it must be when nothing is strange. Or perhaps to them, everything is strange, and the end result is the same. Eric was almost asleep, sated, she was sure, but still reluctant to be taken from her breast. She held him patiently, waiting until he was deep enough asleep so it would make no difference.

"Lullay, lullay, my love. . . ." She looked down into Rich's crib, close at her knee. He'd already achieved that enviable oblivion that seemed to come automatically with a full stomach.

She looked at these infants and thought of the many lives entwined in theirs, and they blithely unaware of them all. One day they would know. One day they could be told and would understand about their namesakes, Rich and Erica, about Malaki, and about Val Severin, who suffered so much to bring Adrien to Alexand so that he might live, and Mariet, who died in a sense so that these babies might be born. Adrien felt the blunted ache of grief with that memory. And the twins must know about Sister Thea, and Lectris, who was so lost now without Mariet, his little sister. He was still at Saint Petra's in the sanctuary of Thea's solicitous care. *He's a child of the Mezion, as we all are, and needs comforting.* Lectris would be safe there until . . .

It must be night on the surface; the chill in the air was beginning to penetrate her robe. She reached over to pull the blanket up around Rich. He didn't stir. Dreaming. She could see the faint movements behind his eyelids.

What do babies dream about? Sensations, perhaps; needs. They were savage creatures who must be táught love, even if the potential was there. She could look at them now and call them beautiful, an unspoiled harmony of form, a tactile feast, but they hadn't been beautiful when she first saw them, only defiantly *alive.* She remembered their first cries, and remembered wondering if they were expressions of fear, or anger, or simply mindless affirmations of life. A common sound heard thousands of times every day, and still extraordinary, as the phenomenon of life was extraordinary for all its ubiquity.

As ubiquitous as death, the other side of the coin.

Her eyes closed on an unexpected wave of fear; she held Eric close, warm against her body.

"Lullay, lullay, my little tiny child. . . ." She rearranged the blanket around him and smoothed the cap of curling dark hair, smiling again. They were her best defense against fear. For two weeks, she had been happier than she remembered being in all her life. Content. Content even now on the eve of war. The clock on the linen chest was set for TST; it read 12:35.

It was already Concord Day.

She looked into the other half of the room where Alexand lay sleeping. Or perhaps only resting. Many times this night as she lay beside him, sharing the undemanding communion of the warmth of their bodies, she knew he was awake, but he didn't speak or move, and not because he was afraid of waking her. He knew she was awake, too. He was only savoring this contentment as she did.

The sound screen was on, but not the vision screen; she wouldn't cut herself off from him now even to that degree. She sang in a lullaby whisper a song out of the ages and looked beyond the bed to the uniform hung on the wall. It was only a pale shape, gleaming faintly with silver.

Alexand despised it, recognizing the tasteful flair of its design and the quality of its cloth as he might the workmanship and efficiency of a laser cannon. It had hung there for three days with the shining black boots and black cloak, both regulation SSB design, although the latter was lined in the same blue as the uniform. But tomorrow—no, today—he would wear that uniform with the style bred to him.

A movement in the soft light. She watched him as he sat up, noted the hesitation while he remembered to make allowances for his arm. He turned back the blankets, then paused, looking into the nursery.

The arm was dimly white in the twilight light. He despised it, too. At first, he wouldn't let her see the wound under the bandages. It was Erica who resolved that. An extraordinary woman, and Adrien was every day more satisfied that this child bore a masculinization of her name. On the grounds that she couldn't always be available to do it, Erica had insisted that Adrien learn how to bandage and exercise the arm. Alexand had submitted, however reluctantly, and perhaps he was beginning to understand that she couldn't regard any part of him as distasteful; she could only feel his pain.

For that, Alexand set special store on the ointment Malaki had given him. Adrien smiled faintly as she thought of it; she always found solace in its source as she rubbed it into the wound before each bandaging, as Alexand found relief in its analgesic properties. It worked, he said, and refused to ponder why or how, as if that might negate its effect or dishonor its maker.

Alexand rose now and came into the nursery, stopping for a while to look down at his family. It would be an image for him to remember; a good memory. Then he leaned close to kiss her cheek.

"Who's this?" he asked in a whisper, although both the twins were too deep asleep to be disturbed by anything less than a shout. "Rich?"

She laughed. "No, your second born. Don't feel badly; I still have to check the ident bands. Or their heads."

"Their heads?"

"Rich's hair grows in a clockwise whorl, Eric's counter-clockwise."

He knelt and smoothed Eric's fine, dark hair. "So it does. Look at that hand. As exquisite as a sea shell." He put his finger against the tiny hand resting on her breast. Even in sleep, the hand closed around his finger with the faith of instinct. He said absently, "The grip of life. There was a time when survival depended on that, on an infant clinging to his mother while she fled the predator."

There were still predators. Adrien knew his thoughts, knew he was trying to hold this moment in the present, yet he couldn't keep the future out of it. He looked over at Rich, watched him dreaming for a while, then turned to her.

"Adrien, little mother..." He laughed softly, brushing a straying wisp of hair back from her cheek. "I always knew you had more courage than I, and now I'm grateful."

She freed one hand to hold his hand against her cheek. "Oh, Alex, it wasn't courage. I don't know what it was, but not courage."

"Faith, perhaps. It's all part of the same thing, and I doubt it has a name. Except perhaps... love."

She closed her eyes to find his lips soft against hers.

PART 6: APOTHEOSIS

●❶●○

PHOENIX MEMFILES: DEPT HUMAN SCIENCES: BASIC SCHOOL
(HS/BS)
SUBFILE: LECTURE, BASIC SCHOOL 11 AVRIL 3252
SUBJECT: POST-DISASTERS HISTORY:
THE PELADEEN REPUBLIC (3135–3210)
DOC LOC #819/219–1253/1812–1648–1143252

Simon Ussher Peladeen was a lucky man. As you may recall, it was Simon who married his daughter to the new Lord Orabu Drakon (or, properly, Drakonis) and established his House on Centauri's lushest site, Pollux, where it prospered with its zinc, tin, and copper franchises. Simon built his Home Estate on the mountain-girt Pangaean Straits in the new city of Leda, lived in it for seven years, then at the age of seventy-four, died quietly in his sleep. That was in 3101, three years before the Mankeen Revolt. It was left to his son, Quintin, to deal with the problems that created.

Our histories tend to leave the impression that the Cen-

tauri System was untouched by the Revolt, suffering no
more than a long period of isolation from the Concord. That
isn't quite true. Some of the major battles in the Revolt
occurred there, and four of the five inhabited Centauran
planets were vacuum colonies, dependent on the mainte-
nance of habitat systems. Fortunately, those four were thinly
populated (in fact, the population of the entire Centauri
System at that time was no more than three million), and
could be successfully evacuated to Pollux. Quintin Peladeen
was a man of ability and flexibility, who organized the
evacuation and accommodated the vacuum colonies' population—as well as their resident Elite, including the First
Lord of Drakonis, Konrad—with a minimum of disorder
and remarkably few casualties. One of Quintin's and Drakonis's most difficult problems initially was maintaining the
solar power stations on the Inner Planets, but they managed
it, although at first, only those in Drakonis's Estate city of
Danae on Perseus could be kept functioning, and they were
operated by techs living out of ships and working in vacuum
suits.

The Battle of Pollux in 3112 is the generally accepted
date of beginning for Centauri's period of isolation, but
even after that there was some communication between the
Two Systems. However, it became increasingly sporadic;
the Concord was too preoccupied with its own survival and
later its recovery to care what was going on in Centauri,
and the Centaurans made do very well. Theirs was a select
population chosen for the rigors of colonization, and I think
after the first few years, when they discovered how well
they could manage without the Concord, they rather welcomed their isolation. After 3120, the year of Mankeen's
death, no attempts were made by the Centaurans to establish
contact with the Solar System. Perhaps the Concord, in the
throes of the Revolt and during the long, painful recovery
period afterward, *did* forget about Centauri, but I think it's
equally true that the Centaurans made no effort to remind
the Concord of their existence.

At any rate, Centauri prospered in its isolation, but the
most important development in this period is the founding
of the Peladeen Republic in 3135. It was a Fesh innovation,
of course, and Fesh made up nearly three-quarters of Centauri's population. The Republic's orderly development and

its peaceful acceptance by the System's resident Lords must be credited to Elgar Conant, who became its first Prime Minister. Conant was an econotech in the House of Peladeen and one of Quintin's closest advisors before the Revolt.

Quintin was, by the way, very much the Lord of Centauri, as historians like to call him, even though he wasn't the only Lord in the System. He and Drakonis were, however, the only First Lords, and most of the VisLords cut off by the tides of war from their Terran Houses eventually aligned themselves with one or the other, and many in the second and third generations adopted the Peladeen or Drakonis names. Neither Konrad Drakonis nor his heirs contested Peladeen's leadership; the relationship between the two Houses remained cordial until the War of the Twin Planets. From the beginning of that conflict, Drakonis, then under Lordship of Maxim, allied itself with the Concord, which might seem dishonorable, but insured the House's survival, and as I've noted before, the Drakonis Lords were all very pragmatic men.

Quintin did not embrace the Republic wholeheartedly from the beginning, but I'm sure he realized that he didn't have a great deal of choice in the matter. If he resisted and drove the Republicans to outright revolt, it was unlikely that he could depend on his Fesh House guards to put it down; too many of them were also Republicans. He was fortunate that Elgar Conant was a reasonable and determinedly peaceful man, who even went so far as to enlist Quintin's aid and advice in the formation of the Republic. The government that emerged was essentially a monarchal republic, which left the Houses with some of their powers intact, but dissolved the Fesh allegiance system and gave the Fesh a voice, through elective processes, in their government.

The Bonds were the one problem Quintin and Conant found most difficult to resolve. Most Republicans wanted to dispense with the Bonding system at the outset, but Quintin balked. Bonds were only a quarter of the population, but he was convinced that they would be a disastrously disruptive influence if suddenly set free. Ultimately, Quintin and Conant reached a compromise, and a wise one. Bond education and training programs were instituted immediately under the aegis of the Republic, but the actual liberation of Bonds didn't take place for another thirty years.

In 3172, when the Concord began the first trade exchanges with the Republic, the transition had been made, and the only distinct class to be found in Centauri was the Elite. The Concord made what might be called diplomatic contacts with the Republic as early as 3160, but those were almost entirely with Elorin Peladeen, Quintin's son, and it wasn't until trade relations were established that the Concord became fully aware of the nature and scope of the Republic, and it must have been a shock. Confederation and Concord sociologists had for centuries predicted the "inevitable" consequences of a social experiment like the Republic, agreeing unanimously (with themselves and their Lords) that the results would be reduced productivity, lawlessness, rampant immorality, and ultimately anarchy. Then in 3172 the Concord came face to face with such a social experiment in full flower, its laws respected by its citizens generally, although it had its lawless element—the "Outside" existed in the Republic as it does now in the Concord, as it probably always has in one form or another—but that element was no larger than in any other human society. As for immorality, that's a subjective term, but the Concord couldn't take exception to the Republic's moral codes—they were essentially its own—or to the fact that the Orthodox Church was very strong in Centauri. And certainly the Concord couldn't reasonably assert that productivity had lagged. The Republic had not only reestablished the vacuum colonies, but achieved a high degree of industrialization that no doubt amazed the Lords of the Concord. It frightened some of them. The Republic was already manufacturing its own MAM-An ships. They weren't armed, but clearly the Centaurans were capable of arming them if they so desired.

There was a movement among some Concord Lords at that early date to take the Centauri System by force *before* the Republic could arm its ships, but the Concord was still in its recovery period and the majority of its Lords didn't feel they could afford a war of any sort at that point. And the cause of peaceful moderation had an eloquent spokesman in the new Chairman, Constan Galinin, Arman's grandson. But his eloquence in time lost its effectiveness against the increasingly warlike temper of the Lords as the Concord's recovery proceeded and the Republic became more and more a misunderstood threat to their way of life, and thus their very existence. Constan couldn't stop the War of the Twin Planets. He tried and nearly lost his Directorate seat. Perhaps he succeeded in delaying it, but that only made it more destructive in the end. He is one of those tragic historical figures caught in a trap of circumstances, and his son, Mathis, our present Chairman, remembers seeing his father weep when the Directorate voted the declaration of war.

The Concord bided its time until after the turn of the century, but the Peladeen Lords and the leaders of the Republic didn't. Elorin initiated a program of intensified industrialization so the Republic could not only build more ships, but arm them. His son Morgan, on becoming First Lord in 3175, began building the army to man these ships. He asked the Parlement to augment the police force with what he called the Interplanetary Guard, which the Parlement and citizens of the Republic readily acceded to; there seemed to be a unanimous cognizance on every level of the Republic of the impending threat presented by the Concord. At this point, there was some complaint from the Directors that the Republic was creating an army, but Morgan insisted the Guard's only purpose was to protect the Republic's burgeoning trade from pirates.

When Elor Peladeen became First Lord in 3202, twenty-seven years later, he not only enlarged the Interplanetary Guard, but called it what it was: the Armed Forces of the Republic. It was too late for pretense then; Elor, the Parlement, the Prime Minister, Lair M'Kenzy, and every citizen of the Republic knew what lay ahead for them.

CHAPTER XIX: 14 Octov 3258

●H●H●H●H●H●H●HO H●H●H●HOH●HOH●HOH●HOH●HOHOH●HOH●HOH●H●

1.

The countdown clock read zero — 06:00: 04:00 TST. At 10:00 Predis Ussher's war would begin.

Commander Alex Ransom stood in the middle of the COS HQ comcenter, out of the way, yet close enough to the screens and scanners so he could see them all. He was wearing a headset; endless toneless exchanges whispered in his ear. With a word, he could give orders, ask or answer questions, check sequences, and monitor any communications, but for now he was silent, isolated in a pocket of calculating tension, his mind geared solely for computation as the digits of the countdown clock ticked over.

This comcenter had become an inadvertent extension of Fina's. Alex paced the length of the bank of consoles, looking over the heads of the intent monitoring crew. Most of the exile staff was at the consoles, monitoring Phoenix, Conpol, SSB, and Confleet frequencies, the PubliCom System, Brotherhood and private House channels, and the special code frequencies used by loyal members throughout the Centauri System.

SynchCom frequencies were open on the same levels to the Solar System.

On the stone wall above the consoles, two large screens were mounted. One limned the countdown schedule direct from Fina, the hour-by-hour, minute-by-minute listings of deadlines set and met, calculated demands sorted into precisely detailed allotments of time. Most of the deadlines on the screen now were for FO. SI's preparatory sequences were almost entirely accomplished. Like FO, its staff had been augmented by volunteers from other departments. These, with over two thousand regular agents, were already deployed, their assault on a subversive level as minutely calculated as FO's more straightforward military assault.

Zero hour was 10:00 TST.

The countdown would reverse itself then, counting up to a new zero hour: 16:00. The offensive would be over by then; must be, if the Phoenix fleet hoped to retreat safely to Fina and the Rhea base before Confleet reinforcements arrived from the Solar System.

In that six-hour span, Jan Barret would field a fleet of 325 Falcons and 150 Corvets, each carrying a lethal load of propulsion bombs, each armed with pulsed lasers with twice the power-to-weight ratio of any Confleet gun, each with its multiple objectives set in a calculated lattice of time sequences coordinated to the second with SI's.

Alex had read the preliminary strat seqs with frank admiration. To accomplish the same objectives, a Confleet commander would need ten times the men and matériel. Alex took pride in the design of the campaign both as a member of the Phoenix and as Jan Barret's erstwhile tutor, and that only added to his disgust at the necessity of sending exiles, in an incredible alliance with the Brotherhood, out to do battle with Barret's ships. Yet the Drakonis power plants must be protected, or Ussher's myopic ambition could cost hundreds of thousands of lives. Alex could only hope that when the Phoenix ships met strong resistance on their approach to the Inner Planets, Barret would order a withdrawal, content to give up one objective for the sake of his ships and crews and the other objectives programmed for them.

The tactics of conservation. Jan had learned that lesson the hard way; he wasn't likely to forget it now.

"Commander Ransom..."

The voice wasn't from his earspeaker. Dr. Lind at the MT console. Alex walked over to him.

"Yes, Doctor?"

"Chan Orley's on the Fina MT. He's ready to start transing the first FO members."

"Good." He turned the control ring on his mike. "Tel, get me Commander Blayn, please."

"Yes, sir. He's in the hangar. Just a moment."

A click, then a brief pause, and, "Blayn on line."

"Vic, your FO auxiliary will begin transing in a few minutes."

"Yes, sir. I'll be right up."

Alex studied the second countdown screen. The next six hours were parceled out as precisely for the COS HQ as they were for Fina. The deadline that concerned him at the moment was 07:00. The Fina fleet would begin its slow exodus then, the ships leaving the lock a few at a time, moving under water on different courses, emerging at irregular intervals at points separated by thousands of kilometers. A third of Barret's fleet was hangared in the Rhea base in the Solar System, and they had already begun accelerating toward SynchShift and Centauri.

07:00 and the beginning of the Fina launch was important to the exiles because the fifty FO crewmembers needed to augment the exile and Brotherhood crews for the Inner Planets operation must be transed into the COS HQ from Fina before that deadline, and the evacuation would have to be slow and sporadic to avoid alerting Ussher with a mass exodus.

Alex saw Blayn emerging from the hangar entrance and went to meet him.

"Any problems downside, Vic?"

Blayn smiled at that Outsiderism and answered with another.

"No, but maybe that's asking fate. If there's any choice in the order for transing, we should get the navcomp personnel in first, just in case all of them don't make it. Navcomp's where we're short."

"I know, and they know at Fina, but I doubt there'll be

much choice. It's a question of who can slip away when without attracting too much attention."

"Well, let's hope opportunity favors navcomps. Any changes on the Inner Planets op schedule?"

"No. Jael's talking with Amik now. He'll smell out any problems. But, Vic, be sure the new men understand they'll have to take certain precautions working with the Brothers."

"Don't worry. Anyway, we'll have at least three exiles assigned to every ship." His gaze shifted to the MT. "Here comes the first FO deserter. That's Pete Jason." He set off toward the MT, adding with a sidelong glance at Alex, "Navcomp, and a hell of a good one."

Alex laughed, but a moment later he was distracted when Telstoi's voice sounded in his ear.

"Sir, I have Kahn Telman on line from the Eliseer Estate. You said you wanted to talk to him when he reported."

"Yes, Tel. Can you give me an interconn?"

"Right. Stay on receive."

Alex moved back out of the noise of greetings; two more FO men had transed in. The blue uniforms seemed jarringly out of place here. He thought only fleetingly of the one that waited for him in his room.

"Commander? Telman on line."

"What's your situation there, Kahn?"

"On sequence. Lord Eliseer and his sons just got back from seeing Lady Galia and Patricia and Annia off at the IP port. It's 12:30 local time, and no guests, meetings, or social events are scheduled for the evening. Eliseer and the boys should be sound asleep by 09:30 TST."

"You're lucky, Kahn. It'll be early evening in Leda, and Danae runs on TST; Drakonis and his family will be at the beginning of their day."

Telman laughed. "Oh, I'm grateful, and maybe you—or whoever's in charge of the 'guest' quarters—should be grateful Galia finally decided to take the girls to Paykeen. She changed her mind twice today. What about Lazar Hamid?"

"He's in Concordia, thank the God, but I wish he'd taken his family. I doubt Lady Falda will be any more gracious about being kidnapped than Galia would be." He hesitated, seeing

Andreas approaching. "Kahn, you have an open line to me any time, and both Jael and I will be on stand-by for the abductions. Good luck."

"Thank you, sir. You, too."

Alex reset the control ring on the mike, frowning briefly; everything seemed backward with his left hand.

"Good morning, Andreas."

"That's an optimistic greeting. Did you get any sleep last night?"

Alex smiled at that. "Did you?"

"I've had better nights. Is there anything I can do? I seem to be—" He stopped as another FO crewman left the MT. "Those damnable uniforms." Then he broke into a smile. "Ah— that's young Dalis. His father was an old friend; Charter member. Excuse me."

Alex smiled to himself as he watched Andreas hurry to the MT, watched the transformation in the faces of the new men. Faith can move anything, even the stars, so the Shepherds said.

"'Day, brother."

Jael was waiting at the hangar entrance when Alex emerged from the TacComm meeting. The exile fleet's newly enlarged staff followed to form a loose crowd at the back of the com-center chamber. The ampspeakers were on now, broadcasting from the FO frequency.

The time was 06:55. Five minutes before the Fina fleet began its ship-by-ship launch.

Alex glanced up at the countdown clock before asking of Jael, "How's the old Ser?"

"Grateful."

"For what?"

"Confusion." Then, with a crooked smile, "The old Ser always welcomes times of official confusion, and he's smelled out enough of what's coming down today to tally it as an ungilt gift." The smile faded as he looked up at the countdown screens. "Anyway, the guest quarters are ready. Do you want me on top of that gim?"

"Only until the guests are settled in, then Erica will take over."

"All right." He was listening to the ampspeakers, his attention divided. "Any word from Ben?"

"Not directly. He sent the final plan of attack on the PubliCom studios in Leda, Helen, and Danae. We'll get a warning to Conpol fifteen minutes before zero hour. That will put enough uniforms in the studios to discourage any SI agents other than the loyals Ben has already warned."

"Ussher'll howl when he doesn't see his face and hear his call to arms on the vidicom."

Alex didn't reply. The first two Falcons were leaving Fina's lock. The countdown clock ticked over its implacable digits.

Zero −03:00.

Alex was thinking of Jan Barret. His was one of the voices on the ampspeakers, orders given with the clarity and restraint of confidence.

Jan had been an apt pupil, and now he led his fleet, proudly marked with the triangle-flame symbol of the Phoenix, into battle with the Concord. Jan Barret would do his duty as he saw it, his duty to the Phoenix.

Predis Ussher was chairman of the Phoenix Council, and Jan would die, if need be, for Ussher, not because he believed in him, but because he believed in the Phoenix.

Alex felt a chill at the thought, the possibility of Jan's death. It had the irrational weight of premonition.

The third and fourth Falcons were leaving the lock. Alex closed his eyes, felt the floor shifting and humming under his feet, so vivid was his sense of being there, of moving out of the lock, out into the black eternal night of the sea, moving toward the distant eternal night of space.

Jan . . . Jan, fortune, brother. . . .

2.

The countdown clock read zero +00:45: 10:45 TST.

Chairman of the Council Predis Ussher stood in the middle of the Fina comcenter, out of the way, yet close enough to the screens and scanners so he could see them all. He was wearing a headset; endless toneless exchanges whispered in his ear. With a word, he could give orders, ask or answer questions, and monitor communications, but for now he was silent.

The officers and techs were furiously intent at their tasks, but he knew they were aware of him, standing behind them, ready and watchful. He turned to look out the windowall into the hangar, hugely empty now that the fleet had embarked toward its destiny of victory. A crowd had gathered beyond the deck. Only a few hundred. Fina, like the hangars, was nearly empty, and for the same reason. Those who weren't presently on duty had naturally gravitated here. He knew they would. Here they could get news of the offensive, and here they could await the triumphant return of that brave fleet.

Ussher glimpsed a flashing reflection in the glass; light catching on the gold braid of his uniform. He pushed the cloak back a little further on his shoulders as he turned, surveying the quiet, orderly, concentrated activity around him.

Yes, this was the way it should be, the way he knew it would be. Every man and woman properly uniformed, their exchanges terse and restrained, the pervading undercurrent of tension disciplined into alert efficiency.

"PNX-C289—*Esme*. Damn it, Scott, come *in!*"

Ussher frowned, finding the source of that jarring note with no difficulty. Commander Emeric Garris at the GroundComm console, his angry words directed into his headset mike.

"I don't care if your captain was on line to the Mezion, I gave you a Pri-One signal. Put Captain Stern on. I have a scan from Omega. A Confleet unit on intercept course . . ."

Ussher mentally tuned out the rest. He didn't understand why Jan Barret insisted on putting Garris in charge here. Perhaps just to keep the old soldier occupied. No doubt he was harmless enough, and even served some purpose. The FO staff seemed to like him.

Ussher didn't, and he fervently wished Garris had seen fit to stay retired from FO as he had from the Council. A scarred old curmudgeon, stubborn and set in his ways. One of Riis's cronies.

Ussher took a deep breath and looked up at the progress screen, the corners of his mouth tightening with a smile of satisfaction as he automatically translated the abbreviations: F

into Falcon, C into Corvet, TCC into Troop Carrier Corsair;
fac dam est, he read as facility damage estimate; Pol as Pollux,
Cas as Castor, InP as Inner Planets. The heading on this group
was: Conflt Bss—ss dam/des/fac dam est. Confleet bases; ships
damaged and destroyed and facility damage estimates. He read
the figures hungrily as they ticked across the screen.

Pol Leda	F 127	C 22	TCC 3	fac dam est 70%
Pol Hallicourt	F 18	C 4	TCC 1	fac dam est 50%
Pol Hamidropolis	F 15	C 2		fac dam est 45%
Pol Riollegro	F 23	C 6	TCC 1	fac dam est 60%
Cas Helen	F 118	C 20	TCC 4	fac dam est 65%
Cas Pendino	F 44	C 11	TCC 3	fac dam est 55%
Cas Fiorenz	F 10	C 2		fac dam est 30%
InP Danae	F 52	C 8	TCC 2	fac dam est 45%
InP Thymbris	F 18	C 3		fac dam est 35%

　　ss dam/des total + 00:48:

　　　　　　　F 428　　C 79　　TCC 14

Ussher clasped his hands behind his back, shifting his weight
to his toes and back again. Rather impressive for a war less
than an hour old.

A new line appeared as those moved off the screen: PNX
ss dam/des/cap. Phoenix ships damaged, destroyed, captured.
This was the first Phoenix casualty report.

ss dam	ss des	ss cap
F 10　C 1	F 3　C 2	F 2　C 1

He sighed. That wasn't so bad, especially compared to the
Confleet casualties, and that was only the on-base ships.

The abbreviation "cap" wouldn't be included in any Confleet
listings. The Phoenix didn't have ships or men enough to ex-
pend on capturing enemy vessels in this campaign. Unfortunate. But perhaps next time . . .

The countdown clock read zero + 01:00: 11:00 TST.

Predis Ussher made a tour of the scanners and consoles,
offering occasional words of encouragement to the techs, but

when his eye chanced on the countdown clock, he went immediately to the chair placed for him in the center of the arc of consoles where five intercom screens and a small vidicom had been installed, and his secretary, Alan Isaks, was on duty as his personal communications officer.

He sat down, frowning at the vidicom, at the harried newscaster trying to make sense of a disaster whose dimensions the Concord was only beginning to assimilate.

But he was a regular PubliCom 'caster.

The face Ussher expected on that screen at this time was his own in a pretaped broadcast. This was the only way to reach the Fesh, to make them understand that this wasn't a disaster for them, this was their day of destiny, the day when they could strike off their chains. They *must* understand that, and getting that message through to them was vital to the offensive.

He waited, staring at the vidicom, for five more minutes, then said sharply, "Alan, get me Ivor in Communications."

"Yes, sir."

Isaks moved smartly about his business, but to Ussher it seemed he was unusually slow and bumbling. Finally, Ivor's face looked out at him from one of the intercom screens.

"Ivor, the PubliCom Systems operation—*what happened*?"

"Sir, I don't know. I've been waiting for an all-clear signal to switch in the override. There's been nothing. I tried to 'com Commander Venturi—"

"Never mind. Alan, get Venturi on line."

"Yes, sir."

Something had gone wrong, and his first thought was betrayal. Venturi. And Radek. Ussher glared at the vidicom. Shaky images from the Confleet base at Leda, the on-scene reporter shouting hysterically against the uproar of sirens, spewing firecars, distant explosions. Isaks's voice seemed to have an edge of the same tense panic.

"What? No. Commander Venturi." A pause, then to Ussher, "Sir, will you speak to Haral Wills?"

"*No!* I want Venturi!"

"Yes, sir."

Apparently someone got the message. Within a minute, Venturi's face appeared. He was looking off-screen, features set in hard, tight lines.

"...pull out *now*. They've got MT fixes. Trans them out. Two minutes, Ced; that's all they have."

"Commander Venturi!"

"What do you want, Predis?"

Ussher felt his cheeks go hot. "Damn it, I want to know what happened on the PubliCom System operation."

"So do I. I've got sixty agents on that. They ran into a stone wall, Predis. All the studios were swarming with Conpol men."

"What? That's impossible! Venturi, if you purposely—"

"Holy God, what did you expect? Hundred percent success on every operation?"

"But that one's too important! It's the key—"

"Predis, I have a Pri-One call. You'll get more info on the PubliCom op when *I* get it." With that, the screen went dark.

Ussher stared at it for a moment, then surged to his feet and again took up his position in the center of the chamber, jaws tight to the point of pain. New figures were appearing on the progress screen. Selasid Mercfleet hangars and ships. First Line freighters; Second Line freighters; tenders. He was thinking that he'd like to see Orin Selasis's face when *he* saw those statistics.

Pol Leda	FLF 24	SLF 42	TDR 53	fac dam est 85%
Pol Telhamid	FLF 1	SLF 18	TDR 27	fac dam est 50%
Cas Helen	FLF 18	SLF 33	TDR 47	fac dam est 75%
InP Semele	FLF 7	SLF 15	TDR 31	fac dam est 35%
ss dam/des total +01:15:				
	FLF 50	SLF 108	TDR 158	

Well, perhaps Venturi was right. You couldn't expect one hundred percent success. After the offensive, another attempt could be made on the PubliCom studios. Conpol's guard would be down then. In fact, the taped speech might be even more effective then, when the Fesh had seen more of what the Phoenix was capable, more of the Concord's failure.

The countdown clock read zero +02:00: 12:00 TST.

Ussher checked it against his own watch, then stood silent, absorbing the purposeful hum of voices and machines. Any Confleet commander would give his stars for a comcenter run with such devoted efficiency.

But Garris seemed incapable of staying where he belonged. He kept pacing behind the monitoring crews, peering over their shoulders at the screens and scanners. Fortunately, his duties kept him confined to the GroundComm console most of the time. Ussher heard him in a brief exchange with the flagship interconn officer, Calvet Lanc, both looking up at the progress screen. The latest report was on Confleet observational satellite stations.

Pol	Polar Obsat	fac dam est	70%
Cas	Equatorial Obsat	fac dam est	80%
InP	Dionysus Equatorial Obsat	fac dam est	40%

Three out of seven. Ussher nearly laughed aloud. Almost half Confleet's eyes in the skies blinded. Following that came a report on House facilities engaged in storing or producing war matériel.

Pol	Leda	Elisr	Wrhs—ref met	fac dam est 65%
Pol	Leda	Elisr	Smltr—mlydm	fac dam est 50%
Pol	Leda	DeKW	Wrhs—com eqmt	fac dam est 70%
Pol	Petrovna	Ivnoi	Wrhs—ref met	fac dam est 60%
Pol	Telhamid	Cord	Wrhs—petrochem	fac dam est 85%
Cas	Helen	Elisr	Wrhs—ref met	fac dam est 50%
Cas	Tremper	Ivnoi	Smltr—pltnm	fac dam est 45%

That would give those high-nosed Lords something to think about. The screen remained blank, awaiting correlation of new statistics. Ussher looked for Garris; he was wandering from his post again.

"Commander Garris, I've seen no recent statistics on Confleet ships damaged or destroyed in combat."

Garris shot him an impatient look, then with a negligent wave toward one of the comptechs, "Talk to Janie."

The woman looked around inquiringly, and Ussher said in clipped tones, "Ferra Browning, may I see the latest report on Confleet combat casualties?"

"Just a moment, sir. I'll see what's come in."

And, finally, the figures paraded across the screen.

Confit ss dam/des in cmbt:	F 73	C 11	TCC 1
Total + 02:05:	F 121	C 27	TCC 1

Add that to the on-base casualties, and already the Phoenix had taken nearly twice its numbers in—

"How the hell did *that* happen?"

Garris again. He was standing behind Ussher's empty chair, staring at the PubliCom screen. Ussher approached to see what elicited the resounding outburst.

"A direct strike on the Eliseer Estate!" Garris turned on Ussher, the scar cutting across his eye white against his anger-flushed face. *"How did that happen?"*

Ussher didn't deign to respond until he heard the stumbling account from the 'caster. The family wing. And it was night in Helen. The Lord and his twin heirs had been sleeping peacefully.

"You're asking *me* how it happened, Commander?"

Garris, with a choked expletive, stormed to the Ground-Comm console.

"Kyser! Put me on line with Cornel Simon. No—it'll be Major March on that op. The *Hopewell*."

Ussher restrained his smile as he sat down in front of the vidicom. The family wing. For that, Major March would have his cornel's wings. That operation had gone better than he expected, but he was waiting for news of another, news that was overdue.

"Alan, get me Rob Hendrick. He's in Communications."

When Hendrick's face appeared on one of the 'com screens, it offered no encouragement.

"Well, Rob? I expected a report on the Bond operation half an hour ago."

"Uh . . . yes, Predis, I know, but I've been checking with all the field agents I could reach, and—"

"The microspeakers activated as planned?"

"Oh, yes. We've got agents in thirty key compounds: twelve on Pollux, eight on Castor, four on Perseus—"

"I *know* that." Something was wrong; Rob had never learned to control his eyes when he was nervous.

"Well, the speakers activated on schedule in all compounds, but the . . . uh, results are rather . . . inconclusive."

"Rob, damn it, stop hedging!"

"I didn't mean . . . well, I think it's a little early yet for any overt response, but we know the Bonds heard the 'voices.' Naturally, there's been a lot of confusion in the compounds. When the offensive began, House guards poured in with orders for the Bonds to get to their quarters."

Ussher's hands curled into white-knuckled fists. First the PubliCom Systems operation, and now this. It was intolerable!

His first thought, again, was betrayal. Radek and Venturi had been opposed to appealing to the Fesh and Bonds from the beginning. They were willing to throw away a key weapon against the enemy for some esoteric ethic, a meaningless piece of dogma mouthed by Riis.

But, after a moment, his anger ebbed. They *couldn't* sabotage this operation. He'd put it in the hands of people he could trust, and the speakers *had* activated.

"Rob, there must be *some* reaction somewhere."

"Well, I have a report—just got it in—from Hamid's Estate compounds in Leda. His guards have met resistance there, and they seem to have the beginnings of an uprising on their hands."

Ussher sighed. "Well, perhaps that's a beginning for us. All right, Rob, keep me up to date on this." He nodded to Isaks, and the screen went dark.

A beginning. Yet a nagging canker of doubt was festering in his mind. If the Bonds were going to react—and it was inconceivable that they wouldn't—why the delay? Was it too early, or too late?

3.

Nothing made sense.

Dreaming. Must be still dreaming.

"Father? Can you hear me?"

A face loomed over him. Galen. He recognized his voice before his face came into focus.

At length, with his son's help, Loren Eliseer managed to sit up and swing his legs over the edge of the couch. A small room, full of color. That was all that registered at first. When his eyes finally began to function properly, he stared around him incredulously.

It still didn't make sense. This lushly extravagant room wasn't in the Estate. He had never seen it before in his life.

"Just don't move too fast, Father. You'll feel better in a few minutes."

Galen, still bending over him. Renay was across the room at a comconsole; harried voices buzzed from a vidicom. Eliseer wondered what Renay found so fascinating, but his mind was clear enough now to realize his first born's interest in the screen indicated no lack of concern for his father. That was verified in the anxious glances he sent him.

Eliseer asked of anyone who might venture an answer, "What in the God's name happened?"

It was Galen who replied, "I don't know, Father. We've only been conscious about fifteen minutes. I don't know where we are, either, or why we're here. I can only estimate that we were taken from the Estate two to three hours ago. It's 20:30 Helen Standard—12:30 TST."

"At least we've been left the time. But why? Who's behind this? And how—" He stopped, struck by alarm. Galia. And the girls. Then he sagged with relief, remembering they were in Paykeen. They'd be safe there. Or would they?

"I think the answer to who's behind this," Renay said quietly, only the slightest edge of tension in his voice, "is here. We've been left the PubliCom newscasts, too. Galen, you'd better tell him about the woman."

Eliseer started to rise to go to the screen, but at that he paused, looking questioningly at Galen.

"What woman?"

"She said she's a doctor. She came in about the time Renay and I were coming around and checked us—and you—with a biomonitor cuff and offered some pills for our headaches."

"You didn't take them, did you?"

"No, of course not. She didn't argue; said we'd recover soon enough without help." He winced as he rubbed his forehead. "It *is* easing up."

Eliseer was acutely aware of the pounding ache of his own

head as he commented sourly, "That's encouraging. What else did she say? Did you recognize her? I suppose she was face-screened."

"Yes. She didn't say much, other than to point out the available comforts here."

Renay put in with a short laugh, "Three rooms incredibly furnished, an elegant bath, a liquor cabinet like I've seen in only the grandest Houses, and a cooler stocked with a few 'snacks' that make Master Duvo look like a Bond hall cook."

Galen nodded. "This is kidnapping in style, anyway."

"But it's still kidnapping," Eliseer said angrily. "This woman, she must've given some hint—"

"Nothing. She said she'd be back soon to check on you."

"Father!" Renay motioned to him, eyes fixed on the screen. "Galen, they're showing the sequence on the Estate again. Father, hurry."

Eliseer wasn't yet capable of hurrying, but he managed the few meters without blacking out. The image on the screen made no sense, either; not at first. A night scene, artificial light fragmenting it, making it harder to read. An aerial view of buildings; immense, billowing clouds of smoke, firecars like airborne fountains dancing among riven ruins.

The Estate. His own Estate.

"Holy God, that's the family wing!"

Renay only nodded without looking at him. "That *was* the family wing. They're searching for us in the rubble, Father. For our bodies." He paused as the images on the screen changed. "Good. They're giving us a recap and update."

For ten minutes, Eliseer stood transfixed, watching the screen, listening to the garbled, incomplete reports read in a consistent tone of bewildered panic. Confleet bases and arsenals, IP ports, Selasid Mercfleet hangars, Robek Trafficon centers and Transystems terminals, Confleet and Conpol com- and compcenters, House warehouses, even three Eliseer smelters—bombed, strafed, crippled. The reports poured out from Castor, Pollux, Perseus, Dionysus, Pan, from every city on every inhabited planet in the Centauri System.

The name of this disaster was war.

And if the 'casters seemed incredulous of almost everything

they reported, there was no doubt about the source of this incomprehensible attack.

The Society of the Phoenix.

A fleet estimated at anywhere from a thousand to three thousand ships had been unleashed on the Centauri System, and every vessel bore the name and symbol of the Phoenix.

And he had always regarded the Phoenix as simply another pirate clan, possibly with radical political leanings. But this was no pirate raid; it was a war, and a stunning revelation.

Apparently this war was limited to the Centauri System. He grasped at that as hungrily as the 'casters. Help was on the way. Confleet was sending a full thousand-ship wing from the Solar System. Again and again, the 'casters insisted that reinforcements would arrive within four hours.

Renay said coolly, "It seems the Concord has underestimated the Phoenix all these years."

Eliseer was amazed and proud of his son's calm, and it served as a reminder to put his own thoughts in order.

"So we have, and I assume we're prisoners of the Phoenix. Or hostages. I wonder what they hope to gain from that. Or any of this, for that matter."

A warning chime from the door precluded any reply Renay might have made. They all turned, waiting silently as it opened.

The first to enter was a face-screened man carrying a gun with an unusually wide muzzle. He didn't speak, but stepped aside for the woman, also face-screened, who followed.

Renay said, "Father, this is the doctor. With friend."

Eliseer studied her. Tall and slender, dressed in a standard slacsuit. The 'screen didn't hide the silver hair coiled in a thick braid at the crown of her head. She and the guard both bowed respectfully, but apparently she was the spokesman here; the man remained silent.

"My lord, Sers. . . . I'm sorry I can't give you my name. The gun my 'friend' is carrying, by the way, is armed with stun darts. They aren't lethal, but I must warn you, they'll stop you in your tracks in five seconds."

Eliseer moved casually toward the couch, separating himself from the twins. The guard, he noted, shifted position to keep all of them in range.

"I appreciate the warning, Doctor. Now I would appreciate an explanation."

"Of what, my lord? Your abduction?" There was no antagonism in her tone, rather a hint of sympathetic amusement.

"I see you don't balk at calling it by its true name."

"No, but if I said you're in protective custody, that would also be true. I assume you've been told about—"

"The war going on—" He waved a hand in an indeterminate motion at the windowless walls. "—out there. I've seen a sampling of it on the newscasts."

"Then you understand the situation. You've also seen what happened at your Estate?"

"Yes, I've seen it," he said, his tone more cutting than he intended. The woman unnerved him, perhaps because she displayed no hint of the maliciousness or arrogance he expected.

"I'm sure, my lord, you realize that if you and your sons hadn't been *abducted*, you'd undoubtedly be dead. That's why you're here."

"Well, Doctor, please don't think we're ungrateful, but I can't believe that's the only reason we're here. And why go to the trouble of . . . putting us in protective custody if you intended to bomb my Estate?"

"Because we didn't *intend* to bomb your Estate. We only recognized that in war, errors are possible. It might interest you to know that we also abducted Lord Drakonis and his family, as well as Lady Falda and her children. Lord Hamid, fortunately, is safe in Concordia."

"Fortunately?" He took a step toward her. "What about my wife and daughters? Are they also *safe* in Paykeen?"

"To my knowledge, yes, my lord. We'll set up an interconn so you can speak with them as soon as possible."

"And relay your demands to the Directorate, I suppose?"

"No. You may relay the assurance that you and your sons will be released as soon as it's safe to do so."

"Safe? For whom?"

"For you, my lord."

The woman was maddening. Eliseer glanced over at his sons, both listening attentively, carefully expressionless.

"It doesn't make *sense*."

Eliseer was vaguely surprised that he'd spoken aloud the

thought that haunted him since he awakened.

"I know, my lord," the woman replied, "and I'm sorry I can't tell you more." Then her head turned toward the twins. "And now, Ser Renay, Ser Galen, I must ask you to go into the next room for a short while."

"Why?" Eliseer demanded, instantly suspicious.

"Only because I have someone with me who wishes a private audience with you, my lord. Nothing more sinister will come between you and your sons than a closed door. If it were our purpose to harm you, or if we had a nefarious purpose in separating you, we'd have done so before you regained consciousness."

Eliseer sighed, reluctantly admitting the logic in that.

"Who asks a private audience of me *here*?"

"I'm not free to tell you, but she asked me to give you a message. 'The long months of secret waiting are over.'"

Adrien.

It could only be Adrien. Eliseer didn't realize how apparent his shock was until Renay started toward him.

"Father? What is it?"

After a moment, he had himself in rein again. "Renay, you and Galen go into the next room."

"What? But we can't—"

"Please."

The brothers exchanged glances; twin's glances, Eliseer called them, then reaching a silent accord, they retreated into the adjoining room.

Galen paused at the door. "We checked our 'coms and yours, Father. They're all working."

Eliseer smiled at that. "Thank you, but I don't think you need to worry. Not about this, at any rate."

When the door closed behind Galen, Eliseer turned to see the guard opening the outside door.

She was face-screened when she entered, but Eliseer knew he'd have recognized her even without the message as a cue. He looked down at her hands. She was wearing the ruby and sapphire betrothal ring; wearing it on her left hand.

He waited, motionless, hardly aware of the departure of the doctor and the silent guard.

Finally, he whispered, "Adrien..."

The face-screen went off, but still Eliseer was incapable of movement, and she seemed equally constrained.

"Father? Oh, Father..."

Then she ran to him in a rush of tears and laughter, and he held her in his arms, laughing and crying with her.

4.

The countdown clock read zero +03:00: 13:00 TST.

Ussher frowned at the coffee Isaks had brought him; it was cold. He put it down by the vidicom, then tilted his chair back to read a new series of figures appearing on the progress screen.

Robek Plan Transys Trafficon cntrs fac dam ests:

Pol		Cas		InP	
Leda	75%	Helen	80%	Danae	90%
Hallicourt	95%	Tremper	70%	Titania	60%
Telhamid	95%	Cuprin	95%	Thymbris	45%
Omega	60%	Oriban	85%		
Lamont	80%				
Petrovna	45%				

Those figures meant aircar, 'train, and pedway traffic in all those cities had been brought to a virtual standstill. He smiled, his gaze shifting to the vidicom. He didn't have to leave to his imagination the incredible snarls of traffic and the resulting confusion and panic. The bewildered newscasters were telling the story in words and pictures. They also told another story that he found equally satisfying.

The Hamid Estate in Leda had suffered serious damage from propulsion bomb strikes. Not as serious as the Eliseer Estate, but official concern was being voiced for the survival of Lady Falda and Lord Hamid's heirs. There were no reports of damage to the Drakonis Estate in Danae, and he couldn't ask about that. Garris had been too suspicious of the Eliseer strikes. Fortunately, he was occupied at the GroundComm console now; he had missed the Hamid Estate reports.

Isaks said quietly, "Sir, the first casualties will be coming through the lock in a few minutes."

"Casualties?" For a moment, Ussher was distracted. He looked at Isaks and saw that he was intent on his earspeaker. "Oh. Put me on the ADCon frequency."

Some of the voices in his ear were echoes of those only meters away on the Approach and Docking Control board. He rose and went to the windowall. The crowd around the deck had dispersed, called to their duties. Towcars and crews waited near the lock tunnel, some of the 'cars equipped with pressure winches and cutting lasers. Across the hollowly empty vault, red-tunicked medsquads waited by the corridor entrance with ten loaders, two piled with emergency medical equipment, the others filled with empty stretchers.

He looked away, toward the lock tunnel, listening to the voices in his ear. Nine Falcons and two Corvets; damage and casualty assessments; order of arrival decided on the basis of proximity and extent of damage.

"ADCon—Pri-One override! This is Major Dylon, *Eliad*."

"PNX ADCon on line, *Eliad*."

"Hull damaged. Emergency bulkheads going. We're one minute from locks. For the God's sake, keep them clear!"

"Locks clear, *Eliad*, and open. Subtugs deployed on—" A burst of static; a dim voice buried in it. Ussher looked around at the techs on the ADCon board. He couldn't be sure which was the source of the strained voice.

"*Eliad?* Major Dylon, come in! *Eliad!*"

Silence. Then another voice.

"ADCon, this is Subtug Squad 3. Corvet *Eliad* on visual. She . . . she's disintegrating. Pressure implosion. We'll try to— to get any survivors into our pressure chambers."

Survivors. Ussher turned, staring blindly out into the hangar. Survivors in two hundred meters of water?

Someone came into the comcenter, and in the few seconds the door was open, he heard a whoosh like a muffled explosion, then a prolonged shriek. The first sound was the opening of the lock gates, the second he only understood when a ship lurched out of the tunnel. Corvet *Ranger*, listing so far to one side, her steering vanes were dragging, burning a line of sparks on the floor. Tow crews and medsquads swarmed toward her,

the latter boarding even as she was dragged into the hangar,
.out of the way of the next ship emerging from the lock.
Ranger's side was a wreck of crumpled, fused metal; sea water
gushed from torn holes between the struts.

". . . Dr. Cabot in the infirmary to expect thirty-three injured.
Fatalities estimated at twelve."

Ussher's hand jerked up to his headset to switch it off. He
looked around the comcenter distractedly, finally fixing on the
progress screen.

Confleet arsenals hit; facility damage estimates. Yes, he'd
been waiting for those figures.

Pol		Cas		InP	
Leda	70%	Helen	65%	Danae	60%
Telhamid	80%	Tremper	70%		
Lamont	75%	Oriban	55%		
Petrovna	85%				

That was every Confleet arsenal in Centauri. He took a deep
breath. A few casualties were unavoidable. *Victory has its
price.*

"Your signal's clear, Jan. Right."

Ussher frowned, attracted first by Garris's stentorian tones,
then by the familiar form of address. That was First Commander
Barret he was speaking to.

"What? No, our reports from Danae and all the Inner Planets
bases say that sector should be clear."

Garris was unhappy; more than that, alarmed. Ussher caught
Isaks's eye and with a hand signal directed him to put him on
line with Garris and Barret.

Barret's voice came through first. ". . . check with our Inner
Planets agents. Cornel Demerin came out of SS into an attack
wedge of Confleet Falcons. Twenty-two of them."

"Jan, it had to be an accident; pure chance. There's no way
Confleet would have any of our emergence coordinates."

"I know, Emeric. Confleet probably deployed extra ships
in that sector specifically to guard the power plants. I would
in their place. Demerin pulled out of the engagement with
minor damage and no casualties, but I'm afraid we can count
on extra steel around the Dionysus and Pan plants, too, so that

scraps the power plant op. Tell TacComm that Demerin and his unit will shift to the Pan Obsat op, and I'll—"

"You *can't* scrap the power plant op!" Ussher reached the GroundComm board in a few strides, all but shouting into his mike, and Garris whirled, face scarlet to the roots of his grizzled hair.

"What the *hell*—"

"Damn it, those power plants are vital!" Ussher stared into Barret's face on one of the screens. "You can't give them up just because you ran into a few Confleet ships!"

Barret's voice cracked in his ear, his face was almost unrecognizable in his sudden fury. That was something Ussher had never seen, or ever thought to.

"Predis, this is *my* decision."

"And you've made the *wrong* decision!" Even before the words were out, Ussher realized his error, but he didn't have time to amend it.

Barret snapped coldly, "Captain Lanc!"

Calvet Lanc, at his console only a meter from Ussher, responded with a quick, "Yes, sir?"

"Get him off my lines and *keep* him off!"

Ussher stood rigid, hearing a sharp click, then silence from his 'speaker. Garris sent him a single, baleful glance, then resumed his dialogue with Barret, and finally Ussher stepped back, finding nearly everyone in the comcenter staring at him incredulously, then turning away with something like embarrassment.

An error. Yes, it was an error, but damn it, those power plants *were* vital. And Jan—who did he think he was, talking to the chairman of the Council like that?

The countdown clock read zero +04:00: 14:00 TST.

Ussher again occupied his chosen position in the center of the chamber, hands clasped behind him. A new set of figures appeared on the progress screen; another report on the Obsat stations.

Pol	Equatorial Obsat	fac dam est	70%
Cas	Polar Obsat	fac dam est	55%
InP	Perseus Equatorial Obsat	fac dam est	45%
InP	Pan Equatorial Obsat	fac dam est	50%

Now all the eyes were blinded, or at least dimmed. Two
more equally satisfying reports followed.

Selsd Interplan Sys Ports fac dam ests:

Pol Leda	80%	Cas Helen	65%	InP Danae	50%
Pol Telhamid	closed	Cas Tremper	70%		
Pol Lamont	closed				

Selsd Mercfleet ss dam/des off-planet:

	FLF	8	SLF	20	TDR	26
Total +04:03:	FLF	16	SLF	35	TDR	38

The screen remained blank only long enough for Ussher to
savor those statistics before the next ones appeared. Those he
couldn't savor. Phoenix casualties.

ss dam	ss des	ss cap	ss unactd
F 13 C 7	F 9 C 4	F 3	F 7 C 3
Total +04:04:			
F 34 C 11	F 21 C 10	F 6 C 2	F 10 C 7

Ussher frowned over the last division. Unaccounted for.
Inevitably, that meant ships either destroyed or captured. He
turned, bracing himself mentally, and looked out into the
hangar. Fifteen falcons and four Corvets had already come in,
carrying a total of twenty-three dead and sixty-two injured.
More crippled ships were out in the sea depths making their
way toward the lock.

But victory has its price.

The medsquads and towcrews went about their work with
the same concentrated efficiency as the staff here in the comcenter. The Phoenix would bear its casualties as it must, even
proudly.

After a moment he said to Garris, "I'm going out into the
hangar. Perhaps I can help in some small way . . . a few words
with those brave young men."

Garris gave him such a blank look, Ussher wondered if the
old man might be getting deaf. Or just senile. Ussher turned
on his heel and went to the door.

The noise was staggering. Soundscreens insulated the comcenter from the onslaught, and Ussher wasn't prepared for it.
The low-pitched thump of the pumps, the thunderous clank of
the lock gates opening periodically with a huge rush of air;
there wasn't time to wait for the pressure to equalize. The
whines of loaders, towcars, winches, the explosive hiss of
cutting lasers, the shouted exchanges of orders, questions, demands. The sounds reverberated in the great vault where the
helions were dimmed in a fog of acrid smoke from burning
metal as the docking crews cut open the smashed sides of ships
to get at survivors trapped behind jammed locks.

Ussher held on to the railing as he descended the steps to
the hangar floor. A grating shriek and a crash brought his head
around abruptly. A Falcon had slipped its tows and careened
into the wall of the tunnel into Hangar 2. Towcars and crews
rushed to its assistance. The tunnel was blocked; more ships
were stacking up behind the slewed Falcon. Another Corvet
rumbled through the lock tunnel, sending a miniature tidal wave
across the water-washed floor.

The towcrews shot out their snakes of cable and magnetic
hooks and hauled the ship into the hangar. A medsquad was
at the ship's lock before it had come to a stop, and by the time
Ussher reached the ship, the crew was already disembarking,
the injured carried out on stretchers by the medtechs. Ussher
looked up at the bow of the ship. The *Hopewell*. From the
outside, only a seared concavity was visible, but through the
lock, he could see that the explosion had made a shambles of
the condeck; he wondered vaguely how the ship had managed
to get back to Fina.

"Excuse me, sir . . ."

Ussher stepped back as two medtechs brought another
stretcher and hurried up the ramp into the lock.

"Yes, of course, men. It looks pretty bad in there."

One of the techs nodded. "It is."

"Fer Ussher?"

He turned. One of the crew; a young man, Second Gen.
Strange, he was having a hard time remembering names.

"Corpral Stennis, isn't it? Looks like you took a bad lump
on your head there."

He smiled dazedly. "I guess . . . I was lucky. Sir, how is it
going? The offensive?"

Ussher put his arm around Stennis's shoulder, smiling.

"We've got them howling, Corpral. They don't even know what hit them, and we're *still* hitting. Now, you'd better get to the infirmary. You've done your part, and I want you to know I'm grateful. The Phoenix is grateful." And with a pat on the shoulder, he sent him on, turning as another stretcher was maneuvered out of the locks.

"Dr. Huxley, any problems in the infirmary?"

The doctor looked up, then, on recognizing him, smiled fleetingly.

"Not yet, Fer Ussher. This is just the beginning."

The beginning? Ussher blinked at him, frowning.

"Well, let me know. Is this . . . Major March?" The man on the stretcher was unconscious, half his head covered with a blood-soaked temporary bandage.

"No. Major March . . . well, he'll leave the ship last. Excuse us, sir. We've got to get this man to the infirmary."

"Oh . . . yes. Of course." Last to leave the ship. March was dead, then. He'd never get his cornel's wings.

"Sir! Watch out!"

A tow cable sprang to singing tautness directly behind him, a towcar swished past, people were running through the treacherous skim of water, shouting back and forth. The 'car driver leaned toward him.

"We've got to move her out of the way, sir. More ships coming in!"

Ussher stumbled, dodging men and machines until he was finally clear of the *Hopewell*. One of her steering vanes sliced within centimeters of his head. He retreated toward the corridor entrance as a rush of air and a resounding clank marked the opening of the lock. He looked back. Two Falcons. One was towing the other.

Near the corridor doors, medtechs were lifting stretchers onto the specially designed racks on the loaders. Each machine could carry six wounded, but only one was present, and four men lay on stretchers on the floor propped on makeshift supports to keep them out of the water.

"Dr. Kaosu, where are the rest of the loaders?"

A harried woman was bending over one of the stretcher-borne wounded, ripping open the front of his uniform. She glanced up at Ussher, but only briefly.

"Jerris, a coag injection. Hurry. Where's that antisep sheet? And, Del, you'd better give him some pentaphine." She rose as two medtechs knelt by the stretcher to carry out her orders. A warning beeper announced the arrival of an empty loader.

"Oh, thank the God." She snapped off her reddened plaskin gloves, took another pair from her pocket, tore off the protective envelope, and pulled the gloves on as she went to the next stretcher. "I 'commed John M'Kim, Fer Ussher. He's sending more loaders. Oh, damn—the tourniquet slipped."

The man she was leaning over was already covered from the chest down with an antisep sheet. One sleeve had been cut away, his forearm loosely bandaged. She tightened the strap and turnbuckle above his elbow, and his head rolled toward her, mouth taking the shape of a smile, eyes glazed with pain and terror. The tourniquet slipped loose again.

"Damn thing won't hold. Fer Ussher, hold this tight until I get another one."

Her tone broached no argument, and before he realized it, he was kneeling beside the man, holding the strap tight, and Dr. Kaosu had vanished.

Names—why couldn't he remember names today?

"Fer Us-ussher? 'S 'at really . . . you?"

"Yes, Sargent. You just relax now. You've done your part, and I want you to know : . ." He swallowed hard, looking down at his boots. The water around them was red. "You—you'll be all right. This arm doesn't look too bad. They'll have you up and . . . and . . ."

The man was coughing. Horrible, retching sounds. Blood sprayed from his mouth, his free hand was locked on Ussher's arm.

"Help m-me . . . help . . . me . . ."

Ussher felt droplets on his face and hands, burning like acid. He tried to pull away, but the man's grip seemed unbreakable; his body heaved and shuddered.

"Doctor!" Ussher shouted in a frenzy of desperation. "Doctor—help! Help me!"

"Let him go, Fer Ussher. Let him go. There's nothing more' you can do for him."

She was kneeling on the other side of the stretcher, fingers pressed to the man's throat. He was still now.

Ussher drew back. His uniform. Blood. It was spattered with blood.

"Is he . . . ?"

The doctor nodded. "Yes, sir. I'm sorry. He's dead."

"But he—he can't be. That arm . . ."

"It wasn't just the arm." Before she pulled the sheet up over the man's head, she turned it back so Ussher could see the chest and abdomen.

"Oh, Holy God . . ."

He staggered to his feet, doubled over with cramping nausea. There was no place in this pounding cacophony to be sick, but he couldn't hold it down.

The countdown clock read zero +05:00: 15:00 TST.

A new report was materializing on the progress screen.

Conflt Bss—ss dam/des/fac dam ests:

Pol Telhamid	F 42	C 10	TCC 1	fac dam est 80%
Pol Lamont	F 110	C 18	TCC 2	fac dam est 75%
Cas Tremper	F 52	C 15	TCC 2	fac dam est 70%
Cas Santalena	F 18	C 3	TCC 1	fac dam est 50%
InP Titania	F 12	C 2		fac dam est 30%

ss dam/des total +05:01:

F 662　　C 12/　TCC 19

Ussher devoured the figures. Against those losses of facilities and ships, the Phoenix had gotten off easily, and the statistics from the Confleet bases didn't include the ships lost in combat off-planet. He smiled grimly. The latest figures on that came next.

Conflt ss dam/des in cmbt:　F 18　　　C 3　　TCC 2
Total +05:22:　F 287　　C 55　　TCC 9

Let the Lords think on *that*. Over 1,200 ships damaged and destroyed. So Phoenix casualties were running higher than he expected. What were those losses laid against the Concord's? Victory has its price. He looked down at the PubliCom screen, one side of his mouth twitching again into a smile.

The frantic 'casters babbled reports of new disasters every minute, of rampant confusion and panic, of cities paralyzed, while Concord officialdom flailed about helplessly, feeding the 'casters the only salve it could think of.

Confleet was sending a thousand-ship wing from the Solar System. Over and over, the 'casters spewed forth that pap. It would be here soon; within the hour.

Ussher laughed. Where did they think Confleet would find a full wing? In the ruins of Mars? And did they think that creaking dinosaur could organize a thousand ships and the twelve thousand men to staff them in so short a time? It would take days, even weeks.

"Sir, there's a call . . . *sir?*"

He frowned irritably. How did Isaks expect him to hear anything in this hubbub of voices, gabbling out of the screens, buzzing in his ears. And why in the God's name wouldn't they keep the comcenter door closed?

"What is it, Alan?"

"Dr. Cabot in the infirmary. For you, sir."

Ussher nodded, then Cabot's face appeared on a screen. At first, he didn't recognize him. The man looked like a specter.

"Yes, Dr. Cabot?"

"Sir, we've run out of room in the infirmary, so we're setting up an auxiliary station in the SMR level dining hall."

"You've run out . . . oh, well, that seems a . . . a very sensible decision, Doctor."

Cabot frowned, as if he weren't sure he'd understood him correctly.

"The problem is, the med staff and aid-trained volunteers are up to their necks here. I need more volunteers to help set up in the dining hall. We've got wounded on the floors; we can't even get to the critical cases without stumbling over—"

"All *right*, Doctor." Ussher was looking down at the cuffs of his uniform. Couldn't get the stains out. "'Com John M'Kim. Yes, he's the one you should've called."

"But, sir, I thought you—"

"M'Kim! 'Com M'Kim. Doctor, I have my hands full here. Surely you realize that."

Cabot didn't respond, but something in his cold look set Ussher's pulse pounding. He signaled to Isaks, and his breath came out in a sigh when the screen went dark. What did Cabot expect? That *was* M'Kim's department, wasn't it?

The PubliCom 'caster was babbling about the coming arrival of the Confleet wing again. Might as well look for the second coming of the Mezion.

He should have ordered SI to try again on the PubliCom Systems operation. He stared at the haggard face of the 'caster, and a dread conviction overwhelmed him. That was an irremediable loss, not getting his appeal on the vidicom screens. Later, after the offensive, *wouldn't* be soon enough. It was too late *now*.

And those damned Bonds, What had happened? No use talking to Hendrick again. Ussher had 'commed him four times and listened to him hem and haw, and the substance of it was that there had been minor uprisings in four Hamid and three Drakonis compounds. *Minor* uprisings, the worst of which had lasted half an hour.

And the ROM, which might have taken this opportunity to lead the Fesh students at the Leda and Helen Universities into open revolt against the Concord masters they professed to despise—the leaders of the ROM weren't leading anyone anywhere.

Pampered young hypocrites. Spoiled whelps of the Fesh rich. Couldn't trust their sort to come through when—

"What did you say, sir?" Isaks leaning toward him, frowning questioningly.

"I didn't say anything. Damn it, why don't they keep that *door* closed?"

He didn't look behind him at the door. A new report was posted on the progress screen.

PNX ss dam/des/cap/unactd:

ss dam	ss des	ss cap	ss unactd
F 26 C 13	F 22 C 14	F 9 C 4	F 6 C 4
Total + 05:10:			
F 60 C 24	F 53 C 24	F 15 C 6	F 16 C 11

He stared at the figures, and he didn't want to add them, but the total materialized, unbidden, in his mind.

209.

That was almost half the Phoenix fleet, damaged, destroyed, captured, unaccounted for.

The countdown clock read zero +05:30: 15:30 TST.

Ussher paced the comcenter floor. There were thirty-five ships in the main hangar now. He glanced that way only briefly.

Then he stopped his pacing, distracted by Calvet Lanc's voice from his post near the GroundComm console.

"... FS *Demond*. For Leftant Condo, Navcomp."

Demond. That was the flagship. Jan's ship. Ussher looked for Garris, finding him near Lanc at a printout transceiver. Garris was speaking into his headset mike; a radio 'com apparently. Ussher approached, listening intently.

"... coming through clear as glass, Met. Damn, you should get a medal for this." A pause and a short laugh, then, "Well, we'll stamp out a few for SI. All right, is that the lot? I've got it all taped; we'll send it straight to Jan. Take care of yourself." He turned his mike control ring. "Line clear, Ben. Thanks. Cal?"

Captain Lanc turned. "*Demond* navcomp is on receive."

Garris took a printout spool from the console and tossed it to him. "Roll it out, Cal. Roll it out."

Ussher asked sharply, "Roll what out, Commander?"

Garris· looked around at him, his smile turning cool. "SI came through with flags flying. One of their agents just handed us the SynchShift emergence coordinates for that whole damned Confleet wing."

Ussher's throat seemed to close, stopping his breath. "What ... wing?"

"I thought you were at least keeping up with the newscasts, Predis. The thousand-ship wing Confleet's sending from the Solar System to relieve Centauri. They'll be emerging—" He checked his watch. "—in forty-seven minutes."

"That's impossible. They can't send that many ships."

Garris said to Lanc, "When you're through, I want to run that tape through a comp analysis. Predis, what do you mean? How many ships did you ask for?"

At that, Ussher felt the heat rushing to his face. "Commander, this is *not* a laughing matter."

"Who's laughing?" He studied Ussher a moment, frowning.

"You mean, you didn't . . . you didn't *realize*—"

"I certainly didn't believe that pap the PubliCom System is putting out. A thousand-ship wing, indeed! The Concord couldn't get that many ships and men together in a week, much less a few hours!"

Garris only stared at him, mouth sagging, and Ussher became aware of a silence around him, of other gaping stares. But what had he done? What was his error this time?

He blurted, "The Concord is a creaking, senile dinosaur! It can't even keep order in the Solar System. How can it possibly put together a full wing in this short a time?"

Garris shook his head, his tone flat and curt. "Well, Predis, there's life in the old fossil yet. The mobilization order went out from FleetComm HQ at 10:30 TST. Oh—thanks, Cal." This as Lanc returned the tape spool.

Garris in turn gave the spool to the officer on the navcomp console, who inserted it into a slot and began playing the keyboard as deftly as if it were a muscial instrument. Ussher stared over his head as numbers and abstract figures drawn in light began to dance across the three screens. He couldn't have guessed how long he stood watching, incapable of even the smallest motion, but when at length the silent concert ended, he recognized the impossible as a reality.

But why hadn't Jan told him? Between his TacComm staff and SI, he must have had some idea of the size of the retaliatory force Confleet could send and how soon. Of course, Jan had given him those sheafs of comp read-outs, as if he expected him to be a comptech and make sense of that mishmash of numbers. But Jan should have *told* him. Or it should have come from SI. Venturi had held out on him from the beginning.

". . . on line for you, sir. Commander Barret."

Ussher roused himself, but Lanc was talking to Garris, who was already on his way to the GroundComm console, where Barret's face looked out from one of the screens.

Ussher said to Lanc, "Put me on line, Captain."

"Uh . . . I'm sorry, sir, but I have orders."

"I don't give a damn . . ." No time to argue with Lanc. He'd settle that later.

"Yes, Jan, we've run a fast analysis," Garris was saying. "What do you think?"

Ussher glared at the screen, watching the reply he couldn't hear, seeing Garris nod agreement.

"There's been too much steel dropping into the water in this general area as it is. Somebody up there's going to notice. You've knocked out the Obsats, but these coordinates spell a heavy concentration of ships around Pollux."

Ussher took another step closer, straining at Barret's silenced response.

Somebody up there's going to notice.

That meant notice *Fina*.

Garris was mumbling into his mike. ". . . get as many ships into the hangars as possible, but we've only got forty minutes."

Ussher tried to control his voice, but it came out as a shout.

"You can't let those ships come *here*! They'll pinpoint Fina for Confleet!"

Garris turned, glaring angrily at him. "Predis, by the God— either shut up or get out of here!"

"But he's going to betray Fina! Jan! You can't do that! Damn it, I want on line. Rhea—send them to Rhea! Anywhere! Just don't let—"

"Predis, *be quiet*! Janson—and you, Corbet."

Two FO officers appeared at his elbows, and Ussher realized they were prepared to take him away forcibly. The chairman of the Council. The first born of—

Ussher drew himself up, not so much as glancing at the two men, saying with cool precision, "That won't be necessary."

Neither they nor Garris commented, the latter turning away to resume his conversation with Barret, while Ussher stood rigid, pulse pounding, hearing Garris's words, but incapable of assimilating their meaning.

Finally, Garris ended with an odd, tight break in his voice, "Jan . . . well, there's nothing else to do. But be careful. We'll be . . . waiting for you."

The screen went blank, and Garris turned away from it, looking every day of his seventy years.

Ussher said curtly, "Commander, I demand an explanation!"

Garris stared at him, his scarred face suddenly white.

"An explanation! For what? Holy God, you don't understand *anything*, do you? You've been living in your little dream world so long, you don't know what's—"

"Garris, damn you!" One of Radek's puppets, her trained lackeys! But that Garris would dare, at this time, in front of the members, to insinuate that— "Let me *go*!"

The two officers were gripping his arms. It was intolerable. Inconceivable. Garris's face was only centimeters from his, and his eyes burned with naked contempt, his voice rasped, constrained to a guttural whisper.

"You want an explanation, Predis? Then listen! Jan Barret carried out a six-hour programmed offensive with ninety percent success. *Your* offensive, Predis! He did it for you, and did a hell of a good job of it. Now Confleet's sending reinforcements, and that was programmed, too. What *wasn't* programmed was the concentration of ships around Pollux. They'll cut off the rest of the fleet's retreat to Fina if—"

"But they *can't* retreat to Fina! What about—"

"The Rhea base? Damn it, if you had the vaguest idea what's going on here, you'd know that every ship capable of SS acceleration *is* going to Rhea. But that still leaves more than sixty damaged ships that can't make it into SS. What are they supposed to do, Predis?"

There was a buzzing whine in his ears. He couldn't find its source. Garris bored on, and Ussher felt the words pounding in his head.

"I'll *explain* what Jan's going to do, Predis. Four hundred Confleet ships are homing in on the Pollux sector. He's going to take twenty Falcons and ten Corvets and set up an SS emergence ambush. He's going to buy some time. Time for the damaged ships to make it back to Fina before Confleet can get close enough to see where they're headed. He's going to buy that time with . . ." A silence trailed out with those words, then he turned abruptly.

"Predis, get away from me."

It was spoken in a curiously mild tone, and Ussher realized he was free of restraint now. He stood a moment, but no words would take shape against that strange, sourceless whining. He made his way back to his chair.

The countdown clock read zero +06:19: 16:19 TST.
Ussher's eyes were turned up to the progress screen.

PNX ss dam/des/cap/unactd:

ss dam	ss des	ss cap	ss unactd
F 32 C 13	F 28 C 18	F 12 C 5	F 6 C 4
Total + 06:20:			
F 92 C 37	F 71 C 42	F 27 C 11	F 22 C 14

The figures vanished off the top of the screen, and he couldn't have recalled any of them. The newscaster's voice impinged just as lightly on the surface of his thoughts.

". . . with the arrival in the Centauri System of a full Confleet wing led by Commander Delin Borudo, enemy resistance has virtually evaporated. Concord officials have not yet determined the motive behind this unprovoked attack, but the Phoenix has long been recognized as a revolutionary . . ."

Ussher stared at the smoothly handsome face on the screen, heard the glib phrases, and nothing in his mind balked or reflected surprise that the face was becoming increasingly familiar as he watched it. The dark hair and arching brows, the frigid blue eyes, the hawklike cast of the bones. The face looked out at him with smug contempt and said in clipped, precise accents, "*I* am the Lord Alexand, first born of the Lord Phillip DeKoven Woolf, grandson of the Lord Mathis Daro Galinin. . . ."

But Alex Ransom was dead.

Of course he was. There—Garris had just said it. He was dead.

Someone near him whispered, "Oh, Holy God . . . oh, no —"

Isaks, staring dazedly past Ussher. Around the comcenter people were turning, all looking in one direction, all looking toward the GroundComm console. Toward Emeric Garris.

Ussher came slowly to his feet, turning by small degrees until finally he found Garris looking directly at him.

As if Ussher had asked a question, Garris said, "I just had a report from Leftant Commander Gavin. *Demond* took a direct barrage and exploded. First Commander Barret is dead."

"No . . . no . . . no . . . no . . . no . . . *NO!*"

Ussher pressed his fists to his head, his brain was exploding, shockwaves of agony rocked the room. He saw the door, stumbled toward it. He ran, staggering, panting. No air. They were choking him. He ran, fell against the door as it opened, reached out for the railing. The smoke blinded him, seared his lungs. And he ran.

5.

16:45 TST. Emeric Garris sloshed through the oil-skimmed water to the steps of the comcenter deck, content to leave the final berthing operations to Commander Gavin and the able-bodied survivors.

1,609 were no longer able-bodied or survivors: 901 dead, 214 wounded, 254 captured, 250 unaccounted for. Altogether, nearly half FO's staff.

And out of 2,270, SI had sustained 528 casualties. But ninety-six were only wounded; most of them would recover.

Garris leaned heavily on the railing as he climbed the steps. Lord Predis had shown his colors, and there was no one in Fina who wasn't bitterly, painfully, aware of it. Their leader had no lofty speeches for them now, no golden promises, no stirring predictions of *victory*. Their leader had turned tail and run.

He was hiding in his office now. Garris had that from Isaks; Ussher had 'commed him. To the young man's credit, he elected to stay in the comcenter and relieve the ADCon staff rather than obey Ussher's summons or answer his questions.

Garris paused outside the comcenter door and surveyed the hangar, feeling the pain in his gut he called old age, although he knew better. At least he'd lived long enough to see FO through this, but perhaps that was because he knew about Alex Ransom and Andreas, knew this wasn't all in vain.

The men and women out there among the wrecks, driving themselves doggedly past the limits of endurance, didn't yet know. He wondered what kept them going. The demands of the moment; nothing more. He'd seen a doctor break down in tears when one of the wounded died in his arms.

The sound of footsteps roused him. Ben Venturi. Garris wondered vaguely at his expression of anxious concern.

"Emeric, are you all right?"

"What? Oh—of course. You find Marien and M'Kim?"

"They're both helping out in the infirmary, but they'll be here in a few minutes. I paged Hendrick and got no answer. He's with Predis." Ben looked at his watch. "We'd better get into the comcenter."

Garris nodded and led the way. The officers and techs looked around, eyes lifeless with numb weariness. No one spoke. Alan Isaks, he noted, was back by Ussher's empty chair, staring bleakly at the PubliCom screen.

Garris made a round of the scanners and screens, asking a few questions, getting unelaborated answers. Pollux's skies were swarming with Confleet recon flights, but there was no hint that the quadrant of the Selamin Sea around Fina was attracting any undue attention.

A few minutes later, Marien Dyce and John M'Kim arrived. With Venturi and Garris they made up the Council at the moment. Garris had called them here as councilors and let them assume he was taking FO's vacant seat.

Vacant. The very word made an anguished void. And yet you'd think an old soldier would finally become immune to grief.

Marien Dyce came over to Garris, asking, "Where's Erica?"

He knew, but couldn't tell her. Not yet. "Uh . . . she must be in the infirmary."

"Oh. I didn't see her there. Surgery, probably."

It was revealing that Marien didn't ask about Ussher or Hendrick. Neither did M'Kim. He stood near the door, looking out into the hangar, and for the first time Garris saw past the ever pragmatic accountant's facade.

"Sir, I'm picking up something here."

A woman looked up from a prox scanner, and that quiet announcement was electrifying and drew every eye to her. Their fear didn't need words; fear that Fina was discovered.

Garris looked over the tech's shoulder, studying the star of light on the edge of the screen.

"What does the comp ident say, Jen?"

"Single ship; mass indicates a Falcon, on direct approach vector. Altitude . . ." She faltered a little then. "It's submerged. Minus fifty meters. Speed, three kps."

He nodded. "Carl, are the approach shock screens on?"

"Yes, sir."

Garris watched the moving star, frowning to mask his relief. In the tense quiet, the voice that came from the ADCon speakers might as well have been on ampspeakers.

"Calling PNX ADCon . . . come in, ADCon."

At the ADCon console, a startled comtech fumbled at the controls, then stopped, looking around at Garris.

"Sir, all the fleet ships are *in*."

"I know, Sim. Try to find out who it is—and put this on tape."

He nodded and set the controls.

"PNX ADCon on line. Requesting vessel identification."

The response was immediate, flat, and matter of fact.

"Sargent Simmons, this is Commander Ransom aboard Exile Fleet Falcon *Phoenix One*, requesting lock entry. We are . . . eleven minutes and thirty seconds from the lock tunnel."

In the stunned silence, only the hummings of machines were audible. Simmons finally found his voice, but not to reply to that request. Again, he looked to Garris.

"Sir? What . . . what are your orders?"

Garris turned to another tech. "Max, get me a VP ident on that voice. Hurry. Sim, just tell him to hold."

While they waited, the tension nearly tangible, Garris looked at Dyce and M'Kim, and what he saw in their faces called up a sigh of relief. Hope. Aching hope that pleaded to be fulfilled. And these had been Ussher's strongest converts on the Council.

"Sir, here it is!" Max, gesturing wildly at a screen. "The VP ident. It's *him*. It's Commander Ransom!"

Garris's orders were almost lost in the resulting confusion, but he didn't try to quiet it.

"Sim—entry request granted. Carl, deactivate the approach shock screens and alert the lock crew. Janie—where are you? Call a general assembly in the hangar. All members. And for those who can't get loose, switch in the intercom screens."

He could smile now, and he took particular satisfaction in the last order. Ussher had vidicams installed in the hangar so his speeches, those damned rallies, could be heard even by those members whose duties precluded their attendance. Now

Ussher could watch this one from his hiding place, watch Fina's last rally.

Isaks was making a 'com call. The screens were dark, but Garris had no doubt Ussher was on the other end of that dialogue. He frowned, then with a shrug dismissed it. What he read on Isaks's face assured him it wasn't a friendly gesture. A challenge. He wondered if Ussher would meet it.

The pumps had finally succeeded in clearing away the water, but at the moment that was hard to ascertain. Those parts of the floor that weren't occupied with ships and machines were filled with people, including the ambulatory wounded.

Emeric Garris stood at the deck railing, listening to the ADCon frequency on his headset. Dyce and M'Kim were waiting near him. Venturi had been here, too, but a minute ago departed suddenly with a monosyllabic explanation.

"SI. Willie says Pri-One."

Garris only nodded absently. He was thinking about Andreas. To see Andreas again, alive, here where he belonged—

An echoing clank, a rush of air and water. *Phoenix One* was coming in. A towcrew hurried toward the tunnel, shouting warnings to the crowd to make room. That blue-uniformed crowd. Garris felt the weight of his own uniform, and he wanted to strip it off on the spot.

The ship emerged into the hangar, and the only sounds in the great vault were mechanical; cables shooting out, thudding home, towcars whining, lock gates closing, pumps thumping, the ship's generators rumbling. She came to a stop a short distance beyond the tunnel, turned with her side and lock toward the comcenter.

The crowd shifted, everyone vying for position to see the lock. Yet they were so quiet. Garris studied the faces he could see, trying to understand that silence. Shock was part of it, but beyond that he read the aching hope he'd first seen on M'Kim's and Dyce's faces.

The tongue of the boarding ramp slid out as the lock opened. A whispering swept through the waiting crowd. Three men were standing in the lock.

One of them Garris didn't recognize at first. It had been nearly five years since he met Jael the Outsider as a new recruit here in Fina. But he spared Jael little attention now, and he stayed a pace behind the others as they descended the ramp.

Andreas—there was Andreas. . . .

Garris held on to the railing, putting down the urge to weep or laugh or shout aloud. Yet he found his attention drawn to Alex Ransom. He watched him, forgetting to breathe.

He was wearing an ordinary slacsuit; Garris noted that because it came as a surprise. His first impression was of a cloak and dress boots, and he was reminded of the night Alex Ransom first came to Fina. It had struck him then, too, that aristocratic bearing that fell short of arrogance only because of the years and generations of stringent discipline behind it.

The blue-clad crowd stirred and shifted, and finally wonder found expression; finally the pendant silence was washed away in a flood of voices, and the vault that had echoed in the last few hours with the clangor of disaster, reverberated with the laughter and accents of hope.

There were no concerted cheers from this crowd, only a formless, continuous clamor, intensely individual articulations of joy and relief, an ultimate, exhaustive resolution. It was a long time before Alex and Andreas could make their way through the crowd to the deck, and they seemed in no hurry. Garris waited, thinking Andreas hadn't looked so well in years. Jael, he noted, stayed close by Alex's right side when the crowd began to press in on them.

But now they had finally reached the deck. Andreas saw Garris and left the others behind, then, when he was only a pace away, stopped. They stood silent, memories and hopes shared in the exchange of fleeting smiles.

Andreas said, "Emeric, I'm glad to find you still here." Then he put out his hand, closing the distance between them.

"Welcome home, Andreas. Welcome *home!*" Garris took both his hands in his, laughing, shouting words he wasn't even aware of, but no one heard him in the clamor or cared if he was making sense. Andreas understood, and so did Alex, whose left-handed grip said what words couldn't.

The comcenter was nearly empty as officers and techs left their posts to join the celebration. And Ben was back. Garris was too swept up in the noisy enthusiasm to wonder why he seemed so grim until he saw him push his way close enough to Alex to say a few words into his ear, and Alex suddenly became equally grim.

It was then that Alex turned to the railing, his raised hand and sober expression finally bringing quiet out of the pandemonium. Garris, with the others on the deck, drew back, waiting expectantly, but Alex's first words were not at all what he anticipated.

"I've been informed," Alex began in a quiet tone that still projected to the edges of the crowd, "that the Phoenix must now add three more deaths to its casualty lists. Marg Conly, assigned to SI, and councilor Robert Hendrick were found dead in the Communications department offices. They were killed by laser beams at close range."

Garris stared at him, and neither he nor the other members had recovered from that shock when Alex went on, "I've also been informed that twenty minutes ago the man who called himself Predis Ussher ordered himself transed to Leda. He used one of the MT techs on duty as a hostage to force the other to carry out his orders. The hostage, Jeris Sanders, is also dead. We don't know where Ussher is now, but we know he cleared his personal lock box and took with him a suitcase filled with commutronics equipment."

The incredulous silence that followed was broken by a stricken cry.

"He's bolted! Run out on us!"

It came from John M'Kim, which was another shock for Garris; M'Kim was the last person he expected to be first to voice that angry realization.

It was absorbed instantly by the members, and the enraged repetition of the accusation exploded into a torrent of sound that set Garris's pulse pounding with a kind of fear he'd never in a long soldier's life experienced. He looked down at the open-mouthed faces contorted in rage and knew that if Ussher were to appear here at this moment, this vengeful crowd, this mob, would literally rip him apart.

Alex raised his hand again, his voice cracking against the massed roar.

"Have you forgotten who you are?"

Garris saw the faces turn, eyes come into focus on Alex, and the storm of anger ebbed enough for them to hear and understand him when he repeated that uncompromising demand.

"Have you forgotten who you are?" And finally, as the roar ebbed into a low murmuring, he answered himself. "You are the Phoenix. You are the hope of the future. You are the last bulwark between civilization and anarchy."

The murmuring died in a long sigh; a curiously gentle sound, as his tone had become gently understanding.

"You've been betrayed, but you haven't been defeated. Ussher's misguided ambitions have served a purpose for the Phoenix, although not the one he intended. He led you, drove you, to the brink of disaster, but it may also be the brink of success. Not victory. Success. To a point, we might even be grateful to him. The Phoenix is now within striking distance of Phase I."

Alex paused to let that sink in, to see hope and curiosity rekindled, but when it began to take the form of shouted questions, he again held up his hand for quiet.

"A great deal has happened in the last few months, and will happen in the next few hours and days. We come bearing hope, but I'll surrender the privilege of explaining that hope to the man who most deserves it." He turned and looked behind him. "Andreas, the . . . podium is yours."

And the audience was his. Quiet now, the blind emotional charge spent. Garris was so intent on Andreas as he moved, a little self-consciously, to the railing, that he was startled by Alex's voice close to his ear.

"Emeric, I need a place for a private conference."

Garris looked around at him, finding him tensely grim again, sharing none of the pervading spirit of joyful gratitude that filled this great chamber.

"Oh. Well, there's your—I mean, Jan . . . Jan's office. It won't be locked."

No one seemed to notice his departure with Jael and Ben; everyone was listening to Andreas. Garris tried to concentrate on what Andreas was saying, but he felt the chill breath of fear casting a pall of doubt on this gathering of hope.

Alex switched on the monitors behind the desk, leaving the sound off, then turned and surveyed the mirror-walled room

that had once been more his home than the rooms he slept in.
A working space, yet oddly impersonal. He found almost nothing to assert its recent occupation by Jan Barret, certainly nothing of Alex Ransom, or even Emeric Garris, who had occupied
it for thirty years.

No. There *was* something testifying to Jan's presence.

The desk was conscientiously cleared, and in the center was
a tape spool. Alex picked it up and read the words under the
seal. "For Nina Barret."

Jan's handwriting. A parting message for his wife.

Alex put the spool back on the desk, wondering who would
have to give it to Nina, recognizing his own cowardice in
hoping it wouldn't be left to him.

On the other side of the desk, Jael stood waiting, only the
narrowing of his oblique eyes betraying his anxiety. Ben had
all but fallen into a chair where he sat with his elbows on his
knees, head in his hands. He was haggard with exhaustion.
And more. There were few of the SI casualties he hadn't known
by name, and too many had been friends.

Finally, Alex said, "Ussher will go to Selasis."

Ben looked up at him, then pulled in a deep breath. "Probably. That's our working premise, anyway."

Jael said, "I wonder if he didn't set up his in-lines with old
Cyclops a long time when."

Ben shrugged listlessly. "Alex, we've got every available
agent looking for him, but right now that's not very many.
We're concentrating on the Selasid estate and the hangar and
warehousing facilities in Leda." He paused, jaw muscles tens-
ing. "All our agents have orders to kill on sight."

Alex nodded. "I'd like to talk to Erica. She could give us
some idea how much he can tell Selasis—how well his conditioning will hold."

"I talked to her. Only had time for a fast run-through. She
says there are two negative factors. First, it would be voluntary
revelation; that tends to loosen conditioned restraints. Second,
she diagnoses him as a paranoid schizophrenic, and she doesn't
know what effect that'll have on conditioning. Her guess is his
conditioning won't hold on anything having to do with you,
and that covers a lot of ground. But basic conditioning probably
will hold. In other words, he probably can't tell Selasis where

Fina is, but he can spill the lot on who you are and what you intend to do. At least, in general terms."

Alex's eyes were drawn to the screens. Andreas on the deck, his audience rapt.

"Ben, Ussher may be able to tell Selasis about my intentions in more than general terms. He took enough Phoenix commutronics equipment with him to set up a small comcenter, and he knows all the frequencies and codes; he can tap any Phoenix transmission. All we can do is conduct as much of our business as possible in the next few hours without any kind of radio or vidicom communication, but we can't avoid it entirely. For one thing, I'll need monitoring and MT contact with the Concordia chapter."

Jael folded his arms and said firmly, "You can't toss that, brother. We aren't sending you into the Directorate Hall without a door."

"I'm not suggesting I go in without one, Jael. We'll just have to use our personal 'com seqs when we can, and hope we can successfully jam the frequencies Ussher has access to, or hope we find him before he reaches Selasis." He hesitated, frowning; it was like entering a fencing match without knowing how high the charge on his opponent's foil was set. "Ben, can Ussher tell Selasis that we're sure of Karlis's sterility?"

Ben considered that a moment, and not happily. "He did manage to slip some monitors past us occasionally, and there was something we picked up once, something he said to Hendrick. He called Karlis 'Orin's pretty eunuch.'"

Alex nodded. "Then he knows." The opponent's probable charge set was approaching lethal level. He checked his watch. "I'll be lifting off for Concordia in a few minutes. Jael, you'll be—"

"Alex, can't you hold off for a while?" Ben asked. "Maybe we can corner Predis in Leda before he finds a ride to Concordia."

"He may already have found a ride. The passenger lines are shut down, but the Leda IP port isn't entirely closed. A Selasid freighter or charter could lift off any time. No, Ben, a delay would only give Ussher more time to reach Selasis, and Selasis more time to make his plans."

Ben accepted that finally. There was no real choice.

"I'll do what I can here, and we've got some top people in the Concordia chapter. We'll try to keep you out of trouble."

"And the Phoenix, too, I hope. Jael, you're in command here. Leave a skeleton crew in the COS HQ and trans everyone else back. They'll be needed here."

He nodded. "What about the old Ser's 'guests'?"

"Send them home as soon as possible; back to their Estates."

"And your Lady and heirs?"

Alex took a deep breath. "Send them home, too. Here. Home to Fina."

6.

The Lord Mathis Daro Galinin looked up over the six screens and across the cluttered surface of his desk to the chair where First Commander Lear Aber of Confleet sat stiffly erect, as if he were at attention, or as if the black uniform, weighted with gold braid and epaulets, allowed him no laxity.

"Commander, it isn't up to me to comment on the advisability of sending another Confleet wing to Centauri. That decision is yours."

"Yes, my lord. I realize it's an inordinately large expenditure of men and matériel, and we're reduced to conscripts in the reserves now." Aber's hands seemed to twitch on every fifth word. "However, I feel we must be in a position to deter or effectively deal with further attacks in the Centauri System should they occur."

Galinin nodded, his eyes straying to the screens before him. Reports from Centauri. The clock panel told him the hour, local time, in the major cities on every planet and satellite in the Two Systems. It was 05:30 in Leda, 09:30 in Helen, and 21:30 in the subterranean cities of Danae, Semele, and Thymbris. And in Concordia. He had been at this desk almost continuously since the reports of the first attacks came in from Centauri, more than eleven hours ago, watching the statistics of ruin accumulate on the screens, and he was too numb to feel anything; he was beyond despair.

And Lear Aber—a man who usually made decisions quickly

and with a certain brazen confidence—Aber was at a loss now, shuffling about verbally and mentally, helpless and hopeless. As Aber continued enumerating the pros and cons of sending more ships to Centauri, Galinin sighed; another old man's sigh. He found his thoughts turning constantly to Rich, who had given all that was left of his life for the Phoenix. Would he condone this taloned Phoenix unleashed in Centauri?

Perhaps he would accept it. Galinin wasn't yet so numbed that he didn't recognize its political implications.

The small PubliCom screen on his desk caught his eye. A newscaster questioning Isador Drakonis about his "kidnapping." The 'caster seemed disappointed with Lord Isador's answers. Galinin had already heard them: he and his family had been treated well, and no demands had been made of them, nor any conditions imposed on their release. Galinin had those answers from him, as well as Eliseer and Hamid's first born, Kasmer—Lady Falda was under sedation—when he spoke with them after they were returned to their Estates three hours ago. He found the implications in that puzzling.

He frowned as he turned off the vidicom.

"Commander, I leave it to you to decide what proportion of your forces you wish to concentrate in Centauri, but let me remind you that the Martian situation isn't entirely resolved yet, and this new crisis has set off violent reactions—" He stopped, distracted by the intercom buzz. Selig's face appeared on a screen.

"What is it, Master Selig?"

"Uh...my lord, I'm sorry to disturb you, but there's a Major Ransom of the SSB here. He has a message from SSB Central Control. Priority-One, my lord."

Galinin frowned irritably. More official panic, no doubt. Selig had managed to divert most of the flood of queries and demands from Concord officials and nervous Lords, but he couldn't ignore that Pri-One rating.

The Chairman could, however, if he chose to, and Galinin was on the verge of refusing the message when the name Selig had used finally came through to him.

Major Ransom of the SSB...

Ransom.

A coincidence, of course. Still...

"Very well, Selig, send him in. Commander, I hope this won't take long."

Aber nodded distractedly, not even bothering to look around as the doors opened, but Galinin was intent on the man who entered, inwardly cursing the face-screen: the SSB image of anonymity. Nothing could be read in the shadow face under the black helmet, nothing in the figure under the black cloak. The only indication that a human being existed under all that anonymous black was the fact that he'd removed one glove; he wore a flat-stoned ring on his left hand, and it *did* seem to be a living human hand.

"My lord . . ." He stopped in front of the desk, bowing to Galinin, giving Aber a respectful nod.

And that was curious. A salute wasn't mandatory between members of the military and police, but when one was ranked First Commander, it was customary.

Galinin asked, "You have a message for me, Major?"

"Yes, my lord." He reached under his cloak with his left hand and took out a plaseal packet. "I was instructed to wait for a reply."

"Very well." Galinin was all too familiar with these SSB packets. Tamper-proof seals keyed for him, detailed indentification of the source and messenger, an earspeaker with the tape already inserted. As he placed the 'speaker in his ear, he studied the messenger, standing patiently at attention.

Ransom.

It *must* be a coincidence. Not that he'd be surprised if it weren't. He was past surprise today. And the man's voice; there was something disarmingly familiar about it. Galinin leaned back, resting his hands on the carved arms of his chair, as the tape began.

"To the Lord Mathis Daro Galinin, Chairman of the Directorate . . ."

Even at those introductory words, Galinin felt a chill settling between his shoulder blades. It was the messenger's voice.

". . . Curiosity will no doubt prevent you from sounding any alarms at this point. I hope wisdom will induce you to maintain the same attitude when you've heard this out. I've come in the name and hope of peace. As for my identity, I'm sometimes called the Brother of the Lamb, a name I know to be familiar to you. I wish to speak with you alone, my lord, in the interests of peace. That's all I ask, and that's the only reason I'm here. I assure you, you'll be quite safe. If it were my intention to harm you, I wouldn't bother to identify myself at all, or give you so much opportunity to signal for help, or waste your time with this little dissertation. I must warn you that *I'm* quite safe, too. If you choose to alert anyone to my presence, I'll simply cease to be present. Nothing would be gained for either of us.

"If anyone else is in your office now, I must ask you to send them away and, to further insure our privacy, to switch off all monitors and recorders. I'm well acquainted with your monitoring system, including the backup panel in the compartment under the intercom console. I must also ask you to turn off the peripheral shock screens if they're on.

"My lord, I come in peace, and I come in the Name of the Lamb. I beg of you, have faith enough to hear me out."

The tape ended with a faint click, and Galinin became aware of the pressing silence in the room. And he'd been right about one thing: he was past surprise, and far past personal fear.

There was something ironically ludicrous about the whole situation. A man dressed in SSB black, calling himself the brother of a saint, delivering a message that could only come from the enemy without uttering a word aloud, and in the presence of Commander Aber, who sat muddling in his own indecision, oblivious to it all.

The messenger still stood at attention, an enigma in black, and any inclination to laughter of any kind faded; Galinin felt within him a vague uneasiness like a premonition, a cognizance on a level too far below the rational to make sense.

He allowed himself another long sigh as he removed the 'speaker and turned to Aber.

"Commander, something important has come up, and I must deal with it immediately. When you've reached a decision on your future course of action in Centauri, let me know."

Aber came to his feet and bowed. "My lord, I'll be in touch with you within the hour." He glanced at the messenger, then marched to the doors.

Galinin opened them with the control on his desk, closed them behind him, then reached for the intercom. The messenger didn't move, and Galinin knew he wouldn't until his demands for privacy were met.

"Master Selig, I will accept no calls, and I want no interruptions for any reason until further notice."

Selig blinked, then nodded dutifully. "Of course, my lord."

Galinin then methodically turned off every monitor, including the backup system. The peripheral shock screens weren't on; they seldom were. He noted that the messenger leaned forward slightly to make sure of them.

"I assume, Major, you wish the doors locked?"

"Yes, my lord. Who's on guard at your private entrance?"

Galinin laughed. The door behind his chair was quite invisible, he knew, and its existence, with the corridor that connected it to a lift giving access to a private landing roof, he had always considered a well kept secret.

"At this time Captain Tedlock is on duty. He's from my House guard, and he's there because I have ample reason to trust him. Now, Major, your terms have been met. Will you introduce yourself to me?"

He took off his helmet with his left hand, then pushed the cloak back from his shoulders. The uniform under it wasn't SSB black, but a light blue decorated with silver braid. He made a formal bow, a hint of irony in it, as there was in his tone when he said, "First Commander Alex Ransom, Fleet Operations, the Society of the Phoenix."

Galinin leaned back, smiling faintly.

"I see the SSB let a large fish slip through its nets when they lost you, Commander. If I say it's a pleasure to meet you, don't think I'm being facetious. I've found you of some interest."

"So has the SSB, my lord."

Galinin laughed appreciatively, but he was wondering why he still had his face-screen on. The glove on Ransom's right hand drew his attention; it wasn't a regulation SSB glove. That in turn reminded Galinin of the salute Ransom *hadn't* given Aber, and the fact that he used his left hand exclusively.

"Pendino." Galinin found himself smiling again. "You were wounded in the course of rescuing Dr. Andreas Riis."

"An interesting conjecture, my lord."

"Indeed. At any rate, I'm duly impressed. I must also admit I'm impressed with your skills as a tactician in view of today's events in Centauri. But you said you've come here in the interests of peace."

"I've come to ask you, as the Chairman, to grant me official recognition as an envoy of the enemy."

"I see. And as an envoy of the enemy you wish to initiate negotiations with the Directorate?"

"Yes, my lord. That was the purpose of today's 'events' in Centauri. To bring the Concord to the bargaining table with the Phoenix so that we may, in the age-old custom of merchants and princes, haggle over the fate of civilization."

Galinin's hands tightened on the arms of his chair. He remembered very well when he had last heard those words, remembered who had spoken them.

"You're the second envoy the Phoenix has sent me, although I'm not sure the first could be described in exactly that term."

"Richard Lamb was very much an envoy, my lord."

"You . . . were a friend of his?"

A long pause, then, "Yes, my lord. I was a friend."

Something in his tone gave Galinin an atavistic sensation of rising hackles; something about his voice. He *knew* that voice.

"Well, Commander, thanks to your first envoy all this isn't entirely unexpected—although it's still a shock. However, you must be aware that if I choose to grant you envoy status, I'll be in effect aligning myself with you and the Phoenix in the eyes of some of the Directors, and considering the precarious balance of power at the moment, that could be disastrous for me. I'm willing to take that risk, even to put the Chairmanship on the line—and that's what it will come to—in the name and hope of peace, but only if I have some confidence in what, and with whom, I'm inadvertently aligning myself."

"I know, my lord, and one of my purposes here is to outline the terms the Phoenix will present to the Directors and to assure you the risk is worth taking."

"Very well. But I'll find it difficult to muster any confidence if I'm forced to make judgments of a face-screened man."

"I . . . don't expect you to do so, my lord." His left hand moved toward his neck, yet with a constrained hesitancy Galinin found disturbing. Why did he seem so reluctant to show his face?

"My lord, I live a somewhat . . . schizoid existence."

"If you mean 'Alex Ransom' isn't the name you were born with, I assumed that, and I don't ask another."

"But it's the name I was born with . . ." An uncertain pause, then, "The name will be evident in my face, and it will inevitably be a shock for you, my lord, but I don't know how to prepare you for it, except . . ." He was unfastening his collar, and Galinin expected the face-screen to go off, but it didn't. He had something in his hand; he put it on the desk.

"The Brother identifies himself to the Shepherds with this talisman."

Galinin looked down and saw a small disk of gold. Then he surged to his feet, staring at it, a painful constriction binding his chest, choking off his breath. He reached out for it, turned it over in a shaking hand.

The wolf and the lamb. Rich's gift to his brother, and his brother's most precious possession.

Yet no one, except those closest to Alexand, had known about this medallion, known what it meant to him. From the day it was given to him, he had always worn it. It wasn't among the effects sent the family from Confleet; no one expected it to be. Alexand would have been wearing it when he died.

Galinin looked up at Commander Alex Ransom, standing expectantly silent, hands at his sides, perfectly still. He looked at the one exposed hand, the dark skin, the long bones; a hand with the power in it to make machines or make music.

He became aware of a peculiar resentment inspired by the barrier of space created by the desk, that pretentious fortress behind which he seemed condemned to spend his life. He moved haltingly around it, feeling his way, every breath an effort. When at length he stood close enough to touch this silent enigma he said in a level tone that surprised him, "You may turn off your face-screen."

Finally, the hand moved to the 'screen ring; finally, the shadow vanished.

"Alexand . . ."

The name came out on a long breath, a sigh of spent fear.

Galinin looked into a face he had never, even in despairing fantasies, hoped to see again, never asked of fate or the God to see, relegating this possibility to the absolute realm of the impossible.

Now I can die content.

He couldn't explain why that thought came to mind, and he didn't try. Only one thing was important now. Alexand. Alexand alive. That he wore the uniform, declared himself a member and leader of the Phoenix was important only in that it was part of the fact of his presence, of his living.

That fact changed everything: the crisis in Centauri that brought him here, brought him to life; the chronic crises that wracked the Concord, that Galinin knew himself no longer capable of containing; even the future of the Concord. He saw everything in a new light now, although he couldn't have explained that, either; not in terms that could be expressed in words.

The medallion in his hand had been a gift to Alexand from his brother, from a saint. And now Rich, by his brother's hand, offered this gift to his grandfather, the gift of hope, to a generation preceding him for generations to come.

"Grandser?"

An asking whisper, and Galinin reached out to him, embracing him, resorting to laughter, the surrogate of tears.

"Alexand—oh, Alex, thank the God!"

Even when they drew apart, Galinin still found it difficult to do more than stare into his face, to absorb every detail of it, the familiar shapes and the unfamiliar lines and shadows that were the toll of the last five years. The resemblance to Phillip was even more marked now, and that thought roused him to a harshly pragmatic awareness of their present situation, and to an aspect of it he hadn't yet considered.

"Alex, does your father know . . ." Alexand seemed to withdraw, but it wasn't antagonism Galinin caught in his eyes before they became coolly expressionless; only regret. That was reassuring. "No, of course you haven't told him yet. But he'll have to know soon."

"Yes, Grandser, but I must leave it to you to . . . to prepare him for the shock."

He nodded. "That would be best, although it won't be easy

for him. Still, he's changed, Alex. He's changed."

"Yes. I know."

Galinin paused, assessing his flat tone. He looked down at the medallion, then pressed it into Alexand's hand, gazing at it lying in his palm for a moment, until his hand closed over it, and he reached up to replace it on the chain at his neck, then fastened the collar of his uniform.

Galinin took a deep breath and pulled the slump out of his shoulders.

"Well, I suppose we should get down to business. You haven't taken the incredible risk of walking into the Chairman's office alone simply to renew old acquaintance."

Alexand laughed at that, but it faded quickly into an introspective half smile.

"You're an extraordinary man, Grandser."

"Am I, now? Come, let's sit by the windowall. I'm sick to death of that desk." Then, seeing Alexand's frowning glance toward the windowall, "It's set on one-way opaque. All the people out in the Plaza can see is a dim glow, which assures them that their Chairman is at least awake."

Galinin took the nearest chair, lowering himself into it with a caution that seemed to be an adjunct of age more than a physical necessity. He watched Alexand, noting the cant of his body to the left, the careful positioning of his right arm. That *was* a physical necessity.

"How am I so extraordinary, Alex? Because I don't balk at finding you resurrected in that uniform? Well, perhaps that's because I don't find the uniform surprising once I accept your resurrection. And I've had a few years to think about Rich. The first envoy. That was when you made your decision about the Phoenix, wasn't it?"

Alexand hesitated, his eyes focused inward, then he nodded silently, and Galinin found himself nodding, too, undoubtedly over the same shattering remembrances.

"I've been thinking of Rich all day, through all the..." Then he frowned, leaving the thought unfinished.

Alexand took it up. "Through all the destruction and death? Would Rich approve of that?"

"I... wondered that, yes."

Alexand looked down into the Plaza, and Galinin's gaze

followed his. The white expanse was dotted with dark clusters of people, and there seemed something ominous about them, although most were simply standing, looking up at the Hall. Galinin wondered what they were waiting for. Answers, or perhaps a catalyst. And perhaps it was here.

Alexand said, "Rich would've despised it, but he would have—and did—recognize it as unavoidable, as I do, as the General Plan ex seqs always have, and as I think you will. If we only had to deal with you, it probably wouldn't have been necessary, but unfortunately we must take into consideration the Directorate and the Court of Lords. There was no alternative for achieving Phase I, and without that..." He frowned on a long sigh. "We can only balance the casualties in Centauri today against the casualties of a third dark age. I wonder if they can even be calculated. We did not lightly turn to war as a means to our ends. We are not makers of war by choice or philosophy."

"I can believe that of you, Alex, as I did of Rich."

"Then believe it of the Phoenix, Grandser. I beg of you—believe it."

There was a plea in his words, but in his eyes an uncompromising challenge and a forcefulness that like the unfamiliar lines in his face had also been acquired in the last five years.

Finally, Galinin said, or rather admitted, to himself as much as to Alexand, "I do believe it. I wasn't convinced when Rich came as your first envoy, but now..." Then he shrugged, making his tone lighter as he noted, "Perhaps the pacific nature of your philosophy explains why Eliseer and Drakonis and Hamid's family were released from your 'protective custody' unharmed." Alexand only smiled, ignoring the questions underlying that, and Galinin added, "You have the Directors baffled with that move, you know. They expected them to be used as hostages."

"We never even considered that. It would arouse antagonism on a personal level among the Directors, and we'll have enough impersonal antagonism to contend with."

"True, which brings us back to the matter of the terms of your negotiations with the Directorate."

"Yes, but before we get to that, there are a few things you

must know about, Grandser." He paused, tight lines forming around his mouth. "The first is a warning. Treachery among 'traitors.' It may destroy us all and all our hopes."

"Treachery?" Galinin frowned. "Is this the treachery that put you and Dr. Riis in the hands of the SSB?"

"Yes. In over half a century, the Phoenix has harbored only one traitor. Extraordinary, isn't it? But one may be enough. He escaped us, and this was only a few hours ago. Our Security and Intelligence agents have orders to kill him on sight if they find him, and that's the first time in our history such an order has been given."

Galinin stopped himself when he began unconsciously tugging at his beard. "How does his escape threaten the Phoenix or any of our hopes?"

"For one thing, one of our top psychoscientists diagnoses him as a paranoid schizophrenic. For another, *I* am the focus of his mania. I robbed him of the Phoenix and destroyed all hope of realization of his ambitions."

"That *would* make him a formidable antagonist. If he vents his mania on you, how will he do it?"

Alexand's mouth curved in a bitter smile. "By again betraying me to my enemies. If you grant me amnesty as an envoy, the SSB will no longer qualify as such, so he must betray me to Selasis, who is my enemy—and the Society's—as much as he is yours."

Galinin frowned, feeling out the grim implications in this warning.

"You said you robbed this man of the Phoenix. Can I be sure you speak for the whole of the Phoenix now?"

"Yes. For a reunited Phoenix with the wounds of schism healed."

Galinin gave him an oblique glance. "I appreciate your admission of the existence of a schism. And your warning."

Alexand reached under the cuff of his right sleeve. "Now the second item you must know about before we go on—and this is a much happier revelation."

It was an imagraph he'd taken from his cuff. He studied it a moment with an oddly pensive smile.

"Grandser, I have another ghost to present to you." He

handed him the imagraph. "Adrien is still very much among the living. Master Hawkwood made an error; he didn't succeed in killing her."

Galinin took the imagraph, wondering why it didn't come as more of a shock that Adrien was alive. Perhaps having accepted one ghost, a second seemed quite matter of course.

"Alexand, I couldn't be happier if . . ." He frowned at the square of film. There was Adrien, smiling out at him, even lovelier than he remembered her, and in her arms—

Galinin blinked and brought the imagraph closer. She was holding two infants, each a mirror image of the other, one straining toward a wail of complaint, the other obliviously asleep.

"Alexand, what—they're . . . they're yours? Oh, Holy God. But when . . . how . . . ?"

He laughed. "I'm still nearly as astounded as you, Grandser. They're three weeks old, and I didn't even know about them until they were born, but that's a long story, which I don't have time to recount now." He leaned forward and gestured toward the imagraph. "That's Richard, the first born, on the right, and on the left, Eric. Or perhaps it's Rich on the left and Eric on the right. I still get confused."

Galinin laughed, staring transfixed at the imagraph. "I can understand that. Well, they're . . . very handsome. Oh, Alex, think of it—Elise's grandsons."

"Your great-grandsons," he said softly.

"Yes. My great-grandsons. Well, now I can—" Galinin stopped, frowning. He'd almost said it aloud. *Now I can die content.* A strangely morbid thought.

Still, mortality is a fact of life.

Perhaps he was so much aware of his own mortality because he'd been given in Alexand, and now in his sons, a sense of posterity that had long been absent from his thoughts. And he felt no dread for his mortality now, none of the old, exhausting sense of futility. These two infants, like the fact of Alexand's living, changed everything, and Galinin was close to tears, so overwhelming was the new sense of hope, a sense of the reality of a meaningful future.

He gazed at the imagraph, then, frowning in preoccupation, rose.

"Excuse me a moment. There's something I must have Selig do, and he may as well get started on it." He went to the desk without waiting for any comment Alexand might have made; he was too intent on his purpose. At the desk, he switched on the intercom. "Master Selig, are you alone?"

Selig looked anxiously out at him from the screen. "Yes, my lord."

"Good. Somewhere in your files there must be a proper documentary form for a Chairman's decree of amnesty to an envoy of the enemy."

"Uh... why, yes, my lord. I don't recall ever having need for... for such a document, but I'm sure—"

"Find it, and prepare it in quadruplicate, or whatever is necessary. The name of the decreed envoy will be Alex Ransom, First Commander of Fleet Operations, the Society of the Phoenix."

Selig dutifully wrote it out, but he couldn't conceal his astonishment. Just as dutifully, he asked no questions, except, "When I have the document prepared, shall I bring it in for your signature, my lord?"

"No, I'll 'com you when I'm ready. Thank you, Selig."

Alexand had risen to stand at the windowall. As Galinin returned to his chair, he looked around at him, eyes reflecting amazement, and beyond that, wondering gratitude.

"Grandser, you haven't even heard the terms yet."

Galinin shrugged. "Well, then, perhaps we should get to that—unless you have more surprises for me."

"I do have something else. An offering I make to you personally, not to the Directorate."

"Something under the table to insure my support?"

"That doesn't seem to be necessary. It's more in the nature of something to *free* you to offer support. To free you of Selasis. Grandser, Karlis Selasis *is* sterile. Yes, the rumors are true. I can't provide proof, however; not the kind acceptable to the Board of Succession. But you don't need proof; the Chairman can demand a Board investigation without presenting evidence. The proof will present itself in a simple physical examination."

Galinin felt his pulse quickening, and for a time he could only look up at Alexand, searching his face for an answer that was there, yet he still had to ask the question.

"Alexand, are you *sure* beyond a doubt?"

"I'm sure. I wouldn't offer it otherwise."

"No, of course not." He sagged back into his chair, staring at the imagraph still in his hand. "If only I'd had the courage . . . I came so close to ordering a Board investigation before the wedding." But that, he reminded himself, was weeping over birds flown. His eyes narrowed thoughtfully. "The Directorate is meeting tomorrow morning—as you're no doubt aware. I'll present you as an envoy then, and I think that would be a very auspicious time for the Board to get my investigation order." He laughed caustically. "I hope I don't miss seeing Orin's face when the news reaches him."

"And I hope I'm with you."

"Yes, well, I suppose we must put our grim anticipation aside for now. Is that the last of your surprises?"

"If there are more, they'll be surprises to me, too. So on to the terms." He settled himself in his chair again, facing Galinin. "These things generally fall into three categories: threats, offers, and demands."

"Mm. Well, you may as well begin with the threats."

"That seems to be the accepted order. First, we threaten a continuation of hostilities. Obviously we can't maintain hostilities indefinitely on an overt military level, but you don't know our limits there, and we *can* maintain them indefinitely on a covert subversive level, a far greater threat, since we're already well entrenched in every branch of the Concord." Then Alexand turned to the windowall, putting his face in profile to Galinin, and there was an inexplicable transformation, a forbidding coldness in his eyes as unnerving as it was unexpected.

He said, "The second threat is the Brother."

Galinin stared blankly at him. "What do you mean?"

"You've gone to the trouble of informing yourself about the Brother; you know the extent of his influence among the Bonds." He looked around, regarding Galinin with chill detachment. "I've preached submission and peace to the Bonds all these years, but I can as easily preach resistance and revolt, and I can make it, in their eyes, a holy war."

"Alexand! You—I can't believe you'd do that. You know what it would mean."

"Anarchy? A third dark age?" He shrugged negligently. "Well, my lord, we're already well along that path."

Galinin was incapable of responding to that, a part of his mind assuring him it couldn't be true, another reeling with the realization of a monstrous error in judgment. Then, as suddenly as it appeared, that air of casual ruthlessness vanished, and Alexand shook his head slowly, his eyes haunted with memories.

"No, Grandser, the Brother will never preach war. His power is a gift of the Lamb. I'll admit that to *you*, but to no one else. The other Directors will have to deal with a warmongering Brother as a very real possibility."

Galinin took a deep breath. "Well, you make it a very convincing possibility."

"It *must* be convincing. At any rate, that concludes the list of threats. As for the offers, some are the obverse of the threats, of course. A cessation of hostilities on all levels and the pacific influence of the Brother. We also offer the rather abstract potential of the Phoenix as an ally, as a repository of knowledge, a research institute, and a data gathering and interpretation facility. As such, it has no parallel in the Concord. It's an incalculably valuable tool."

"Yes, I believe that, but it *is* a rather abstract concept."

"True. As abstract as the real aims of the Phoenix—something that will not enter into the negotiations. But we have some offerings that will demonstrate the value of our intellectual and technological capabilities in concrete terms." He reached into a pocket hidden under his belt, took out a tape spool, and handed it to Galinin. "You can scan this at your leisure. It contains descriptions and specifications for various processes and devices ranging from centrifugal ore separators, to power systems amplifiers, to a modified electroharp. In all, there are 1,200 items. They'll be distributed by the Board of Franchises, and there's at least one for every House suitable for development under existing franchises."

"Very politic," Galinin commented wryly as he pocketed the spool. "That should make the Phoenix a bit more palatable to the Court of Lords."

"And the Directors. They haven't been excluded from the largesse. We also have another invention to offer, but it isn't listed on that spool." He paused, looking directly at Galinin. "The matter transmitter."

"Ah. Then it *is* something more than a myth."

"You know it is. Its potentials as a strategic weapon are obvious—and perhaps it should be listed among our threats."

Galinin tilted his head to one side, studying Alexand. "And the Phoenix is willing to surrender this weapon to the Concord?"

Alexand smiled coolly. "Not to *surrender* it; to offer it in exchange for what we want. And the MT is much more than a weapon. It's one of those profound inventions, like nulgrav or SynchShift, that will change the very shape of civilization. It will be a far more practical method of moving goods and passengers over interplanetary or interstellar distances than anything now in existence. And, Grandser . . ." He hesitated, smiling to himself. "Andreas . . . Dr. Riis, who birthed this profound invention, is a man of almost romantic vision. He sees the MT as humankind's door to the stars."

Galinin saw the wistful light in Alexand's eyes and knew Andreas Riis wasn't alone in that "romantic" vision.

"I hope he's right, Alex. But forgive me for bringing you down from the stars so rudely—what about the matter transmitter for planetside transportation?"

At that Alexand laughed briefly, his tone brisk as he replied, "The MT's efficiency drops sharply in comparison to existing modes of transport at distances of less than ten thousand kilometers. It won't be a threat to Hild Robek."

Galinin frowned. "I'm not sure I understand."

"The term 'threat' in this context? There's a stipulation to this offer, Grandser. The MT will be presented *only* to the Concord as a whole, to be operated and administered by a Concord agency comparable to Conpol or Conmed. But, because its efficiency is relatively low at short distances, the MT in the Concord's hands will offer the Robek Planetary Transystems no appreciable competition."

"I see." Galinin frowned on finding himself tugging at his beard again. "But it *will* offer Badir Selasis competition. I'm surprised you didn't include this as an under-the-table offer along with Karlis's sterility. It's as much a threat to Selasis. Alex, this . . . traitor of whom you warned me, does he know about the matter transmitter and this stipulation?"

"Yes, and he can tell Selasis about them."

Galinin felt the static charge of fear; it seemed to come from the very air around him.

"Can he tell Orin what you've told me about Karlis?"

Alexand hesitated, then finally nodded. "Yes."

Galinin didn't pursue the potentials in an alliance between Selasis and the traitor, but he was beginning to understand the real dimensions of Alexand's warning.

"Well, have you any other offers?"

"No, Grandser, no more offers. Which brings us to the demands. First, of course, amnesty for all Phoenix members and the immediate release of any now in SSB custody. Second, the Phoenix will be removed from the realm of traitors and thieves. Or enemies. I don't know what it will eventually become; a working partner of the Concord, ideally, but a kind of silent partner."

Galinin nodded. "Legalization is not, I assume, the end of your demands."

"No. Our second demand is the reinstatement of the Lord Alexand DeKoven Woolf with full powers intact as of his 'death.'"

That wasn't at all surprising; Galinin fully expected it, and yet it brought another frown.

"That might complicate the Woolf succession."

"It will complicate more than the succession. So will our final demand." His left hand closed into a fist, then opened again. "The existing declaration of succession to the Chairmanship names Lord Woolf as your immediate successor, but *I* was to be your true successor by virtue of my Galinin genes."

"Yes. As a matter of fact, that declaration still stands as written. Some of the Directors found it advantageous to leave the question of Phillip's successor to the Chairmanship unresolved for the present. But I'm sure you know that, and I'm wandering. Or perhaps I know what you're going to say, and I'm not sure how to deal with it."

"Would you find it unacceptable?"

"Put it in words so we can both be sure we know what we're talking about."

He smiled at that, but only fleetingly. "The Lord Alexand, fully reinstated, will be made direct successor to the Chairmanship."

Galinin could almost have anticipated the choice of words,

including that depersonalized use of third person, the same formal mode used in reference to "Lord Woolf."

Alexand asked again, "Would you find it unacceptable?"

"No." He pulled in a deep breath. "I wanted you in that damnable chair eventually, Alexand, and your genes were only a convenient rationale. Evin should have fallen heir to it; he was trained and had quite a remarkable aptitude for it. But when he was killed . . ." Strange, the memory was still weighted with pain, even after twelve years. "I took a good look at you then. You were only—what? Seventeen. Still, I saw something in you; recognized it, perhaps. No, Alex, *I* don't find it unacceptable. The problem is that it means bypassing Phillip. It's not that he's so ambitious for that chair. No one in his right mind really wants it, but one must always consider the alternatives. However, if *I'm* willing to accept you as an alternative, I have no doubt he'll accept you."

"Or will he only accept your decision? I can't afford to have the Lord Woolf as an enemy on the Directorate."

Galinin sighed, and it was with a little relief that he saw the mask of detachment slip briefly. What Alexand meant was that he didn't want his *father* as an enemy.

"I think he'll accept *you*. I don't mean to say he'll welcome you immediately. He'll need time to get past the initial shock and that peculiarly parental reaction of resentment when you've suffered grief or fear for a child, then find it well and safe."

Alexand said tightly, "He has every right to resent his suffering. And his grief . . . for Mother."

"Yes, I suppose so."

"Grandser, I didn't know. I didn't know about Mother."

"I'm sure you didn't." Galinin left it at that, saddened by the revelation of the travail of guilt only hinted at with those words. Elise would never have wanted her son to bear such a burden for her. "Let me talk to Phillip, and give him some time, if possible. Once he gets past the shock, he'll see your resurrection as a miracle, as I do. But back to the Woolf succession. Relegating Justin to the position of second born will serve to antagonize Sandro Omer, and you don't want him as an enemy on the Directorate, either. However, there's another possibility. I haven't made a declaration of House succession yet. Rather foolish at my age, I know, but in looking over the selection of nephews and cousins, it didn't really seem to matter whom I named. But you would be a logical—and genetically appropriate—choice. And if you were heir to Daro Galinin, that might make it easier for the Lords to accept you as direct heir to the..." He frowned, realizing he'd lost Alexand's attention.

Alexand held up his hand, asking silence, listening intently to something Galinin couldn't hear, and it seemed to disturb him profoundly. Finally, he turned, eyes narrowed, looking past him to the desk, then around the room.

"Grandser, I'm wearing an earceiver. I've just been told that the peripheral shock screens have gone on."

Galinin became aware again of that prickling sensation of fear that his skin seemed to take up from the air.

"The shock screens? In this room?"

"Does Selig have access to the controls?"

"No one does, except me. Well, there's the emergency control center for the entire building. But, Alex, why—"

"I can't explain now." He rose, a smooth silent motion; he seemed to emanate a feral alertness that only added to Galinin's uneasiness. "I'll leave as I came. We'll have to continue this—"

He had taken two steps toward the doors, but now he froze, staring in the direction of the desk, and Galinin didn't have time to turn and see what fixed his attention in sudden fearful realization.

A dull thud somewhere behind him.

And Alexand was leaping toward him.

"*Get down! Grandse——*"

Galinin was hurled to the floor, the chair toppling under him. He saw the window glass, reinforced with strands of flexsteel, cave outward and turn frosty with millions of bound splinters.

A lightning bolt had struck the room, the thunder of it a crushing blast; his head and ears seemed to explode with it.

"My lord? My lord? Oh, Holy God—*my lord!*"

Selig's voice was dim and distant against a rumbling whine that wouldn't stop, that peaked and ebbed with the agonizing pounding of his heart. Shufflings and murmurings, shouts and pleas. He couldn't make sense of them, couldn't hear.

On his back. He was lying on his back. The very weight of his body seemed to press the air from his lungs.

An importunate voice. "Don't move him! Wait . . . doctor . . . wait . . . doctor coming . . . wait. . . ."

He couldn't see.

"My lord? Oh, my lord, please, don't try to move."

He *couldn't* move. No. His left arm, reaching across his body, encountering a hand. Selig's.

Be quiet, Selig. Be quiet.

I must think, remember, understand, I must . . .

Alexand.

What happened to Alexand, Selig?

He turned his head. Lolling like a broken doll's. But he *could* turn it, and now he could see. At least there were blurred shadows wavering before him.

Where is Alexand? Selig, damn you . . .

He'd forgotten something. Forgotten to make the words into sounds. What if he couldn't—

There was Alexand, a blur of blue in a clot of black. Struggling. Guards. Damn fools, didn't they know about his arm?

The image came into focus, and chagrin locked in a burning band around his stuttering heart. He reached out toward the dim shapes with his functioning hand.

"Stop! Let that . . . man . . . go!"

Had he really said the words? Oh, God, if he couldn't make them understand . . .

Yes, they did understand; the struggle had stopped. But Alexand had fallen.

"Selig, is he . . . alive?"

"I . . . uh, yes, my lord. But, please, you shouldn't—"

"Listen . . . listen to me. Am-amnesty." The word seemed so hard to shape. He strained at it, trying to shout it, hearing only a whisper muffled in the shuffling and rumbling.

Two figures came between him and Alexand. Their faces loomed above him at some incredible distance. Still, he knew them. Did they think he wouldn't?

Orin Selasis.

The waiting vulture.

The other was coming closer. Trevor Robek. Thank the God for that.

"Trevor? Can you . . . hear me?"

"Yes, Mathis. Just rest. You'll be—"

"No. Selig, you *know*. Docu-mm——" Oh, damn, he *had* to get the words out. "Document. I had . . . you draw up—"

"Yes, my lord. The decree of envoy status. Yes, I did draw it up. But, please, my lord, you must—"

"Trevor? Where are you?" It was getting dark in the room. Something had blown the lights out.

"Mathis, I'm here."

"I charge you . . . witness . . . I decreed—that man . . . I granted . . ."

And finally someone was turning off the noise. Well, that was a kindness.

". . . amnesty."

PHOENIX MEMFILES: DEPT HUMAN SCIENCES: BASIC SCHOOL
                    (HS/BS)
SUBFILE: LECTURE, BASIC SCHOOL 18 AVRIL 3252
                    GUEST LECTURER: RICHARD LAMB
                    SUBJECT: POST-DISASTERS HISTORY:
                    THE WAR OF THE TWIN PLANETS
                    (3208–3210)
DOC LOC #819/219–1253/1812–1648–1843252

I've always found comparisons between historical figures tempting, and another one I won't resist is between Lionar Mankeen and Elor Ussher Peladeen. To begin with, they were both the last Lords of their Houses, and both died fighting for the cause of human liberty.

There is even some physical resemblance. Both were tall and fair-skinned, and both had red hair, although Elor Peladeen's wasn't the vibrant color of Mankeen's. And both came into First Lordship of their Houses at early ages with the premature deaths of their fathers, Mankeen at twenty-five, Elor at twenty-four, and both engaged the Concord in hopeless wars.

178

However, there are equally strong contrasts to be drawn.

Elor Peladeen knew his war to be hopeless even before it began; Mankeen didn't.

There is also an obvious contrast between the women they married. Mankeen's marriage to Lady Lizbeth Lesellen was a House union and could never be described as a loving relationship, nor could Lizbeth be described as a true partner and helpmeet. Peladeen's marriage to Manir Kalister was from the beginning a union of love, and she was very much a partner in his affairs, and a fervent partisan in his cause. She was a descendant of a Kalister VisLord, one of those stranded in Centauri by the Mankeen Revolt, and through various marriages—which I won't attempt to unravel—actually carried Peladeen blood herself. Elite marriages in post-Mankeen Centauri involved a great deal of interbreeding simply because so few Elite were available for marriages. But although the Elite generally married within their own class, even after the Republic was well established, those marriages didn't have to be House unions. In this, at least, the Elite were given the gift of choice.

Elor and Manir chose each other when he was twenty-one and she was only sixteen, so it's said. They were married three years later in 3202, the year Elor was so abruptly elevated to First Lordship. They had only one child, a son, Predis, and I doubt his arrival in a world on the verge of collapsing on his parents' heads was intentional. He was born in 3208, six years after Elor and Manir were married, and only a month after the onset of the War of the Twin Planets. It's recorded that Lord and Lady Peladeen were especially loving parents, and I believe that. I'm sure they didn't want a child—not one who would be condemned by his parentage to an early death—but no doubt that made this child, once born, all the more precious to them.

Of particular interest to us is Peladeen's aid and encouragement to the Phoenix. He was a man of extraordinary vision, despite his youth, who recognized in the Phoenix a hope for what he knew he would be dying for. Peladeen bore the title of Lord—and with honor and grace—but he was essentially a Republican and far more a proponent of the human right of choice than any of his predecessors in the House, and even more than many of his Fesh contemporaries in the Republic. You know about his funding of the Phoenix, of his vital role in the building of Fina, and the tight cover of secrecy he maintained to protect it. The nonmembers who assisted in the construction had no idea what they were building—they were told it was a military installation—or even *where* they were building. Peladeen told only two people about the Phoenix: his wife and the Prime Minister at that time, Lair M'Kenzy, who was also Peladeen's closest friend, and it's a measure of his love for Manir and his respect for M'Kenzy that he shared the hope he took in the Phoenix with them.

But the Phoenix was their only hope; there was nothing else they could rationally take hope in.

In one lettape to Andreas Riis, Peladeen says, and seems to find it amusing, "We're giving them a hard run, Andreas, harder than they ever expected." "They" was Confleet, of course, and the Armed Forces of the Republic did indeed give them a hard run. The formal declaration of war was voted by the Directorate on 2 Januar 3208, and that lettape was sent 20 May 3209, and at that point, incredibly, there was still some room for doubt as to the outcome of the War. The Republic's Armed Forces fought with intelligence, flexibility, and courage that Confleet couldn't equal. Ultimately, of course, the brute weight of superior numbers shifted the scales, and in the last six months of 3209, the Republic suffered one disastrous defeat after another. Maxim Drakonis had declared himself an ally of the Concord even before the declaration of war, and the Inner Planets served as advance bases for Confleet that were particularly telling in the campaign, since the Republic couldn't attack them without risking a power outage that would kill millions on Castor and on the Inner Planets themselves. However, it should be noted that Maxim conscientiously maintained the power beams for Castor, although the survival of its population would have had no bearing on his House's survival, and there is evidence that he had the backing of Constan Galinin in this, although some Confleet commanders wanted to cut off those umbilicals, calling it simply a tactical maneuver.

Peladeen ordered the evacuation of as much of Castor's population as possible to Pollux, but he didn't have ships enough to evacuate more than a quarter of its inhabitants. In the last days of 3209, he concentrated the evacuation on

Helen and virtually emptied the city, and on 1 Januar 3210, the New Year Day, he and his top military commanders retreated to his Helen estate. Lair M'Kenzy insisted on accompanying him, as did Lady Manir with their son. After the Battle of Helen—which is a misnomer; it should be called simply the *Destruction* of Helen—on 12 Januar, Elor Peladeen's body was found in the ruins of his estate along with M'Kenzy's. The bodies of Manir and Predis weren't identified, but then few of the bodies cast into mass graves after the Peladeen Purge were.

Yes, there was another Purge, and remember, it occurred less than fifty years ago. There are many people here in Fina now who lived through it. I say remember it in order to remind you that the veneer of behavioral codes that make a "civilized" human being is very thin. We are always only the blink of an eye away from bestiality.

There is so much about the War of the Twin Planets and its aftermath that is unforgivable. Perhaps I feel so strongly because it's so close to me in time. History has recorded worse atrocities. I can't forgive them, either.

And what justification would I have for forgiving the Peladeen Purge? For the systematic execution of nearly every Republic parlementarian and official, and not only the officers, but every enlisted soldier in the Armed Forces, as well as any Elite even distantly related to the Peladeen or a great many who simply happened to be living in Peladeen's Centauri? How can I forgive the looting and wanton destruction of the Peladeen Estate, and particularly its museum with its collection of rare art, some pieces dating to Pre-Disasters periods, or the purposeful demolition of the Republic University and its great library? And how can I forgive Kozmar Hamid when on his occupation of the Peladeen holdings on Pollux he declared all surviving citizens of the Republic resident on those holdings—which included most of the inhabited areas of Pollux—his Bonds, whatever their former training or rank, condemning people who had been free citizens, educated and skilled, to a life of brute servitude, and their children to ignorant slavery. Any who objected went before execution squads, and hundreds of thousands chose that alternative rather than Bondage.

Maxim Drakonis and Almor, Lord of the new House of Eliseer, were far more equitable in their treatment of the defeated. Eliseer imposed Bondage on none of the survivors, nor did Drakonis. Almor brought his Bonds from the Cognate House of Camine, and Drakonis, who actually had little need for a large Bond workforce, was granted five thousand Bonds from the Concord. In every other way Drakonis and Eliseer were more merciful and reasonable in the aftermath of the War, but unfortunately Hamid was made Lord of Pollux by a Directorate strongly influenced by Jofry Selasis, and most of Centauri's population was on Pollux.

Something else I can't forgive is the treatment of Elor Peladeen by the Concord's historians. A small thing, perhaps, yet it rankles with me. He has been consistently pictured as a deluded fool acting under the influence of the villainous masterminds of the Republic, like M'Kenzy. Elor Peladeen deserves better. For that matter, so does M'Kenzy. I say Peladeen deserves better not because I think the opinions of the living mean anything to the dead, but because he was a man of intelligence, foresight, and, above all, of epic courage. Such courage is rare in human history, and it's important that it be recognized and revered. It's important for the living, for the future living, to know that such courage is within the reach of human beings.

I only hope for our sake, for that of future generations, Elor Peladeen will one day be justly and truly represented in history. His courage is a vital part of our human heritage.

CHAPTER XX: 15 Octov 3258

●Ⅱ●

1.

Alexand lay stretched out on the bed scrutinizing the reflections in his boots, his left arm folded under his head, right arm motionless and aching at his side. He'd made himself comfortable to the point of removing his cloak and jacket and opening his shirt. The pursuit of comfort was tolerated in "protective custody," if not the pursuit of sleep. Even at this late hour, the ceiling was a flat glow of light. Darkness was *not* tolerated here; it would blind the monitors.

There were four sensor lenses, one in each corner, and no effort had been made to camouflage them. The audio monitors were a little more difficult to locate only because they were smaller.

His every move, every sound, was duly recorded.

Yet he had an oppressive sense of isolation that stirred memories of the Cliff. He'd been carefully searched and stripped of the two monitors that had been his link with the Phoenix. Only the MT fixes in his boots had been overlooked; they didn't register on the montectors.

Still, his accommodations were in marked contrast to those at the Cliff. The room was relatively large, perhaps four by five meters. The walls were a soft blue, the floor covered with a sienna thermcarpet; the bed was narrow, but passably comfortable; and he was even provided a wall-mounted clock-calendar. He looked up at it and watched the numbers change.

24:01 TST. A new day. 15 Octov 3258.

Concord Day was relegated to history.

Commander Alex Ransom was relegated to this comfortable cell in the Conpol Central DC.

But it wasn't an SSB DC.

He levered himself into a sitting position on the side of the bed, his breath catching at every movement, and surveyed his comfortable accommodations. The bed was placed against one of the shorter walls, the head in the corner. The corridor opening—there was no door; only the shimmer of a shock screen—was directly opposite him. Near the longer wall to his right a round table was placed, suitable, he supposed, for dining. Two chairs flanked it. Perhaps they thought he'd be having guests. He enjoyed the further luxury of a private bath. At least it adjoined the room and was separated by a solid door. No square centimeter here was in fact private.

He pressed his hand gingerly to his forehead. He'd survived unscathed the lethal rain of debris from the explosion, but somewhere in the struggle with the Guards, he'd taken a blow to the left temple to add to the aching of his arm. But he was probably fortunate to be alive, and he wasn't sure why he was. The Conpol officers who brought him here made it clear, if only by innuendo, that they considered him condemned in his guilt.

Yet they wouldn't tell him whether Galinin was alive or dead.

Grandser—

The image of that white-locked head, carmined with blood, leapt out of the dim fragments of memory. It was the last thing he remembered seeing before he lost consciousness.

He *must* live. He *must* be alive.

Panic. It waited in ambush at every junction of thoughts. He counted out ten deep, spaced breaths until he had it under control, then rose and went to the window.

It was just beyond the foot of the bed, a rectangle two meters long and one high, affording a splendid view of Concordia from this point on the fifteenth level. He could see parts of the Plaza complex, the shining white shaft of the Hall of the Directorate, and the triple spires of the Cathedron. And he could see the warning lights of emergency vehicles flashing along the traffic grids, watch the Conpol patrols pass in grim formations, and in the distance, see erupting clouds of smoke and fireflies of flame. Probably the Tesmier chemical warehouses. The billow of smoke to the right and half a kilometer beyond probably came from one of the Concord Bond compounds. There were others too distant to identify.

Concordia was no longer the city of lights.

Many of its lights were out by order, he was sure. Curfew. The incessant police patrols indicated that. Some, in broad swaths of darkness, were put out by violence and disaster. And over the city as far as his eye could seek, hung a dirty orange pall, glowing hotly under a burdened layer of cloud.

A cell with a view. A luxury, indeed.

And this hellish view might cost him his life.

The warning was spelled out on the sill: "Caution. This window equipped with shock screen."

That meant that nowhere in this comfortable cage would he be less than two and a half meters from a shock screen. The limit for safe MT transing was five meters.

Selasis had found an invaluable ally in Predis Ussher. Alexand wondered when Ussher would discover that he hadn't been so fortunate in Selasis.

No stars in this sky. He closed his eyes. Stars always spelled freedom.

Adrien, if I die, will you live for our sons?

Perhaps she would, but few human beings could sanely survive the same grief twice.

Footsteps.

The spasm of tension translated into pain. The Cliff. His body remembered. Booted footsteps.

Two booted and one . . . soft-soled shoes.

At length, they stopped outside his door. There were two Conpol guards; one stayed outside in the corridor and switched off the shock screen while the other escorted the third man in.

His white tunic and the red caduceus on his allegiance badge proclaimed him a Conmed doctor. A short, stocky, washed-out man of middle age, he blinked and squinted myopically at Alexand.

"This the patient? Well . . . uh, sit down. Might as well sit down."

Alexand went to the bed and began pulling off the glove, while the guard took up a position a meter to his left, and the doctor looked around helplessly, then brought up one of the chairs from the table. He sat down in front of Alexand, opened his medical case on the bed, then frowned at Alexand's un-gloved hand.

"This has already been bandaged." He looked to the guard for an answer to that enigma.

"Old wound, Dr. Cambry. Captain Edmin said for you to look it over, maybe patch it up."

"Oh. Well. Let's see . . ." He noticed the swollen bruise on Alexand's temple and squinted at it. "Bit of a lump here, I see." He fumbled about in his case. "Dizziness? Anything like that? Double vision?"

"No, only a headache," Alexand replied.

"Oh. Well, uh . . . might as well have a look inside." Cambry gave a short laugh—apparently that was meant to be humor-ous—and took a stylus light from his case, then crouched over Alexand, shining the light into one eye, holding his head steady with a hand on the right side of his head. "Straight ahead . . . don't blink. Good. Well. Now, the other. . . ."

Alexand was finding it more difficult to control his annoy-ance than his blinking, until he became aware of a sensation in his right ear so unexpected, he might have jerked away if the doctor hadn't had such a deceptively strong grip on his head.

Cambry had just slipped a miniceiver into his ear.

He was a Phoenix agent.

The glaring light probing his eye, Cambry's face so close to his, hid his momentary surprise from the guard and the monitors as effectively as they had the actual placement of the 'ceiver.

"Well, everything seems to be . . ." The doctor looked at Alexand's right hand with a sigh of resignation. "So, I guess . . . uh, the shirt. Better get it off. Here, I'll help."

The simple process of taking off the shirt became complicated with Cambry's help, but it was at length accomplished. He sighed again as he examined the bandaged arm.

"Well, you seem to have . . . well. That hurt a bit?"

Alexand was hard put not to laugh. The man was extraordinarily good in his role, but it was an understatement to say his bumbling handling of the arm hurt "a bit."

Alexand's jaw was set as he said, "Yes, it . . . hurts."

"Oh. I suppose . . . well, better give you something for that." He rattled around in his case and brought out a pressyringe. "Allergies to analgesics? Enkephaline?"

"Not that I know of."

As Cambry began the injection into the shoulder joint, Alexand leaned back, making his left arm a prop, reveling in the cessation of pain as numbness enveloped his right arm. Cambry muddled in his case, taking out gauze, tape, scissors, biostatic solution, and ointment. And finally, Alexand heard what he'd been waiting for, preparing himself for; the monitors wouldn't catch so much as a flicker in his eyes.

A voice sounded in his ear, a familiar voice.

"Alex, this is Ben. I'm on a SynchCom interconn through the Concordia chapter on my personal 'com seq. Ussher probably can't tap into this. Dr. Cambry is on line with me, too. I'll give you a fast rundown on the general stat. First, Galinin is still alive."

It was an effort to control his relief, but again, Cambry's ministrations made good camouflage. Alexand watched with the vague interest that would be expected while the doctor, in an apparent funk of indecision, finally armed himself with scissors and began cutting away the old bandages.

". . . He's unconscious and in critical condition; got hit with some of the flying debris. A life support unit has been set up in the infirmary at his Estate, and a top cranial trauma expert called in. Woolf is overseeing Galinin's security, and it's tight. He brought Dr. Stel from his Estate, and except for the specialist and Dr. Perris, Galinin's personal physician, nobody else is allowed anywhere near him. Woolf's taken over at the Hall, too; Chairman Designate, and he's got his hands full. The news about the bomb leaked out and hit the vidicom screens before he could do anything about it, and set off mass panics and riots in nearly every major city in both Systems. He ordered curfews and closed the public transystems except for emergency use, and he went on the screens himself. That probably did more good than anything else, along with getting a good tight hold on the 'casters. According to them, everything's under control, both in Centauri and the Hall of the Directorate. . . ."

Cambry had the old bandages off and was studying the arm with a fastidious frown. Some of the grafts hadn't held. In accordance with his orders to "patch it up," he simply closed the reopened wounds with temporary tape sutures. No doubt his superiors would consider more permanent repair a waste of time.

Alexand watched him, ever conscious of the monitors, the questions in his mind multiplying, straining to be voiced, but he could only listen and hope Ben would answer them.

"We don't have much info on what happened in Galinin's office, Alex. A bomb, of course, and it hit dead center on the desk. It had to come from the private entrance, and one thing that's been overlooked in the confusion is that the Galinin House guard on duty there has disappeared. But nobody's interested in that. The case is closed, and you're the one trapped in it. You probably would've been shot down on the spot, or turned over to the SSB, except Galinin *did* manage a few words before he passed out. An interesting little sidelight is that Selasis just happened to be on his way to see Galinin when the bomb went off. He had Robek with him; wanted a witness from the other side, I guess. Anyway, that backfired to a point. Galinin told Robek he'd granted you amnesty as an envoy, so Selasis couldn't ignore it."

Grandser . . . thank you for my life. And I brought that bomb to you almost as if I delivered it with my own hand.

"That still hurting some?"

Alexand focused on the doctor and his indirect warning. "Some, yes."

"Oh. Well, I could give you another shot, I guess. Maybe the dosage . . . hard to tell sometimes . . ."

"That won't be necessary."

Cambry shrugged indifferently and went on with his work, and Alexand waited for Ben's voice, for answers.

"That bomb came from Selasis; you know it as well as I do, but we can't prove a damn thing, and nobody seems to be interested in looking past you for the guilty party." He paused, his breath coming out in an audible sigh. Cambry had begun rebandaging the arm, starting, as Erica always did, at the shoulder.

"Alex, I wish to hell you could answer some questions for me; if you saw something or somebody. At least Galinin is still alive, and he bought us a little time with that amnesty decree. Selasis will have to get a Directorate majority to override that. Meanwhile, we've got four agents in the DC, and you've still got your MT fixes. Cambry will leave a monitor in the room so we can... uh, hold on a second."

Alexand waited, his gaze shifting disinterestedly to the guard, whose attention was wandering, his boredom evident.

Then Ben's voice again. "Got word through the Concordia chapter—Phillip Woolf just arrived on the landing roof at the DC, so brace yourself. Let's see what other news I've got— oh, our agents in the Selasid Estate say Orin's hosting a very secret guest in the Security wing with nobody but Hawkwood's top staff in attendance. It has to be Ussher. No real news from here. Fina's more or less back in one piece; the recovery's going well. I—uh, asked Lady Adrien if she wanted to talk to you, but she thought maybe it'd be better... well, she said you'd understand. Erica moved her into HS 1's guest room with your sons. You don't need to worry about them, and Lady Adrien... took it well. About you."

Ben paused then, searching for words, Alexand knew, words of encouragement. There was no way to let him know they weren't necessary; he had faith that the Phoenix would do everything humanly possible to save him. And he knew exactly how little was possible.

"Alex, just remember, we're... with you." Then, after a short, unsuccessful laugh, "Anyway, we can't afford to lose you now. So... later..."

The doctor was mumbling to himself as he worked a strip of gauze around the elbow, the guard was tapping impatiently on his holster, and in the distance, the multiple thuds of booted feet echoed.

Father, this wasn't the way I wanted it.

The guard roused himself and went to the door to confer with the other guard in the hall. Dr. Cambry seemed oblivious. It wasn't until the beat of booted steps stopped outside the door that he finally looked up, sought the guard where he had been standing, then peered around at the door.

"Oh, dear. What . . . oh . . ."

The Lord Phillip DeKoven Woolf strode into the room, flanked by two scarlet-uniformed House guards and a perspiring Conpol captain. The doctor stared with sagging jaw, then scrambled to his feet, bowed jerkily, and dropped the roll of gauze; it unfurled silently and spent itself at Woolf's feet.

The captain snapped, "Cambry! I thought you'd be finished by now!"

While the doctor nervously made excuses and tried to collect the gauze, Alexand waited silently, looking up into his father's face.

It was a mask, perfectly controlled, expressionless, unreadable. Only when he first entered and his eye chanced on Alexand's arm, still exposed below the elbow, was there a hint of reaction, but it was too fleeting to be interpreted.

The mask was enough.

No frown of rage, no glare of chagrin, no accusing stare was necessary. Alexand knew the mask from childhood.

You're as much a traitor as your brother.

He heard the words echoing down the long corridors of memory, while Woolf said quietly to the captain, "Let the doctor finish. I'll wait."

Within a minute, Cambry was back in his chair hurriedly finishing the bandage, the House guards were waiting in the hall, the captain had been sent back to wherever he came from, and the Conpol guard was back in his position at Alexand's left, rigidly at attention. Woolf was sitting by the table, adding nothing to the silence in the room.

At length, Cambry completed his task, mumbled vaguely about an oral analgesic as he put a pill bottle on the bedside table, then stuffed his equipment into his case, and fled to the door, bowing repeatedly to Woolf. The guard, at Woolf's gesture of dismissal, followed him.

By no stretch of the imagination could they be considered alone. The guards waited outside the open door, and the room

was crowded with mechanical eyes and ears. Yet again Alexand
felt that profound sense of isolation, the heritage of the Cliff.
He rose, and it seemed an overwhelming effort, found his shirt
and pulled it on, leaving it unfastened, then put on the glove;
it hid the bandages. He wondered if Woolf would speak at all
if he didn't initiate it. He still hadn't moved, his eyes were still
fixed on him.

Alexand asked, "Is Lord Galinin alive?" The ears behind
the monitors would wonder if he didn't ask that.

"Yes. He's alive."

Alexand's relief wasn't feigned; only a delayed response.
"Thank the God."

"Indeed, Commander Ransom," Woolf said coolly. "Certainly the thanks for his survival aren't due you."

Commander Ransom. Alexand nodded and went to the window to look out at Concordia palled in disaster.

"Then Lord Galinin is still unconscious."

"Is that a question or a guess?" Or a known fact to which
he shouldn't have access; Woolf didn't voice that alternative.

"It's a deduction based on the fact that I'm imprisoned here
and obviously convicted beyond a doubt in your mind of the
attempted assassination of the Chairman." He turned, leaning
back against the window frame. "Why are you here?"

For a long time Woolf only stared at him, his weariness
evident in the shadows under his eyes, the white line around
his mouth.

"I suppose I had to . . . to see you with my own eyes." The
mask slipped then, revealing bewilderment and pain, and behind that true recognition; he was for this moment looking at
the son whom he had sired, nurtured, loved, and grieved.

He said dully, "I was called to Mathis's office and found
him lying unconscious in his own blood, and I was told . . . I
was told that my son is alive. Alexand is *alive*." He laughed,
a hollow, despairing sound, and Alexand closed his eyes wearily.

"Father, I'm sorry. I didn't intend for you to learn of my
living so . . . brutally."

"How could it have been anything *less* than brutal when the
next thing I was told was that my son—my resurrected son—
was responsible for Mathis's . . ." His jaw clamped tight and

he shook his head dazedly. "I thought it had to be an error in identification. Even later when I was given proof from the VP ident taken here, I still couldn't believe it. I had to . . . see you."

Alexand took a step toward him. "And can you believe I'm guilty of trying to kill Grandser? Isn't there any doubt in your mind about that?"

Woolf rose abruptly. "How *can* there be?"

"How can there *not* be? Father, you . . ." He started to say, *You know me; I'm your son.* But the mask was in place again, and what he read in his father's eyes made those words meaningless.

"Commander Ransom, the man who tried to kill Mathis Galinin is not my son."

Alexand turned away, toward the window, and finally he nodded.

"No . . . my lord. He isn't." Then he heard a movement behind him; Woolf starting for the door. "In the God's name, at least let me—"

"Defend yourself? You'll have an opportunity for that—"

"When my case comes to trial? You aren't so naive. At least consider the fact that Galinin instructed Selig to draw up a decree recognizing me as an envoy."

"And under what duress?"

"You know Mathis Galinin better. What kind of duress could I possibly use to induce him to do anything he considered a betrayal of the Concord?"

"What kind of duress? No doubt that would come under the general heading of what you call 'conditioning.'"

"My lord, you are, naturally enough, ill informed on that subject. Mathis Galinin is highly resistant; I doubt he could be conditioned at all, except in consent. But you still haven't suggested an explanation for my trying to kill him *before* he *signed* the decree, or, in fact, why I'd detonate a bomb while I was still in the same room."

At that, Woolf only shrugged. "I'm quite sure you didn't *intend* to detonate it at that time, but accidents and errors do occur. You can't deny the fact that when that bomb went off, you were alone with Mathis in a locked room to which no one else had access."

"Have you forgotten the private entrance? Did you question

the guard? You know the guards at that entrance always carry lectrikeys in case of emergency."

"I didn't question him personally. I've had other more pressing matters to occupy me—like riots in every major city, and the Centauri System in shambles."

"Still, I'd advise you to talk to the guard, because the bomb *did* come through the private entrance. I saw it."

Woolf eyed him impatiently, but after a short pause folded his arms across his chest and asked mockingly, "You *saw* it? Well, Commander, how did it enter? By balloon, no doubt?"

"Nothing so colorful, my lord. It was thrown into the room by a human hand. Lord Galinin and I were sitting by the windowall. He suggested that. But whoever tossed that bomb into the room expected him to be at his desk, and I should've been there, too. The door is directly behind his chair, which has a very high back. The would-be assassin couldn't see that the chair was unoccupied. But I had a better vantage point; I saw the door open, and I saw the bomb tossed over the back of the chair and onto the desk. It went off within a second of impact."

Woolf wasn't convinced, but Alexand didn't expect him to be; that explanation was more for Ben Venturi than for Woolf.

"All right, Commander, who threw the bomb into the room? The guard, perhaps?"

"All I saw was an arm and hand. It wasn't the guard, unless he bothered to take off his uniform. The sleeve was dark. Black, I think. No—it was brown."

"Brown. Well, I must immediately order Conpol to seek out all brown-sleeved men—or perhaps it was a woman?"

Alexand replied in the same cool tone, but without the sarcasm, "My lord, you'll give no orders to seek out anyone. Why should you? You have the culprit already, delivered by some very convenient twist of fate. You'll play out this little charade exactly as scripted; you'll dance like a puppet until you find out who's pulling the strings, but it'll be too late then. Scapegoating is a dangerous practice." He wondered if Woolf would remember those words from Rich's lips on that last night, the night at the nexus of their lives. "It too often lets the real culprit escape unnoticed and unpunished."

"Am I supposed to regard you as another—sacrificial..."

He hesitated over the word. ". . . lamb being led helplessly to the slaughter?"

"That's exactly what's happening, only I won't be the only one led to this slaughter. There are factors involved in this you aren't even aware of, and they can destroy you and ultimately the Concord, as well as me and the Phoenix."

"In other words, you intend to have your revenge if—"

"*Revenge?* After five years, you *still* don't understand?" Alexand brought himself up short, feeling the tension-induced ache in his arm radiating across his shoulder. "I beg of you— don't dismiss so lightly the possibility that I'm being made a scapegoat. I'm well aware of the highly emotional responses aroused in this situation, and equally aware that they're being expertly used. You haven't been given time to consider the events of the last few hours rationally or logically."

Woolf raised an arched brow. "I suppose you intend to enlighten me—rationally and logically?"

"I'd at least like to point out that to accuse me and the Phoenix of trying to kill Mathis Galinin is a logical absurdity. First, consider the assassination attempt itself. If it were our intention to kill Galinin—and it certainly is not—it wouldn't be necessary for any Phoenix member to enter the Hall of the Directorate, much less the Chairman's office. We have the matter transmitter. You know that. We could trans a bomb into his office—or into the Directorate Chamber, for that matter— at any time, and none of us would have to be within a thousand kilometers of the Hall. And even if it *were* necessary for a Phoenix member to enter the Chairman's office, consider the absurdity of sending *me* on that high-risk mission. It must be obvious that by an accident of birth, I am of some value to the Phoenix."

Woolf's nostrils flared briefly, but otherwise the mask was well under control now.

"In view of the unprovoked attack on Centauri, I'm not sure I understand your definition of absurdity."

"There was nothing absurd about that. Its purpose was to force the Concord to recognize the Phoenix as an enemy power." Then with a faint, oblique smile, "The Concord doesn't bargain with thieves and pirates, does it, my lord? But it *will* bargain with an enemy, and I think you'll concede that a small

power must, when putting itself at odds with a megapower like
the Concord, depend ultimately on achieving its ends through
negotiation."

Woolf remained silent, conceding nothing. But he was still
listening, and Alexand accepted that small favor with bitter
gratitude as he continued, "Consider our position, facing negotiations with the Directorate, negotiations vital to us. Would
we have any conceivable reason for killing Galinin—for removing him from the negotiation process—when the alternative
to Galinin will inevitably be Orin Selasis? Bargaining with the
Directorate under Galinin's leadership will be difficult enough,
but under Lord Orin's leadership, negotiations won't even take
place. *That's* why I say it's absurd to accuse me or the Phoenix
of trying to do away with Galinin. We have everything to lose
by his death, and nothing to gain!"

Woolf had stiffened, and now he said curtly, "May I remind
you, Commander, that *I* am Chairman Designate—*not* Orin
Selasis."

Alexand studied him, recognizing that as a reflex defense
mechanism. Unfair, unjust, cruel beyond expression, that any
human being should be subjected to this sanity-shattering combination of stress, shock, and grief.

"My lord, you may be Chairman Designate, but if Galinin
dies, the balance of power on the Directorate will shift in
Selasis's favor, and you'll never be Chairman, especially not
when Selasis can use my identity against you. If you even hope
to survive, for your House to survive, you'll have no choice
but to come to terms with Selasis."

"Never!" The word was a rasping whisper of contempt.
"That would be a betrayal of everything I believe in, a betrayal
of Mathis Galinin."

"'Never' is asking fate, my lord. Now I ask you to consider
something else. Who is it who has everything to gain by Galinin's death, and everything to lose if he lives? The answer
will be obvious if you understand two things. For one, Galinin
planned to order a Board of Succession investigation of Karlis's
capacity to sire heirs, and that—"

"Karlis's capacity...Commander, I'd advise you not to
toss out innuendoes on a Lord's virility with such incredible
abandon."

Again, reflex. Alexand could only laugh, because he found it so bitterly sad. He turned to the window, watching a Conpol patrol, bristling with warning lights, pass in V formation a few levels below.

"Karlis's virility—or lack of it—isn't at issue here except as a threat to Selasis. The Chairman can order a Board inquiry without offering evidence. So can the Chairman Designate." He looked around at his father, and that possibility might not have existed for any interest he displayed in it. "Another threat to Selasis is the second item you must understand. One of the offerings the Phoenix intended to make at the bargaining table was the matter transmitter. As an extraplanetary commercial transport system, the MT will be far more efficient—and less costly—than the Selasid InterPlan System." He paused, noting the narrowing of eyes that was Woolf's only outward recognition of the implications in that.

"There was a stipulation to this offer. The MT would only be surrendered to the Concord as a whole, to be controlled by a Concord agency. It would *not* be allowed to fall under the control of any single House. So you see, my lord, *Selasis* is the one man who has everything to gain by Galinin's death. If Galinin lives, Orin faces public revelation of Karlis's sterility, and in all probability, the loss of his First Lordship. And if negotiations with the Phoenix proceed, the House faces ultimate bankruptcy with the development of the MT as a commercial transport system. But if Galinin dies, Selasis will realize his lifelong ambitions—the destruction of the Houses of Galinin and Woolf, and above all, his ascendancy to the Chairmanship."

There was a silence then, in which neither of them moved. It was Woolf who finally broke it.

"The problem with your logic, Commander Ransom, is that there is no evidence to substantiate it. Or am I in error? Have you anything at all to support this *logical* edifice of cause and effect—other than *your* word?"

Alexand became aware of the sourceless constraint that had kept him nearly motionless all this time, that still bound him. He felt the appeal under those coldly pronounced words, and again the mask had slipped, if only slightly. Woolf was appealing for proof. But Alexand took no hope from that.

"No, I have nothing to support it. Only my word." If that wasn't enough, there *was* no hope.

Woolf hesitated, then turned to the door.

"You'll have your opportunity to present your defense tomorrow morning when the Directorate meets."

"Tomorrow morning you will sign the order for my execution."

Woolf stopped short. "What?"

"That decision will be arrived at by a majority vote of the Directors. You won't oppose it."

It was some time before Woolf replied to that, and it was short and curt, spoken as he strode out the door.

"Time will be the test of your clairvoyance. Goodbye, Commander."

Alexand saw the shimmer of the shock screen go on in his wake, closed his eyes to listen to silence finally swallow up the thud of booted footsteps.

He whispered, "Goodbye . . . my lord."

Woolf had to tell Captain Edmin twice to be quiet before they reached the landing roof entrance, the second time with no hint of courtesy. Finally, as he crossed the roof to his 'car, the Conpol escort was left behind; only the two House guards accompanied him. He didn't even notice the second Faeton-limo waiting near his. Not until a shadowy figure emerged from it and approached him. He was only vaguely irritated; he didn't at first recognize the man.

Master Bruno Hawkwood.

Woolf felt his guards draw closer behind him, as if Hawkwood's very presence constituted a menace to him.

At two meters' distance, Hawkwood stopped and bowed.

"My lord, the Lord Selasis sent me. He begs a few minutes of your time in private conference at his Estate."

Woolf said brusquely, "Orin knows I haven't time to confer with him at his Estate. Tell him I'll be at the Hall." He started to go on to his 'car, but Hawkwood, with only a confidential lowering of his voice, stopped him.

"Lord Selasis fully understands the value of your time, my lord, but he asked me to convey to you the importance of this meeting."

One of the guards behind Woolf shifted nervously, and Hawkwood's tawny eyes moved, fixed briefly on him, then slid back to Woolf's face.

"Lord Selasis has already spoken with some of the other Directors. The Lords Shang, Fallor, and Omer. They seem quite disturbed about the . . . identity of Commander Ransom."

Nicely put, Woolf thought bitterly. Shang, Fallor, and Omer, the traditional fence riders. They were disturbed, and that meant Selasis could depend on their votes, which left Woolf with only two possible allies on the Directorate: Honoria Ivanoi and Trevor Robek. They'd be fools to remain allies at those odds.

You'll have no choice but to come to terms with Selasis.

"Very well, Master Hawkwood. I'll talk to Orin."

Hawkwood inclined his head in polite acceptance, showing no hint of emotion, neither surprise nor contempt.

"Lord Selasis sent one of his 'cars for your convenience, my lord."

Woolf was on the verge of balking at that, of insisting on traveling in his own 'car, but it seemed too small a point to be worth making. He turned to his guards.

"Captain Sier, come with me. Sargent, take my 'car to the Hall. Wait for me there."

They hesitated, eyeing Hawkwood warily, until Woolf without another word struck off toward the Selasis 'car.

2.

"The meeting lasted forty-five minutes." Ben was at the 'spenser; he punched for coffee, but almost forgot to pick up the cup. "We don't know what happened. We only got a monitor in Selasis's private office once, and Hawkwood found it within two days."

He remembered the cup and took it to Erica. She put it down on her desk, wondering why she'd asked for it; she was too exhausted for its mild stimulant to have any effect.

"Thanks, Ben."

He nodded and sank into the chair to the right of the desk. His ulcers were bothering him. She knew the signs, just as she

knew there was nothing she could do for him. She looked up
at Jael, perched on the left side of the desk, outwardly at ease,
but in his oblique eyes was the feline alertness that seemed to
be for him a natural state.

Her office had become an informal conference room, perhaps out of deference to Lady Adrien, so she could be near the
twins, asleep now in HS 1's guest room. The doors were open;
Adrien could hear them if they cried. Erica looked across at
her, sitting in splendid calm, dark eyes like unruffled pools,
reflecting light blindly and absorbing none, and an image
shaped itself out of memory: Alex's nerveless hand caressing
the white petals of an orchid, while Erica told him the Lady
Elise was dead, and why.

Adrien was looking at Ben, a direct, unblinking gaze he
seemed uncomfortable with; he didn't understand it.

She said, "You know what happened at that meeting, Ben.
As Alexand said, Lord Woolf had no choice. Will Alex
be ... surrendered to the SSB when the execution order is
signed?"

Erica flinched inwardly and reached for her coffee cup. She
saw Ben's glance of appeal, but avoided it.

He said dully, "Yes, my lady. Probably so."

"I see. He'll be stripped of the MT fixes if that happens,
so if he's to be rescued, it must be before he's transferred from
the Conpol DC to the SSB DC. Can it be done?"

Ben tried an offhand smile. "We've pulled people out of
the Central DC plenty of times. We've got four agents in there,
monitors and MT fixes on Alex, and time. Seven hours before
the Directorate meets."

Adrien listened, unmoved, and when he finished, repeated
her question.

"Can it be done?"

Jael rose and propped his fists on his hips.

"She wants a straight say, Ben. It's hers to ask." Then to
Adrien, "We don't have the odds with us. You know about the
shock screens in his room. The only way we can turn them off
is to get at the central control board, and that's sealed tight.
We can't even get near Alex; they cleared that corridor and
sealed it up, too. We're lucky we had a doctor inside, or Alex
would still be in limbo."

Her hands were folded in her lap. Erica saw them tighten,

one on the other, but that was all.

"The doctor can't do anything more?"

"He might be able to get into the room again if Alex ran a sick gim, but he can't touch the shock screens, and that's Alex's only door."

"The doctor couldn't leave MT fixes somewhere outside Alex's room so you could . . . trans more men in?"

Ben braced himself to answer that question.

"My lady, we thought about that. We could mount an armed invasion inside the DC, but the trouble is . . ." He needed a deep breath before he could go on. "His room is equipped with cyanide gas sprays. The standing orders are to kill him before taking a chance on letting him escape."

Erica tensed, seeing Adrien turn even paler, but she didn't give way; she looked up at Jael as he said, "We gave a long thought to snuffing old Cyclops. It might be a blessing for humankind, but even that wouldn't turn a 'cord for Alex. In fact, we'd better send up a few prayers that Selasis doesn't die a natural death in the next few hours. He could choke on a fish bone, and the Directors would lay it to the Phoenix."

"And cry all the louder for Alexand's blood." Adrien nodded, shifting her blind gaze to Ben. "What else is left us?"

He spread his hands, palms up. "We can hope Galinin regains consciousness long enough to tell somebody what really happened, or we can hope Woolf . . ."

"Will have a change of heart?" she asked caustically. Then she frowned. "That would be more likely if he could be convinced of Orin's vulnerability. Karlis; his golden eunuch."

Ben nodded. "Woolf's acting Chairman now—until Selasis makes his bid, and that probably won't be before Galinin dies. As long as Woolf has the title, he can order a Board of Succession investigation." His voice betrayed his skepticism, and no hope was kindled in Adrien's eyes.

"Is there nothing else?"

"Taking Alex by force. If he's moved to the SSB DC, we might have a chance during the transfer, unless they're smart enough to use portable shock screens and keep a gun at his head."

"They're at least that intelligent, Ben."

He shrugged wearily. "Well, then our last chance will be

at the ... the execution. With that many people around, shock screens won't be practical. Besides, once they get him on that stand, they'll probably depend on the fact that he'll be surrounded by fifty Directorate guards."

Adrien's eyes narrowed. "Won't they be justified in depending on that?"

"Not if enough of them happen to be Phoenix members." Then, having finally said something that inspired some hope, he seemed to feel a perverse obligation to dampen it with qualification. "It's a long chance. He'll be exposed, and there'll be plenty of authentic guards around him, all armed."

She gave a short laugh, devoid of amusement. "Still, planning for that will be more productive than simply hoping for Galinin's recovery or Woolf's change of heart."

Jael looked at his watch. "I'll have to ex out now. I'm lifting off for Concordia in half an hour."

Erica saw a tension in Adrien's features that served as a warning. She rose, facing Jael.

"I'm going with you."

At that, Ben came to his feet, too. "Uh ... my lady, I don't think ... I mean, the Concordia chapter's a double ident operation, and—"

"And I wouldn't be *safe*?" The mordant meaninglessness of that word was evident. She turned to Erica, a gentle light shining fleetingly in her eyes. "I must leave Rich and Eric in your care, and I know it will be loving care."

Erica managed a smile. "It will be, my lady. Always. Whatever happens, you may depend on that."

"I do. And whatever happens ..." She hesitated, then turned to Jael. "I'll be ready to leave when you are."

3.

Alexandra stirred, but didn't wake. Only dreaming.

04:10 TST. Phillip Woolf pushed back his sleeve to check his watch, then looked again into his daughter's face, softly lit in the changing light of the lumensa; shimmering warm blues and greens for peaceful sleep. The music shaping the colors was so low it was nearly inaudible. An imp, Mathis called her, a young witch, and she had power to charm, even in sleep. She'd be a beauty one day; Olivet's fair skin, and the black hair and clear blue eyes of DeKoven Woolf. One day.

But now, Alexandra, two years old, lay absorbed in dreams, dark hair curling against her cheek, and Woolf found himself looking not into the future, but into the past. It might have been Rich, this sleeping child; Rich at two, before...

Woolf turned and crossed to the smaller bed in another alcove where Justin lay asleep. So much Olivet's child, golden haired, his eyes exactly the same deep, lavender blue as hers. It had seemed fitting that this, their first born son, should be so evidently her child.

Olivet Omer Woolf was the embodiment of a second life for him, one he never hoped for when the first ended; a second chance at happiness for himself, and for the House—

Survival.

The word was a black weight in his mind. In the end, was that all it came to?

He heard a whisper of sound and turned. Olivet was standing in the doorway, the brighter light behind her making a diaphanous glow of her robe, sheening the aureate sweep of her hair with silver.

Was survival so much to be scorned?

"Phillip...?"

He went to her and put his arm around her shoulders, waiting until they were in the sitting room before he spoke.

"You needn't have waited up for me, Olivet."

"I found sleep a little elusive tonight. Phillip, are you... are you all right?"

He knew what she meant, and he couldn't answer the real questions any more than she could ask them.

"Yes, I'm all right. I've done what I could to restore order, so I thought I'd better get a few hours' rest."

He walked with her out onto the balcony adjoining the sitting room, a favorite personal place of theirs. It looked out over an informal garden scented with acacia and rock daphne and beyond to the lights of Concordia. But in the darkness before this dawn, the air was acrid with smoke, an oppressive layer of cloud containing and reflecting a sickly light.

For a time he stood at the railing, Olivet silent beside him, until at length she asked, "Any news of Mathis?"

"I stopped at his Estate on my way home. No change. Dr. Perris seems to consider that encouraging, but I don't think Stel agrees."

"Phillip, is . . . Alexand really alive?" Then, when he frowned questioningly, she added, "Father 'commed me. He's worried about the succession; about Justin. As if Justin would even know the difference if he weren't the first born."

Woolf paused, struck by the beautiful naïveté of that.

"I doubt Sandro is concerned for Justin's feelings." He took a long breath, resenting the caustic smell of the air. "Yes, Olivet, Alexand's alive. He calls himself Commander Alex Ransom. Of the Phoenix."

She looked up into his face, then with a sigh turned away.

"Oh, it seems so . . . what a bitter thing, that such a miracle should be turned into a tragedy."

"A miracle?" The word didn't seem to make sense.

"Alexand. To have someone you loved and thought dead restored to you. That *should* be a miracle. Phillip, I'm sorry."

He nodded numbly. "I know. Thank you."

"Do you think he really tried to kill Mathis?"

For a moment, Woolf considered the question, seeking within himself for his inner convictions. *Alexand* could not have raised a hand against Mathis, but Commander Alex Ransom . . .

I don't *know*. And the question was totally irrelevant now; he wondered if Olivet would ever understand that. A new era had been ushered in this day; an era in which the savage exponent of violent death had entered the equations of human interaction on the highest governmental level, and the restraints of law and convention no longer restricted the pursuit of power.

Power and survival were synonymous.

In this new era, politics had reverted to the basic natural criterion of success: survival.

Olivet said regretfully, "Forgive me, I shouldn't force you to talk about it. I was only . . . surprised."

"Surprised? What do you mean?"

"I just can't believe it of Alexand. I didn't know him well, but we were so nearly the same age, we met at quite a lot of social events. Sometimes I'd catch a glimpse of him when he thought he was unobserved." She hesitated, looking out toward the smoke-palled city. "How much can you really learn about a person in that sort of situation? I think all I was really sure of was that he was . . . lonely. Profoundly lonely."

That word, that concept, was entirely unexpected, and so was his response to it. Like a physical blow; his breath caught, and he had to stop himself from doubling over.

She reached out for his hand. "You must get some rest now. Please."

"You go on to bed. I'll be there in a short while. I need a few minutes alone to . . . think."

She didn't argue, not by word or gesture; she had a gentle capacity for accepting without question even what she didn't fully understand. Woolf cupped her face in his hands, watching her lips shaping a smile while her eyes brimmed with tears. He kissed the smile.

"A few minutes, Olivet."

"I'll be waiting."

He turned to the railing, listening to the silken sounds of her departure, trying to hold on to that; the only sound that filled the vacuum was the rumbling hum of the city, dimmed by distance and disaster.

Can you deny your genes in every cell of his body?

Why can't I forget? The back of his hand tingled with the impact of a blow struck five years ago.

I am betrayed. Betrayed then as I am now.

Sardonic laughter welled within him. Have I not betrayed Mathis and myself, made a pact with evil? And what is betrayal? An abstraction as meaningless as faith in a world where the only criterion of success is survival. Survival at any cost, because not even the cost is meaningful.

Then, abruptly, his every muscle tensed in alarm.

The hum of the city no longer reached him; someone had activated the sound screens. The artificial silence made him all the more aware of a sound directly behind him. A light footstep.

Orin won't kill me now. That was part of the pact.

Olivet. It must be Olivet.

He turned, one hand raised, ready to snap the small laser into his palm; he'd worn the spring sheath since the attack in the Directorate Hall. Someone was standing in the doorway, framed in light, but it wasn't Olivet. He stared at the woman before him, at an apparition, and wondered why at first he thought she was robed in lambent sheaths of pearls. She was, in fact, dressed in a simple slacsuit.

Adrien Eliseer.

His hand groped backward, seeking the support of the railing. She took three steps toward him.

"Forgive me, my lord, but I had no way to warn you of my coming, or of my living."

He asked haltingly, "What do you want?"

That seemed to surprise her; perhaps she expected him to question her identity. He didn't. There was only one thing he was sure of at this moment. He knew who she was.

Finally, she answered him.

"My lord, I've come to ask for my husband's life."

"Phillip? Is something... what happened?"

He closed the door behind him and leaned against it. There was no light in the room, but the windowalls were clear. The pallid glow from the city sketched Olivet sitting up in the bed. She was frightened. That was in her voice.

"Nothing... happened, Olivet. Nothing's wrong."

She would hear the lie of that in *his* voice, but how could he even begin to tell her what had happened? How could he find the words to encompass what was wrong?

He went to a chair near the door and began stripping off his clothes, trying to remember when he had put them on. Yesterday morning. Concord Day. Somewhere in that dim past era of a day ago. Olivet was still waiting, still afraid, but he couldn't say anything to reassure her. He could only ask for her silence with his.

Dear wife, I just had a little chat with a ghost who told me an enchanting tale of a place called Saint Petra's of Ellay, of the secret birth of twin infants, and the first born was called Richard. And you, my lady, who haven't yet seen three decades, are by a magical stroke, a grandmother.

And I... am a grandfather.

Then there was a charming little coda. By another magical stroke, it was given unto me the power, by the utterance of a single order, to destroy the great one-eyed ogre, Selasis.

The rumors are true, my lord.

What *isn't* true in the enchanted world on the other side of the rainbow?

But dear wife, I had to tell that lovely ghost that *I* live on *this* side of the rainbow, where there is no truth, only . . . survival.

She didn't understand; didn't understand that I can't believe her—not in this world, in this new era.

But Alexand is innocent.

She didn't understand that Alexand's father couldn't believe that, and even if he did . . .

He tugged off his boots, let them fall, and sagged against the arm of the chair. Never since Elise's death had he endured anguish so mordant.

The ghost left me with a curse; a potent curse.

He heard Olivet stirring and forced himself to rise. He tossed the rest of his clothing onto the chair, then stood naked, looking out into the dull glow that should have been the coming of dawn. His eyes were adjusting to the darkness, as Olivet's already had. He saw her there, waiting; she didn't move except to tilt her head back to watch him when he went to the bed and leaned over her.

"Olivet . . . I love you. Don't be afraid."

She reached up and touched his cheek.

"If love were enough, *you* wouldn't be afraid."

But what else do we have?

He leaned closer until his lips touched hers. Trembling. He could feel it in that light touch, and knew no other way to stop it, except to seek something else in it. Slowly, savoring the languid distraction of the kiss, he carried her, let her sink with him, down into the cushioned warmth of the bed.

What else do we have?

My lady wife, love me, make love with me. It will be enough.

And yet it wasn't.

Later, when she lay beneath him, and he lay closed in the soft constraint of her arms and thighs, when the darkness seemed to constrict and beat with a single impulse, he pulled away from her with a harsh cry he couldn't restrain and lay panting, teeth clenched, eyes squeezed shut. All that stopped him from weeping for that encompassing realization of failure, even of shame, was some vague conviction that to give way to tears would be an even greater failure, a greater shame.

Never before. Never had this happened. Never.

Even my body betrays me.

Olivet stirred, took a long breath; she spoke not a word, moving in the darkness, drawing close to him, asking no more than his shoulder for her head, his hand in hers.

Here was love, warm and accepting beside him, but it wasn't enough.

He stared up into nothingness, aware of an incipient nacreous glow. Dawn. It was coming finally.

The first dawn of the new era.

4.

It was 07:30, only half an hour before the Directorate meeting. Still, when Phillip Woolf arrived at the Galinin Estate, he took time to check the security procedures in the infirmary wing and discuss them with Galinin's Chief of Security. He was satisfied with Master Devron's efforts, but well aware that total security was an impossibility.

He kept thinking of Commander Alex Ransom's offhand assurance that the Phoenix could trans a bomb anywhere, even into the Directorate Chamber.

He encountered Galinin's brother, Emil, and Rodrik, his first born, as they were leaving the infirmary wing, Emil bent and bewildered, too distracted for more than a few words. Rodrik seemed preoccupied, and Woolf noted the pretentious gravity in his bearing. No doubt he thought it appropriate to the probable heir to Daro Galinin.

Woolf passed down a long corridor filled with House guards into an anteroom where his sleevesheath gun was duly noted by a detector, and after an examination with a montector and a personal search, which he insisted on, he was allowed to pass into Galinin's room.

Futile, all futile, the guards and detectors and searches. Mathis was safe now, made safe by the shadow that hovered over him almost perceptibly: the shadow of death.

Only Dr. Marton Stel, Woolf's personal physician, kept vigil by Galinin's bed. Above the head of the bed, a biomonitor screen registered in ticking calligraphy the wavering signals of his living. His face was almost hidden. An ugly turban of bandages bound his head, angling down over the left temple; a respirator mask covered the lower half of his face, the sigh of the pump audible in the pendant quiet.

Woolf looked down at Galinin's hands, motionless against the sheet. Broad, strong hands, more the hands of a craftsman than a statesman. On the right was the topaz Crest Ring of Daro Galinin, on the left the golden seal of the Chairmanship.

"Marton?"

Dr. Stel understood that unstated query. He turned away, staring bleakly at the monitor.

"He's a man of courage, my lord; the will to live is there. Otherwise, I doubt he'd be alive now. If he were twenty years younger . . ."

"But he's not." How often had Mathis, in rueful annoyance, called himself an old man. Woolf had never believed it until now.

"No, my lord, and I . . . can't offer any hope for him, short of a miracle."

Stel seemed silenced by his own pronouncement, then he roused himself, a bitter hatred taking shape in his features that was stunning in someone so typically reserved and conscientiously detached in his demeanor.

"The man who did this—I wish to the God there was some way to make him pay for it with more than his life. That's not enough!"

Woolf nodded, wondering how Stel would feel if he knew the real identity of the man who had done this. At least, the man who *would* pay for it with his life. Stel had brought Alexand into the world.

But he would never know. No one outside the Directorate would know. That was part of the pact.

Woolf went to the door without looking back.

"'Com me if . . . if there's any change."

5.

Alexand spent most of the hour between 08:00 and 09:00 at the window, watching morning come to Concordia in murky veils of rain. The city roused itself from the long night, not to full wakefulness, but, like an invalid, to pendant alertness, feeling out its aches and pains.

Ben's voice sounded intermittently in his ear. Once it was Erica. Never Adrien. That was an act of mercy on her part, and he understood it, as she knew he would.

There was nothing new or unexpected in the reports, and finally he stopped listening to them except as a link with hope, an axis of assurance to keep his thoughts aligned.

The other axis was Rich.

Rich his brother, not his son.

Reach out to me, Rich, my linked-twin soul; reach out and give me your courage.

Fear was an alien entity taking possession of him, cell by cell. Already it occupied his heart and commanded the quickening beat of his pulse; it had seized the fragile network of his nervous system, distorting the signals of his senses. He couldn't depend on his muscles to function as he ordered them, and he knew if he lowered his defenses for an instant, it would take up tenancy in his mind.

At 08:45 Alexand turned from the window, tucked his shirt under his waistband, fastened the cuffs and collar. Then the uniform jacket. He worked with little success at restoring a strand of braid loosened in his encounter with the Directorate guards. He had to concentrate on it; it was one of those small tasks his left hand was unaccustomed to, made all the more difficult by its wayward trembling. The front fasteners presented no problem, but the cloak was more difficult. It slipped off his left shoulder twice before he got it snapped in place.

At 08:50, Ben warned him that the SSB 'car had landed on the roof.

That was the last message he heard from the miniceiver. If the SSB found it, they'd wonder where it came from, and suspicion would fall inevitably on Dr. Cambry; no one else had been close enough to him. Cambry had also left a monitor in the room, but Alexand couldn't risk searching for it, and he assumed it had a destruct mechanism.

The ear 'ceiver couldn't be so equipped, however. Alexand went into the bathroom, where he removed it under the guise of washing his face and smoothing his hair with his fingers. His comfortable accommodations did not include a comb or anything that could conceivably serve as a weapon.

The 'ceiver went into the syntegrator with the disposable towel. The bottle of pills Cambry had left waited by the soft plasex cup. The pills were exactly what they seemed; oral analgesics. He knew that from Ben, and he'd already taken one this morning. Now he studied the pills through the transparent walls of the bottle. There were at least ten left. He filled the cup with water, then swallowed them all at once. Within half an hour, he would be very nearly unconscious, but that didn't concern him. Within a few minutes, he could be unconscious in another sense. The TAB would be in effect.

He knew what he had to look forward to, and knew the pills were only capable of blunting pain, and would be effective only until the SSB psychocontrollers recognized their symptoms and administered a counterstimulant. Still, it might mean a few minutes' delay, a few minutes' relief. In an SSB interrogation room, minutes become important.

At 09:00 Alexand was again at the window, studying the exquisite patterns of raindrops on the glass, moving lenses transforming the cityscape into an abstraction of subtle grays. The thudding of booted heels was distant thunder.

His last thoughts would be of Adrien, but he willed himself not to think of her now. The rain; silent, silver streaks on transparency. Rain shaped this planet, made the seas, the cradle of life; rain had fallen here millions of years before he had been alive with eyes to see it, and rain would fall here millions of years after he was gone.

Three pairs of booted footsteps—no. At least four. Too many to be sure.

Soon. He was dizzy, mouth and throat parched, his eyes slipping out of focus unless he concentrated on it.

Soon. He wondered why he looked forward to the TAB.

It wouldn't reduce the fear, or the pain. But it would make them meaningless. Perhaps that was it. It would make *him* meaningless.

"Commander Alex Ransom?"

Rich...oh, Rich, reach out to me....

Alexand turned. There were four men aligned just inside the door; black boots, black cloaks, black gloves, black helmets, black shadows where their faces might be. One of them spoke, reading from a vellam sheet.

"First Commander Alex Ransom, the Society of the Phoenix, you are under arrest, and, by decree of the Directorate of the Concord of Loyal Houses, condemned to execution in just punishment for the crimes of treason and the attempted assassination of the Lord Mathis Daro Galinin, Chairman of the Directorate. Said execution, by Directorate decree, will take place on this day, 15 Octov 3258, at 20:00 TST in the Plaza of the Concord in the city of Concordia."

The man who stood staring in stark incredulity at the four shadow figures heard the words, each one sharply enunciated, solemnly spaced.

He heard every word, but understood only one of them.

Execution.

6.

At exactly noon, Bruno Hawkwood entered Master Jaid Garo's interrogation room, which was relegated to the first level of the Estate Security wing, twenty meters underground. This was one part of the Badir Selasis Home Estate no visitor ever saw. And none who knew about it wanted to see it; it was not a place that was visited voluntarily.

In shape, the interrogation room was a half circle. Centered on the straight wall was a metallic disk two and a half meters in diameter, its perimeter bulked with inputs and outlets for a variety of instruments and mechanisms. On that disk, limbs spread to make a living X, the victims were mounted. Master Garo liked to call them "subjects," but Hawkwood was impatient with euphemisms; he didn't need them, and it surprised him that Garo did, until he realized his error. "Subjects" were exactly what they were to Garo.

Master Garo was not sadistic.

Hawkwood wouldn't have tolerated that. The revelations made in this room were never appropriate for public consumption, and the man who heard them had to be worthy of trust. A sadist couldn't be trusted, and his psychosis inevitably negated his efficiency.

Garo might be termed psychopathic in that he was incapable of empathy for other human beings, but that increased, rather than diminished, his efficiency. In fact, he might have written the definitive text on his art, if it weren't so clandestinely practiced. He approached his work with methodical detachment, never losing sight of his purpose, always working through an ordered sequence of operations, which he graded on a numerical scale from one to twenty; he seldom found it necessary to go beyond ten. He made only three parts of the human anatomy sacrosanct: the ears, the mouth, and the eyes. The subject must be able to hear the questions asked him, and able to answer them. And he must be able to see.

Master Garo was ever sensitive to the psychological aspects of his work.

The eyes are windows to the imagination, he propounded, with no philosophic or poetic intent, and imagination augmented his persuasive processes as effectively as a nerve-sensitizing injection. That was why the curved wall of this room was lined with mirrors so his subjects might look out from the wheel and see themselves reflected a hundredfold at every stage of mutilation, from the initial threat operations, through the secondary pain infliction levels, to the permanent injury stages.

But Master Jaid Garo was faced here with ultimate failure.

The man now mounted on his wheel was impervious to his arts. Garo hadn't believed that possible, nor had Selasis, when Hawkwood warned them of the futility of subjecting this man to Garo's methods. The only hope of getting more information from him was through voluntary disclosure, and that might have been accomplished by playing on his mania.

But the Lord Selasis was not a patient man.

Hawkwood went to the control console where Garo sat in

numbed bewilderment. He had reached, and passed, operation twenty.

The air was fetid with the sweat of fear, with urine, feces, and blood. Hawkwood looked up at Garo's subject with cold disgust, not for the man himself, but for the shortsightedness that had put him there.

His hair seemed a startling orange flame under the penetrating lights. There was a spiderish aspect about him, limbs splayed, stretched beyond the tolerance of the joints, swollen with blood. A web of tubes, wires, clamps, probes, and automated appendages radiated inward from the edge of the wheel to adhere to the acid-blistered, blood-scaled body or obtrude into its every orifice.

Unnatural, unmanned, unhuman, this slab of flesh was only living because of the paradoxically sustaining functions of some of those mechanical appendages. A delicate balance, and Garo couldn't maintain it much longer.

Hawkwood asked softly, "Well, Garo?"

"He . . . the man is—it's incredible!"

"You haven't worked with Phoenix conditioning before."

"But the man's *insane*. Conditioning shouldn't hold—listen. Just *listen* to this!"

He turned up the audio pickup. The man's voice was too weak for the words to be audible without amplification, and even with it they were barely intelligible, garbled in red froth, disrupted by heaving muscular spasms, his body's revolt against what was happening within it.

"I am . . . the Llllord . . . Predis Uh . . . *Uh* . . . Ussshhh . . . Pela—Peladeeeeen. . . . I am firsssst born . . . of—of—of Lorrrr . . . Elor Pel-Pelah—ah . . . *ah* . . . *AH*—"

Garo switched off the audio, and the broken sounds could be heard only as a hiccoughing mumbling.

"That's *all!* Six hours, and that's all he ever said. I can't— there's nothing more I can *do*."

"There was never anything you could do. Kill him."

"But I have no orders from Lord . . ." He stopped and, when Hawkwood turned on him, went pale.

"Master Garo, I am still Chief of Security. You take your orders from me. I take mine from Lord Selasis." So, the word was already out, filtering down through the ranks.

Hawkwood reached for the red lethal-shock button.

"The order is mine, Garo. The deed is mine."

The man's body bucked and beat against the wheel, then hung limp. The chamber was silent except for an incessant dripping sound.

"Garo, call the disposal squad, then you may go."

Garo sighed out his relief and snapped a curt order into the intercom, then rose stiffly.

"Uh . . . good day, Master Hawkwood."

Hawkwood nodded. He didn't turn to see him go, nor did he move when the four Bond mutes came in. They eyed him warily, but when he showed no interest in them, went on with their work, communicating with each other with hand signals.

It wasn't Hawkwood's custom to watch this culmination of the interrogation process, yet he felt a certain obligation to this man, and he noted with satisfaction that the Bonds showed a vestige of the respect for the dead their religion taught them as they disengaged the body from the web-work of the wheel.

Perhaps the man *had* been a Lord's son. He had certainly been mad, and that was a key Sign.

Hark to the voices of madness, for they may be the chosen vessels of the Word of the All-God.

This man was a signpost.

Orin Selasis, being both self-indulgent and self-blinded, had only seen him as a tool, one he carelessly destroyed in his impatience, but Bruno Hawkwood looked beyond the utility of the man and found the signpost.

They called him the Master of Shadows; he knew that. He also knew, now, that he'd only been his Lord's shadow, following blindly as he led down a False Path into Chaos. But a junction had been reached. He and his Lord would no longer walk the same path, and this man, whose broken body the mutes were lowering onto a sheet of black plasex, had been a signpost and a catalyst. He had set in motion the sequence of events that led Bruno Hawkwood inevitably to the Prime Sign.

Adrien Eliseer was alive.

Orin Selasis regarded that as an unforgivable failure on Hawkwood's part; nothing more. He didn't consider the chain of occurrence linking this man with that revelation.

Hawkwood wasn't a Reader, but sometimes the gift of Sight is fleetingly bestowed even on the Unsighted.

Selasis would never, if this man hadn't in his madness come to him, have ordered the assassination of Mathis Galinin. The result of that, Selasis only regarded as another unforgivable failure, giving no thought to the fact that Hawkwood had failed because of a turn of Destiny he couldn't have foreseen: Galinin had chosen to sit by the windowall, not at the desk.

There was a purpose to that as there was to all things.

If the assassination attempt hadn't failed, Selasis wouldn't have found the imagraph, face down on the floor, snatched from Galinin's hand and thrust into his by the invisible hand of Fate.

Adrien Eliseer had not been meant to die by Bruno Hawkwood's hand, and with his new Sight, he read a corollary in the two infants pictured in her arms. Her husband, her Promised by blessed vow, was not meant to die. To attempt his death would be to knowingly follow a False Path.

Orin Selasis wouldn't be turned from that Path, but his shadow might escape now to seek a True Path.

Escape was an appropriate term.

Hawkwood knew himself to be a condemned man. Perhaps that was another reason he stayed for the shrouding of this man's body.

He stood condemned for the two failures Selasis couldn't accept as Written, and he was alive now only because Galinin was still alive. At the first hint of his recovery, another assassination attempt must be made, and Selasis preferred to limit the risks of revelation by entrusting the second attempt to the same man who had made the first. Thus he let Hawkwood live. But it was only a temporary stay of execution. Hawkwood knew that as he knew this day was inevitable. He expected it and had prepared for it.

Ten years ago, when he married Margreta, he had experienced what Selasis would derisively call a religious ecstasy; a vision. Hawkwood called it an Insight. Now, in a remote mountain valley in Newzelland, a house had been built on a Concord land grant. The owners were established as a University professor nearing retirement and his fair young wife.

The gardens and pastures were tended by two Bond couples whose silence and service were guaranteed by gratitude and an awareness of their fate should they try to leave the retreat. They had been condemned to death and were presently on the runaway lists. And they knew Margreta and loved her as sick, needy, and frightened creatures inevitably did, sensing instinctively that she loved them.

That capacity for love seemed innate in her. Who else would see the need in a man like Bruno Hawkwood and answer it with love?

Two of the mutes carried out the shrouded body; they seemed to find it a heavy burden. The other two, with vacmops and antisep sprays, began the cleaning up, and Hawkwood wondered why the odor of blood seemed as hard to eradicate as the substance itself.

He turned and left the room, closing the door behind him. As he rode the pedway down the corridor, he was thinking of Margreta and conscious of the time. At 12:30 she would be calling on a private frequency, and he could only take that call in his office, which he had over the years made a sanctuary, an electronic fortress.

Galinin still lived, and thus Bruno Hawkwood still lived, and in the chain of occurrence, Margreta lived. Two hours ago she had left the Estate bound for the University Hospital, a commonplace errand since her surgery, which would attract neither Selasis's attention, nor that of the secret guards who always watched her. But she wouldn't return to the Estate. There were means of evading even the closest surveillance. Margreta should at this time be safely resting at the farm retreat.

He reached a lift, pausing before he entered it. He wasn't a Reader; he couldn't be sure the cloying uneasiness he felt now was simply a normal response to anxiety or the warning of Sight.

Listen. That is the first lesson, the hardest lesson, and the last lesson.

Listening demanded solitude. He stepped into the lift and floated up four levels to the Security Administration section.

The sensed equivocation was associated with Enid Gysing, he knew, but he still couldn't be sure of its real cause. He'd have preferred to send Margreta away alone, but that was impossible. She was only a month out of the hospital, and it had been a difficult surgery. Beyond that, her vision, though improved, was still impaired. She might be willing, but she wasn't physically capable of making her escape alone.

But wasn't that simply another link in the chain? And Enid Gysing seemed so inevitable a choice as her escort, he thought that could only be another link.

Ferra Gysing, like Jaid Garo, was congenitally incapable of empathy, but she had a strong sense of loyalty. She was trained as an intelligence agent, and Hawkwood had come to depend on her for the most critical assignments. He often trusted her with information he wouldn't consider trusting even to Helmett Ranes. Master Ranes was his second-in-command and inevitable successor, and Hawkwood trusted him to the degree he trusted anyone in spite of that fact.

But with Enid Gysing, loyalty was again inspired by gratitude.

An attractive woman, darkly handsome, she had several years ago caught the eye of Karlis Selasis, who lured her to a room he called the Velvet Pit, where he occasionally indulged himself and some of his Lordly peers in various sensual games.

Hawkwood never expressed an opinion on his Lords' choices of entertainment, nor would he have interfered in Karlis's games if one of his agents hadn't been made the object of them. He made his point to Selasis finally; the training and talents of someone like Ferra Gysing were not to be wasted on casual entertainment for Karlis and his friends. They must look elsewhere for their playthings. And perhaps it was only pique at his son's excesses, but Selasis had conceded the point. Enid Gysing declared herself forever in Hawkwood's debt, and had demonstrated her gratitude in steadfast loyalty since.

Hawkwood checked his watch before he made a short detour into the comcenter. There was still time enough, and it took only two minutes to determine that his agents in Daro Galinin had reported no change in Galinin's condition. He was still medically classified critical.

As Hawkwood was leaving the comcenter, he paused. Helmett Ranes was coming down the corridor from the lift. No wonder the word had already filtered down through the ranks; Ranes walked like a newly dubbed Lord.

Until he saw Hawkwood.

Ranes had always had good facial and eye control, but in

that moment of surprise, something very much like embarrassment was briefly revealed.

"Good afternoon, Master Ranes."

Ranes smiled pleasantly enough but didn't stop, only slowing his pace.

"Afternoon, Master Hawkwood. Afraid I'm running a little late. Had to check something down in the interrogation level."

"Ussher, you mean?"

"Why . . . yes. He hasn't broken yet."

That was a careless lie and indicative of uncertainty. Hawkwood only nodded and waved him on, then set off down the corridor toward his office, wondering why Ranes had lied to him. Where had he actually been?

12:25. Just time enough to check the sec-systems in his office before Margreta's call.

At exactly 13:00, Hawkwood rose from the altar in the corner of the windowless, white-walled room that had for twenty years suited his purposes and sensibilities so well. The altar, like the rest of the office, was cleanly functional, devoid of excess decoration. Seven candles were aligned on it, and in the center, point poised in a sphere of water-clear quartz, stood the Dagger of Will, thrice seven centimeters long, shaped of blue jade, the hilt and guard forming a translucent crucifix with the seven-spoked Wheel of Destiny carved into the intersection.

He wasn't a Reader. His new Sight was imperfect. He hadn't read the signs correctly.

Margreta hadn't called.

Twice he had tried to reach her, but there was no response, not even a call buzz.

He turned and crossed the winter-white carpet to the com-console behind his desk. He wouldn't try to call her again. A question must be answered now.

Where had Helmett Ranes actually been?

There was a shielded panel under the console counter; not even X-rays would reveal it. Orin Selasis was jealous of his privacy, particularly in the small chamber he called his private office. Hawkwood had set up the sec-system, but with typical mistrust, his Lord periodically had Ranes check it, with Hawkwood as a countercheck on him. Since Hawkwood had designed the system, Ranes was at a disadvantage. He found the monitors left for him to find, but, predictably, didn't show them to Selasis, choosing instead to insure his position as second-in-command with blackmail. He didn't find the monitors operated through this hidden console.

Now Hawkwood set the tapes on replay, sampled earlier conversations between Selasis and Hamid, then Cameroodo. Helmett Ranes had entered his Lord's private office at 12:10.

The preliminaries were short, interesting only in that Selasis's confidential tone was revealing. Hawkwood wondered what lever he would use to hold Ranes's loyalty. Ranes had no wife; he loved no one. Mastèr Garo might suffice for him.

And, finally, the answer beyond the answer.

"Well, Master Ranes, I understand you have something to show me."

And Ranes responding with smug eagerness, "Yes, my lord. It arrived a few minutes ago."

"Ah. From Ferra... what was her name?"

"Gysing, my lord. Enid Gysing."

"Well, Ferra Gysing deserves a commendation, Helmett. What's this? *'Ab initio, ad infinitum.'*"

There was the answer.

Hawkwood closed his eyes, corded hands clenched.

Ranes voice again. "I checked that. Old Latin. Means something like 'from the beginning to the end.'"

And Orin Selasis replying, "No, Helmett. *To infinity.*" Then he laughed.

That inscription was etched inside the wedding ring Hawkwood had placed on Margreta'a hand ten years ago.

"MARGRETAAAAA!"

The cry reverberated in the ordered white silence. His fists crashed down, a double hammer, smashing out the voices from the console.

> *Holy Lord, mover of stars, move my hand in thy will.*
> *Mover of suns, move my arm,*
> *Mover of worlds, move my body...*

He had misread the Signs. Bruno Hawkwood wasn't a Reader. His new Sight was imperfect.

Maker of Order, align my thoughts...
Holy Lord, Author of Fate, make my Destiny...

But now he was cleansed in the purifying flame of agony. Now he looked back on the chain of occurrence and read every link with perfect clarity, and looked ahead into the future, and saw every link starkly revealed.

I am thy body, I am thy arm, I am thy hand...

Hawkwood crossed as silently as a fall of snow to the altar; there he knelt, eyes fixed on the Dagger of Will.

In the name of Gamaliel, sainted of the All-God.
Ahm.

At length, he rose and his right hand went out, closed on the cool blue hilt of the Dagger. It slipped easily out of its crystal mount.

He put on a cloak; brown; the color of earth. At the console, he pressed certain buttons, and by the time he left the room, the air was acid with the odor of burning circuits. He walked down the corridor to the lift, speaking to no one he met along the way. On the landing roof, he passed the 'car he usually used and went to the one assigned to Master Ranes. He could trust it not to be sabotaged.

Another 'car lifted off within thirty seconds of his departure. He watched it, but took no evasive action. In ten minutes, he was in the heart of Concordia on the landing roof of the Central Transystem terminal. He set the 'car's navcomp system on automatic return. It hummed away into the Trafficon grids as he walked into the terminal.

At that point, as far as Lord Orin Selasis could determine, Bruno Hawkwood vanished into vacuum.

7.

Jael stood waiting, hands on his hips, surveying the com-center, a cramped, low-ceilinged room crowded with only ten techs on duty. But he was used to small, subterranean spaces, and he wondered why he felt so uncomfortable here. This was the Concordia chapter's main comcenter, and it had been running for fifteen years without ever pulling a look from the Shads.

But they only looked under rocks they didn't like.

This hide was Concord built; the apartments above it housed Concord Fesh. The Concord-approved architech who designed it specified a subbasement for storage, but no one seemed to notice, when the apartment complex was finished, that there weren't any accesses to the storage area. The Concord forgot it existed.

So the Phoenix had itself a nice safe hide, and the only way into it was by MT through apartment 373-T.

Dovey. But something about it still hackled him.

Then he sighed and checked his watch: 18:02.

Look it in the eye, brother. What's hackling you is that Alex Ransom is on an SSB rack right now, and in two hours he has a meet with a laser beam on a black stand in the Plaza of the Concord.

A public execution. No trial, not even a gimmed play-through. By Directorate decree. Selasis was pushing the buttons now, and he and the other Directors wanted the whole damn Concord to see how quick they were to turn out justice. The vidicom time spent on the impending execution told the story again; Woolf had stepped aside to let Selasis push those buttons, too. The Plaza would be packed.

Jael felt a chill at the back of his neck. A warning. He was alive today because he'd paid heed time and again to what his body told him.

Selasis had private plans for the execution. Jael had no idea what they might be, but he was sure snuffing Alex wasn't enough for old Cyclops. An agent in Badir Selasis had picked up a conversation between Orin and Karlis. The talk hadn't turned up anything specific; father didn't confide in son, which showed Orin hadn't slipped his senses entirely.

Selasis had said, "This day, Karlis, the day of Alex Ransom's execution, will be remembered in the history of the Concord as a day of perfidy..."

True enough, but he didn't mean it straight. There was more.

"Jael? I have Ben on line."

One of the comtechs was rising to give him his place at the SynchCom screen. Jael moved to the chair hurriedly; this was what he'd been waiting for. Ben was only five minutes late, but it read like an hour.

"Thanks, Gil. Ben?"

His face had a gray cast, due only in part to a slight peripheral interference.

"Give me what you have first, Jael, then I'll give you some good news."

Jael sighed, content to wait with that assurance.

"From Badir Selasis, not much, except I think we can count Ussher dead now. I guess he didn't talk fast and long enough to suit Orin. He was probably a long time dying, if you can take any comfort from that. Nothing on Hawkwood. Orin and his blade, Ranes, are still in a red panic."

"What the hell is Bruno up to? What about his wife?"

"Margreta's gone, too, and the way we've put it together, she's not coming back; it's a one-way trip to the Beyond."

Ben hesitated, eyes slitted. "Then that explains why Bruno slipped out on Selasis." He shrugged irritably. "Any other time, I'd have the whole department zeroed in on this. What else have you got?"

"Nothing you can lay hands on, but I don't like the way Orin's filling up the Plaza for..." He paused as another tech signaled for his attention. "Hold on, Ben. You have something, Renna?"

She nodded. "A report from Seton at Daro Galinin. The High Bishop Simonidis just arrived."

Jael felt his throat constricting. "For Last Rites?"

"I suppose, but Lord Woolf's still at the Hall with the Directorate."

Jael turned to the screen and relayed the information to Ben, whose eyes narrowed even further.

"Well, Jael, as long as Woolf hasn't been called in, it probably just means Galinin's not getting any better."

"Probably. Now, give me your good news."

"It all gets to be relative, doesn't it? The good news comes from SSB Central Control. We got the phony orders through, and not an eyebrow raised anywhere along the line. Commander Hensel of the Directorate Guard will be expecting a forty-man

Special Riot Control unit from the SSB, and his orders suggest
the best deployment of the unit will be on the execution stand."

"I hope he takes suggestions well."

"He'll take this one. The name under it is First Commander
Aldred, Conpol, and it's cosigned by DeSen of the SSB. Have
you got enough men there? And what about uniforms?"

"Brother, we could send twice forty in." Then he added
with a shrug, "Well, at least sixty. After that we might have
to put them in Ussher's little blue suits."

Ben did a fair imitation of a smile on that. "All right. Any
changes in the plans?"

"None we can see coming. What about the MTs?"

"Every MT-equipped ship will be in the Solar System, and
we're setting up a comp program to phase with the terminals
there in Concordia. We should be able to trans all forty men
off that execution stand, once you get Alex clear."

If it came to taking Alex out by force, the odds went against
all forty men surviving to be transed. Jael regarded half that
number as an optimistic estimate. Ben was no more optimistic,
he knew; not underneath the big face-show.

"Ben, I'll need my ident info from SSB CC soon. I've got
to put in some mem time if I'm going to pull this captain gim."

"You'll have it in less than half an hour, with copies of all
the orders—everything you'll need. You're still planning to go
for Alex yourself?"

"That one's mine by soul-right, brother. Besides, I'm
damned fast in a short sprint."

"You'll have to be." He pulled in a long breath, then nodded.
"You will be. Jael, Erica's here with me. She wants to talk to
Lady Adrien."

Jael frowned. "Well, she went to one of the sleeping rooms
about an hour ago. I doubt she's managed any sleep; maybe
she just wanted to be alone." And out from under eye, Jael
added to himself, where she wouldn't have to keep her face
up all the time. But she'd probably keep it up in the dark.

Ben turned off-screen for a brief consultation with Erica,
then he turned to Jael again. "Ask her to call Erica as soon as
possible. Nothing important; Erica just wants to check on her.
But don't tell her that."

"She'll tally it. Anyway, I'll give her the message. Anything
else?"

"No, not now."

"All right, then. Fortune, brother."

"You, too. Later, Jael."

The agent in SSB Central Control came through with the vital orders and information Ben had promised in less than five minutes. Jael was still immersed in it half an hour later when he was distracted by someone calling his name; one of the techs at the intercom board.

"Dana Lamodo for you, sir. She says it's Pri-One."

Jael went to the console, frowning. "Who?"

"Dana Lamodo. In the access apartment."

"Oh." He sat down at the console, where a middle-aged woman looked out from a screen. He remembered her now. "What's wrong, Ferra?"

"Sir, it's Lady Adrien. She's . . . gone."

For a moment, he could only stare at the woman blankly.

"She's *what?* How could—never mind. Just say it out."

She did, haltingly. A few minutes ago Adrien had asked to be transed up to the apartment. She wanted to be in a room with windows. Everyone on the staff knew who she was and what Alex was to her; it was no surprise she pulled the gim so easy. Uplevel, in the Lamodo apartment, Ferra Lamodo, in motherly style, made her comfortable by a windowall overlooking a park court, then offered refreshment. No surprise that the Lady smiled gratefully and asked for a cup of tea. And, when Ferra Lamodo went to the kitchen to prepare it, the Lady Adrien walked out the front door.

"Damn her. *Damn* her."

Dana Lamodo's mouth sagged open. "I . . . I'm sorry, sir."

"Well, don't worry. We'll . . ." What? Find her? Before the SSB or Selasis did? "Was she carrying anything?"

"I'm not really sure. She was wearing a cape, and I suppose she might've had something hidden—"

"A cape?"

"Yes. An ordinary woman's style. She said she was . . . cold. Oh, Jael, she looked like a lost child, but with never a tear. It didn't occur to me . . ."

"I know, Ferra. You were gimmed by an expert. Don't let it hackle you." He signaled to the tech. "Get me Daly. He's at the Directorate Hall."

And that's where Adrien would be as soon as she could reach it. Perhaps she could. She probably had a cover disguise under the cape; there were no locks on the doors here, and she'd had plenty of time to locate the costume and disguise ident room. She had sense on her side; she'd step light. And she had will, the kind that looked at death as no more than an impediment to her purpose.

Jael knew her purpose, and whatever it might mean to the Phoenix, to the Concord, to history, he couldn't find it in him to wish failure on her.

The Lady Adrien Eliseer Woolf didn't intend to let her husband die unavenged.

8.

Within the great shaft dominating the Hall of the Directorate was a circular well thirty meters in diameter extending from the first level to the twentieth, the topmost, where it was capped with a dome of red-amber glass. It was encircled at every level with balconies, their balustrades and supports forming an interlocked pattern of arching lines and faceted planes, white marlite and polished steel washed in the rubescent light, so that to stand on the lower balconies and look up to the distant source of light was like standing within the magnified heart of a crystal lattice.

Adrien Eliseer Woolf stood thus on the second level, hands locked on the railing, and she seemed to feel a vibration in her palms, as if the whole of the lambent lattice sang with some silent music of its own making. She looked up into its carnelian heights through the blue haze of the veil of her Sisters of Faith habit.

It had seemed fitting when she found this habit in the Phoenix HQ disguise ident room. She had her choice of Orders, in fact; there were habits for six Orders among the costumes and uniforms. She also had her choice of ident cards, including those suitable for the various Orders.

And her choice of weapons.

But she had only brought some stun darts with her into this

building. She chose the nun's habit in part because she knew it would allay suspicion on the part of the Directorate guards—and it did; they had been consistently solicitous and accommodating—but their attitude would have changed abruptly if the metal detectors had discovered a gun under the habit.

Still, she must have one, and soon.

She pushed her sleeve back to look at her watch. One of the entrance guards had frowned over that, but he wasn't sure enough of the Order's restrictions to venture a comment.

19:10. She had been in the Hall nearly an hour.

And from one of the windowwalls overlooking the Plaza, she had watched the Bond workcrew setting up the execution stand, seen the Plaza in the waning light of the afternoon filling with a restless, waiting crowd, and she had thought of Concord Day, of the many times she had sat with her family on those tiers of steps among the Concord's glittering Elite, looking down into the Plaza brimming with tens of thousands of Fesh and Bonds gathered for the celebration.

And this year they gathered to celebrate Concord Day belatedly, and not with spectacular fireworks, but with—

Alexand—oh, my Promised, my husband. . . .

She clung to the railing, body bent with palpable pain; her skin crawled with chill, her forehead seemed locked in a constricting band.

She knew what he was going through at this moment as she had every moment of the last ten hours. Sometimes she could hear screams. They were born in her own mind, she knew, yet again and again, as she waited in the close-walled confines of the Phoenix HQ, she had looked around her to find the source of those terrible cries.

Sharing only doubles the pain, and yet it makes it easier to bear. A paradox, that.

He had spoken those words on the night she became his Promised. But the paradox failed when pain passed a certain level of intensity. And who would share with her the pain of grief when he was dead?

I can't survive this twice.

But neither would Orin Selasis survive it.

And Phillip Woolf?

She straightened, pulling her shoulders back, looking up

into the red-gold crystal well. Trembling still; every smallest
muscle in her body trembling.

She looked up through the haze of her veil and saw the
adamantine face of Phillip Woolf.

"How *can* I believe you? How can I believe him? Don't call
him my son! My son lies sleeping there in the nursery—my
only son!"

Had Woolf any right to survive Alexand?

She heard voices, low and tense, as all the voices seemed
to be in this Hall today. She turned. Three Concord Fesh: clerks
or techs. They glanced indifferently at her as they passed and
walked away down one of the radial corridors.

"... if I could get off duty, I'd sure as hell be out there,
too...."

Why? she wondered. To see justice done? Or simply to see
death done?

She started down another corridor. It didn't matter. Orin
Selasis would see justice done. Nothing else mattered now.

Still, the three Fesh reminded her that she must keep up her
guard. She had encountered few people once she left the front
windowwalls where the curious gathered to look down on the
Plaza. But there would be Phoenix agents in this building
searching for her. That was one reason she had stayed toward
the front of the Hall, stayed with the crowds. And one reason
why she had spoken to no one—not even to answer the most
casual courtesies—except the entrance guards. The Phoenix
agents sent to find her would have recognition conditioning for
her voice.

Jael, forgive me for burdening you with more anxiety, but
I have no choice. Save him if you can, and if you can't...

Jael would understand.

Now she hurried down the halls, and she was herself searching. She must find a guard; she had to arm herself if justice
were to be done.

There were few guards in the Hall; most of them were out
in the Plaza. That made it more difficult to find one in an
advantageous situation, but it also meant that where there would
normally be two posted, she would find only one now, and at
length, after she had walked what seemed kilometers of white
corridors, she found one stationed at an emergency-use lift on

a narrow, less frequented hallway, and he was alone.

One of the stun darts was hidden in her right hand. She'd had no instruction in its use, but the mechanism seemed obvious enough: hold the narrow end, where the needle was sheathed, against the victim's skin, and press the flange at the other end that fit so comfortably under her thumb.

The guard was a young man with fair coloring; he reminded her of her brothers. She approached him slowly, her steps faltering, and when he looked around at her, pressed her left hand to her heart. He started toward her, frowning.

"Sister? Is something wrong?"

A few more stumbling steps; she was gasping for breath.

"Is there—a doctor . . . an infirmary or . . . ?"

"Yes, Sister, on Level 5. Let me help you." As he spoke, he closed the distance between them. *"Sister!"* He was close enough now to reach out and catch her when, with a choked cry, she stumbled and fell.

She clung to him, still gasping, while he eased her down to the floor. He didn't even seem to notice the prick of the needle in his arm, and for a moment she was chilled with fear that the stunner hadn't worked, that she had picked the wrong type, or hadn't used it properly.

Until his mouth sagged open and he stared at her with suddenly glazed eyes full of startled reproach, then she was in turn easing him down to the floor.

She crouched over him, looking up and down the hall, holding her breath to listen. Nothing; no one approaching. Then she turned him on his back and unsnapped his holster and took out the X^2. Her hands were shaking, but she couldn't control it. She dragged him to the lift. Only a few meters, but the effort left her panting. The up lift. It was empty; that was assured by its emergency-use designation. She pushed him out into the void of the shaft where he floated, supine, rocking gently on nothingness. She held on to the lift wall while she reached out and gave him an upward push. He began drifting leisurely toward the next level.

She didn't know how long he'd remain unconscious or how soon it would be before he was discovered. It didn't matter. She wouldn't need much time.

She stripped off the blue habit, thrusting the gun into the

waistband of the slacsuit she wore under it. She still wore the
cape, too; it would hide the gun. Finally, she tossed the habit
and koyf into the lift where they billowed, cloudlike, seeming
more alive than the unfortunate guard.

Then she turned and struck off down the corridor. 19:40.
She must find a public lift to take her up to Level 3. The
Chamber of the Directorate was on that level.

And Orin Selasis would be there, and Phillip Woolf.

Alexand, I won't survive this grief, but neither will they.

Above all, Orin Selasis won't survive it.

My sons, Richard and Eric, forgive me. Forgive your mother
her frailty.

You will be loved, and perhaps one day you'll understand
that your mother loved you, but could not survive the grief of
another love. Not twice.

. . . I take this vow for life and unto death. . . .

9.

"Marton?"

Dr. Stel had fallen asleep in the armchair he'd drawn up by
the bed. At the sound of his name, he roused with a start.

"Is it time?"

Dr. Perris was standing on the other side of the bed; it was
his voice that had wakened him. Perris frowned at the question,
and Stel realized it wouldn't make sense to him. He looked at
his watch: 19:44.

"I . . . must've been dreaming, James," he said, but that was
a lie. He was waiting for 20:00 TST. Perris might understand,
but Stel didn't try to explain.

At 20:00 the man who had done this, who had destroyed
one of the finest human beings, the greatest leaders, the Concord had ever known, would die. It wasn't enough, but it was
all that could be exacted of him as retribution.

At the foot of the bed, the High Bishop, the Revered Eparch
Simonidis knelt praying. He hadn't said the Last Rites yet, but
he would before this day ended.

"Marton, I think . . . look at the brainwaves."

Stel came fully alert, staring at the biomonitor screen in amazement. Lord Galinin was fighting his way toward consciousness.

"Holy God, James, I'd never have thought it possible."

Perris was bending over Galinin now; he only nodded. The Bishop's murmur of prayers stopped; he rose slowly, and for what seemed a long time, the three of them waited, listening to the quickening signals of life, watching the burgeoning of a faint flush in Galinin's face.

"The respirator mask," Perris whispered. "I'd better get it off."

Stel helped him ease it off, waiting anxiously to see if Galinin's lungs would take up their function adequately. A few irregular gasps, then his breathing settled into a steady rhythm; shallow, perhaps, a little too fast. Then, as if he himself had been waiting to be sure of his breathing, Galinin opened his eyes.

Stel thought fleetingly that he should notify Woolf, but he was afraid to leave Galinin even for that short a time. He wasn't deceived by this resurgence of strength. The phenomenon was too often a precursor of death.

"James? Is that . . . ?" Galinin's voice was a rough whisper.

Stel offered him some water from a spouted vaccup while Perris replied, "Yes, my lord. Just relax, now, and try to—"

"Ah, the counsel of . . . old men. Dr. Stel . . . thank you. Dry. Little dry." Then he peered for a time toward the end of the bed. "Simonidis? Come to . . . pray me out?"

The Bishop bowed, pinched mouth drawn down.

"Yes, my lord. I've come to ask the blessings of the Holy Mezion and the All-God on this their faithful—"

"Wait till . . . I'm ready to meet them. Where . . . where's Emil?"

Perris answered, "Your lord brother is in the anteroom with Lord Rodrik. Do you wish to speak to them?"

His eyes closed on a frown. "No, not . . . not now. First I must see . . . Escondo. And hurry. Not much time."

Perris glanced meaningfully at Stel, and both recognized Galinin's purpose. A death testament of some sort. Lamet Escondo was Galinin's personal barrister-counsel.

Perris started for the door. "I'll call Master Escondo, my lord. He's in the anteroom, too."

"Good. And tell Emil... I put him off not... not for lack of love. Only lack of... time."

"I will, my lord."

Simonidis remained standing but resumed his prayers, and, after a minute or two of that, Galinin opened his eyes and rasped irritably, "For the God's sake, Frer... at least for *my* sake, stop... stop all that mumbling."

The Bishop stiffened, chin quivering, but refrained from comment, and at that moment Perris returned with Escondo. The barrister was carrying a flat case; he approached the bed hesitantly, his dark skin nearly as gray as his sparse, kinky hair.

"Oh, my lord..."

Galinin winced as he turned his head a few degrees.

"Lamet? Is that you?" Then a long sigh; Escondo was on the verge of weeping. "My friend, get hold of yourself. Please. I... so little time. Things I must do."

Escondo, with an effort, got himself under control.

"Of course, my lord. How—how may I be of service?"

"I must make... declaration of House succession. No time for... fancy documents. A recording. Can you make it proper? Legal... whatever?"

Escondo put his case on a chair and opened it.

"Yes, my lord. Recorded testaments or declarations *are* accepted by the courts and Board of Succession. I'll need two witnesses to the recording. They'll make statements both at the beginning and end of the tape, and they must have copies made simultaneously, and then—well, your thumbprint sealing the spools. That will make it sufficiently... uh, proper."

Galinin smiled. "Then let me... rest a bit while you take care of the preliminaries. You have three witnesses. Doctors Perris and Stel, and the Revered Frer. Might as well... use all of them. But, Lamet... hurry."

Escondo hurried, and within five minutes the recorders were activated, he had read a prefatory statement of amazing brevity, considering its legal nature, and the three witnesses had made their statements. For a moment, Stel feared that Galinin had lapsed again into unconsciousness, but when Escondo told him he might now make his declaration, he opened his eyes, seeming perfectly aware of his surroundings, alert and calm.

Perhaps that was why Stel was so shaken by the declaration that followed. He'd have sworn any oath that Galinin was entirely sound of mind at this moment. In fact, he *had* sworn it in his statement as a witness.

"I, the Lord Mathis Daro Galinin, First Lord of the House of Daro Galinin, being without a living son and direct heir, do hereby exercise my obligation to name my successor to the position and title of First Lord of the House of Daro Galinin." He stopped then for a few breaths, still calm, and Stel's only concern at that point was for his physical state. The shock was yet to come.

"I hereby name . . . as my successor the Lord Alexand DeKoven Woolf, my grandson by my eldest daughter, Elise Galinin Woolf, and/or the Lord Alexand's . . . sons and heirs. May the Holy Mezion and the All-God grant him and the House . . . peace."

Escondo stared at Galinin, but before he could object, Stel caught his eye and stopped him with a shake of his head. If Lord Galinin in the confusion of illness and injury thought his grandson still alive, then let him think it. He was dying. Let him die content in this delusion.

His breathing was increasingly labored. He closed his eyes, exhausted as if he had just completed some demanding athletic feat.

"Lamet . . . the final . . . statements of witness. Let me . . . hear them."

They repeated their oaths, swore to the veracity of a pain-born delusion. What else could they do? Then Escondo took the four tapes from the recorder and Galinin sealed them with his thumbprint. Escondo had to help him, holding the spools against his thumb until the print was made. Finally, he gave the witnesses their copies with solemn instructions for their safekeeping, then turned to Galinin with the fourth in his hand.

"Do you wish . . . uh, should I . . . ?"

"Give it . . . to . . . Phillip. Lord Woolf. And, Lamet . . ." A long pause while he fought for breath. "Message for him. For Phillip. Tell him . . . to listen. Alexand is our . . . hope. Tell him to—to love his . . . son."

Stel felt tears scalding his cheeks. He didn't try to hold them back. Galinin was beyond seeing them now.

Simonidis asked, "Is he finally . . . gone?"

Stel shook his head. "Not yet. He's unconscious. But perhaps you should go ahead and . . ." He couldn't speak the words aloud. *Say the Last Rites*.

Escondo was staring at the spool in his hand. He asked of no one in particular, "What should I do with this?"

The Bishop answered with a weighted solemnity that at last seemed fully appropriate, "You will give it to the Lord Woolf, Master Escondo, exactly as your Lord instructed you."

And Lord Woolf must be called, Stel reminded himself.

But Simonidis was kneeling to begin the Rites, and Lord Emil and Rodrik and Lady Marcessa were coming in. Perris must have summoned them. They were all kneeling with Simonidis, and Stel could only kneel, too.

After the Rites. There was nothing Lord Phillip could do, at any rate.

Stel glanced at his watch before he closed his eyes in prayer. 19:58. His prayer wasn't for the soul of Lord Galinin; that he left to the Bishop. His prayer was one of bitter gratitude.

Justice, however inadequate, would be meted out in the Plaza of the Concord within minutes.

10.

The black 'car had no windows.

When the door slid open, a furious rush of wind swept in. But he couldn't feel it. Only hear it. He looked up and saw a fragment of sky, and knew he had never seen anything so beautiful. Ruby pink and opal orange clouds curdled on azure. A silver sliver of moon danced among them.

Two dark shapes came between him and the sky.

"Come on, you. No good giving us trouble now."

You. Why didn't they call him by his name? He had a name now. He knew who he was, where he was, why he was here.

The span of chain between his manacled hands rattled when he raised them for assistance, teeth clenched as the SSB guards pulled him out of the 'car. They weren't unnecessarily rough, it was simply that the smallest movement, even breathing, even the hammering beat of his pulse, was painful. The SSB psychocontrollers had been given less than eleven hours and a man who admitted himself military commander of the Phoenix.

And now Alexand sagged, doubled over in his guards' support, and wondered if he could even stand upright.

The wind was a battering roar; it evoked some new shape of fear in him when he thought he knew all its shapes. Yet he couldn't *feel* it. He could feel the chill of the spring evening, but not that howling wind.

"Can he stay on his feet?" He could barely hear that indifferent question over the wind roar.

Alexand answered it. "Yes . . . I can. . . ."

Rich—oh, Rich, help me. Reach out to me. . . .

Rich had been here, looked out at this world from this place, looked out from within a body flayed with a different kind of pain, looked out at his own death without fear.

The wind beat louder as he straightened, testing his balance, making sure he had both feet squarely under him.

Rich, stay with me; let me see this, understand it, accept it, meet it, with your eyes.

And the pride that's my only heritage from my name.

He wore the blue-and-silver uniform the Concord recognized as evidence of one identity. In the SSB DC, when he was ordered to put the uniform on, he didn't recognize or understand it. He did now.

But he would die as the Lord Alexand DeKoven Woolf.

The helions were on, washing white the red reflections of sunset on the buildings, and the Plaza was a solid sea of humanity.

Concord Day, and the Fesh and Bonds gathered to see their rulers in splendid panoply, gathered to see and cheer, and he wondered why they cheered.

But the Fountain of Victory was stilled.

It wasn't Concord Day.

And the wind he could only hear, bludgeoning his ears, wasn't a wind.

The crowd wasn't cheering on this day. Another sound he couldn't name; something pounding with brute ferocity. The crowd had become that equivocal entity he had always recognized as potential behind the cheers. He stood in a space of white solitude. Between him and that unkenned entity, a barrier of black shapes, golden-helmeted Directorate guards, a motionless line that, followed to its culmination, brought his eye to the lightless monolith of the execution stand.

Rich, stay with me. . . .

He took two steps and nearly fell; his aching nerves seemed incapable of conveying his commands from brain to muscle.

I will *not* be carried to that stand. Rich was carried only because he had to be. I can walk. I *will* walk.

I'm not a saint; all I have is pride.

Pride on the one hand, Rich on the other, and Adrien as a presence realized without conscious thought behind every thought, Alexand walked, step by step.

Rich *had* been afraid. Only now did he understand that. Rich had chosen the manner of his death, yet when he crossed this endless few meters, he was afraid.

How could the space take so long to traverse?

At first he tried to count his steps, but after six lost track. The physical act of making them took too much concentration, and the wind . . . no, the crowd. It was an aural centrifuge. He looked out through the barricade of guardsmen. Faces, unique, individual, yet in their open-mouthed, shrieking fury, they forfeited individuality and humanity to become mere fragments in a blurred tapestry.

"It *is* the Brother!"

That shard of sound caught at him. He stumbled, depending on his guards for support until he reestablished the nerve-muscle sequences that moved his body forward.

"The Brother! It *is* the Brother! The Brother of the Lamb!"

One face loomed out of the tapestry. An old man robed in the green and brown of a Selasid Bond, stretching forward, crying out, while the guardsmen pushed him back.

"It *is* the *Brother!*"

Alexand turned away.

Impossible. Hallucinating. He was hallucinating.

Why did they make this distance so long? Why stretch it when he was so near the end of his strength and will?

"The Brother! The Brother! The Brother!"

Bruno Hawkwood used one of the side entrances into the Hall of the Directorate, but the hood of his cloak was back, and he wore no face-screen. He'd have used the front entrance if it weren't closed, and the Conpol officers and Directorate guards he encountered didn't concern him.

Orin Selasis would pay any price for Hawkwood's head, but he didn't dare seek assistance from the Concord. The last thing he wanted was for Hawkwood to fall into Concord hands. Master Ranes would be charged with procuring his head. He would fail. Like his Lord, he never truly understood human nature, only human weaknesses. Ranes wouldn't look for Hawkwood here any more than Selasis would.

There was only one guardsman at the entrance, and one inside at the check station. Guard ranks in the Hall had been stripped to fill those outside in the Plaza. Hawkwood studied the screens behind the station desk; the prisoner was being escorted to the execution stand. The volume on the speakers was low, yet something in the quality of that mass roar aroused an ambiguous uncertainty.

Had he read the Signs correctly?

In two hours of alpha meditation, the alignments of the metagraph had yielded the same results thrice times three. Adrien Eliseer Woolf was the Prime Sign. As long as she lived, the Lord Alexand could not die. That was the first link of predication.

The images were wavering. He blinked to clear his focus and reminded himself to make allowances for the poison. It would slow his reflexes.

"Evening, Master Hawkwood." The station guard greeted him with wary courtesy. "Uh . . . your business here, sirra?" Standard procedure. Still, he seemed reluctant to pry into Bruno Hawkwood's affairs even so circumspectly.

Hawkwood said for him and the recorders, "I have an important message to deliver to the Lord Selasis."

The guardsman nodded and waved him to the position marked on the floor in front of the metal detector.

"I'll have to run you through the scanner, sirra. Any metal on you?"

Hawkwood opened his cloak and let him see the Wheel of Destiny medallion.

"This. And my wedding ring."

"Um-huh. Right." He checked a screen on the desk in front

of him. "You're clear, sirra. Thank you."

The green light went on, and the shimmer of the shock screen barricade disappeared. Hawkwood stepped onto a pedway that carried him toward the center of the Hall.

Perhaps he should wait until the execution resolved itself. That was a key link in the chain of occurrence, one that read dimly. He was only sure that it wouldn't play itself out as the Concord, and Orin Selasis, expected it to.

Still, he wasn't a Reader. Perhaps he should—

No. He'd calculated the time and the amount of poison closely. He couldn't change his plans; this was now Written. Under his cloak, his hand went to his waist and the crucifix of the Dagger of Will.

This was Written.

"The Brother! The Brother! The Brother!"

Hallucination. That wasn't even the same voice, wasn't even one voice. The black barricade ahead sagged, then with a fusillade of laser flashes and anguished cries, restored itself.

The process of moving his body within the strictures of pain and pummeling sound occupied his mind totally, yet he must free part of it to understand this phenomenon.

The old man. Alexand focused in near memory on that one face. He knew it; he'd seen it before.

"The Brother! It *is* the Brother—the Brother—Brother—Brother—"

New voices. More voices.

Izak. There was the name. Izak, Elder Shepherd of the Selasis Estate Compound B.

Izak had looked at the man named by the Concord and uniformed as Commander Alex Ransom of the Phoenix, and had recognized the Brother. Impossible. The uniform alone would blind Izak to the face of the man in it.

It *is* the Brother.

The emphasis on the verb. Verification of something doubted, but something he'd been led to expect. Izak had been *told* that Alex Ransom was the Brother.

No one outside the Phoenix could tell him that. No one except—

Orin Selasis. Ussher knew.

The steps to the execution stand. Alexand had to devote his full attention to them and to containing the surge of nausea.

Seven steps. He remembered that; Rich remembered it. Rich remembered the figure standing at the top of the steps dressed in mourning black, face-screened, motionless, present as a testament of faith.

Alexand looked up and saw the figure there, looking down at him, and at first it didn't seem unreasonable. But this man wore the black helmet of the SSB.

The stairs. If they'd give him a little time, he could manage them, and if he could explain to the guard on his right that holding that arm only made it harder.

Rich, stay with me. I've made it this far. . . .

That battering wind of sound. He *could* feel it now. The stand vibrated with it; he felt it through the soles of his boots, and there was terror in it. He was panting; not enough air. Not enough air in this huge Plaza for their rage and for him.

And was it not a righteous rage?

Overhead in hovering 'cars, peering out from alcoves and windows, PubliCom vidicams were recording the execution of justice for all the Concord, for history.

A righteous rage, and he understood it.

"The Brother! Brother! Brother! Brother! Brother of the Lamb! The Lamb! Lamb! Lamb! Lamb!"

That he didn't understand.

Or perhaps he only feared it more.

He paused when he mastered the last step, and his escort allowed him that. Perhaps they needed the pause, too, to try to make sense of what was happening in this crowd.

The sky was a glory of pink and scarlet, and from this level, the whole of the vast tapestry of beings filling the Plaza was visible, dazzling under the helions. Along the promenades were lines of Directorate guards, gold helmets flashing, and on the roofs above them, white-helmeted Conpol squads manned X^4 laser cannons. The execution stand was lined on three sides with more black uniforms. SSB. He noted that as an anomaly. Below the stand, stretching all the way across it, was a close-spaced rank with helmets of gold. At the top of the tiers of steps, guarding the entrance to the Hall, was a Conpol rank armed with shoulder-mount X^3s. Above them in the clefts of the Hall, more X⁴ squads were posted, and above the buildings, black Conpol aircars hovered.

The Concord was ready.

But for what? Who had foreseen the metamorphosis taking place in this crowd now?

The roar was stunning, mounting incredibly beyond the limits of tolerance, but it was no longer a shapeless sound that might be mistaken for a storm howl.

"The Brother! The Brother! The Brother! The Brother!"

It beat back and forth across the expanse of the Plaza, smashed into the faces of the buildings, recoiled, swept back to strike another wall, recoiled again.

This righteous rage belonged to the Bonds, rage against the man they called holy because he was the brother of a saint; the man who betrayed them by being someone else, by being a man arrayed in uniform, a man who commanded war and death, and a man who tried to kill the noblest of the noble, the strong and gentle father-leader of the Concord.

The tapestry was shimmering like a desert mirage; the hammering clamor seemed to set the air in motion. Great masses of double hues were coalescing, Bonds in their House tabards, consolidating into solid entities within the larger entity. And as those took shape, the excluded particles, the Fesh, shifted toward the periphery of the mass, making room for the expanding bicolored aggregations creeping amoeba-like toward the execution stand.

"Oh, 'Zion, we're down for it now!"

The voice was less than half a meter away or he wouldn't have heard it. One of the SSB escort.

Alexand turned, trying to keep his eyes in focus as he looked toward the center of the stand. The faceless man in the red uniform waited there by the stabile laser.

Rich, I'm afraid. Where did you find that light that was never quenched until death put it out?

Was I not proud, too, my brother? Did I not know how many people depended on my courage, then and for the future?

You were one of them.

Alexand took the first step toward the executioner.

•   •   •

This was Written.

Bruno Hawkwood looked down into the Plaza from a sec-
ond-level windowall where a place was made for him by the
Fesh crowding for a view without his asking it by word or
gesture.

The brute volume of the sound from that vast multitude was
audible even behind glass ten centimeters thick. It was a sound
to inspire fear, and he felt it around him, passing like an electric
charge from one person to the next.

It was happening, the turn of Destiny the Concord and Orin
Selasis hadn't foreseen.

Yet something in that reading sounded a dissonance.

> Weaver of Now, let me see
> The warp of then since past,
> The woof of then to be.

The scene shifted out of focus, and that served as a reminder.
He counted out ten beats of his heart, gauging the intervals.
Time enough, but not time enough to answer questions already
answered.

Two narrow halls took him back to the central well and the
lifts. He'd made a brief detour to seek that vantage point at the
windowalls and, once away from them, found himself virtually
alone. When he reached the lifts, he floated up one level, then
traversed a short arc of the well and turned into a broad hallway
of white marble, as solemnly proportioned as a cathedron nave.
It was fifty meters long and ended at the great history-carved
doors of the Chamber of the Directorate.

A silent place now; he could hear the roar of the mob outside
as a malevolent murmur. Normally, there would be guardsmen
at the lifts and at least four at the Chamber doors where only
one occupied the check station; he was apparently immersed
in the screens behind him.

The sixty fluted columns ranked along the hall seemed delicate, even airy, in proportion to the height of the ceiling, yet
they were two meters thick at the base. Hawkwood walked
among them in dwarfed silence as he might in a forest. But he
wasn't entirely alone.

Behind one of the columns, ahead of him and to his right,
someone was hiding. He heard soft footsteps, glimpsed some-

thing dark disappearing behind the column.

Perhaps he had underestimated Master Ranes.

His pace didn't falter, but he veered closer to the column as he proceeded. If someone were waiting in ambush for him, he would probably delay until Hawkwood passed and had his back to him. Hawkwood let the regular beat of his footfalls serve as reassurance until he reached the column.

Then he lunged around the near side, and in a few quick, precise movements had the potential assailant pinned against the fluted marble, his hand at the throat in a grip that with a slight increase in pressure could be lethal.

Hawkwood also had the muzzle of an X^2 pressed against his own chest at the level of his heart.

Yet he loosened the grip on the throat that might have provided a bargaining lever with the laser. The woman caught in his counterambuscade looked at him with a fearless, unwavering gaze that bespoke deadly intent, but she hadn't come here to kill Bruno Hawkwood.

He stepped back, hands falling to his sides, and bowed.

The Lady Adrien Eliseer Woolf.

The Prime Sign.

Now he could be sure.

Alexand took the first step toward the executioner.

Had they forgotten the drum roll?

Official murder needs ceremony to make justice of it.

No doubt they hadn't forgotten, but even on ampspeakers it was too frail a sound to assert its presence in this battering torrent.

The face of the Shepherd, Izak, flashed in and out behind the rampart of guards as he flailed through the crowd, staying abreast of Alexand in his long, last walk. When Izak saw Alexand looking down at him, he flung himself at the living barricade, arms outstretched, hands reaching out, palms up.

"My lord! Oh, my lord . . . my lord . . ."

Alexand couldn't hear the words, but he recognized the shape of them on the old man's lips before he disappeared, thrust back into the tumultuous human currents.

The words, the hands reaching out, not in angry fists, but in open-palmed appeal, and the grief written in that ancient, skeletal face, stopped Alexand in mid-step.

"Izak! The God help me—*Izak!*"

Rough hands pulled at him, impelling him forward, toward the executioner.

"Come on! No help for you out there!"

He fought for balance, staggering with the impact of realization. The guard was wrong; he was only stating negatively what he feared.

There *was* help for him out there.

He had misjudged the timbre of the voices when the Bonds took up the name of the Brother. He'd thought it anger, thought they believed themselves betrayed by their holy man.

Had he learned nothing about them in all these years? The judgments of the Concord were as incomprehensible to them as if they were spoken in an unknown tongue. These Bonds were calling out the name of the Brother in resounding shock and grief, and their rage wasn't for him, but for those who brought him here to kill him.

Rich had a year to prepare his followers for his apotheosis; they expected it and understood it as his Testing. Still, violence had almost erupted in the wake of his death, and there weren't three thousand Bonds in the Plaza that day. Today there were twenty times three thousand, and they hadn't been prepared for this Testing. They were told Galinin's assassin would die here today, and came to find the Brother. It wouldn't be conceivable to them that the two could be one and the same.

Alexand reached the center of the stand, and the SSB escort retired, leaving him to the Directorate guard captain and two sargents. They wore no face-screens to hide the stark fear in their faces.

The sargents came up on either side of him, but the moment they touched him, the sound that seemed at absolute maximum peaked to an even higher volume, the line of guards in front of the stand sagged and strained to hold. The two sargents seemed paralyzed, staring out at that clamoring mass as they might at an approaching tidal wave.

Alexand felt his lips draw back, felt a cold elation within him that might have been laughter.

No help for me out there? I have an army, tens of thousands ready to die for me, convinced that would buy them a piece of sainthood in the Beyond. With a gesture, I could unleash that savage tide to sweep onto this flimsy box and smash it, to surge up the tiers of steps and batter down the great doors of the Hall, sweep on, pounding through the marble corridors until it reached the Directorate Chamber itself.

He saw the blue lightning of lasers as the guards fought off an assault on the steps, heard screams, not of anger, but of agony. And the smell—

"No—oh, God, no! *No!*"

He swayed, felt his knees on the verge of giving way. Izak, I'm not a saint; my visions are imperfect.

But this one was becoming acidly clear.

He might unleash this pent, ravening tide, and it would overwhelm the execution stand. It might even take him with it, carried along in a protective eddy, and the MT fixes were probably still in his boots. There was a chance—

But the tide would never reach the Hall.

Before that, the orders would be given. The lines of guards at the doors and along the promenades would close ranks and open fire. The X^4 canon squads on the roofs would turn their guns down into the Plaza and open fire. The 'car squads overhead would converge and open fire.

This vision was perfect and so horrifying, he began to weep when he realized it hadn't yet transpired. There were skirmishes along the barricades, but they still held.

And he understood now the how and why of this.

Izak, and probably other Shepherds, had been told that Alex Ransom was the Brother for the sole purpose of making this hideous vision come to pass.

Selasis. Ussher knew about the Brother. Selasis meant to create an Armageddon here that the Concord would never forget. The Bonds might hold the Lords responsible, but *they* would blame the Phoenix. They would never forget and never forgive.

Alexand sought Izak and found him only because he was so close; the black barrier had been forced back against the stand.

"*Izak! Stop! You can't let this—IZAK!*"

But Izak didn't hear; he wouldn't stop shouting.

Hands clamped on Alexand's arms; faces pale and rigid

with terror under golden helmets loomed only centimeters away.

"An ampmike! Get me—let me *talk* to them!"

The guardsmen didn't hear; they were too frightened. They were pulling him toward the executioner.

"No! Let me—not *yet!* Don't you *understand*?"

They didn't understand; they didn't hear.

Yet if they let the executioner carry out his duty now, there was no way to stop the tide. The vision would come to pass, the tide would become a horror of carnage.

He channeled every vestige of strength left him to pull himself free of the hands that would drag them all to death. He couldn't hear his own cry of pain and despair.

Free. Only for seconds. Alive and free. Seconds.

He stumbled to the edge of the stand, swayed there, shouting into that raging, booming tide, crying out in the Name of the Lamb for peace.

They didn't hear him; his voice was drowned in the howling roar. Too late. Too late. . . .

Rich! Help me! Oh, my brother, my sainted brother—

Now he could be sure.

Bruno Hawkwood looked into the face of Adrien Eliseer Woolf, the Prime Sign, and his elation took the form of a sensation of vibration, as if he were a bell struck in a vacuum.

He said in a near whisper, "Forgive me, my lady, for laying hands on you so roughly. I didn't expect you here."

But wasn't it right that she was here? If he were a true Reader, he'd have expected her.

Her chill gaze didn't waver, yet she was so pale, she seemed near fainting, except the fierce will possessing her eyes wouldn't tolerate that. A Berserker's rage was confined in those black orbs, and her gun was still aimed at his heart.

"My lady, you'd be justified in killing me, but I beg of you, don't kill me now. I'm a condemned man by my own choice. You'd only be hastening an event already Written, and I have a path I must follow to its end before I die."

Still, she didn't move; her voice was as soft as his.

"*I* have a path to follow, too, Master Hawkwood."

"Death is at the end of your path, my lady."

"Yes."

"I mean *your* death."

"But I won't die alone."

He closed his eyes, warned by a fleeting dizziness that he couldn't delay too long. A dull rumble reached his ears; something in it quickened his already erratic heartbeat. Some unfathomable terror was taking shape outside, and he knew by Insight that if he didn't pursue his Written path, the very fabric of past, present, and future would be torn.

"There's a purpose to our meeting here and now, my lady. You're here as a signpost to me on my path, as I'm a signpost on your path."

"I don't know *your* purpose here, but I do know mine."

"They're one and the same, but this is *my* path."

Her deadly intent gaze seemed to probe into his soul, and perhaps she believed him, but she didn't understand yet.

"If we're on the same . . . path, Master Hawkwood, you won't try to stop me from reaching the end of it."

He shook his head. How could he make her understand that he *must* stop her? Their purpose was the same, but not their paths. He couldn't let her die, and she would if she tried to walk this path; *his* path.

A True Path can only be walked alone.

Rich! Help me! Oh, my brother, my sainted brother—
Falling. All his strength gone. What was left?

The Brother sank to his knees in the path of the apocalyptic tide that wouldn't hear him. He lifted his chained hands and crossed his arms, forcing the right arm with the left, hands reaching for his shoulders.

The Lamb died praying, and the Brother knelt for prayer, but sought nothing behind his closed eyes except the dark silence he found there.

Rich, there's nothing left. Forgive me. . . .

Perhaps he was close to shock; he didn't know, didn't care. Perhaps his senses were too numbed to continue submitting signals to his mind, or perhaps his mind had stopped the input of signals it could no longer sort into coherent order.

He didn't know, didn't care.

He didn't know his few seconds of freedom were becoming

many seconds. He didn't know that something was happening outside his senseless husk self that every non-Bond witnessing it would call a miracle.

The Brother knelt in the path of the tide, and the men in black uniforms surrounding him, charged with his death, made no move to touch him; no move at all. The Brother had stopped time on this black stand. He held it, unknowing, while he communed with darkness and a dead saint.

He heard the drum roll.

His senses roused to submit that signal, and his mind succeeded in translating it into a question: How can I hear it now?

And an answer: The crowd-tide had receded, quieted enough to let that sound become audible.

He opened his eyes.

The tapestry had changed, a new texture imposed on the double-hued masses. Arms crossed, forming repetitious zigzags, faces tilted up to the light of the helions as if it were sunshine. And a new texture in depth. They were kneeling. He heard the murmuring of a new kind of wind; it moved out from him like a summer wind bending grasses in its invisible passage. When the wind reached them, the Bonds knelt, one by one, rank on rank, thousands upon thousands. Their voices, their anger, stilled, they knelt to pray with the Brother in answer to his unasked prayer.

But the Brother didn't call it a miracle.

These people had been left nothing of their own but their religion. From childhood, they had accepted the guidance of the Shepherds, the embodiment and arbiters of all that was holy, in every aspect of their lives and particularly in the ceremonies of worship. When the Shepherds knelt for prayer, they knelt. The response was reflexive. It was inconceivable that they could see that physical signal given by a man they called holy, the brother of a saint, without responding by imitation.

The response was inevitable.

The miracle was that he had given them the one signal that would be comprehensible in spite of the mass rage that had shaped them into a tide of disaster, that would quell the rage with the reminder that it was not righteous, it was a sin against all they held sacred.

Perhaps that came of communion with a saint.

The drum roll thrummed. His body trembled with it; fear and pain together reclaimed their holdings.

A muttering undercurrent of sound entered his awareness. The tide had been stopped, but the tide was Bond. On the borders of this crowd, fifty deep under the promenades, looking out from every window, the Fesh waited. And at hundreds of millions of vidicom screens in every city, every human habitation on every planet and satellite in the Two Systems, the Fesh waited.

The man declared guilty of attempting the assassination of the Lord Galinin still lived; that outrage was unavenged.

The Brother meant no more to them than Alex Ransom did to the Bonds.

The Concord waited to mete out justice, and the one man who knew the injustice of it because he knew his own guilt, would remain silent while the Concord slaughtered its scapegoat in faith that it would thus be cleansed of fear and delivered from disaster.

It would be, must be, done. The Concord had no choice.

A True Path can only be walked alone.

And his time was growing short. Bruno Hawkwood knew he might render the Lady Adrien unconscious without harming her, yet he hesitated at that; it would mean leaving her here, helpless and vulnerable.

"My lady, I can't let you walk with me on this path. I can't let you ... die. ..." He stopped; he was forgetting to keep his voice down. Or was it—no, he only heard his own voice more clearly now because of the silence.

Lady Adrien started to speak, but he said sharply, "Listen!"

"To *what*?"

To nothing; to the silence. That ominous, fearful murmur was gone. Something had happened out in the Plaza, the unforeseen turn of Destiny—

Abruptly, the new silence was broken with a sound so unexpected, both of them froze into taut stillness.

The doors of the Directorate Chamber had opened. Hawkwood couldn't see them from behind the column, but he didn't move. A better vantage point would also expose him.

Voices in an impassioned exchange came from the Chamber, echoed in the white recesses of the hall. He recognized one. His Lord. Orin Selasis in a vituperative rage, bellowing, "Traitor! Do this, and you show yourself the traitor you are to *all* the Concord! By the God, a traitor will never hold this chair as long as *I* live!"

And another voice, nearer, probably at the Chamber door. "A traitor *will* hold it as long as *you* live!"

Hawkwood recognized that voice, too, but above all, he recognized the free ring of defiance in it.

Now he could be doubly sure.

Lady Adrien also recognized the voice, and she reacted so swiftly, Hawkwood didn't have time to think out his own reaction. He caught her wrist, twisted it to turn the gun upward, his right hand closed over her mouth as he forced her back against the column with the weight of his body.

"Wait! Wait, my lady!" A frenzied whisper that stopped her struggles.

Perhaps she was simply surprised to find herself so suddenly immobilized. She stared up at him, then at the sound of hurrying footsteps, the focus of her gaze shifted inward, the Berserker's rage flashed from the black depths of her eyes. The footsteps echoed like hammer blows, quickening as they approached. There was a point at which Hawkwood knew he might be seen, and his one hope was immobility. He couldn't relax his hold on Lady Adrien, only pressing harder against her when she renewed her struggles.

He whispered into her ear, "I can put you out without making a sound, my lady. Don't force me to that."

She stopped fighting him, but he could still feel her tense readiness. The pounding footfalls passed; Hawkwood turned his head to see the Lord Phillip Woolf, cloak whipping behind him, break into a run as he neared the lifts. He plunged into the first one and sank out of sight.

The hall was silent again; the Chamber doors had closed.

"My lady, we are *not* on the same path if Lord Woolf is your target."

Hawkwood knew she'd have killed him then if she could, but the moment passed, and when he released her, she sagged limply, face contorted as if she were struck with pain.

"Not *just* Woolf! But he *let* Selasis—oh, Holy God, *why?* Why did you stop me?"

"Didn't you hear what he said to Lord Selasis?"

Her features lost their agonized tension. "What he . . . said?"

She'd heard nothing but the sound of Woolf's voice, the identity of it. Hawkwood understood that; he understood every nuance of grief. He was only grateful their paths had crossed so he might turn her from her False Path and save the life he had once, in mortal error, tried to take.

"My lady, follow him and you'll know why I stopped you. Your lord husband lives as long as you live."

That didn't make sense to her, not even the fact that she was free of any restraint. He took the gun from her; she seemed to have forgotten it was still in her hand.

He said, "Your path leads to life, my lady, mine to death. Go now."

She stared at him, still dazed, then broke away and started to run toward the lifts. But after a few steps, she stopped and looked back at him, and he saw her lips silently form a word, a name, in sudden comprehension.

Margreta.

He didn't wonder how she knew; he was only sure she did know. He saw tears in her dark eyes.

Her last words were spoken aloud.

"Lord bless, Bruno Hawkwood."

Then she turned, running, leaving a renewed silence in the marble solitude when she stepped into the lift.

Hawkwood turned in the opposite direction, feeling the soundless resonance vibrating within him.

Now he could be three times sure.

A True Path.

It would be, must be, done. The Concord had no choice. No choice.

And I shall die with that, when all I asked in the beginning was my birthright of choice.

Words blurted from the ampspeakers. The formal charges. To the Fesh, they were affirmations of the rationale, part of the ceremony for just murder. To the Bonds, they were only meaningless sounds. The Concord was full of meaningless sounds.

Alexand searched the faces below him and found Izak's, but until the words ended, only looked down at him, and the

Shepherd looked back, tears finding their way down the furrows of his cheeks.

The rattle of words stopped; the drum roll resumed. Alexand heard movements behind him, brusque orders.

"Izak . . . can you hear me?"

The Shepherd's hands together reached out to him.

"Oh, my lord, I hear you."

To make the words audible over that shivering staccato demanded an effort of will Alexand wasn't sure he could sustain.

"Izak, were you witness to my brother's Testing?"

"I was, my lord, I was."

"This is *my* Testing. Don't betray it with violence; don't betray me. Remember . . ." A ringing sound in his ears; his voice faded against it.

Rich, hold on to me. So little time. . . .

"Izak, remember me as you . . . remember my brother. Remember my words as you remember his."

"We will remember, my lord. We will remember."

Booted footsteps behind him. He ached with every one.

"A sanna . . . my friend, a sanna for my passing."

He couldn't hear. The ringing in his head pulsed with the pounding of his heart and the endless drum roll.

"The Lord is my shepherd; I shall not want . . ."

There, at last. Izak's frail voice joined by tens more, then hundreds, and, finally, thousands. A melody as poignantly beautiful as this evening sky. The new moon had found a clearing in the violet cloud, amethyst upon sapphire, and a single star to accompany it.

". . . He maketh me to lie down in green pastures: he leadeth me beside the still waters . . ."

The sky faded into a *lapis* blur; his eyes were failing, but he could hear his sanna, the voices tens of thousands strong, echoing among the white facades.

". . . He restoreth my soul: he leadeth me in the paths of righteousness for his name's sake . . ."

The drum roll had stopped. Soon. They would come for him soon, take him to the executioner.

"*...Yea, though I walk through the valley of the shadow
of death...*"

Footsteps. Boots. Every thudding impact set off blue light-
nings of pain along his nerves. Knife-edged voices sounded in
unintelligible crossfires.

"*...I shall fear no evil: for thou art with me; thy rod and
thy staff they comfort me...*"

Adrien, my second linked-twin soul...I had to try. I had
to try. Adrien, my love, my wife, mother of my sons, who
will be the only testament to my existence...

"*Thou preparest a table before me in the presence of mine
enemies...*"

He felt the presences behind him, sure of their pending
nearness, yet no one touched him.

Now. Take me now, in the name of mercy. I can't hold the
fear and pain at bay past the end of the song. For all those who
depend on my courage, now and in the future, test it no further.

"*Thou anointest my head with oil...*"

Even the sanna was faltering. Please. Now. *Please.*

The cadence was falling into disarray. Behind him, voices,
words, shouts. And, always, the pounding of boots.

"But, my lord..."

Only the Bonds called him that now, and they were all
kneeling out there, singing. Except they weren't. The song was
raveling out before its end.

"Yes, my lord."

"*...my cup runneth over....*"

He raised his head, wondering if he could, by some effort
of will, see why the sanna came to an end in a murmuring like
a gentle summer surf. There was Izak kneeling, looking up in
wondering awe. Yet he'd stopped singing.

More amplified words barked out. Is that how they killed

the sanna? Strange, when it survived the drum roll.

Go home.

He thought he heard that among the word/sounds. No. He must be hallucinating again. The words stopped. He closed his eyes again; only the murmuring surf was left.

He felt a hand on his left shoulder.

Now.

Finally, it was now, and the sanna was gone.

Adrien, for our sons, then. I'll die with my courage intact for them. He gathered himself, waiting for the hard grip on his arms, the jerking upward pull.

It didn't come.

The hand still rested on his shoulder. A presence. Close enough so he could hear a long, aching sigh. Alexand opened his eyes, waited until dim shapes materialized before them, then turned his head. For a long time, his mind wouldn't accept the image his eyes presented it.

It admitted recognition. This was one of the first faces he'd ever learned; that code would never be lost. But his mind balked at recognizing this face in this context, at finding it here so close he might have kissed that cheek, as the child Alexand had done so many times. And his mind balked at seeing those eyes drowned in tears; there was no code for that anywhere in his memory.

Yet, in the end, it had to be accepted.

His mind conceded, *This is your father.*

Phillip Woolf looked out at him down a long tunnel of years and said, "Alexand, forgive me."

A True Path.

Even the doors that would otherwise be closed to him were easily opened.

As he approached the check station, Bruno Hawkwood studied the guardsman. He was close to panic, left alone at his post with a near disaster occurring in the Plaza, and treated only minutes ago to a heated exchange between two Directorate Lords.

And now Bruno Hawkwood.

"G-good evening, Master Hawkwood." Then, with a furtive glance down the hall, "Who was . . . I mean, that woman—was she . . . uh, someone you—"

"An acquaintance of mine, Leftant." He looked past the guardsman to the screens, to the one focused on the execution stand, and permitted himself a smile.

His Sight hadn't failed him. This death that would have torn the weave of Fate had been averted. Already the Conpol ranks were dispersing, the guardsmen filing back into the Hall, the crowds shifting and fragmenting, the exodus begun. In the center of the stand the Lord Woolf knelt holding his son in his arms. The Bonds were singing. Even at low volume, the exultant ring of the song could be heard. Hawkwood felt cool resolution in his veins. A True Path.

And even as he watched, a slight figure ran down the white tiers of steps, a woman with dark hair catching the wind of her precipitous descent. At the execution stand, one of the SSB officers met her—and there was an oddity: the man had switched off his face-screen and he made no effort to stop her, but escorted her to the spot where Woolf knelt supporting his son. She made it three kneeling figures, a composition of fortuitous grace and balance, something that should be transmuted into stone or bronze by a comprehending artist's hand.

In the dark beginning of this day, after his meeting with Lord Woolf, Orin Selasis had for Hawkwood's edification congratulated himself on his acuteness in judging human nature.

"What the unfortunate Lord Woolf likes to call *honor*, Bruno, is a luxury. In poor times, one learns that luxuries must be put aside if one hopes to survive. But Phillip is learning that lesson, however reluctantly."

Perhaps honor *should* be considered a luxury, it was so costly.

When Lord Woolf left the Chamber with that defiant affirmation of a truth, he couldn't have been unaware of the price of this luxury. Orin Selasis, in his rage, spelled it out: Woolf had forfeited the Chairmanship and thus surrendered himself and his House to ruin.

But Selasis had also spelled out his own fate.

". . . as long as *I* live."

The guardsman, noting Hawkwood's interest in the screens, turned to see what roused it, and that was all Hawkwood needed. The leverage was bad since he had to reach across the counter, but within seconds the guardsman crumpled to the floor. He would be unconscious at least ten minutes.

Hawkwood paused to gauge his own physical state. His range of focus had shortened, his pulse was fast and erratic, and the constriction in his throat made breathing difficult unless he paced it carefully.

Still, there was time enough.

He pushed his cloak back from his right shoulder—he would need his arm free—then took the Dagger of Will from the sheath at his waist. The translucent blue blade was marred with an oily stain. He found the Chamber door control behind the counter, and with a soft rumble, the panoplied panels slid back.

The carpet was a golden, harvest-ripe field, the windowall a panorama of purple sky still lighted with sunset, the Plaza a multicolored montage with the ten Directorate chairs stark, dark silhouettes against it. The chairs were empty, the Directors stood at the windowall, all intent on the execution stand.

His Lord was at the center of the panorama.

"I *believed* him! But he's demonstrated the error of *that!* The Chairman Designate in collusion with the enemy! And how long have he and his traitor son been planning his ascendancy to the Chairmanship over the dead body of Mathis Galinin?"

Lord James Cameroodo was a looming shadow to the left of Selasis; near him stood Lazar Hamid, the nervous movements of his hands casting off jeweled reflections. Next, Charles Fallor, gray and stooped, then Sandro Omer, urbanely aloof, his anxiety evident only in the tense set of his shoulders. On Selasis's right, Sato Shang, as gray and bent with age as Fallor, but still in command of his dignity, and, finally, Honoria Ivanoi and Trevor Robek. Robek seemed to be attending Lady Honoria, as if she might need support, but Hawkwood knew that was unlikely.

None of them heard the doors open, or Hawkwood's footsteps, quieted by the harvest carpet. He moved through the circle, then stopped, a distance of four meters separating him from his Lord. His time was calculated, the remainder of minutes and seconds left him diminishing, yet he wasn't impatient. He waited, the Dagger of Will in his right hand at his side, and listened to his Lord rage against treachery.

The Lady Honoria was the first to sense his presence. Garbed still in mourning, pale hair drawn back under a black-veiled koyf, she turned from the windowall, eyes fixing briefly, contemptuously, on Selasis, then moving in an unbroken arc backward, resting finally, as if on something she sought, on Bruno Hawkwood.

Her breath caught on a question, not surprise, but she didn't ask it. She didn't even speak his name. That was left to Trevor Robek, who was standing close enough to be alerted by the turning of her head.

"Hawkwood!"

All the Directors turned, their eyes making the same arc. Hawkwood waited for his Lord to recognize him.

Heavy robes fanned as he whirled. Black. Why did he choose that color today? Premature mourning for Mathis Galinin? Or perhaps Selasis was granted Sight on some level he would never understand or admit.

"Bruno!"

The name hissed explosively, his single eye glittered, half hidden in its pouched socket.

Hawkwood bowed. "Yes, my lord."

Then, because he had no intention of drawing this out, nor time to waste explaining what would be inexplicable to his Lord, Hawkwood raised his right hand, concentrating on the Dagger, its trajectory, and its target, and his arm made a quick, downward snap. The knife flew free.

It made no sound on impact; none audible over the cry of chagrin wrung from his Lord's open mouth, echoed by the other Directors. The left shoulder. He'd aimed for the heart, but it didn't matter.

Selasis staggered, right hand seeking the hilt; he seemed relieved that it had only lodged in his shoulder.

That passed an instant later when he began choking for breath, when he tried to free his laser from its sleeve sheath and his muscles wouldn't respond, when he tried to take a step toward Hawkwood and his knees buckled under him.

"You—I . . . I'll kill—kill you! *Kill* . . . you!"

"No, my lord." Hawkwood turned to Robek and Cameroodo, who were moving warily toward him. "You can do nothing for him, or to me, my lords. I've taken the same poison with which that blade was tipped. It has no antidote."

They stopped, staring incredulously at him, while Selasis

fumbled at the knife, face wrenched and reddened, head lolling, taking his eye in a circuit of his fellow Lords.

"Do . . . some-something! Why are you . . . damn you! *Damn you all!* Damn . . . da——"

No one moved or spoke. He toppled, hitting the floor with an impact that forced a guttural shout from him. He floundered like a beached sea beast, until in a flailing frenzy he turned himself on his back so he could fix his eye in dumb rage on Hawkwood. But with that his strength was nearly spent; he lay quivering, chest heaving with every desperate breath.

Hawkwood heard his own rasping breath, felt the solid pain occupying his heart and lungs. When he reached into a pocket under his cloak, his muscles responded errantly, and when he crossed the few steps to Selasis, his feet dragged, his knees wouldn't hold. He sank beside his Lord, kneeling as if in prayer.

"Take comfort . . . my lord." His numb lips defied the words. "Even in this, your . . . shadow follows. My lady Honoria? Where . . . where are you?"

Perhaps he wouldn't see Selasis die. The poison worked more slowly when taken orally, but there had been delays.

A shaft of black appeared before him. He looked up and at length found Honoria Ivanoi's face.

"My lady, I have . . . no right to ask anything of you, and yet I must . . ." He paused for breath, and as he spoke, had to calculate the words to coincide with each labored exhalation. "I ask a . . . death boon."

A soft rush of satinet; she knelt so he wouldn't have to strain upward to see her, yet her voice was distantly cold. She despised him passionately; he knew that, but he would trust no one else here to honor this death boon.

Honor. It was her name.

"What boon, Master Hawkwood?"

"This . . . tape spool" He reached across the black, heaving bulk of his Lord. "My lady, give it . . . to the Lord Woolf. The . . . elder Lord Woolf. No one . . . else."

Honoria Ivanoi took the spool. It couldn't weigh more than a gram, she knew, yet it seemed an icy weight burdening her palm. Hawkwood's hand fell away from hers, dropping against his thigh; his pale eyes, the color of winter grasses, looked out of shadowed sockets in a face in which the bronzed planes seemed dusted with silver.

She stared down at the spool, and found words almost as difficult to shape as he did.

"What . . . is this?"

He said, "My death testament. The attempt on Galinin's life, Lord Karlis's . . . illness. And more. My lady . . . the truth."

"Nooohhhhhh—"

Honoria rose, recoiling in frank fear. Selasis heaved himself up, clawing toward her, toward the spool.

It was his last living movement.

He fell back, head thudding against the floor, his eye turned upward, and a cryptic stillness seemed to descend upon him. Honoria stared, transfixed, and as it always seemed inconceivable that the living could cease to be living, now it seemed inconceivable that this silent object had ever sustained a motive force called life.

In some dim distance, a bell began tolling.

A single bell monotonously repeating its one doleful tone. She recognized it. It had only to be heard once to fix itself forever in memory. It came from the Cathedron.

The death knell.

Perhaps Hawkwood heard it, too. He drew a long, painful breath that whispered out with his last words.

"Destiny writes itself out in paradox. . . ."

He sank within himself, sagged slowly forward, and at length fell across the lifeless mass that had been his Lord. Honoria watched the inconceivable process of death a second time, finding some elusive meaning in the stark patterns of black and brown against gold. Hawkwood's left hand was flung out toward her, nearly touching the hem of her gown. There was a narrow gold band on the fourth finger.

Paradox.

Nothing within her cognizance now didn't seem a paradox; the patterns of black and brown on gold, the patterns of lives and deaths, here in this Chamber, outside in the Plaza where the fragmenting crowds, having witnessed the preservation of life, paused to hear the tolling of a death knell.

Paradox, that she had always known, but could never prove,

that Orin Selasis and his henchman, his Master of Shadows, were together guilty of her husband's murder, and now they lay dead before her, she had watched them die, and yet she felt no satisfaction. All she felt was grief, the old grief for Alexis, renewed and even more mordant.

She felt the cold weight in the palm of her hand. The truth. Paradox that Bruno Hawkwood had become a source of truth.

In the Plaza, beyond the listening multitudes, the Fountain of Victory came to life, lifting its exalting white plumes against the indigo sky. She thought of Phillip Woolf, and that dulled the edge of revived grief. Phillip, who had watched his son kneeling in prayer to stop a disaster, and recognized it as an ultimate act of self-sacrifice, who had recognized then that the terms of survival offered him by Orin Selasis were unacceptable.

He is my son, and he is innocent. I will not let him die, I will not let him be sacrificed to the greater glory of Orin Selasis!

Honoria became aware of the other Directors, like somnambulists, rousing themselves to wonder where they were, what had happened, exchanging tentative, consulting glances.

Trevor Robek touched her arm. "Honoria? Are you . . . ?"

"I'm all right, Trevor."

Then Cameroodo, standing over the two bodies, seeming to find their presence here vaguely puzzling.

"We must . . . notify someone. . . ."

A dull rumbling; they all turned. The doors were opening. At first, Honoria didn't recognize the man who entered, he was so pale and disheveled.

Master Selig.

She watched him make his way toward them in odd starts and stops, as if he were blind and seeking the occupants of the room by sound alone. Her heart began pounding in alarm.

The death knell.

Only now did its real meaning penetrate the barrier of mental shock. That mourning bell wasn't tolling for two deaths that no one outside this Chamber could know about.

"My lords, my lords, my lords—*oh, Holy God!*"

Selig came to an abrupt halt when he saw the two silent

shapes on the floor. Trevor Robek went to him and put a bracing hand on his shoulder.

"There's been . . . a tragedy here, Master Selig. We haven't had time to—"

"Tragedy . . ." The word had a strangely calming effect; Selig seemed to lose interest in the incredible fact of two bodies, one a Directorate Lord, in this august Chamber. He gathered himself into a semblance of his usual dapper dignity.

Honoria turned away, hands in fists as if she could defend herself in that sense from what she knew was coming.

She heard Master Selig say, "My lady, my lords, I have . . . I must inform you . . ."

He couldn't seem to manage the words. She understood that; shaping grief into words inevitably destroyed the clinging vestiges of hope.

Honoria Ivanoi looked out at the white affirmation of the Fountain and spared Selig the necessity of speaking the words he found so painfully difficult.

She said them for him.

"The Lord Mathis Daro Galinin is dead."

PHOENIX MEMFILES: DEPT HUMAN SCIENCES: HISTORY
(HS/H)
SUBFILE: PHASE I: HOUSE OF WOOLF GALININ
LETTAPE #6: FROM LORD ALEXAND WOOLF GALININ
TO DR. ANDREAS RIIS 13 OCTOV 3259
DOC LOC #819/8-161-8237-122016 #6: 1237/118-13103259

My dear Andreas,

I'm transmitting an imagraph with this lettape—one that Adrien and I consider the best of the multitude taken of our daughter since her birth a week ago. So here is Elise, smiling winsomely. I think she's well named, and as you can see, she even has red hair, a surprise to all of us, and she already shows signs of an inquisitive nature and an extraordinarily strong will. The twins, by the way, have accepted their sister with equanimity and no hint of jealousy. Eric has displayed his usual heedless curiosity and is inclined to find out how this new creature works by prodding and pulling, sometimes none too gently. Rich seems content to observe from a little distance.

But enough of paternal maunderings. The real purpose of this lettape is that on this day, the eve of Concord Day, it seemed appropriate to take time to look back on the first year of Phase I, and particularly appropriate to share my musings with you, Andreas. Our triumphs are yours, really, and perhaps Elor Ussher Peladeen's.

Yet when I first set my mind to this review, my initial feelings were primarily of frustration. There is so much that hasn't been accomplished yet and Directorate alignments are not as favorable to our goals as we had hoped. The election of Lord Garwin Wale Corelis to the vacated Selasid chair was the first blow, of course, and James Cameroodo's first triumph. Cameroodo has, as predicted, come to the fore in Selasis's absence as the leader of the reactionary faction. He's a forceful man, and has Hamid entirely under his thumb, as well as Fallor, who can no longer be considered a fence rider. Even Shang tends to lean too often toward Cameroodo. Sandro Omer, perversely, still straddles the fence, despite his marriage ties with DeKoven Woolf and his generally cordial attitude toward me. It is, I'm well aware, to his advantage to hold the tie-making or -breaking vote.

But in today's Directorate meeting, with my temper growing short while Shang and Fallor wrangled over a point of procedure, I experienced one of those rare moments of insight when one grasps perfectly the proportion of things, and I realized with a certain awe that I was at that moment occupying the chair Grandser always called so damnably uncomfortable. (He was right about that, both figuratively and literally.)

My occupancy of that chair we owe to Grandser, to the Declaration of House Succession he made with his dying breath, and as I look at this imagraph of Elise, I regret bitterly that he can't see his daughter's namesake. But he knew about Rich and Eric, thank the God, before he died.

And we owe the swift implementation of the lever he gave us to Father. He recognized the period of shock following Galinin's and Selasis's deaths and the revelations of Hawkwood's death testament as the optimum opportunity, and although he refuses to accept due credit, he was instrumental in engineering my ascendancy to the Chairmanship in that first week. To be honest, I remember very little of those key days. I was too ill to make intelligent decisions, and we must all be grateful to Father for making them for me, and for since being at hand to aid in dealing with subsequent decisions.

At any rate, in reviewing our accomplishments, I must mark my occupation of the Chairmanship on the positive side, but I'm also aware that few concrete reforms can be counted for the year, and it's ironic that the only unquestionable success in the area of reform is one that affects only the Elite, and that is the Elite Divorce Ruling. That was as much a tribute to my mother as the naming of our first daughter, so I'm pleased with it for that reason. Another Elite reform issue that has a good chance of Directorate approval now is abolishing the mandatory Confleet service period for Elite males.

As for the Bond Treatment Standard (it's no longer called the G-W-R resolution since Trevor Robek asked to have his name withdrawn from it—another discouraging sign, although he still supports it, however unenthusiastically), it has had one resounding defeat already, and it would be futile to submit it again without major changes in the balance of power on the Directorate.

At least that was the doleful picture until a few days ago, when I had an unexpectedly fruitful private talk with Garwin Corelis—at his request. His election to the Selasid chair may not be as much a blow to us as we thought. He is a conservative, to be sure, but not a reactionary. At any rate, he plans to present an alternative to the Bond Treatment Standard that would not involve penalties of any kind for Houses that fail to meet the standards, but would simply offer tax levy reductions to those that do. The Board of Revenue would be responsible for judging whether a House meets the standards, which will undoubtedly be more acceptable to the Lords than inspection by a Conpol agency.

This is a compromise that falls far short of our hopes. It won't touch the Bonds in the reactionary Houses where treatment is most inhumane; their Lords will pay higher taxes willingly rather than submit to any Concord agency's "meddling in internal House affairs." Yet I regard it as something to be counted among our successes. It is at least a beginning, and from it awareness may grow, and perhaps in the future Lords who do maintain the standards will put some peer pressure on those who do not. Above all, I welcome it because it was proposed by Corelis and offers some hope that he won't be the totally negative factor we feared.

Corelis may show himself an ally in another matter, and that is the resurrection of the House of Peladeen and recognition of Jael as its First Lord. Jael Kalister—and he bears his mother's surname well—has been ever at my side this year not only because I need him, but because it gives him opportunities to meet and to some degree deal with the Directors, and we've made a point of presenting him always as an aide rather than as a servant or subaltern. He is never addressed as Fer, but as *Master* Kalister, although the God knows no guild has ever conferred on him any degree ranking. Perhaps it's indicative of his success in this ambivalent role that no guild—*or* Lord—has questioned that title.

We hope to bring the reestablishment of Peladeen before the Directorate within the next year, and I think if we can make sure of Omer's vote, we'll have a majority because Corelis hinted—obliquely, of course—that he might not oppose it. This is another surprise from Corelis, but indicates no sympathy for me, or the Phoenix, or certainly for Jael, but rather a personal loathing for Lazar Hamid. Apparently, Corelis feels Lazar could use more competition in Centauri.

If we succeed in making Jael Lord of Peladeen, we can count that as another victory, but as the old saying goes, victory has its price, and Jael will pay dearly for this one. The future Lord of Peladeen can't marry as he wishes; he must remain free to make a suitable House alliance. That means he can't marry Val Severin. Jael and Val are entirely aware of this, and both are so poignantly stoic. Since Val is Adrien's personal secretary, I see a great deal of her, and have spoken to her about it. (Jael refuses to discuss it, turning my inquiries with a laugh and the assurance that he knows the tax on the gim.) Val told me once, "I'll always love him, and he'll love me, and perhaps we'll be clandestine lovers—he wouldn't be the first Lord to have a secret mistress—but I'll never bear his children. Still, what we have is enough. It's a gift, and we accept it gratefully."

It *is* a gift, but I'm sorry they must accept so small a portion of its potentials.

But to continue my accounting. One thing can be considered a total success, but since it's a Phoenix program, that's to be expected, and that is the "Acolytes Corps," as Erica calls it, and its success is due to a great extent to her training program. We have thirty graduates of the program in the field now, and where I've been able to make follow-up visits I've been eminently satisfied with the Shepherds's response to the Brother's acolytes, and they deserve a great deal of the credit for the thirty percent decrease in Bond uprisings this year. The fact that the Bonds now identify the Brother with the Chairman—and thus the Concord—has also been a stabilizing factor, but wouldn't be nearly as effective without the constant reinforcement of the Lamb's dictums provided by the acolytes. Erica tells me another class of thirty will be ready to go on line within a month, and I have no doubt the incidence of uprisings will show another marked decline by this time next year.

Another success is the establishement of ConTrans—the agency that will control the MT when it's ready for general use. The Lords who were at first so skeptical of the MT have begun to show lively interest now that working models are available, and it's becoming an index of status to have MTs in one's Estate. Still, it will be another ten to twelve years before the ConTrans system is fully operational, and meanwhile we must keep the Selasid InterPlan System limping along, which is rather difficult when the family is so prone to constant quarreling. Karlis, to our relief, seems content to remain in his exile on Rarotong since the Board of Succession deposed him as First Lord, and has avoided contact with anyone, especially his uncle Godfry, the House's new First Lord. Karlis leads an almost monkish existence, and recent information suggests that he's turning to religion for comfort and is becoming exceedingly fanatic about it.

Perhaps that will satisfy James Cameroodo: A vindictive man, and I'll never forget the icy obduracy in his eyes when he proposed a Directorate decree of execution for Karlis. Cameroodo regarded Orin's death as a divine punishment and obviously felt Karlis deserved the same. I'm relieved that the only Director who agreed with him was Lazar Hamid. The rest of us even at that time, two weeks after Galinin's death, felt for Karlis more pity than outrage. The same pity we in the Phoenix felt for the man who called himself Predis Ussher. He was mad, and didn't deserve to die so terribly.

I'd be very interested, Andreas, in your musings on what has happened in the Phoenix during this first year of Phase I, and I hope it has met your expectations. Certainly the Phoenix has met mine, especially in the way it has assumed the role of secret partner to the Concord. I was disturbed, however, when Ben 'taped me yesterday to tell me that the Council is reconsidering the moratorium on new members. I feel very strongly that it should be maintained for at least another two years. It's too early for us to open our doors to any but special cases; too many people seeking membership now are only caught up in the enthusiasm of the moment prevalent among radical liberals, and now that membership is no longer punishable by death, we must be careful to avoid lowering our standards of admission. Becoming a part of the Phoenix must always be a lifetime commitment, and we must continue to choose our members as if we were still outlaws.

But forgive me that little sermon. I realize you don't need it. However, I'm concerned that Commander Gavin and Haycor of Communications, as well as M'Kim and Marien Dyce—I'm especially uneasy about Marien—*do* need it. If you think it would serve any purpose for me to deliver the sermon to the Council personally, I will, but I won't impose myself on them unless you feel it necessary.

Adrien asked me to extend you her invitation to visit us again. As you said, the Galinin Estate is a most gracious and comfortable place, but your fears that you might get too used to comfort are unfounded; you'd only get bored with it. I second the invitation, and for palpably selfish reasons. I have so little time and my visits to Fina have been necessarily limited. Beyond that, I no longer feel at home there as I once did—again, the tax on the gim—but I miss it, and to be able to talk to you, to spend long night hours at it as Rich and I used to do, brings me home again, home to all that is important in my life, to my very humanity. Don't deny me that.

Andreas, on the eve of this day of celebration, accept my gratitude for giving the Concord—and me—hope; the hope that one day human beings might achieve their birthright of choice. Like Elor Peladeen, I live and, if need be, shall die in that hope.

> Alexand, the Lord Woolf Galinin
> Concordia, Terra, 13 Octov 3259

Historical Chronology

●❙●

2030–2060	Decades of Disaster 2030–2040 The Great Drought 2035–2055 The Pandemic 2044 The Nuclear Wars
2060–2585	The Second Dark Age
2560	*The Revelations,* Bishop Colona (2522–2615)
2585	Founding of the Holy Confederation of Conta Austrail, Lord Even Pilgram (2523–2585)
2761	Invention of the Darwin cell
2875	The Articles of Union, Lord Patric Eyre Ballarat (2839–2920)
2876–2903	The Wars of Confederation
2903	Founding of the PanTerran Confederation

3000	First Post-Disasters Lunar landing
3018	First permanent colony established on Luna: the city of Tycho
3033	First unmanned research stations on Venus
3035	First permanent colony on Mars: Toramil
3051	First permanent colony on Mercury: Solaria
3052	MAM-An drive developed by Fredric Cadmon based on theories published the same year in Ela Tolstyne's *Treatise on Matter/Anti-Matter Interactions*
3055	Nulgrav developed by Domic Peresky
3060	The Drakonian Theory published by Orabu Drakon, the first Lord Drakonis (3025–3098)
3078	First SynchShift ship, the *Double Star*
3078–3104	PanTerran extrasolar exploration phase: eighteen expeditions to Alpha Centauri A, B, and Proxima, Barnard's star, Lalande, Sirius A, Epsilon Eridani, 61 Cygni A, Procyon A, and Kapteyn's star
3079	First permanent colony on Ganymede: New Tycho
3080	First permanent colony on Callisto: Callipolis
3083	First permanent colony on Titan: Titania
3084	First permanent colony in the Centauri System: Leda on Pollux Second permanent colony in the Centauri System: Helen on Castor
3085	First Permanent colony on Perseus, the Centauri System: Danae First permanent colony on Triton: Armentia

3087	First permanent colony on Pan, Centauri System: Thymbris First permanent colony on Dionysus, Centauri system: Semele
3088	First permanent colony on Pluto: New Paykeen
3104–3120	The Mankeen Revolt, led by Lord Lionar Mankeen (3065–3120)
3105	Founding of the Concord of the Loyal Houses
3135	Founding of the Peladeen Republic in the Centauri System
3170	First extraterrestrial colony reestablished after the Mankeen Revolt: Tycho on Luna
3172	First Concord trade exchanges with the Peladeen Republic
3200	Founding of the Society of the Phoenix Last extraterrestrial colony reestablished: New Paykeen on Pluto
3208–3210	War of the Twin Planets
3218–3241	Concord extrasolar exploration Phase: ten expeditions to Sirius A, Procyon A, Kruger 60 A and B, Van Maanen's star, and Altair
3241	Disappearance of the ship *Felicity* on the Altair expedition
3246	Galinin-Ivanoi assassinations
3258	Centauran Revolt

Census of the Concord, 3250 A.D.

Allieged to Houses:	Fesh	651,571,000	
	Bonds	1,780,503,000	
	Total		2,432,074,000
Allieged to Concord:	Fesh	420,722,000	
	Bonds	1,020,170,000	
	Total		1,440,892,000
Allieged to Church:	Fesh	232,803,000	
	Bonds	350,810,000	
	Total		583,613,000

Total number of Elite   98,382

Total number (estimated) "Outsiders"   45,000,000
                                                            _____

Total population   4,501,677,382

The Houses of the Directorate of the Concord, 3244 A.D.

●Ⅱ●

DARO GALININ: Lord Mathis, Chairman of the Directorate
    Franchises: Solar System Power Systems
    Home Estate: Concordia, Terra
    Crest: Lion
    Colors: Purple and gold
    Stone: Topaz

DEKOVEN WOOLF: Lord Phillip
    Franchises: Commutronics
    Home Estate: Concordia, Terra
    Crest: Black Eagle
    Colors: Scarlet and black
    Stone: Ruby

LAO SHANG: Lord Sato
    Franchises: Basic metals: aluminum and some iron
                           and steel alloys
    Home Estate: Paykeen, Terra
    Crest: Dragon
    Colors: Red and green
    Stone: Alexandrite

NEETH CAMEROODO: Lord James

Franchises:	Basic metals: iron and steel
Home Estate:	Toramil, Mars
Crest:	Leopard
Colors:	Yellow and indigo
Stone:	Tanzanite

D'ORD HAMID: Lord Lazar

Franchises:	Foodstuffs, primarily marine
Home Estate:	Leda, Pollux
Crest:	Owl
Colors:	Yellow and green
Stone:	Yellow citrine

ARMENT IVANOI: Lord Alexis

Franchises:	Rare metals
Home Estate:	Tycho, Luna
Crest:	Stag and Hound
Colors:	Violet and black
Stone:	Amyethyst

HILD ROBEK: Lord Trevor

Franchises:	Planetary Transystems
Home Estate:	Concordia, Terra
Crest:	Cock and Serpent
Colors:	Scarlet and orange
Stone:	Garnet

DELAI OMER: Lord Sandro

Franchises:	Computer Systems
Home Estate:	Coben, Terra
Crest:	Winged Warrior
Colors:	White and black
Stone:	Diamond

BADIR SELASIS: Lord Orin

Franchises:	Interplanetary Transystems
Home Estate:	Concordia, Terra
Crest:	Sleeping Bear
Colors:	Green and brown
Stone:	Emerald

DESMON FALLOR: Lord Charles
    Franchises: Foodstuffs: grain and livestock
    Home Estate: Montril, Terra
    Crest: Dolphin and Trident
    Colors: White and blue-green
    Stone: Aquamarine

Standard Concord Uniforms (FESH)

●ǁ●

University System:
> Teacher: Floor-length surcoat. Color: gray.
> Professor: Floor-length surcoat. Color: white.
> Lector: Floor-length surcoat. Color: white with black edgings.

> Conmed: White tunic with red caduceus shoulder patch.

> Conpol: Fitted trousers; long-sleeved, belted jacket with stand-up collar; short gloves; and cloak reaching to the top of forty-centimeter boots; all black. Trim and insignia, gold; helmet, white.

> SSB: Basic uniform same as above, but no trim; rank insignia, silver; helmet, black. Face-screen worn at all times.

> SSB Psychocontroller: Basic uniform same as SSB, but white, including helmet and boots. Face-screen worn at all times.

> Directorate Guard: Basic uniform same as Conpol. Trim and insignia, gold; helmet, gold.

Confleet: Basic uniform same as Conpol except for vertical gold stripes centered in front and back of trouser legs. Trim and insignia, gold; helmet, black with two parallel gold dorsal stripes, two centimeters wide.

Glossary—General Terms

●‖●

ACOLYTE: (Bond Religion) A student and assistant to a Bond Shepherd; acolytes are chosen by the Shepherds and generally succeed them on their deaths.

AGE OF RIGHTS: Age of legal maturity for Elite; it is celebrated on the twentieth birthday.

AIRCARS: Short-range, airborne vehicles powered by nulgrav and generally operated on Trafficon grids. Most personally owned 'cars belong to the Elite or the Concord or Church, although they may be flown by Fesh in their work. Only fifteen percent of the Fesh own 'cars, the remainder depending for personal transportation on Robek Transystems air taxis, subtrains, or intercity shuttles.
   Types of aircars:
AIRDRAY: A large vehicle designed for transporting freight. 'Drays range in capacity from ten to 100 dekatons.
AIRSCOOTER: A small open 'car with a maximum seating capacity of four, generally operated within factories, mines, etc.
AIRSHUTTLE: A vehicle used for transporting large numbers of people. 'Shuttles range in capacity from fifty to 200 passengers.

AIRTAXI: Two- to six-passenger rental 'cars equipped with voice-responsive autonav systems. 'Taxis are activated automatically when money is placed in a designated slot. Cost of 'taxi rental is based on the distance traversed.

ALLEGIANCE: A permanent indentureship to the House (or to the Concord or Church) into which Bonds or Fesh are born; that is, the House to which their parents, particularly fathers, are "allieged." The latter term is generally used in reference to Fesh; Bonds are termed "Bonded" to a House. "Allegiance shifts" from one House to another, or to the Concord or Church, are enacted only on approval of the First Lord of the House.

ALLEGIANCE BADGE: A small cloth insignia bearing the crest of the House (or of the Concord or Church) to which a Fesh or Bond is allieged; generally worn on the left shoulder of an outer garment, such as a cloak or cape.

ALL-GOD: The supreme deity of the Mezionic pantheon.

ANTISEP SHEET: (Medical) A thin plasex sheet chemically treated to act as an antiseptic barrier for the protection of open wounds prior to treatment.

AQ: Aptitude Quotient. A statistical profile, based on standardized test scores, of an individual's vocational aptitudes.

ARCHIVES: An agency of the Concord authorized to file and preserve historic documents and to serve as a data storage and dispersal center for public records and documents. It has close ties with the University System and its Library, but is a discrete agency.

ATMOBUBBLE: An energy field in which the charged interface forms a "bubble" that contains interior atmosphere while excluding exterior atmosphere (or vacuum); it may also be used to selectively exclude particular radiation wavelengths.

AUTONAV SYSTEM: Automatic computerized navigation and guidance system for ships or vehicles.

AUTOSPENSER: Generally called a "'spenser." An automatic dispenser, usually for food or beverages.

BACTERIOSTATIC GAUZE: (Medical) A porous fabric, chemically treated to inhibit bacterial growth, used for bandaging wounds or incisions.

BARRENGORSE: A spiny-lobed, photosynthetic organism, generally classified as a plant, native to the Barrens of Castor and one of the predominant species in the Marching, or Pygmy, Forests. It is a hydrotropic "migrator," moving by a process of rapid growth in low-lying, branching tendrils on the surface, and in deep-probing roots below the surface, both of which are abandoned as quickly as new shoots and roots grow, allowing the plant to follow its underground water sources.

BARRENS: The minimally fertile temperate zone of Castor between the icecaps and the equatorial desert, or Midhar.

BASIC SCHOOL: The educational system for Fesh; specifically, a ten-year mandatory program administered by the Houses (or the Concord or Church), generally following guidelines established by the University System's Department of Education. Additional one- to three-year vocational training programs are also provided by House Basic School systems, although specialized training is often a prerogative of professional Guilds.

BEAMED POWER: Solar energy collected on orbiting satellites (or on surface power-receptor stations on the Centauran Inner Planets), then transmitted to planetside receptors in the form of microwave beams, which power the high-gain kinetic (HGK) generators that produce electrical current.

BELNONG: A vertebrate triped native to Castor, a symbiont with various photosynthetic organisms of the Marching Forests. It is most notable for its capacity to regenerate itself from as little as ten percent of its body, a process that provides one means of species reproduction, although it is also trisexual and reproduces oviparously. The eggs are incubated by certain species of photosynthetic symbionts.

BEYOND: (Bond Religion) The "Realm Beyond the Farthest Star." The Bond equivalent of the Heavenly Realm, residence of the All-God and Holy Mezion and the saints, and place of reward after death for the souls of persons deemed worthy.

BEYOND SOUL: (Bond Religion) A manifestation of a dead person assumed to reside in the Beyond; a ghost.

BIOMONITOR: (Medical) A device for monitoring vital signs generally fitted in a "biomonitor cuff," which is attached to the patient's wrist. Its signals can also be displayed on a "biomonitor screen."

BLESSED: (Bond Religion) *n.* Living persons regarded as especially favored or in some way singled out by the All-God and Holy Mezion.

BOARD OF CENSORS: A committee made up of ten members of the Court of Lords, each of whom serves a five-year term. Its function is to designate Priority ratings for any material published, exhibited, performed, etc. in the Concord. Its prerogatives include destroying or prohibiting the publication, exhibition, or performance of material it judges subversive or immoral and prosecuting persons or even Houses guilty of publishing, etc., or in any way disseminating condemned material. Penalties range from fines to execution.

BOARD OF FRANCHISES: A committee made up of ten members of the Court of Lords, each of whom serves a five-year term. Its function is to distribute and allot House franchises, and to mediate disputes involving franchises. Its judgments are legally binding, and a Lord found guilty of franchise infringement is subject to fines or even imprisonment and forfeiture of First Lordship.

BOARD OF SUCCESSION: A committee made up of ten members of the Court of Lords, each of whom serves a five-year term. Its function is to oversee House successions and to determine whether they are consistent with the successional restrictions delineated in the Concord Charter. Lords judged guilty of perpetrating illegal succession are subject to imprisonment and removal, with their heirs, from their House's succession.

BOND: The term refers to the class or to individuals within it. Bonds are the lowest class in the Concord, an illiterate, slave/serf class comprising approximately seventy percent of the population and functioning as an unskilled labor pool.

BOOKTAPE: A lengthy literary work encoded on tape, from which the text and/or illustrations are displayed on a reading screen.

BORASIL: Boron, silicon, and oxygen glass; in spun form, it is used as a protective and insulating coating.

CAFFAY: A beverage brewed by various methods, most of them involving steam, from the roasted beans of the coffee plant. ("Coffee" has come to refer to a beverage made with synthesized flavoring. Like the original, it also contains caffeine.)

CANTAS: Also "High Cantas." Religious ceremonies celebrated in both Orthodox and Bond Churches commemorating various sacred events or seasons.

CARRAMINX: An organism native to Castor classified in popular terminology as a "plant-animal." It is photosynthetic and reproduces by seeding, but is rootless and mobile, has a rudimentary nervous system, and five compound eyes responsive to both light and color.

CENTAURI SYSTEM: The planetary system of the star Alpha Centauri A. The seven planets in the system are: Perseus, Dionysus, and Pan, the Inner Planets; Pollux and Castor, the Twin Planets; and Tityus and Hercules, the Outer Planets.

The Inner Planets are all small (Perseus, the largest, has a diameter of approximately 4,000 km), rocky, geologically inactive bodies devoid of atmosphere. The distance between their orbits is relatively small, making them markedly erratic.

The Twin Planets, Castor and Pollux, were so named because they are similar in size (approximately 9,000 and 13,500 km in diameter respectively) and revolve around a common center of gravity in a single orbit. Pollux has an atmosphere similar to Terra's and is even more an oceanic planet. On Castor liquid water is found under the surface, depending on the season and latitude, but above the surface it is either vaporized or frozen in the large icecaps. Castor's thin atmosphere is predominantly nitrogen and carbon dioxide with less than 5.3 percent oxygen.

The Outer Planets, Tityus and Hercules, are gaseous giants comparable to the Solar System's three ringed giants, and the main constituents of their atmospheres are hydrogen, helium, methane, and ammonia. The diameter of Hercules, the seventh and largest Centauran planet, is only a thousand kilometers less than Jupiter's. Tityus, Centauri's only ringed planet, rivals Saturn in the extent and complexity of its ring system. Hercules has ten small, icy satellites; Tityus only five.

CHAIRMAN OF THE DIRECTORATE: The Lord elected by the Directorate (although the position is in practice hereditary) as the presiding officer of the Directorate of the Concord of the Loyal Houses.

CHAN D'AMOR: A legendary love story, sometimes in the form of a poem or song.

CHRONO-SPATIAL EVERSION: A principle of the Drakonian Theory applying to time/space modification.

CIRCLE: In fencing, the area to which combatants are confined in a formal fencing match. The established dimension is a diameter of five meters, the perimeter of which is usually marked with a luminescent, photosensitive line; a bell sounds if a combatant steps on or over the line, and a point is awarded his opponent.

CLARIPIPES: (Musical) A small wind instrument made up of twelve metallic tubes of graduated lengths.

CLAVALIER: (Musical) A large percussion stringed instrument played by manipulating a keyboard. The true clavalier employs no electronic amplification.

COGNATE HOUSE: A House related to another by common ancestry.

COMARIS: An herb used as a seasoning, derived from the leaves of a plant (the comara) native to Castor.

COMCENTER: Communications center. A central terminal through which all communications and information pertinent to a particular type of operation are channeled.

COMCONSOLE: A desk-sized unit equipped with various communication devices, such as vidicom, intercom, lettape screen and recorder, reading screen, memfile inputs, and holojector.

COMMUTRONICS: A term encompassing all aspects of the communications industry.

COMPOUND: (Bond) A housing complex for Bonds providing living quarters, dining halls, and all other basic needs. Compounds are invariably walled and each houses eight to ten thousand Bonds.

COMPSYSTEM: Computer system.

'COM SEQ: Pocketcom sequence. The number sequence denoting the microfrequency assigned to an individual's personal pocketcom.

COMSYSTEM: Communications system.

CON-CONDITIONING: (Phoenix) Contingency conditioning. After an initial "set," and with the consent of the subject, the operator can make a conditioned command without going through the usual process of establishing a receptivity state for conditioning.

CONCORD OF THE LOYAL HOUSES: An alliance of Houses founded in 3105, "Loyal" indicating their opposition to the rebellious Houses of the Mankeen League. It is generally referred to as "the Concord," which designates both the alliance itself and the administrative institution created by and governing it. The latter is to a great degree independent of the member Houses and wields some authority over them, although its power is ultimately derived from common consent of the Houses.

CONCORD: Also "'Cord." Monetary unit printed on six by ten centimeter vellam sheets in denominations of one-tenth, one-half, one, ten, one hundred, one thousand, ten thousand, etc., up to one million.

CONCORDIA: Capital city of the Concord, located on the southern coast of Conta Austrail, Terra.

CONDITIONING: (Phoenix) A method of controlling another person's behavior and memory by means of hypnotic techniques augmented by electronic manipulation of brainwave patterns.

CONFLEET: The military branch of the Concord.

CONFLEET WING: A major Confleet tactical division made up of a Command Unit consisting of one TC Corsair flagship with a complement of ten Corvets and eighty-nine Falcons, plus five units, each of which consists of nine subunits of nineteen Falcons under the command of one Corvet.

CON-LEVELS: (Phoenix) Conditioning levels. Four recognized levels indicating degrees of mental control over another person achieved through conditioning techniques.

CONMED: A branch of the Concord providing medical services and research and training facilities.

CONPOL: The police branch of the Concord.

CON-RAD: (Phoenix) A small transceiver worn in the ear and used for identifying fellow agents; it sets up a signal tone increasing in volume in ratio to its proximity to another con-rad on the same frequency.

CONSCRIPTS: Fesh given compulsory allegiance shifts from Houses to the Concord to fulfill tax levies.

CONTACT ALARM: (Phoenix) A warning sensor worn next to the skin; it produces a vibration that can be felt as a "buzzing" sensation.

CORSAIR: Usually designated Troop Carrier (or TC) Corsair, these are the largest of the three classifications of Confleet ships and serve as flagships of Confleet wings. Corsairs are staffed at optimum with a crew of seventy-five, act as battleline supply and medical stations, and can carry up to two hundred troops in excess of the crew.

CORVET: Second largest of the three classifications of Confleet ships, three times the size and weight of a Falcon, a tenth that of a TC Corsair, at optimum staffed with a crew of thirty. A Corvet and a complement of nineteen Falcons makes up a subunit, the Corvet serving as command ship.

COTILONNA: A formal dance traditionally celebrating the betrothal of Elite couples in which the Promised couple and their parents join hands in a small circle within the larger circle(s) formed by guests attending the betrothal ball.

COURT OF LORDS: A governmental body, primarily advisory in capacity, consisting of the First Lords of the Houses of the Concord.

CP-ONE: (Phoenix) The highest Critical Potential rating given an individual, designating an extremely high potential as a socially disruptive factor.

CREST RING: A ring worn by a First Lord; the stone is always the House stone incised with the House crest. It is a symbol of authority passed down from one generation to the next, from each First Lord to his first born upon the former's death.

DAGGER OF WILL: A symbol sacred to the Order of Gamaliel. Actual daggers are usually made of jade, sometimes of other minerals, but never of wood or metal. They are always exactly twenty-one centimeters in length with the symbol of the Wheel of Destiny carved into the cruciform intersection of hilt and guard.

DANAE: Largest city on Perseus, one of the three Centauran Inner Planets, and site of the Home Estate of the House of Drakonis.

DARK SOUL: (Bond Religion) An evil spirit, escaped from Nether Dark, that infests living persons.

DEATH PLEDGE: Also "Death Boon." A promise made to a dying person, generally considered an irrevocable pledge with deep moral and religious connotations.

DECADES OF DISASTER: A historical period, usually dated 2030 to 2060, marked by the dissolution and destruction of the Twentieth-Century civilization, culminating in the onset of the Second Dark Age.

DETENTION CENTER (DC): A Conpol or SSB prison.

DICTUM: (Bond Religion) A pronouncement attributed to a saint or holy man or woman. Dictums become part of the moral and religious code of adherents, and defiance of them is considered heresy.

DIPNOPTERA: An oviparous vertebrate native to southern equatorial areas of the Selamin Sea on Pollux. In its marine stage, it grows to a maximum length of thirty centimeters over a period of two Polluxian years. At maturity it undergoes a rapid metamorphosis, developing breathing sacs and membranous wings, after which it migrates in flocks numbering as many as half a million to breeding grounds in the forests of the Himalya, Comargian, or western Caucasias Mountains. After breeding, only gravid "females"—dipnoptera are actually androgynous—return to the sea, where they die after depositing their eggs to float and incubate in warm equatorial currents.

DIRECTORATE: The Directorate of the Concord of the Loyal Houses, a panel of ten First Lords by law elected by the Court of Lords or by the Directors themselves, although the positions are in practice hereditary. The Directorate is the ultimate governing body of the Concord.

DOC LOC #: Document locator number. A sequence of numbers used to call or locate a particular piece of information from a computer memfile system.

DOLCHETTA: (Music) A hollow-reed wind instrument with a range of three quarter-tone octaves characterized by a "straight" (without vibrato), slightly woody tone.

DOORCON: Door control. A small panel inset, beside a door, that controls its opening and closing, and may include voice-, print-, or lectrilock, and sec-system controls.

DOUBLE IDENT: (Phoenix) A member working outside Fina under an assumed identity.

DOUBLET: An Elite men's sleeveless inner coat, close-fitting, sometimes belted at the waist, and usually decorated with brocade, which is often reinforced with strands of flexsteel to serve as light protective "armor".

DRAKONIAN THEORY: A body of theory, formulated by the physicist Orabu Drakon (the first Lord Drakonis) and published in 3060, dealing with interrelationships of space and time, including principles Drakon called "chrono-spatial eversion" and "synchronal metathesis," the applied principles in SynchShift and SynchCom.

DRENALINE: (Medical) A stimulant chemically similar to naturally produced adrenaline.

ELADANE: (Medical) A strong hallucinogenic drug listed as dangerous by Conpol, which makes its use and possession illegal. It can cause permanent psychosis and occasionally death by hyperallergenic reactions.

ELECTROHARP: (Music) A small, wood or plasteel, oval instrument, sixty centimeters in length, with twenty-four electronically amplified strings, played by plucking with the fingers.

ELITE: The term refers to the class or to individuals within it. The ruling class of the Concord. All Elite are related by blood to the First Lords of the Houses.

ENKEPHALINE: (Medical) An analgesic that functions by stimulating the production of enkephalin in the brain.

ENZYMATIC SOLUTIONS: (Medical) Solutions containing enzymes used in the treatment of injuries to dispose of necrotic tissue.

EPIGRA: A philosophical and/or moral thesis usually expressed in poetic form. The term is associated primarily with adherents of the Order of Gamaliel in reference to a body of Epigra attributed to Saint Gamaliel.

ESTRE: A religious holiday celebrating the Mezionic resurrection.

EX SEQ: Extrapolation sequence. A computer sequence extrapolating results of event interactions based on absolute data.

FACE-SCREEN: A small energy field screen that obscures the face by means of a light-diffusing field projected from a narrow, metallic ring worn around the neck.

FALCON: The smallest of the three classifications of Confleet ships, highly maneuverable even in planetary atmospheres. It is staffed at optimum with a crew of ten.

FER, FERRA: General masculine, feminine forms of address for Fesh, used when other titles—Master or Mistra, doctor, lector, etc.—are not applicable.

FESH: A term derived from the word "professional" applying to the middle class, which comprises approximately twenty-nine percent of the Concord's population. Fesh provide the Concord's skilled labor and technicians, as well as its scientists, scholars, and artists. It is the only one of the three officially recognized classes in which there is opportunity for professional and social advancement within the class.

FIRST LORD: The hereditary ruler of a House.

FIX: (Phoenix) A homing device used to accurately pinpoint transmission points for a matter transmitter.

'FLEETER: A popular term for a Confleet officer or enlistee.

FLEET OPERATIONS (FO): (Phoenix) The military branch of the Phoenix.

FLEXSTEEL: A steel alloy capable of being drawn into fine, flexible threads ranging in diameter from one to one-tenth of a millimeter.

FLOROPTERA: A photosynthetic organism native to Pollux, in general form strikingly similar to many Terran shrubs; notable for the ability of its large (up to twenty centimeters in diameter) blossoms to "fly."

FRANCHISE: The exclusive right held by a House to manufacture, or produce, and distribute a specific product or type of product, or to provide a specific service.

GALININ RULE: A sanction against interference by any Concord agency in Bond religious practices and ceremonies except when they present a clear threat to life or property; formulated by the Chairman, Lord Benedic Daro Galinin, as part of the Civil Standards Code of 3065.

GAMALIEL, ORDER OF: A nonmonastic religious brotherhood whose primary philosophical tenet is absolute fatalism. It was founded by followers of Saint Gamaliel (ca. 2550 to 2610), one of Bishop Colona's first disciples.

GAM CHI EXERCISES: A series of physical and mental exercises expounded by the Thirty-first Century Sinasian philosopher Gam Chi Roon.

GANISTAN CARPETS: Floor coverings woven in traditional designs and employing techniques used by Pre-Disasters cultures in northern Indasia.

GLASSGRASS: A photosynthetic organism native to the Paneast Desert of Pollux. It reproduces by a process analogous to fungal sporing, but is similar in appearance to Terran grasses, except that it is nearly transparent, and, due to its high crystalline silicon content, extremely refractive.

GROUNDCOMM: A combined form for Ground Command used in Confleet and Phoenix Fleet Operations.

GUILD: A Fesh organization made up of practitioners of a particular skill, craft, or profession, which maintains standards of competency and provides supplemental training. Fesh may or may not choose their professions, but once that decision is made, they are admitted into the appropriate Guild as "prentices." Advancement in Guild ranks is by means of competency tests and/or demonstrations of achievement in the profession through three degrees, ultimately to the rank of GuildMaster (masculine) or GuildMistra (feminine). They are subsequently addressed as Master or Mistra unless a higher title, such as lector or doctor, pertains. Fesh Guild rankings usually have a direct bearing on salaries and advancement, in conjunction with tech grade ratings.

Guilds may bring some pressure to bear on their Lords in behalf of members, but only in disputes with executive level (Fesh) superiors. Guild intervention against Elite level decisions, or mass protests or work stoppages, may be legally treated as acts of treason.

HABITAT SYSTEM: The collective mechanical systems—atmobubbles, water cyclers, energy systems, thermogenerators, etc.—necessary to maintain human habitation on planets and satellites where atmospheric or surface conditions are otherwise inimical to human life.

HEAT SHELL: (Medical) A miniature atmobubble used to maintain a controlled temperature around a supine patient.

HEAVENLY REALM: In Orthodox Mezionism, the abode of the All-God and Holy Mezion and, after death, of those deemed worthy.

HELEN: Largest city on Castor and site of the Home Estate of the House of Camine Eliseer.

HELION: A large, extremely bright artificial light source.

HEMUS: A Polluxian vinelike plant, with large (up to twelve centimeters in length) palmate leaves that grow into dense, impenetrable mats on forest floors in moist, temperate climates. Its pulverized "bud" tendrils are used as a topical anesthetic by practitioners of herbal medicine.

HOLOJECTOR: A mechanism for projecting holograms into a hologram chamber.

HOLY CONFEDERATION: An alliance (2585–2903) of all the feudal Hold-Masters and rulers of Conta Austrail; founded by Lord Even Pilgram.

HOLY WORDS: (Bond Religion) A verbal compendium of dogma, parable, moral codes, history, poetry, etc., analogous to the Holy Writ in Orthodox Mezionism, transmitted from one generation of Shepherds to the next solely by rote memory.

HOLY WRIT: A collection of writings and scriptures sacred to Mezionism, it includes parts of the Pre-Disasters Christian "Bible," especially the so-called "New" Testament, and *The Revelations* of Bishop Colona.

HOUSE: A political-economic entity described as a "dynastic cartel," ruled by a single family headed by a hereditary First Lord, and economically based on exclusive franchises for the production and/or manufacture and distribution of specific goods or services.

IMAGRAPH: A color image, appearing three-dimensional, printed on a vellam film.

INDEPENDENT FESH: An unofficial designation referring to Fesh whose lives and work are relatively independent of their House, Concord, or Church allegiances. Most Fesh in the University System are termed Independent, since many are there by virtue of temporary and even permanent allegiance grants from their Houses, the Concord, or the Church. Artists, authors, and performers are included under the broad umbrella of the University, although display, publication, and production of their work falls under House (DeKoven Woolf) franchises. Members of some professions, such as broadcasting and journalism, or artisans and designers in Houses based on "craft" franchises, are also considered Independent Fesh, as are individuals in the upper echelons of House, Concord, or Church administrative hierarchies.

INTERCONN: Interconnection; an intertie between two or more types of communication systems.

INTERPLANETARY TRANSYSTEMS: The interplanetary transport systems operated under franchise by the House of Badir Selasis, including all off-planet freight and passenger services. Selasid franchises also encompass the InterPlan port and terminal systems, as well as manufacture of all vessels used in any kind of off-planet transport, including Confleet ships.

IP PORT: Abbreviation for Interplanetary Transystems port.

IRIS LENSES: Small, plasex lenses, corrective and/or colored, that fit over the iris of the eye.

JAMBLER: A device for jamming and scrambling radio or vidicom transmissions.

JINNI: A mythical supernatural being of mischievous nature that can take animal or human form at will.

KAO-ROSSIC: Thirty-first-Century architech and designer whose work is typified by stringently simple lines and the successful mixture of woods and metals.

KARATT: A formalized style of hand-to-hand combat generally practiced as a sport only by Elite males.

KELP: A marine invertebrate native to Pollux where it inhabits temperate intertidal zones. It is "rooted" and much like true Terran kelp in appearance, but is usually classified as an animal, and in its adult phases is carnivorous.

KOYF: A woman's headdress comprised of a close-fitting band framing the face, often brocaded, jeweled, or otherwise decorated, with an attached veil covering the hair and sometimes reaching waist, or even floor, length.

KRISTUS EVE: A religious holiday occurring at the summer/winter solstice on Terra celebrating the birth of the Mezion as Avatar.

LADY: Any Elite woman over Age of Rights.

LECTOR: A University teacher of advanced degree. The title is more prestigious than GuildMaster or GuildMistra, but is used only in reference to persons actively involved in teaching.

LECTRILOCK: A lock employing electrical field bonds that can only be negated by a lectrikey emitting specific frequency sequences.

LEDA: The largest city in the Centauri System; on the planet Pollux; site of the Home Estate of the House of D'Ord Hamid; and site of the first colony in the Centauri System.

LETTAPE: A communication typed on a special keyboard console, then transmitted onto a tape spool at the receiving console, where it is projected on a lettape screen.

LETTAPE SEQ: A number sequence designating a personal frequency used to direct lettapes to a particular person's lettape console.

LIFE VOW: A religiously sanctioned vow regarded as binding until death.

LIGHTPEN: A pen-like electronic device used to write on photosensitive surfaces, such as vellam or scriber screens, or to write on or manipulate data on a computer data display screen.

LITIGATION BOARD: A House judiciary panel staffed by Fesh; its function is to adjudicate disputes between or involving Bonds.

LORD: Any Elite male over Age of Rights who is a First Lord or the first born of a First Lord. ("My lord" as a form of address is used for both Lords and VisLords.)

LUMENSA: A wall-sized screen that displays varying patterns and colors in response to sound (usually musical) stimuli.

MAM-AN: Matter/Anti-Matter Annihilation. The term, especially when abbreviated, usually refers to the MAM-AN generator and/or drive, developed by Fredric Cadmon, which exploits and controls the massive energy yields of matter/anti-matter annihilation.

MANELA CHANDELIER: A large, intricate light fixture, often referred to as a "canopy" chandelier, created by the Thirty-second-Century designer, Simyon Manela.

MANKEEN REVOLT: A sixteen-year-long (3104–3120) civil war instigated by Lord Lionar Mankeen, leader of the Mankeen League, which was made up of over three hundred dissident Lords of the PanTerran Confederation.

MANTLET: Clothing worn by young Elite males (generally under the age of seventeen), similar to a cloak, but shorter, usually fingertip length.

MARBLEX: A manufactured structural material similar to natural marble in appearance, but more durable and resilient.

MARCHING FORESTS: Also "Pygmy Forests." An aggregation of predominantly photosynthetic species, all interdependent, some true symbionts, found in the Barrens of Castor at altitudes below +1,500 meters (Helen Base Point). The organisms are low-growing, reaching a maximum height of one meter, and migrate collectively across hundreds and even thousands of kilometers in the course of a Castorian year, following the seasonal advance and retreat of the icecaps, which provide their only source of water.

MARICAINE: (Medical) An illegal and marginally addictive drug prized as a mild stimulant and euphoric.

MARLITE: Marblex with a phosphorescent material added to create a perceptible luminescence.

MATTER TRANSMITTER. (Phoenix) Abbreviated MT or, in the long-range form, LR-MT. A device functioning on Drakon's principle of chrono-spatial eversion that transports, or transmits, objects or persons virtually instantaneously from one point in space/time to another.

MEMFILE: Computer memory or data storage file.

MERCFLEET: The Selasid Interplanetary Systems mercantile fleet.

METALITE: A steel alloy impregnated with conductive filaments that when electronically stimulated become luminescent. The stimulus control is generally set to respond to a reduction in the surrounding light level.

MEZION: Yesu Kristus, the Holy Mezion, Avatar of the All-God; an incarnation in human form of the All-God.

MICROSPEAKER: A miniscule tape spool equipped with an audio speaker.

MIDHAR: The equatorial desert of Castor, girdling the entire planet and varying from two to five thousand kilometers in breadth.

MINICEIVER: Also "ear 'ceiver." A radio receiver worn in the ear, its signal audible only to the wearer.

MINICORDER: A miniature audio recorder used for surveillance or espionage.

MOD-STIM DEVICES: (Phoenix) Modulated frequency stimulus devices. Mechanisms emitting aural or visual frequencies that induce synergistic resonances with a subject's brain waves in order to produce the receptivity state necessary to conditioning.

MONTECTOR: A device used to detect the presence of electronic monitors.

MORPHININE: (Medical) A strong analgesic with an alkaloid base chemically related to opium; addictive only when taken in massive doses over a long period of time.

NAVCOMP: Navigational computer; or as an adjective referring to the programs, read outs, etc., it produces. The term is also used to refer to the techs who operate it.

NEOMEDIT: A furniture design introduced in the early Thirtieth Century characterized by use of transparent materials with delicate supports often in the form of the "Roman" arch.

NETHER DARK, WORLD OF: (Bond Religion) In the afterlife, the zone to which sinners and the un-Blessed are consigned; equivalent to Orthodox Mezionism's hell.

NETVINE: A photosynthetic organism native to Pollux found at low altitudes, generally near the sea. It is rootless, with thin, thread-like stems covered with microscopic lobe-leaves. In pursuit of sunlight and atmospheric moisture, it forms fine-meshed nets suspended between any available natural protuberances. Airborne "seed" fronds, carried by winds, have been found at altitudes of up to ten thousand meters.

NULGRAV: A mechanism for nullifying gravity. The first nulgrav generator was designed by Domic Peresky, House of Hild Robek, in 3055, based on principles set forth by Ela Tolstyne in her *Treatise on Matter/Anti-Matter Interactions*, in which she predicted that one such interaction would be repulsion.

OBSAT: Manned observational satellite in stable orbit around a planet or satellite.

ORCHESTRAL ORGAN:(Music) Also "Orchestron:" A large, electronic instrument capable of simulating the sound of any musical instrument as well as producing sounds unique to itself in any combination. Orchestral organs usually require a minimum of three musitechs for live performances. They can also be played by computer-programmed tapes.

OUTSIDE: The term may refer to the state of being "outside" the law or recognized social classes, to the subsociety existing in that state, or to the districts found in most major cities where Outsiders and their illicit businesses are tolerated. Outsiders comprise an officially unrecognized and largely criminal and/or fugitive class with a population estimated at forty-five million.

PAGE: An Elite boy between the ages of ten and fifteen, usually the son of a House VisLord or the scion of a Cognate House, granted the privilege of being educated in the Home Estate of a First Lord.

PANTERRAN CONFEDERATION: A planet-wide union of Houses analogous to the Concord, its political offspring. It was founded at the culmination of the Wars of Confederation in 2903 and flourished until the onset of the Mankeen Revolt in 3105.

PEDWAY: A moving walkway for pedestrian travel.

PELADEEN REPUBLIC: A monarchal republic established in the Centauri System in 3135 under the titular leadership of Lord Quintin Peladeen, terminated in 3210 upon its defeat by the Concord in the War of the Twin Planets.

PELISSE: A light outdoor garment worn by Elite women, typically ankle length, with long, wide sleeves; usually hooded and often made of fur, or fur trimmed.

PLANETARY TRANSYSTEMS: The transportation systems, operated under franchise by the House of Hild Robek, which include any kind of surface transport. ("Surface transport" is interpreted in Robek franchises as any form of non-marine, mechanical conveyance operated at an altitude of less than four thousand meters.) Public transportation systems and metropolitan Trafficon grid systems are included in Robek franchises as well as the manufacture of all equipment necessary to these systems and all vehicles used for surface travel.

PLASEAL: A thin, non-elastic, plasex film that adheres to itself upon the application of heat.

PLASEX: A general term for various synthetic, nonmetallic compounds produced by polymerization of organic compounds. These can be molded or cast into a variety of forms, or rolled into sheets or films.

PLASIFOAM: A packing or insulating material made of air-infused plasex.

PLASKIN: A thin, highly elastic plasex film.

PLASMENT: A cement mixed with certain types of plasex giving it resilience and durability, as well as excellent insulating capacity. It is used architecturally to coat walls, floors, and ceilings, both interior and exterior.

PLASTEEL: A structural plasex reinforced with lattices of steel rods.

PLATINADE: A platinum-titanium alloy generally used for fine tableware or for jewelry mountings.

POCKETCOM: Pocket communicator. A device used for personal communication equipped with a two-way vidicom screen (usually less than ten centimeters in diameter), a radio transceiver, and frequency control.

POINT OF HONOR: A personal challenge to be answered in a formal fencing match. Like fencing, "the Sport of Lords," the point of honor is a custom practiced exclusively by Elite males.

PORCELEEN: An extremely high-fired, nearly translucent ceramic used for tableware or small art objects.

PRESSYRINGE: (Medical) A disposable syringe equipped with a compressed-air capsule.

PRINTLOCK: A lock operated by the reading and identification of thumbprints of programmed persons.

PRIORITY RATINGS: Access ratings given to publications or information by the Board of Censors. Information given a Priority-One (or Pri-One) rating is accessible only to the Chairman, Directorate Lords, and with Directorate approval to certain Fesh, such as First Commanders of Conpol, the SSB, and Confleet. Pri-Two information is accessible generally to any Elite and to Fesh granted specific access permits by a Lord. Pri-Three information is available to any Elite, to ranking Fesh scholars and scientists, or to upper echelon House, Concord, or Church personnel with a blanket access permit, rather than the limited specific access permit necessary for Pri-Two memfiles. Pri-Four information is open to all Elite and Fesh without restriction.

The term "Pri-One" is also used informally to indicate anything regarded as important or vital.

PROX SCANNER: Proximity scanner. A radar system employed for surveillance within a limited area.

PSYCHOCONTROLLER: In Conpol and the SSB, personnel trained in psychoscience and specializing in interrogation procedures.

PSYCHOMAXIC DRUGS: A popular term for hallucinogenic and euphoric drugs.

PUBLICOM SYSTEM: Public Vidicom System. The vidicom broadcasting system operated by the House of DeKoven Woolf under its commutronics franchises.

PULSED LASER: A laser used as a strategic weapon in which emissions are pulsed, creating shock waves within the target. This augments the laser's effectiveness and avoids the tendency of unpulsed emissions to create a plasma in massive, metallic targets, which prevents full penetration of the beam.

RECOGNITION CONDITIONING: (Phoenix) A type of conditioning that enables the subject to recognize things or persons at a preconscious level on the basis of sensory clues—such as the sound of a particular voice—implanted by conditioning.

RELIQUARY RITE: (Bond Religion) A ceremony centered on a relic—usually part of the ashes of the cremated body—of a new saint, marking his or her acceptance into the Bond pantheon of saints.

RIGHTNESS: (Bond Religion) An event deemed ordained by the All-God.

RITES OF PASSING: (Bond Religion) Funeral service preceding the cremation of the dead.

ROCKWOOD: A photosynthetic organism native to Pollux and very similar to Terran conifers in appearance, although its divided, lobed leaves resemble Terran ferns or Castorian barrengorse rather than coniferous needles, and its smooth, cylindrical trunks are invariably double or triple. The trunk tissue is highly siliceous, its structure supporting growth to heights of 125 meters. Rockwood reproduces by means of wind-disseminated spores formed in spore buds on the upper parts of the trunks.

SANNA: (Bond Religion) A traditional chant or song of glorification, reverence, etc.; a hymn.

SANSERET SILK: Ornamental silk brocade from the House of Sanseren, patterned on Second Dark Age brocades found in Ceylonia, and characterized by stylized floral and animal designs.

SCANNER: Any type of system, such as radar, employed in nonvisual observation; specifically, the screens displaying their signals.

SCOUT: A small, short-range Confleet ship generally used for reconnaissance; it is hangared offplanet in TC Corsairs, can be piloted by one person, and will accommodate three.

SCRIBER: A small (usually fifteen by twenty centimeters), flat, photosensitive screen on which a lightpen is used as a writing instrument. The images created are impermanent and can be negated instantly by switching off the screen.

SEANOVA: An invertebrate marine organism native to Pollux, approximately twenty centimeters in diameter, with ten to twenty tentacles radiating from an ovoid body, the epidermis covered with minute spines that are also sensory organs. During its annual mating period, the seanova becomes luminescent and changes color from its usual blue-gray to a reddish orange. Populations estimated at up to five million congregate in the surf off protected, sandy beaches where they link tentacles to form glowing, undulating masses. Seanova "rafts" remain intact for two to three Polluxian days, while both males and females eject quantities of germ plasm, some of which finds its way into the open brood sacs of asexual "mothers," where the young develop.

SEC-CON: (Phoenix) Security conditioning. A form of conditioning that prevents voluntary revelation to any nonmember of information pertaining to the Phoenix.

SECOND GEN: (Phoenix) Second generation. Any person born to Phoenix members after its founding.

SEC-SYSTEM: Security system. A system of locks, alarms, monitors, etc. designed to protect an area from intrusion and/or to identify, disable, or in some cases even kill intruders.

SEMELE: The largest city on Dionysus, the second of the Inner Planets of the Centauri System.

SER, SERRA: Masculine, feminine forms of address used for Elite under Age of Rights.

SHANIDEL: A furniture design characterized by the use of exotic woods carved in strongly curvilinear forms; the original designs were created by the Thirty-first Century sculptor, Orman Shanidel.

SHEPHERD: (Bond Religion) A minister/priest of the Bond Church. He not only conducts religious ceremonies in the church but acts as arbiter of all moral and religious questions for his 'flocks.' Shepherds also preserve and perpetuate the Holy Words by rote memory, and many serve their flocks as practitioners of herbal medicine.

Only men are chosen to be Shepherds although the Bond Church recognizes many women as saints. The Shepherds choose their successors, who begin their training as acolytes at ten to twelve years of age. A Shepherd may choose several acolytes but designate only one to succeed him upon his death. The others continue in the role of acolytes if they remain in the same compound and choose not to marry. Both Shepherds and acolytes take vows of celibacy.

Shepherds and acolytes in most Houses are excused from other work and allowed to live in or near the chapels, and the Shepherds's choices of acolytes are accepted without question by compound overseers. However, in Houses with more restrictive policies, the Shepherds's choices must be approved by the overseers, who may revoke an acolyte's, or even in some cases a Shepherd's, status at any time.

In most House compounds there are ten Bond chapels and Shepherds, one of whom is designated the *Elder* Shepherd, a title of respect conferred by concensus of all the Shepherds in a compound. All the Bonds in a compound are considered to be in the Elder Shepherd's flock.

SIGMOD CIRCUITS: Signal modification circuits. Electronic devices that automatically encode and decode radio or vidicom transmissions.

SLACSUIT: An informal, two-piece garment worn by both sexes in the Fesh class and consisting of pants and pullover shirt of the same material. Some variation in style, material, and accessories is available, especially to wealthier Fesh, with more variation offered in women's styles.

SPIRIT WEFT: (Bond Religion) A bond between individuals, or their souls, that cannot be broken, even by death, and extends into the Beyond, or afterlife.

SPOROWHALE: An invertebrate, marine organism native to Pollux. Its name is a misnomer, although it does reproduce by means of sporelike bodies, but its only relationship to the Terran whale is that both are large marine organisms. The adult sporowhale may be up to ten meters in length, six in breadth. It is a colonial organism more closely related to Terran marine plants than animals in all its diverse stages of development, particularly in the tertiary stage. In the quinary, or adult, stage, it acquires, along with its solid, ovoid form, the typical lateral ridge fins, or megacilia, that enable it to embark on its long migration from the northern Selamin Sea, through the Comargian Straits, to its breeding grounds in the southern Polluxian Ocean, then back to its starting point, two Polluxian years later, for sporing.

SSB: The Special Services Branch of Conpol, a police agency authorized to investigate and prosecute cases of subversion, treason, or other crimes against the Concord.

STARENZA: A furniture design characterized by severe lines and geometric decoration produced by the House of Starenza (now merged with Mays Fedoric) in the Thirtieth Century.

STUN DART, OR STUNNER: A device used defensively to inject a drug into another person. Stunners may be fired from a gun or similar device utilizing a compressed air charge, or when direct contact is possible a device similar to a miniature pressyringe is employed. Drugs used vary in effect, some causing only brief muscular paralysis and/or unconsciousness, while others are immediately fatal.

SUBTUG: A small (maximum length, five meters), powerful subsea vessel generally used for underwater construction, marine farming, anchoring tidal seines, towing fish corrals, etc. Most models can be piloted by one person.

SURCOAT: An article of Elite masculine apparel worn over a doublet or vest; a coat-like garment with long, flared sleeves, usually belted or sashed at the waist. In length it varies from mid-thigh to floor length. The longer styles are generally worn by older men.

S/V SCREEN: Sound/vision screen. (Sound and vision screens are also used separately.) Energy fields that prevent penetration of sound and/or light waves, usually used in windows, doorways—sometimes *as* doors—or as partitions.

SYNCHCOM: Ultra-lightspeed radio or vidicom communication.

SYNCHRONAL METATHESIS: A principle of the Drakonian Theory, also referred to as the time/space transposition or interchange effect.

SYNCHSHIFT (SS): Transition into the ultra-lightspeed "state"; the applied principle of synchronal metathesis, which "makes possible navigation in time as well as in space; that is, the synchronization of one's temporal destination with one's spatial destination." (From *SynchShift Explained*, Laramy Joneson, Archives doc loc #1210/17–1919–2153235–PR–4.)

SYNTEGRATOR: A refuse disposal mechanism that reduces refuse to a fine ash by subjecting it to extremely high temperatures in a shielded laser chamber.

TAB: (Phoenix) Total Amnesia Block. A type of conditioning designed to prevent forced revelation of information pertaining to the Phoenix. The TAB usually goes into effect upon the arrest of a Phoenix member by Conpol or the SSB and induces a selective amnesia that blocks out all personal memory.

TABARD: A garment worn by both male and female Bonds, a short, loose jacket with long sleeves, boldly patterned in the two colors of the Bond's House—or for Concord Bonds, in black and gold; for Church Bonds, in white and gold.

TACCOMM: Tactics Command. In both Confleet and Phoenix Fleet Operations, a department whose function is strategic planning.

TEA BREW: A metal or ceramic pot, equipped with a self-contained heating unit, used for brewing tea.

TECH: The term is exclusive to Fesh and is derived from the word "technologist," although it also refers to trained practitioners of skills outside the applied sciences. It is generally used as a combining form, as in econotech (economist), medtech (medical technician or assistant), stattech (statistician), etc.

TECH GRADE RATINGS: Techs are rated Grade 1 through 10, in that order, on the basis of examinations administered by the University Board of Standards. Salaries and other benefits are usually commensurate with grade ratings.

TENSTEEL: A steel alloy with exceptionally high tensile strength.

TESTING: (Bond Religion) A trial by ordeal regarded as divinely sanctioned.

THERMBLANKET: A bed cover with fine, heat-emitting wires woven into the fabric.

THERMCARPET: A floor covering that like the thermblanket has heat-emitting wires woven into the fabric, but the conductors are heavier and radiate more heat. Thermcarpets are often the principal heat source in residential rooms.

THERMOGENERATOR: A generator/storage system, usually employing beamed solar-powered exchangers to produce and store heat, which is circulated in a vented airflow system.

THRYMBIS: The largest city on Pan, third and smallest of the Inner Planets of the Centauri System.

TITHE BONDS: Bonds given mandatory allegiance shifts to the Church by their Houses. The offering of Bonds, along with monetary donations, constitutes the Houses' annual "tithe" offerings to the Church. Such offerings are usually less than a literal tithe, generally three to five percent of a House's total yearly income. Fesh are rarely allieged to the Church involuntarily as tithe offerings, but in most Houses and in the Concord, they will be granted allegiance shifts to the Church on request if they wish to join a monastic order.

TORAMIL: The largest city on Mars, site of the home Estate of the House of Neeth Cameroodo.

TRAFFICON GRID SYSTEM: A computerized system of radio-transmitted grids controlling aircar traffic in urban areas, operated by the House of Hild Robek. All aircars, 'taxis, 'drays, etc. are equipped with remote guidance systems that permit control by the Trafficon system. Only Conpol, Confleet, and Conmed vehicles may legally operate outside grid control within Trafficon-served municipal areas without special clearance from Conpol. The six basic grid levels in order from the lowest to the highest in elevation are:
Entry-Exit grid
'Dray grid (Freight transport only)
Five-kilometer destination range grid
Ten-kilometer destination range grid
Twenty-kilometer destination range grid
Express grid (High-speed vehicles or those with destinations beyond twenty kilometers)

TRANS: (Phoenix) *n.* or *v.* Travel or transmission via matter transmitter.

TRANSIT PLAZA: A public area at a junction of major urban pedways offering parking for aircars, airtaxi stations, and access to subtrains or 'shuttle terminals; maintained and operated by the Robek Planetary Transystems.

TWO SYSTEMS: The two solar systems—the Sun's and Alpha Centauri's—occupied by extensive human habitation. The term is also synonymous with the Concord.

TYCHO: The largest city on Luna, site of the Home Estate of the House of Arment Ivanoi.

UNDER THE SHADOW: (Bond Religion) A person who is, or lives, under the Shadow is one whose life or soul is in jeopardy.

UNIVERSITY SYSTEM: A Concord agency established in 2903 by Lord Paul Adalay, first Chairman of the Directorate of the PanTerran Confederation. The University provides facilities for higher education (beyond the Basic School level), as well as for scholarly and scientific research, and for endeavors in all the arts. University campuses are found in all major cities in the Two Systems.

VACCUP: A drinking vessel, usually made of plasex, with double walls sealing an insulating vacuum that maintains liquids at hot or cold temperatures.

VACMOP: A cleaning implement with a suction hose, the mouth of which is surrounded by absorbent plasponge bristles.

VACUUM COLONY: Any human habitation (not necessarily a colony in a literal sense) that requires habitat systems in order to maintain conditions suitable for human existence.

VELLAM: A photosensitive laminate pressed into thin sheets and used primarily for printouts and for hand writing with a lightpen.

VF (VISUAL FREQUENCY) CAMOUFLAGE SCREEN: An energy-field screen used to shield an area from long-range visual observation, as from airborne vehicles or ships, by selective disruption of light waves.

VIDICAM: A vidicom image encoder or camera.

VIDICOM: Transmitted electromagnetic signals translated into three-dimensional, color images on vidicom screens, which range in size from a few centimeters in height and breadth to the typical home-use screen of 1.75 by 1.75 meters, to large wall screens up to six by six meters. The term may also refer to the screen receiver itself or to the PubliCom System and its broadcasts.

VIOLAN: (Music) An instrument with seven electronic beamed "strings" over a hollow sounding box with an attached tone or fingering bar. Sounds are produced by drawing a charged rod, or "bow," across the strings.

VISLORD: Any Lord who is not a First Lord or the first born of a

First Lord. He is referred to as VisLord, but addressed as "my lord."

VIS-SCREEN: Visual-image screen. A vidicom screen used to view areas not accessible to direct visual observation, as in space vessels where the only visual access to anything outside the ship is through vidicams mounted on the hull transmitting images to vis-screens within the ship.

VOICE LOCK: A lock that opens only in response to a voice it has been programmed to recognize by VP ident. A special code word is usually programmed as an additional precaution.

VOLANTE: An Elite social dance performed by couples facing each other in two concentric circles, men outside, women inside, to music with a distinctive sequence of rhythms. At the end of each sequence, or chorus, there is a short "allegro" during which the two circles move in opposite directions. When it ends, each dancer takes the person he or she is then facing, as partner for the next chorus.

VP IDENT: Voice print identification. A means of identifying an individual based on the unique spectrogram pattern formed by his or her voice.

WHEEL OF DESTINY: A symbol, in the form of a seven-spoked wheel, sacred to the Order of Gamaliel. The wheel (or circle) represents continuity and eternity; the seven spokes represent the Order's seven secret "logos" (philosophical concepts and/or disciplines), mastery of which, adherents believe, leads to true Insight, a state of total comprehension.

WINDOWALL: A window made of thick (10 cm) glass reinforced with extremely fine, and virtually invisible, strands of flexsteel. Windowalls can span up to six meters in width and heighth without internal structural supports.

Glossary—Outsider Terms and Slang

ASK FATE: To court disaster by naming it beforehand, especially in jest.

BLADE: A knife. Also a member of the Brotherhood assigned to act as a guard or enforcer.

BLOOD EDICT: A decree, order, or command made with the tacit understanding that the penalty for defying it will be death.

BODY-DECKER: A person prone to wearing an abundance of jewelry or other personal ornamentation.

BROTHER: Any male Outsider "cleave" to the Brotherhood.

BROTHERHOOD: A loose but ubiquitous organization dominant in the Outside. Most Outsiders are involved in it directly or indirectly.

BUTTON MAN: Also "Top Button Man:" A person in a position of command or authority.

CALL (A PERSON) FRIEND AND BROTHER, OR SISTER: An oath by which the person named is granted the loyalty and protection usually pertaining only in actual blood relationships.

CAST A SHADOW: To threaten.

CATCH: *n.* An arrest.

CHARM SNAGGER: A swindler who employs appealing personal attributes to dupe his or her victims.

CLAN: An organizational unit within the Brotherhood. The person wielding the most authority within a clan is known as the "clanhead."

CLEAVE: *adj.* Loyal; faithful.

CROSS (ANOTHER PERSON'S) LINES: To infringe on another person's privacy or pry into matters he or she considers personal or secret; also, to infringe on his or her business prerogatives or interests.

DIVVIES: Shared advantage or profit.

DODDER: A person of limited or diminished intelligence.

DOOR: A means of escape.

DOUBLE DEUCE: The number two hundred; "deuce" is twenty.

DOVEY: Easy or pleasant.

DOWNSIDE: Below, on a lower level, or beneath the surface (of a planet).

EAR MAN: A spy.

EYE-OVER: *n.* A close scrutiny.

FACE OFF: A confrontation.

FLOAT: An Outside business establishment vending alcoholic beverages and providing music and/or other entertainment, and characterized by the use of nulgrav mechanisms to create a "floating" environment.

FORTUNE: A wish for another person's good fortune, an expression that serves primarily as a greeting or a farewell, especially the latter.

FRINGER: A person who is an Outsider, but not a born or soul Outsider; usually a runaway or fugitive from Conpol or the SSB.

GAFF: To cheat or swindle.

GIM: *n.* A fraudulent, illegal, and/or deceitful scheme or act, the purpose of which is personal gain for the perpetrator. Also, a scheme or act involving great risk to the perpetrator, but with a more admirable motive.
  v. To deceive, swindle, or cheat.
  A "gim artist" or "gimmer" is a person who gims others; he or she may also be said to "run a gim."

GLIM: Inkling; hint.

HACKLE: To disturb, bother, or arouse suspicion. Also used in the form "to be hackled"; i.e., disturbed, etc.

HEADPRICE: A reward, or the amount of the award, offered, usually by Conpol or the SSB, for information leading to the apprehension of a person on their fugitive or runaway lists.

HOUND: A Brother who specializes in finding and tracking people.

INSIDE: The opposite of the Outside, either as a place or a state of being "Inside"; i.e., a non-Outsider, or someone living within the official or accepted social order in the Concord.

ITCHY NOSE: The state of having suspicion or anxiety about someone or a situation.

KEEP (ONE'S) BLADE SHEATHED: To show restraint or to offer no threat.

KINLY: A feeling of closeness toward another person; a friendly attitude.

LAST FALL: Defeat and/or death.

LAY: To wager.

LIFTER: A space vessel.

LINE IN: To provide information; to make someone privy to a situation.

MAXOBOOTH: A type of entertainment offered in most Outsiders' districts providing, via helmets equipped with electronic beam probes, a choice of simulated sensations or moods.

MOLLY-DODDLE: Nonsense; foolishness.

NOB: To fraternize with, be friendly, or converse with.

NODDY: An informer; usually one who directs Conpol or the SSB to fugitives or runaways in exchange for the headprice.

NUCH: A term of insult (masculine).

OLD SER: Father.

ONE ON: An expression of approbation, encouragement, or agreement.

ON THE SHORT END: At a disadvantage, or deprived.

PASSKEY: The price exacted for providing a "door."

PIN: *v.* To kill, usually purposely.
    n. A killing or murder; also called a "pinning."

POLE, OR POLER: A Conpol officer or agent.

PRICE IN (A PERSON'S) BLOOD: Retribution by death.

PSYGAME HOUSE: A type of entertainment found in most Outsiders' districts offering games based on psychological fantasies realistically staged with a combination of live actors, holograms, vidicom projections, and other visual and aural effects.

PULL A LOOK: To attract attention.

PULL DOWN: To defeat and/or kill.

QUIV: A coward. A person behaving in a cowardly manner is "on the quiv."

RED PANIC: A state of extreme anxiety.

RUN THE GANT: To accept a challenge, or attempt a dangerous course of action.

RUN SHORT: To be deterred, forestalled, or frustrated in one's desires or aims.

SCAN: Also "scan straight:" To understand clearly.

SCREENED AREA: A private or secret part of a person's life.

SEAL: To convict and incarcerate.

SERALLIO: A house of prostitution.

SHAD: An officer or agent of the SSB.

SHIVVY: Dangerous or frightening.

SHOW TOOTH: To object or take exception to someone or something in a potentially violent manner.

SKIMP: Lacking, or in short supply.

SMELL OUT: To find, uncover, or unmask something or someone.

SODDY: Dull, old-fashioned, stilted; sometimes used in the sense of "prim."

SOUL-LINK: A relationship between two or more persons considered more significant and more binding than friendship, love, or even blood ties.

SOUL OUTSIDER: A person born into the Outside and committed to its way of life.

SPIN: A story or tale, often by implication exaggerated or outlandish.

SPOOK: To escape, run away, or desert.

STAT: Status; situation.

STIMUTHEATER: A type of Outside entertainment combining theatrical presentations, usually pornographic in nature, with drug or electronically induced stimuli enhancement.

SWEET: An attractive woman, especially one with an air of innocence or naïveté.

TEN-CARAT BRASS: A term of insult; a sham, false, or faked.

TICE: Attractive; enticing.

TOOK: *n.* A person who is easily deceived; a victim, or prospective victim of a gim. "Tooky" is used as a derisive form of address.

TOOTH MAN: A gim artist or charlatan who uses personal charm to achieve his ends; the "tooth" refers to a habitual smile.

TURN A 'CORD: To make a difference, to change or affect the outcome.

UNMOTHERED: A term of insult.

UPPERCASTE: Elite.

UPSIDE: Above, an upper level, or the surface of a planet. It may also refer to the Inside.

WEAVE: Clothing, especially in the sense of costume.

M. K. WREN

SWORD OF THE LAMB

Book One of THE PHOENIX LEGACY

The House of DeKoven Woolf:

ALEXAND: the eldest. Heir to a great industrial dynasty — and its prisoner. His destiny and his heart are forever at war . . .

ADRIEN: his beloved, rebelling against the law that a woman born to rule cannot give herself to love . . .

RICH: gentlest of the House of Woolf, yet feared. For, as 'The Lamb' and leader of THE PHOENIX, he is the sworn enemy of the most dazzling empire humankind has ever known.

SHADOW OF THE SWAN

Book Two of THE PHOENIX LEGACY

The magnificent saga of a great family and their star destiny.

DR ERICA RADEK: chief psychoscientist and founding member of THE PHOENIX, she had the mind of a computer and the heart of a woman . . .

DR ANDREAS RIIS: frail, elderly genius whose inventions could take humankind beyond the stars — if his enemies would let him live . . .

COMMANDER ALEX RANSON: he had given up his position among Con Fleet's pinnacles of power in the hope of saving the crumbling empire. Yet was he already too late . . .

'Full and satisfying; the society of the far future is superbly extrapolated, the action fast and well-integrated . . .'
Isaac Asimov's *Science Fiction Magazine*

NEW ENGLISH LIBRARY

MORE SCIENCE FICTION AVAILABLE FROM
HODDER AND STOUGHTON PAPERBACKS